THE SPEED OF DEATH

Beyond the burst of glowing cannon shells, little could be seen of the Luftwaffe fighter. Sinclair thought he saw a low-wing aircraft with a triangular fuselage section behind the muzzle blasts, but he had to concentrate on flying his own plane. Then Sinclair heard a strange, hissing whine as the German fighter passed overhead. It was a noise he had never heard before and yet it sparked terror in him. He had an idea of what it was, and seconds later his fears were confirmed when the tail gunner identified their attacker.

"Oh God, I don't believe it! Commander, it's a bleedin' Nazi jet! I can see the glow of his jet pipes!"

THE BEST IN SUSPENSE FROM ZEBRA
by Jon Land

THE DOOMSDAY SPIRAL   (1481, $3.50)

Tracing the deadly twists and turns of a plot born in Auschwitz, Alabaster — master assassin and sometime Mossad agent — races against time and operatives from every major service in order to control and kill a genetic nightmare let loose in America!

THE LUCIFER DIRECTIVE   (1353, $3.50)

From a dramatic attack on Hollywood's Oscar Ceremony to the hijacking of three fighter bombers armed with nuclear weapons, terrorists are out-gunning agents and events are outracing governments. Minutes are ticking away to a searing blaze of earth-shattering destruction!

VORTEX   (1469-4, $3.50)

The President of the US and the Soviet Premier are both helpless. Nuclear missiles are hurtling their way to a first strike and no one can stop the top-secret fiasco — except three men with old scores to settle. But if one of them dies, all humanity will perish in a vortex of annihilation!

MUNICH 10   (1300, $3.95)
by Lewis Orde

They've killed her lover, and they've kidnapped her son. Now the world-famous actress is swept into a maelstorm of international intrigue and bone-chilling suspense — and the only man who can help her pursue her enemies is a complete stranger . . .

DEADFALL   (1400, $3.95)
By Lewis Orde and Bill Michaels

The two men Linda cares about most, her father and her lover, entangle her in a plot to hold Manhattan Island hostage for a billion dollars ransom. When the bridges and tunnels to Manhattan are blown, Linda is suddenly a terrorist — except *she's* the one who's terrified!

OPERATION NIGHT HAWK

By John-Allen Price

ZEBRA BOOKS
KENSINGTON PUBLISHING CORP.

To Alexander Malec, because he was the first one to tell me I wouldn't be a fluke.

ZEBRA BOOKS

are published by

Kensington Publishing Corp.
475 Park Avenue South
New York, NY 10016

First printing: November 1985

Printed in the United States of America

Chapter One: The Encounter
The Hawk Is Lost

To: Oberstleutnant Gunnar Heinrich, Commander X/NJG 1.

Esbjerg, Denmark.

From: Reichsluftfahrtministerium, Berlin.

Project Nacht Falke has now reached its advanced phase. Tomorrow, at 0700 hours, you'll receive the first production example of the Nacht Falke. It will be flown to your base from the Vienna-Schwechat test center. After familiarization trials, we expect you to have the Nacht Falke operational by no later than the first of next year. You're to test the aircraft under all combat conditions, using a variety of flight crews. Two weeks after testing has commenced, you will make a final report to us on the suitability of the Nacht Falke for Luftwaffe use. Since this is the reason why your group was originally formed, we hope your evaluation will be a swift and very successful one.

signed,
Generalleutnant Barkhorn
Nacht Falke Project Chief
Dec. 16th, 1944.

"Pilot to tail gunner, how does the target look?"

"Fully involved, sir. The pathfinders are still dropping markers over the refinery but the way it's burning, the rest of our bombers will see it by the time they reach Hamburg."

"Navigator to pilot, we've reached the coast. I have several courses prepared, Geoffrey, which would you like?"

"One that will take us out to sea. Several lads from our wing have reported heavy anti-aircraft fire from the Peenemünde area. I say it's best not to tempt fate."

Less than a minute later, the Avro Lancaster banked gently, changing to a more northerly direction. Its war load of incendiary clusters and high explosive bombs now gone, the Royal Air Force bomber climbed swiftly. Miles behind it lay its target, the Poelitz oil refinery, near the town of Stettin, East Prussia. The refinery was completely ablaze, an intense storm of fire that lit up the surrounding countryside and lower cloud layers. Above the compact inferno glittered a multicolored display of star bursts and flares, pyrotechnic markers dropped by the pathfinder force. Also over the refinery were more R.A.F. bombers. Part of the hundreds which had come to Poelitz and the hundreds more that would arrive before the night ended.

"Navigator to pilot, our H2S gear is picking up

Bornholm Island and the southern coast of Sweden. In the next five minutes we'll have to change course or we'll run the risk of being fired on by more German batteries."

Out in the Baltic, the Lancaster found the skies to be far less congested. Most of its companions in the bomber stream had turned south after hitting Poelitz, as had the Luftwaffe's night fighters. The Lancaster's radar emission detectors fell silent and the gunners relaxed at their stations, though their pilot ordered them to stay in their turrets.

It banked gracefully again, its wings barely falling out of line with the horizon. This time the black giant turned due west, toward England. When it finally completed its maneuver, the dark coast of Germany sat off its left wing and the light-sparkled coast of Sweden lay on its right.

"Things have quieted down, Mister Sinclair," said the flight engineer. "Would you like me to fetch you a cup of coffee?"

"Please, when we're in the aeroplane it's Geoffrey," the pilot replied. "Only on the ground is it Commander or Mister Sinclair. You've been with me on five missions so far, you should know that by now. And the answer is no, I'd rather not relax until we reach the North Sea."

Once the Lancaster reached its optimum cruise altitude of fifteen thousand feet, Sinclair levelled it off. The burning refinery at Poelitz had since retreated to a small though distinct glow in the southeast. At its current cruise speed, Sinclair would have his aircraft and crew back in England in a little over two hours.

But before they could reach their home, before they could reach the North Sea and relax, they had to cross Denmark. Its thumb-shaped peninsula and archipelago of hundreds of islands glowed brightly on the navigator's radar screen, though it was nearly invisible to Sinclair and the gunners.

"Navigator to pilot, approaching Danish archipelago. You better put the gunners back on alert, Geoffrey."

"They're already on alert," said Sinclair. "One of our radar emission detectors went off a few seconds ago. Whether it's a gun-directing Würzburg or interception radar on some night fighter we can't tell. I wish these damn boxes were more accurate."

The nose, tail and top turrets on the Lancaster swept the skies continuously. For all their usefulness, the plane's radar detectors could not be relied on to give more than a general warning about enemy activity. If there were night fighters in the area, the gunners would only catch a fleeting glimpse of moonlight being reflected off canopy glass, or the faint outline of the fighter as it closed for attack. They had mere seconds to decide if what they saw was real, or just an odd shadow.

"Mid-upper turret to pilot, there's activity on our port side, nine o'clock low. I think some poor bastard's buying it."

Whatever was happening was invisible to Sinclair, hidden by the Avro's broad left wing. He dipped it until he saw what appeared to be an aircraft, another bomber, drawing fire from a point several hundred feet behind it. One of its engines was already on fire, partially illuminating the doomed ship.

"It's a Halifax," Sinclair identified, "outbound like us. His starboard inner engine has been hit and his wing's going to buckle. I'm afraid you're right, Tony, he has bought it. Can you see the night fighter?"

"No, just a point from where the tracers are coming. Wait, wait a moment. He just flashed by the Halifax, he's moving at a tremendous rate. It's not a

Ju-88 or a '110, it's a small plane. Maybe it's a day fighter on a wild boar operation?"

"The Luftwaffe only uses those tactics in the target area, I never heard of them using it outside the area. We better hope it is a day fighter, in any event. If not, we're likely to be the next plane he stalks."

The Halifax managed to remain in level flight for just a few seconds longer. Fire spread from its right inboard engine to the wing; somewhere in it, the flames made contact with either severed fuel lines or a ruptured tank. The resulting explosion tore the wing off between the engine nacelles. As it fluttered away, the rest of the bomber rolled to the right. Eventually, it would enter a lopsided spin. Sinclair could only give the Halifax's death a lingering glance. Like the rest of his crew, he searched the skies for the fighter that had killed it.

"Tony, what was the bastard doing when you lost track of him?" he asked.

"Climbing, I think. He was going very fast."

"Nose gunner to pilot, I've found your bogie. He's after another of our ships, twelve o'clock level."

Several miles in front of the Lancaster, and at its same altitude, was another R.A.F. bomber. The distance was too great to identify what type it was but Sinclair could definitely tell it was under attack.

From just below and behind the bomber a tight stream of tracers leashed out at it. Again, the attacking night fighter could not be seen, though its effectiveness was plainly evident. Tracers sparkled over the bomber's right wing root; barely a second later a brilliant white flash separated the bomber from its entire right wing. The doomed aircraft snapped onto its back and tumbled to the ground, reaching the earth some time ahead of its wing. The tracers stopped at the moment of the explosion, its source remaining invisible to Sinclair and his crew.

"Good God, how could he have crossed that distance in so short a time?" the flight engineer asked. "He has to be doing better than four hundred miles an hour. How many night fighters can do that?"

"Not many can," said Sinclair, "and I've lost track of this one. Pilot to gunners, I've lost the bastard, stay on alert. Whoever it is, he's good and whatever he's flying is dangerous."

Beyond the waxing moon on the western horizon, Sinclair could see nothing. He knew the fighter could be anywhere, below him, above him, maybe even behind him with the speed it had so far exhibited. A wave of relief flashed over Sinclair when his mid-upper gunner informed him that he had spotted the night fighter again.

"I can't be sure it's the same one," the gunner advised. "But with the speed he's been flying at it has to be him. Another aircraft is buying it on our port side, ten o'clock high."

Just above the whirling propeller disc of the left outboard engine, Sinclair watched what looked like a distant burst of fireworks. The blossom of flames was beautiful and yet he knew it signalled the death of another British bomber. As quickly as the explosion had flared to life it died out, with the exception of a long plume of fire that fell to earth like a giant meteor.

"Now I really understand why the Americans like to fly in big formations," said the flight engineer, glancing past the headrest on Sinclair's seat. "I wish we were in the middle of a nice, big, fucking formation."

"So do I, but all we have are ourselves," Sinclair replied. "Keep your eyes open and search. Spotting the bastard means half the battle is won."

For his part, Sinclair carefully swept the horizon in front of the Lancaster. The waxing moon's pale light was the sole illumination he could use. For an instant, he caught sight of a shadow moving across its face. Sinclair blinked his eyes and it was gone, as if it had never been there. But he was certain it had, and that the shadow flew on swept wings.

"Pilot to mid-upper, swing your guns around!" Sinclair shouted. "Enemy straight ahead!"

He pushed his control yoke forward as he shouted, and swung it to the right. The Lancaster responded by dropping its nose and entering a diving right turn. The maneuver had scarcely commenced when a burst of red tracers erupted out of the night. They flashed over the Lancaster's canopy, filling the air space where the bomber would've been. Its nose and top turrets answered with their own twin streams of tracer fire.

Beyond the burst of glowing cannon shells, little could be seen of the Luftwaffe fighter. Sinclair thought he saw a low-wing aircraft with a triangular fuselage section behind the muzzle blasts, but he had to concentrate on flying his own plane. Keeping it under control and waiting for the sickening jar of a shell strike. However, neither plane managed to hit the other in their opening engagement. Sinclair heard a strange, hissing whine as the German fighter passed overhead. It was a noise he had never heard before and yet it sparked terror in him. He had an idea of what it was and seconds later his fears were confirmed when the tail gunner identified their attacker.

"Oh God, I don't believe it! Commander, it's a bleedin' Nazi jet! I can see the glow of his jet pipes."

"No wonder the swine looked so small to Tony," said Sinclair, "and no wonder he climbed after us so quickly. He must have a two hundred mile an hour edge on us."

"But, Geoffrey, jets are day fighters," the navigator pointed out. "How could he have tracked us so accurately?"

"He must have a radar set aboard his aircraft. That's what our detector must've picked up. Pilot to tail gunner, what's he doing now?"

"I'm sorry but he moved so fast I lost track of him."

"Wait a sec, Geoffrey. Monica has just come on," the navigator warned. "Our friend is on our tail, at maximum range."

"All right, I'm levelling her out. Stand by for corkscrew."

Sinclair had to use his flight instruments to bring the Lancaster back to level flight. Once it was in normal attitude again, he had only enough time to note that the bomber was heading north before the navigator gave him an update.

"Distance is down to two thousand feet," he said. "If he's carrying thirty millimeter cannons, we'll be in range soon."

"Understood," Sinclair replied. "Tail gunner, are you ready to call it?"

"Ready, Geoffrey."

"Pilot to mid-upper, have you spotted the bastard?"

"I think I have him. He's dead astern and closing."

"Tail gunner to pilot, roll down port!"

The Avro giant responded to the tail gunner's first call by dropping its left wing and sliding away, starting the corkscrew. It was more of a slide to a lower altitude than a flat out dive. Partway through it, another burst of red tracers were fired by the nearly invisible night fighter. They fell wide of the bomber, the tail and top turrets of which returned fire with their own multiple streams of yellow tracers. They would've trapped the jet, if it hadn't been moving at almost twice the Avro's speed.

"Tail gunner to pilot, change up port."

After sliding a thousand feet, the Lancaster changed its attitude and, instead of diving to the left, climbed to the left. Sinclair used the momentum built up during the descent to make his aircraft climb as if it were a four-engined fighter and not a lumbering, twenty-five-ton bomber.

"Pilot to mid-upper, where's the bastard?"

"I'm sorry, Geoffrey, I lost track of him as well. He should be in front of us. We should see the glow of his jet engines but I can't. Perhaps we did hit him and he went down?"

"I wouldn't wager on that. I hope he hasn't maneuvered under us and has a pair of 'jazz-music' cannons."

"Tail gunner to pilot, if you think he's underneath us we should do the third part of the corkscrew. Roll up starboard."

The Lancaster continued climbing, only now Sinclair made it slide to the right. It rounded off the top of its ascent, having regained all the altitude lost since the start of the corkscrew. To complete the maneuver, the tail gunner would next call out for the bomber to change down starboard and Sinclair would dive it to the right. The crew could then repeat the maneuver, but the top turret gunner interrupted the procedure as they were readying for the final part. He had at last spotted their adversary.

"Good God, he's diving on us! He's coming out of a loop!"

The tracers came from above and behind the Lancaster, which for the first second or two gave no answering fire. That was all the time the jet needed, part of its stream of thirty-millimeter cannon shells

13

walked through the bomber's right wing. From trailing edge to leading edge they marched, with one or more of them striking the outboard engine. It sputtered, then burst into flames as several fuel, oil and coolant lines sprayed their contents over the damaged Merlin.

Sinclair pulled his control yoke to the left, instead of right as he had been anticipating, and the shuddering bomber swung away from the lethal barrage of cannon shells. A moment later it was entering a steep dive and Sinclair was struggling to save his crippled ship.

"Feather starboard outer prop!" he shouted at his flight engineer, while he shut down the master fuel valve and throttle to the stricken engine. "Hit the fire extinguisher!"

Immediately below the propeller feathering buttons were the ones for the fire extinguishers. As soon as the flight engineer had feathered the right outboard propeller, he punched the extinguisher button to save the rest of the engine. Enough of the Merlin's systems were still intact for the propeller blades to be rotated until they were knife edge to the wind and had stopped rotating. The engine nacelle was flooded with carbon dioxide, dampening and eventually killing the flames which had erupted from it. They were still dying when the flight engineer finished the shut down by flipping a pair of toggle switches.

"Ignition switches are off," he told Sinclair. "The fire's burned out. Has there been any other damage?"

"Plenty, we've lost our mid-upper turret."

"But I don't recall hearing Tony say anything about it?"

"He doesn't have to. When we lost that engine we lost hydraulic power to his turret. The only way he can turn or elevate his guns is by manual control.

14

He's next to useless."

Sinclair still kept the Lancaster in a steep bank. Instead of a flat out dive, he spiralled the bomber toward the Baltic Sea. Speed and g-forces increased rapidly; Sinclair felt himself being pressed against his chair's right armrest and could see his flight engineer was having trouble remaining on the simple bench seat next to him.

"Mister Sinclair. Geoffrey, our air speed's moving past three-sixty," the flight engineer warned.

"I know, the Lanc's becoming nose heavy and the elevators are stiff," said Sinclair. He reached beside his chair for the elevator trim wheel and wound it back to relieve the pressure on the control yoke. "I know the problems I'll have on recovery but we need to reach sea level as quickly as possible. Our friend knew exactly how to hit us in the middle of a corkscrew. In all the sorties I've flown, only once before did I encounter someone this good."

"So he's our friend now. I thought he was a bastard."

"He still is, but he's also an experienced pilot and he deserves my respect. We're dealing with an expert flying the deadliest night fighter in existence. We won't evade him using normal tactics. We have to try something extraordinary to escape or we'll be up the spout."

From twelve thousand feet, the Lancaster spiralled steeply toward the Baltic. Sinclair pushed it until its air speed was hovering at four hundred miles an hour. It took less than half a minute for the bomber to make the full descent and, as Sinclair had said, he had difficulty levelling off.

The control pedestal felt as though it had been set in concrete. Sinclair wanted to put his feet on the instrument panel and get his full weight behind the yoke but he needed to keep them on the rudder pedals to compensate for the loss of the engine. By throttling back the remaining three, he was able to slow his aircraft slightly and raise its nose a little more. The Avro giant groaned as it slowly pulled out of its dive, just a few hundred feet above the calm, black waters of the Baltic Sea.

"Mid-upper to pilot, I've lost hydraulic power. I can only use manual controls to rotate my turret."

"I know, but you can still be useful to us. Have you been keeping track of our friend?"

"He's diving after us. He'll be on top of us in a few seconds and he's making it a beam attack."

"Very well, I'm taking us down to the wave tops," said Sinclair. "Prepare to join the Royal Navy."

The Lancaster eased closer to the sea. Close enough for its crew to see the moon shimmering on its surface, close enough for the propwash of the three good engines to roil it. The night fighter made its attack on the bomber's port side, opening fire while still several hundred yards out.

Its barrage of cannon shells left a trail of geysers in the water as they raced for the bomber, intersecting it just aft of the wings. A few shells exploded inside the Avro's fuselage, spraying the interior with shrapnel and glowing fragments of white phosphorous. There was a cry on the intercom. Whoever it was didn't give his name, but Sinclair identified him immediately.

"That was Tony. Les, go see if you can help him," he ordered, "and take the first-aid kit with you."

There was a harsh, eerie glow coming from the aft fuselage as the radio man climbed out of his seat. At first he thought an incendiary shell was lodged in the plane, then he realized it was something far worse.

"Wireless to pilot, our signal flares've been ignited!

You better send someone back to help me," he urged, before he broke his intercom connection and left his station.

"Pilot to navigator, go back and help Les! Take the fire extinguisher with you and jettison those flares! Whichever way you can." Sinclair glanced over his shoulder as he gave his latest command. Under the rear canopy decking, he glimpsed the navigator scrambling from his seat and taking the fire extinguisher off the starboard wall. Then Sinclair turned to his flight engineer. "If they don't take care of those flares, they'll burn our ship in half. Another pass or two like this and our friend will put us on his victory tally."

"What can we do? If we drop any lower we'll become one of His Majesty's submarines."

"There's a shore line ahead. Once we cross it, we'll do some low-level sightseeing. And our friend's great speed advantage will be of little use to him."

The radio man and the navigator crawled over the wing's main spars to reach the burning flares. Already several had ignited, their incandescent glare was blinding to look at and their growing heat had already started to melt the fuselage skin.

"Fetch the second fire extinguisher, Les," said the navigator. "And the crash axe. Don't worry about Tony, right now we have to save everyone."

Once he pulled the safety wire off his extinguisher, the navigator aimed it at the sputtering flares and fired it, spraying them with a jet of carbon dioxide. The radio man squeezed around the bulky, mid-upper turret, taking only a moment to look at the limp, bleeding body resting in it. Back beside the main entrance door he snatched a small, oddly shaped axe out of its wall brackets and made his way forward, picking up another extinguisher as he rejoined the

17

navigator.

A jagged, mountainous coast line sprang in front of the Lancaster, forcing Sinclair to put it into a climb. Its still-considerable air speed allowed the crippled bomber to leap over the peaks and settle inside a shallow valley before the jet returned.

"At least he can't make a beam attack while we're down here," said Sinclair. "Pilot to gunners, stay on your toes. He'll try either a head-on or a stern attack."

"Use the axe to lift each flare out of its mounts and push it out one of the holes!" the navigator shouted at the radio man. "Let's start with this one, Les."

The navigator aimed his extinguisher at one of the ignited flares and fired it. The carbon dioxide dampened the white-hot inferno; even so, the radio man pulled his tinted goggles over his eyes before approaching the flare rack. In spite of his insulated flying gloves and sheepskin-lined jacket, he could feel the intense heat. The flare had already burnt part way through its mountings, the radio man had only to tap it with his axe and it fell onto the bomb bay roof, where the navigator was able to kick it out one of the holes which had been melted in the fuselage skin.

"Good work!" he exclaimed. "Hand me the other extinguisher, this one's almost out. Let's try another one."

"There he is," said Sinclair, pointing at the left side of the windshield. "Pilot to gunners, our friend's making a head-on pass. Port side. Watch your leads."

At the far end of the valley a dark, swept-wing shadow dove out of the sky on a collision course with the Lancaster. As it passed over a heavily illuminated town, Sinclair briefly had a clearer view of his adversary. It was a low-wing, twin-engined aircraft with

18

black under surfaces and mottled gray top sides. Sinclair could even see the array of wirelike radar aerials around the fighter's nose. Moments later it was reenveloped by darkness and spitting cannon shells.

The jet had opened fire at long range and Sinclair could see that its tracers were flashing toward his left wing. He had just enough time to tip his wings before they reached him. They streaked harmlessly past the Lancaster, between the port inboard and port outboard engines. It was several more seconds before the night fighter had come within range of the nose gunner's machine guns and he returned fire.

This time it was the jet that took a few hits and he broke off his attack. He climbed away steeply, drawing more fire from the tail gunner when he fell behind the Avro giant.

"I don't think I damaged him greatly," said the nose gunner. "He'll be back, Geoffrey."

"I know," said Sinclair. "What you've done may have merely made him angry. And I'm counting on that. I'm hoping he'll become reckless."

By the time he disposed of the third flare, the radio man had become adept at lifting them out of their mountings and pushing them through one of the holes burned in the fuselage side.

"Excellent, just one more to go," advised the navigator. "Jettison this one and you'll save the ship."

Temporarily dampened and cooled by a spray of carbon dioxide, the radio man hooked the last sputtering, hissing flare at its front end. He lifted it out of the front bracket and, by twisting the axe slightly, he maneuvered its burning end out the hole it had created. Then he grabbed the tail of the flare with his hand and pushed the rest of it out of the plane. With all the ignited flares now gone, the fuselage fell strangely dark and quiet, except for the radio man screaming to have his hands sprayed with the fire extinguisher.

"Thanks, mate, that I really needed," he sighed after the navigator had complied with his demand. "That axe was red hot and my fingers were broiling."

"I'll dispose of the remaining flares," said the navigator. "Those mounts are still hot and they could set them off. As soon as you're ready, see to Tony."

"Someone isn't obeying the blackout laws," said the flight engineer as the Lancaster thundered over the brightly lit town. "Some poor chaps'll pay for this when the Germans find out."

The valley was not a very long one and soon gave way to rolling lowlands dotted with farms and towns. In the distance was a city, glowing with subdued though extensive illumination. The weak, ambient light allowed the bomber crew to spot the night fighter getting into position above them.

"He's trying for another beam attack," said Sinclair. "He must realize that we lost our mid-upper turret or he wouldn't be trying another deflection shot. This may be our chance, he's growing reckless. Pilot to tail gunner, stand by for port turn. Our friend's making a beam attack again. Once he's committed, I'll make the turn."

High above the Lancaster, the night fighter swung around and lowered its nose to begin a dive, just like a hawk going after its prey. In seconds its speed had increased by more than a hundred miles an hour. Sinclair kept his eyes on the descending fighter, so much so that the flight engineer had to tell him when he was losing proper flying attitude. When it seemed like the jet was bottoming out of its dive, Sinclair finally reacted, throwing the control yoke to the left and shouting at the tail gunner that now was the time.

The Avro giant banked steeply and entered as tight a turn as its airspeed and airframe would allow. Sinclair even advanced the throttle on the one good starboard engine to power the bomber through the turn. The centrifugal force of the maneuver proved too much for the battered engine, however. There was a sharp, jarring snap and the outer starboard engine — its cowling, its propeller, everything forward of the fire wall — was torn completely away.

Sinclair felt the control yoke jump in his hands as the Merlin detached and the wings wobbled but he steadied them and righted his ship. Behind him he could hear the chattering of the tail gunner's Browning machine guns. His trap had been sprung and he prayed it would work.

The jet opened fire while the Lancaster was still in its turn. His burst fell wide of its mark, however, and the Lancaster's tail gunner used the muzzle blasts as the aiming point for his fire. A quartet of .303-caliber Brownings didn't pack the punch of four thirty-millimeter cannons but they sprayed the night fighter with great accuracy. Strikes sparkled along its nose, left wing and engine pod. Almost at once it stopped firing and veered away, breaking off its attack. The bomber crew began cheering, though Sinclair did want to know how much damage their adversary had received.

"He broke away when I started hitting him, Geoffrey," said the tail gunner. "For a second I saw a jet of flame and then, nothing. He was climbing when I lost track of him."

"I hope that means he has engine damage," Sinclair replied. "Pilot to radio man, how are you dealing with the fire?"

"Andrews here, Geoffrey," the navigator answered. "We've jettisoned all the marker flares and the fire's out. We have a bit of damage in this section, though I think the structure's still sound. Les is now seeing to Tony. I'm afraid he's in a rather bad way."

"Tail gunner to pilot, I have him! Our friend's approaching that city we saw lighted up. His undercarriage is down, I think he's landing."

The crew cheered again over their apparent victory, everyone except Sinclair joining in. He swung the Lancaster around and flew toward the same strangely illuminated city. The navigator came forward, stopping at his station for a look at his radar screen and to pick up a map. He came into the cockpit and crouched behind the flight engineer.

"Our friend's on final approach to an airfield," said Sinclair. "It's as brightly lit as that blasted city. What's happening here? Doesn't anyone in Denmark realize the war's still on? An airfield with that kind of lighting would attract our Mosquitoes like moths to an open flame."

"I think sharks after the smell of blood would be a better comparison," said the flight engineer. "When I was with my first crew, I saw what they can do to a Jerry base."

"There's a very good reason for all that light. This isn't Denmark," the navigator informed, folding his map and showing a small section of it to Sinclair. "I checked our H2S and we're here, over the Skåne Peninsula of Sweden. That's not Copenhagen we're looking at, that's Malmö. And the airfield our friend's on final to is called Bulltofta."

In the glow of the runway lights, the German jet could at long last be clearly seen. The navigator immediately identified the fighter as an Me-262, a designation which had eluded Sinclair. In addition to its gently swept wings and bulbous engine pods, the jet's nose-mounted radar array and elongated canopy

22

were readily visible. It didn't have the simple, seg-mented bubble of a single-seater; instead its canopy was heavily framed and nearly extended back to the tail plane, spoiling the aircraft's otherwise clean lines.

"So it's a two-man version," said Sinclair. "Well, this certainly is something new. I don't believe I ever heard anything from intelligence about a two-man version of the '262."

"If we can, we should head back to England," the navigator added. "What's happened to us will be very valuable to R.A.F. intelligence. Can we make it, Geoffrey?"

"I've brought home aircraft that were in worse shape than this. What I'm more worried about is whether or not Tony can make it. How is he?"

"I helped Leslie bring him out of the turret and set him down but I couldn't tell you how bad he is. Les should be plugged into the intercom now, perhaps he can tell you."

"Pilot to radio man, how's Tony doing? Les, are you on the line?"

"I'm here, Geoffrey and I'm afraid Tony's in rather a bad way," the radio man eventually answered. "He has shrapnel wounds in his stomach and legs and he's bleeding rather heavily. I don't think he'll make it to England. He needs medical attention right away."

Sinclair looked out the canopy and gazed at the airport where the Me-262 had finished its landing roll. If he were to follow him in, his wounded gunner would receive excellent and immediate medical treat-ment. However, it would also mean internment and it might be several days before they could meet with British officials. Even then, Sinclair wondered if the Swedes would allow them to say anything about this new German fighter.

"I'm afraid Tony's going to have to wait until we

reach England," he said regretfully. "The information we have is too valuable to be lost. Make him comfortable and later I'll send you back some help. Pilot to nose gunner, return to your bomb aimer's station. Stand by on bomb recording cameras."

Sinclair banked the Lancaster gently and circled the airport's perimeter. He kept an eye on the Me-262, watching it taxi up to the control tower where it shut its engines down and was surrounded by airport personnel. Where it stood, the jet was bathed in light from the terminal. It made the perfect subject.

"Bomb aimer to pilot, cameras on. Ready to open bomb bay doors on your command."

When the Lancaster fell in line with the terminal, Sinclair racked it through a hard right turn. The moment its wings had levelled, he called for the bombardier to start his run. The twenty-foot-long bomb bay doors snapped open, giving the cameras inside a clear field of view.

The Avro giant roared across Bulltofta airfield, little more than a hundred feet off the ground. Its sudden appearance, the sight of an R.A.F. bomber thundering in with its bomb bay doors extended, caused everyone to scramble for cover. It made its photo run without interference; not until reaching the opposite side of the field did the Lancaster draw any fire from the defending anti-aircraft guns. By then it was too late. The tracers and flak bursts were no more than a nuisance to the departing bomber.

"If we avoid Malmö, we shouldn't receive any further attention from Swedish defenses," said the navigator, now back at his station. "When we reach Saltholm Island, we'll have crossed into Danish air space. I'm working on a course that will allow us to avoid Copenhagen. Especially the harbor and the air base at Vaerlöse. There are German warships in the harbor and a night fighter group at Vaerlöse."

"Understood," Sinclair replied. "We'll stay at low altitude until we reach the North Sea. Pilot to gunners, remain at your stations. We're not out of danger yet."

On the ground, as the sound of the Avro's engines died away, the Swedes and Germans came out of hiding and gathered around the soon to be interned Me-262.

"Major Peltz, I am told that you are the pilot of this remarkable aircraft," said a Swedish military officer, the highest ranking one to appear so far.

"Yes, I'm the pilot," one of the two Luftwaffe officers dourly answered.

"I am squadron leader Erik Lindh, of the Royal Swedish Air Force. You and your radar officer are under arrest for violating Swedish air space. We shall inform your embassy in Stockholm of your arrival and later today you'll be allowed to meet with your air attaché. In addition to surrendering your aircraft, you are to immediately surrender all your personal weapons to me."

With a little grumbling, the Luftwaffe crew handed Lindh their service pistols and survival knives, still in their sheaths. They were then led into the terminal by a detail of Swedish border police while Lindh walked up to the jet to admire it better.

"A very remarkable aircraft, squadron leader," said a subordinate officer, echoing Lindh's earlier remark. "The most advanced fighter in the world and it's ours."

"Yes, I only hope it does not become a sleek albatross around our necks," Lindh admitted. "The possession of this fighter could give us nothing but trouble."

"Ian, good to see you," said the Royal Navy officer

25

behind the desk. "Please come in, we've been waiting for you."

Cmdr. Charles Cox rose out of his seat and extended a hand to the newest visitor to his office. He wore the same uniform as Cox, stood several inches taller than him and, though his hair curled slightly like Cox's, his was dark brown instead of sandy-colored. They shook hands quickly, then turned to the first visitor in the office.

"You must be one of the members of Cox's Threat Evaluation team," the new visitor remarked, looking over the other officer's uniform. "We usually don't see many R.A.F. types here in the Admiralty."

"Squadron leader Embry represents Royal Air Force intelligence on my team," said Cox. "He's from their Photo Reconnaissance unit at Medmenham. John, this is Lieutenant-Commander Ian MacAlister. Like me, he's with the navy's intelligence division, though he's not a former pilot. He was a reporter before the war and I dare say he'll be one after it's over. Ian's a good friend and more than that, with his background he'd be perfect for our mission."

"Mission? And I thought you had asked me over for just a chat and morning tea. What type of mission do you have? Sinking another German battleship?"

"Not quite, but it could be of enormous importance to us. I think John should explain the situation to you. Since he was the one who brought it to me in the first place. John?"

Cox handed the squadron leader one of two folders laying on his desk. Embry opened it and pulled out several sheets of paper. He took a few moments to sort them to his liking, then began reading the top page.

"At zero-two-thirty hours, the air attaché at our

Stockholm embassy reported that an Me-262 had made an emergency landing at Bulltofta airport in Sweden. The jet had been in a dogfight with a Royal Air Force bomber and took a number of hits in one of its engines. It landed safely and its crew has been interned by Swedish authorities."

"A jet fighter? How on earth can a jet fighter do a night interception?" MacAlister asked. "As I recall, Charles once told me those jets could only fly day operations."

"I know, this first report is somewhat sketchy. But I do have a more extensive one from the pilot of the Lancaster the jet tried to down." Embry quickly shifted the top page to the bottom of his stack. "This is from Wing Commander Geoffrey Douglas Sinclair. His aircraft was heavily damaged but he managed to land it at an emergency airfield in Scotland. He gives a very good description of the night fighter and also managed to shoot a few photographs of it."

"These should give you a better idea of what this jet looks like," said Cox, opening the second file. He handed MacAlister a set of four black-and-white prints. Of them, only the third was a clear shot of the Messerschmitt jet but it was enough for MacAlister. "Essentially it's a two-seat version of the Me-262 but with much more sophisticated electronics. It has an elongated canopy for the pilot and a radar operator and the antennas you see mounted in the nose are radar aerials. From their design, both Royal Air Force and Royal Navy intelligence say they're part of a completely new radar system. One which would be immune to our jamming.

"With its performance and that new system, this aircraft could be extremely dangerous. If the Germans could produce just a hundred or so of them, they could destroy most of the Royal Air Force's bomber fleet. That would do more than kill thousands of our air crew. It would end half of our joint bombing campaign with the Americans and seriously affect the outcome of the war. There are many vital targets in Germany we must still hit. If we fail to destroy them, it will definitely prolong the war and could change its outcome. Nazi Germany may be a cornered animal, but that is the most dangerous kind."

"I see, it would be a fantastic prize," said MacAlister, returning the photographs to Cox. "Perhaps the most important of the war."

"It's the only production prototype of Germany's latest and most advanced fighter," Embry added, closing his own file. "If we were to have it, we'd not only save our bomber fleet, we'd seriously disrupt Germany's night fighter program. We must have this aircraft, and Charles says you're the man who can get it."

"But why me, Charles? I don't know much about airplanes, ours or theirs. Why, your former assistant knows more about aircraft than I do."

"You've been to Sweden before, Ian," said Cox. "You've done several assignments there and you're familiar with our military attachés. I'm told the attaché who sent that first report is a good friend of yours. Greg Parry."

"What, Greg's still in Stockholm? I thought he would've been transferred months ago. It'll be nice to see him again. Who else will you use on this mission?"

"Who else do you think? Those Americans I worked with several weeks ago would be perfect. Colonel Lacey and his men have been working on the continent for over a month now, retrieving German aircraft for that Enemy Aircraft Evaluation unit of theirs. You've met them before, what do you think of their suitability?"

"They're certainly an odd crew," MacAlister admitted. "Colonel Lacey not only has Army types under his command but U.S. Navy and Marine Corps officers as well. They're a mixed and very talented team, I especially remember that Navy test pilot, Commander Norris. Do you know where they are?"

"Yes, I'm sending Constance back to the continent for them," said Cox. "Since she hasn't been with Lacey for the past fortnight, she was becoming rather 'anxious' to see him. I'm also contacting an old friend of ours. Captain Roberts, he's still assigned to the Special Air Service."

"Wait, now I remember." It took MacAlister a few seconds to search his memory for the name Cox used. "He was that American Ranger assigned to the SAS as an exchange officer. Good God, he's been with them for more than two years."

"I know and I'm trying to locate him. He's on leave somewhere." Cox handed the photograph folder back to MacAlister and indicated to Embry to give him the reports as well. "You better study those while you can. We've booked you a seat on the Swedish air lines flight to Stockholm. You have a new assignment, Ian. You're going to be the new naval attaché to our Stockholm embassy. We'll all have to work fast on this one, such opportunities don't last very long and we can't afford to let another slip through our fingers."

Chapter Two: Day One
On the Continent

"Oberstleutant Heinrich, I am Klaus Lossberg," announced one of the men who had entered Heinrich's office. "Gestapo commander for Denmark. From your appearance, I take it that you didn't get much sleep last night either."

Lossberg walked up to Heinrich's desk where they shook hands. They both looked haggard and tired; there was stubble on their faces and dark circles under their eyes. Their handshake was civil and perfunctory, but in Lossberg's eyes Heinrich could see anger, and he was sure in his own a little resentment showed as well.

"Of course, they were my men that were missing and my plane," said Heinrich, offering the Gestapo chief a seat. "I'm thankful they're safe. If only they had managed to land a few miles farther to the west."

"This is not a matter to be treated lightly, Herr Oberstleutnant," Lossberg snapped. It didn't take much for his anger to show. "Berlin considers this to be an extreme crisis. The only operational prototype of our most advanced night fighter has been interned in Sweden. Luftwaffe headquarters, the RLM, the Foreign Ministry and even the Führer himself are involved. This crisis must be resolved immediately. The aircraft in question must either be returned to us or destroyed."

"I'm sure that is what will eventually happen and please refer to me as Kommandeur. It is my courtesy title, everyone in the Luftwaffe uses it for *gruppen* commanders, so have the courtesy to use it. Why are you and Berlin so nervous about this incident? The Swedes have handled dozens of similar ones before. They've almost always returned or scrapped the aircraft which have come down in their country. And though I don't expect them to scrap the Night Hawk, even if they did there are still two additional prototypes being built. What's happening now that is making Berlin so nervous? Is it my air crew? Except for defectors, air crew are always returned."

"The Swedes are returning your men. They'll be back in our hands in another two or three days. We'll demand a full report on the incident when they return. We want to know how a group of experienced pilots, formed specifically to fly this new jet, could've blundered so badly. What is disturbing to Berlin is the way the Swedes are handling the aircraft.

"This Me-262 is more than the first prototype of the Night Hawk, it's the first jet aircraft of any kind to land in Sweden. We know the Swedes want to produce their own jets and are understandably interested in it. They claim the runways at Bulltofta aren't long enough to allow the Me-262 to take off after it's been repaired, so they're going to dismantle it for shipping to another field. We suspect either their Malmslätt base, near Saab's Linköping plant, or Norrköping, where the Swedes store a large number of interned aircraft.

"We know that the British and the Americans are interested in somehow either obtaining the jet or closely inspecting the aircraft to learn its secrets. This is something we of course cannot allow. Berlin has placed you and I in charge of returning the Me-262 to Germany, or at least preventing it from falling into Allied hands. All

German agents in Sweden, all SS and Luftwaffe units in Norway and Denmark will be at our disposal. As will the services of the other armed forces."

"And who shall we report to?" Heinrich asked, "To whom are we answerable?"

"I'm to report directly to Himmler," said Lossberg. "You're to report to Hermann Goering. Not Generalleutnants Kammhuber or Adolf Galland, your normal superiors, or Generalleutnant Barkhorn, Nacht Falke project chief. Our Stockholm embassy will report directly to Foreign Minister Von Ribbentrop. They, in turn, will report to Adolf Hitler. It is us, however, who'll be responsible should our attempts to regain the jet fail. Am I clear, Herr Kommandeur? I do not want to explain failure to Hitler."

"All right, make sure the harness around the nose section is secure before we start lifting," said Lacey. "How about it, Vince, are you ready?"

"I'm all strapped in, Colonel," Capollini answered, looking out the cockpit. "Ready when you are."

Lacey stepped off the wing of the Me-410 and ordered the rest of his men to move away from it. Only Capollini remained, sitting in the downed fighter's cockpit. Lacey walked over to the crane operator and, once they were sure the aircraft was clear, gave him the signal to raise it.

Slowly, the twin-engined Messerschmitt was lifted off the deep bed of snow it had crash-landed on. As it gained its altitude by inches, Lacey ordered some of his team to grab hold of the fighter's wing tips and steady it. The aircraft was airborne once more, in spite of the fact that its engines were silent, its propeller blades twisted and bent back and its undersides peppered with fifty-caliber shells.

"Hold it there, Al," Lacey ordered. "OK, Vince. Hit

the landing-gear lever."

The Me-410 had made a wheels-up crash landing after being damaged by anti-aircraft fire. Lacey was having it raised so its landing gear could be lowered and the aircraft towed away. When Capollini pulled the gear-retract lever, the gear doors under the engine nacelles and the tail plane cracked open. Without hydraulic pressure, the landing gear had to rely on its own weight to bring it down. That would take time and even then, weight alone wouldn't lock the gear.

"This hand pump ain't working, Colonel," said Capollini. "I guess the hydraulic lines must've been shot out too."

"Then we'll have to help them down," said Lacey. "Sergeant, get your men under the plane."

Another part of the recovery team split into three groups and pried open the gear doors by hand. Those working on the left nacelle were splashed with oil and engine coolant as they struggled with the doors and the landing gear itself. The group working on the tail wheel had the easiest time. Scarcely more than one man was needed to pull the wheel down and lock it in place. The main gear needed more effort and Lacey assigned additional men to help with them.

"OK, Colonel, I got three flags showing on the indicator," Capollini advised. "They're locked."

"Everyone move away from the plane," said Lacey. "We're going to bring her back down."

Except for the men still holding onto the Messerschmitt's wing tips, the team cleared the area. The crane operator put his controls in reverse, slowly lowering the fighter.

"Stop the crane, Colonel!" one of the other team officers shouted. "I think I hear an airplane coming in."

When the crane motors ceased whirring, a weak buzzing became more distinct. It didn't sound very powerful, certainly not the roar of a Merlin or a Pratt and Whitney radial, but it was an aircraft engine and growing louder by the second.

"Well it's not an A-26 from the base," said Lacey, "or anything else that's big. But I don't like it. Some of the guys from the bomb group told me the Germans like to use trainers and light transports to make sneak raids. This could be one of them. Grab your weapons and scatter."

"Hey, what about me?" Capollini asked, the buzz becoming a loud, omnipresent drone.

"You got your service pistol," said Lacey. "Now's your chance to play fucking Patton. If it is an enemy plane, we'll take care of it."

Lacey unslung the M-3 submachine gun he'd been carrying and loaded a clip into it. Cocking the weapon as he ran, he moved over to the line of jeeps and trucks which had brought his team to the crash site. Standing beside the lead jeep, Lacey could see the entire field, the road cutting through it and the trees lining it.

The drone was now clearly coming from one direction, due north. Beyond the northern tree line was the Ninth Air Force bomber base the Me-410 had been attacking when it was shot down. Lacey couldn't hear the sound of anti-aircraft fire from the base but that didn't mean the approaching aircraft wasn't German. Not until it popped over the tree tops was Lacey able to identify it.

"Don't worry, Vince, it's one of our grasshoppers. An L-4," he advised. "It looks like it's going to land. I'll find out what he wants. Chris, you're in charge."

After Lacey safetied his submachine gun, he walked out to the center of the field. By then the L-4 had circled the crash site, so low one could hear wind whistling through its struts, and was coming back around with its engine barely muttering. The Piper glided in for a landing, the snow muffling the thump of its main wheels as they touched down. Rather than wait for Lacey to reach it, the L-4 taxied across the field to him. The pilot switched off the engine when he was just a few feet away and opened the plane's side hatch. The passenger was still climbing out of the Piper when Lacey caught a glimpse of her face and her short, red hair; he was able to identify her immediately.

"Connie! My God, I thought it'd be days before I saw you!" In a few strides Lacey reached Constance Smythe and was embracing her, practically lifting her off the ground. "It feels so good to have you in my arms again."

"And I can't tell you what it feels like to have you do it," she replied, kissing Lacey. "When you can't be with the one you love, you really miss the simple pleasures."

"Hey, Colonel, shouldn't you have saluted her first?" Capollini purred, even though he was almost out of breath from running. "Ain't there something called protocol?"

"It's funny to hear you mention protocol," said Lacey, "Between us it's not necessary, except if it's official. Tell me, Connie, is this official or not?"

"In a way it is, Dennis. Charles sent me here to collect you. How else do you think a mere Royal Navy sub-lieutenant can obtain the use of an American liaison aircraft?"

"I see. What does Charles want me for?"

"Yeah, Lieutenant, what's the lowdown?" Capollini interrupted.

"For the moment, that's restricted," said Constance. "Only Dennis and Commander Norris are to hear the full details. For now, all I can say is a German aircraft has made an emergency landing in a neutral country. There's a chance that we can obtain it. Charles would like to know if you're interested and would you be willing to help?"

"It depends on what the plane is," said Lacey. "But if

35

Charlie wants it, you bet I'm interested. When would he like to hear from me?"

"If you're interested, he wants to see you immediately. And since you are, can you leave now? We could use my aircraft and return to Paris where we could catch a transport back to England."

"I don't think so. With three people in it, I wouldn't trust a Piper Cub to make it out of this field. And at its maximum speed, we'd need an hour to reach Paris. In that time we could be halfway to London in my plane. There's a Lockheed Lodestar sitting at a bomber base just a few miles away and it's at my team's disposal. C'mon, if we take one of the jeeps we'll be there in ten minutes."

Lacey took Constance to the crash site where there were more, though less emotional, reunions with other members of the team. By now the Me-410 was sitting on its landing gear; the team only needed to remove the outer wing panels and it could be towed to the air base.

"Connie and I will be flying to London," Lacey informed the others. "Chris, you'll remain in charge of the recovery. When you get back to base, Norris will be waiting for you. By then I might have a new assignment for us."

"Aw, Colonel, why are you leaving the major in command?" Capollini asked, "he's a Marine and we're Army."

"Shannon's in charge because he is a major. He's the highest ranking officer here and he's recovered more enemy aircraft than we have. Will you have any trouble, Chris?"

"I don't think so," said Shannon. "We'll be at the base in time for lunch. See you later, Colonel."

Lacey and Constance hopped into the lead jeep and drove back to the road, squeezing past the row of other vehicles parked behind it. The jeep had a heavy canvas canopy enclosing the passenger section. It wasn't particularly warm inside but at least it kept out the bone-chilling winter winds. It also allowed Lacey and Constance to have a normal conversation. At last she could give him all the details without compromising security.

"Whatever this plane is, it must be important," said Lacey, "for you not to tell Vince or Chris about it."

"Believe me, it is," Constance replied. "It could be the most advanced aircraft in the Luftwaffe. Last night, an R.A.F. Lancaster was attacked by an unknown fighter after it had bombed an oil plant in Germany. The battle raged from fifteen thousand feet to sea level and managed to wander over Sweden. There, the fighter was damaged and forced to make an emergency landing at Bulltofta airfield, near the city of Malmö. Only then could it be identified as an Me-262 jet. It was a two-seat version of the fighter, outfitted with a new radar system. The Swedes have interned the jet and are planning to move it to a more secure field. Charles believes it's the prototype for a Messerschmitt project called Night Hawk.

"If we could somehow obtain this fighter, the benefits would be enormous. First, we'd learn the latest secrets of German radar technology. Second, we'd have a flyable example of their most advanced airplane and, third, we would delay the Night Hawk project by stealing the only existing prototype of it. This could well change the outcome of the war and will definitely save the lives of thousands of Allied air crew. What do you think, Dennis?"

"Well, we already happen to have an Me-262 at the Patuxent Air Test Center. It's a single-seat, day-fighter version of the jet. It's faster than the Night Hawk but nowhere near as sophisticated. In addition to the radar, it probably has one of the most advanced blind flying systems in the world. We may already have an Me-262, but getting this one will be a coup and a half. Possibly the

37

greatest coup of the war. Do you know what condition it's in and what about that Lancaster? How on earth did it survive a tangle with a jet fighter?"

"None too well. The bomber had one of its engines blown off its mountings, its mid-upper turret was put out of action and its fuselage was badly damaged by a fire. Two of its crew were injured and a third died of his wounds before the aircraft could land in England. The only reasons the Lancaster survived were luck and the experience of its crew. As for the jet, it was engine damage that forced it to land. The pilot and radar operator are being returned to Germany, though the Swedes are retaining the Me-262. Since this is the first jet to land in Sweden, they're as interested in it as we are."

"I wonder why?" Lacey asked. "Apart from being a curiosity item, what good would such an advanced airplane be to them? I recall at the beginning of the war, they were buying P-35s off of us and biplanes off the Italians."

"Sweden's aviation industry is more modern than you think. Charles is having a report compiled on it for the meeting."

"Do we have anyone in Sweden who's working for us? Or are we going in alone?"

"Hardly. Both British and American military attachés are working for us," Constance answered, "and soon we'll have our own men in Stockholm. Charles is sending an old friend of his to Sweden to be Britain's new naval attaché."

"Swedish air lines is pleased to announce the arrival of Flight One-forty-five from London, England. Passengers will deplane at Gate Three, prior to processing by customs officials."

The bright orange Ju-52 taxied across the concrete

tarmac to Bromma's main terminal. It swung around sharply and shut down with its tail only a few feet from the glass-walled terminal building. Parked next to it was a DC-3, wearing a German civil registration and the markings of Deutsche Lufthansa. A small set of boarding stairs was wheeled up to the Junkers's exit door as the plane's stewardess pushed it open. The passengers began appearing immediately and made a short dash through the snow flurries to the gate door. Inside the terminal, they fell in line at the customs station, right behind the passengers from the Lufthansa DC-3. Most of those who arrived on the Ju-52 were civilians, but one wore the deep blue uniform and gold braid of the Royal Navy.

"And you are?" asked the customs inspector at the desk.

"Lieutenant-Commander Ian William MacAlister, of His Majesty's Navy," the officer replied, handing over his passport. "I'm His Britannic Majesty's new naval attaché to your country. There should be somebody here from the embassy to pick me up."

"Yes, your air force attaché is waiting for you." The inspector gave the passport a cursory exam and quickly stamped it. Next, he turned to the customs personnel who were busy opening the luggage of the recent arrivals. "There's no need to search the commander's belongings. I sincerely hope you enjoy your stay in our country, Mister MacAlister."

"I trust I'll find it more peaceful than London has recently been," said MacAlister, slipping his passport back in his jacket. "Thank you so much, goodbye."

MacAlister had his suitcases placed on a dolly and he pushed it into the lobby himself. He had barely entered it when another officer in a similar uniform approached him. At more than six feet, MacAlister was some six inches taller than the R.A.F. officer who met him. They gave each other a formal salute, then embraced like old friends.

"I feel like I'm standing in a hole every time I meet you," said the Royal Air Force attaché. "But it's good to see you again, Ian. It's been months."

"I know, the weather's gone from slightly chilly to unbearably cold," said MacAlister. "I find it rather ironic that I should arrive in a Junkers tri-motor and the Germans in a Dak. Tell me, Greg, when did Lufthansa start using a DC-3?"

"After their Focke-Wulf Condor crashed late last year. They'd been using an Fw-200 since the end of October and it crashed after leaving Berlin one day. We believe the Dakota they're using was one of the airliners they captured off the Dutch. Here, let me help you with this. I have the car parked in the reserved area, it's not too far."

The air attaché, squadron leader Greg Parry, took over the luggage dolly and pushed it through the lobby, selecting the exit door closest to the row of reserved parking spaces. He wheeled it up to a dark blue Bentley sedan and unlocked the car's trunk. MacAlister and Parry quickly loaded his suitcases inside and while MacAlister returned the dolly to the lobby, Parry started the Bentley. They barely uttered another word to each other, not until both were in the car.

"I noted that the chauffeur of the Mercedes parked near us took quite a bit of interest in our activities," said MacAlister, looking back at the car in question. "I also note it has diplomatic plates, German."

"Yes, the Nazis are watching us very closely," Parry answered, "the Americans as well. It just started today. It no doubt has to do with the 'arrival' of their Me-262 at Malmö last night."

"The Mercedes isn't following us. Why? Will the Germans have another car tail us to the embassy?"

"No, they probably expect we'll go there first. What a surprise they'll have when we don't show up. I suspect that car is busy collecting some diplomatic personnel from Lufthansa's Berlin flight."

"Has there been any recent developments with the jet?" MacAlister asked. "What are the Germans up to? Since they've been watching us, I hope we are watching them."

"The Swedes are going to dismantle the Me-262 and they'll move it to their Norrköping base. The airplane could be moved sometime tonight. The Swedish air force would like to keep it under cover as much as possible and moving it from a field that's half civilian is most prudent. This will also allow the Swedes to have their experts from Saab pick over it, and allow us to inspect the jet as well. A friend of ours is discussing this with Swedish officials. The Nazis are also talking to the Swedes, and doing some snooping around Bulltofta."

"Which 'friend' are we talking about?" There was a tremor of foreboding in MacAlister's voice; he could just guess who it was.

"Carl Drache," said Parry. "He contacted us this morning about the jet. He knew quite a few things we didn't."

"I just knew it would be him. Any time we have an incident involving Nazi or Allied airplanes he turns up, always so eager to help. I've said it before and I still maintain it, I don't trust the man. In the past, a good deal of the information Drache gave us proved to be useless or, worse yet, dangerously misleading. Remember the Gräsdal incident of last June? We gave Sweden a dozen mobile radar sets in exchange for the wreckage of that V-2 and paid Drache a considerable amount of money to find out if indeed the rocket was a radio-guided weapon. Only recently have we found that it's not, after wasting millions of pounds trying to develop electronic countermeasures."

"I'll admit what happened there was something of a red herring but even our own scientific team agreed with what Carl found. Those are the chances you take when you obtain information on the enemy. It could be erroneous."

"It could also be deliberately planted," MacAlister countered. "When I was a Reuters correspondent in Moscow, I came across the term *dezinformatsiya*. It was something the Russians pulled on us regularly, it means 'disinformation.' I wonder if the Germans picked up that little practice from them? After all, before the Bolsheviks were our ally, they were Germany's ally."

"That's a rather extreme charge to make, Ian. You know we've done checks on his background; he's as clean as either of us. A Swedish-born aristocrat, member of a titled family with relatives throughout Europe, connections in almost every country on the continent, and he was known before the war as one of Sweden's most ardent anti-fascists. He couldn't be more perfect."

"I know, his background is impeccable. Not a single flaw or gray area. Almost as if it were written that way. To me, there's something unsettling about him. My neck hairs raise whenever I meet the man."

"Well, be on your good behavior for me, all right?" Parry requested. "We're on our way to meet Drache."

"So that's why we're not going to the embassy first. And it won't be to the ambassador's residence, the Ministry of Defense or Swedish air force headquarters. The Germans will be surprised. Where, precisely, are we going?"

"To the English-Swedish Club. Drache said he might be late, so we're to take a table at the bar and wait for him to show. He said he wouldn't be long."

"Well, the Nazis will be surprised, but it won't take them long to find us. When will we meet with the American attachés?" MacAlister asked.

"Once we've been to our embassy. At some point we do have to follow protocol, old chap."

* * *

From northern France, the Lodestar took just over an hour to reach Heathrow airport, outside of London. The drive to the Admiralty building in downtown London was almost as long, which meant Lacey and Constance didn't arrive there until nearly noon. Though they half expected not to find anyone in the Intelligence Division offices, Cox and the rest of the Threat Evaluation team were waiting for them.

"Dennis, I believe you know the members of my team," said Cox, as they all took their seats around the meeting room's table. "From the intelligence branches of our armed forces, our civilian intelligence services and French intelligence. And, gentlemen, you should remember both Colonel Dennis Lacey and Sub-lieutenant Constance Smythe, we're so glad you could finally make it.

"This emergency briefing is now in order. You all know the situation we're facing. It's both a profound crisis and an occasion of fantastic opportunities. If we succeed, we'll have the only flying example of the Reich's most advanced fighter and the latest in German electronics. If we fail, if the Reich regains the Night Hawk, it'll go into production and R.A.F. Bomber Command will be shot out of the sky. That could well affect the outcome of the war and will certainly kill thousands of men. We have some clear and hard choices to make. Squadron leader, could you show us where the jet came down?"

"The aircraft landed here, at the Bulltofta airport, outside of Malmö on the southern peninsula of Sweden," said squadron leader Embry, half turned in his chair and using a pointer to show the location of Malmö on Sweden's Skåne peninsula. When he turned to face the table again, Embry handed out several copies of a photograph to the officers and civilians seated around him. "And this is the aircraft in question. It's a two-seat version of the Me-262 fighter. We in the R.A.F. and the Eighth Air Force believe this is a modification of the Me-262B, an operational conversion trainer. A number of these trainers have been built, it'd be easy to modify one of them to be the prototype for a jet night fighter. The Messerschmitt company proposed this several months ago, they called it the Nacht Falke Projekt. It appears as though the Germans have finally built themselves a Night Hawk."

The photograph Embry distributed to the other members of the team was one from the series Cox had shown to Ian MacAlister a few hours earlier, the only one with a clear, overhead view of the jet stranded in Sweden.

"What do you estimate the performance of this version to be?" Maurice Bertrand of French Military Intelligence asked.

"The performance of the '262B was similar to the single-seater," said Rick Striver, from Eighth Air Force G-2. "But the second seat did reduce internal fuel capacity. So to compensate, it has to carry a pair of drop tanks on fuselage racks. We think the radar array on the nose will reduce the plane's maximum speed some thirty to forty miles an hour and lower its service ceiling a few thousand feet. Even so, the fighter is still a hundred miles an hour faster than the fastest night bomber in service, the De-Havilland Mosquito. If we could grab this plane, or get some good photographs of it, we could find out where this version is being built and flatten the factory."

"Not to mention unlocking the secrets of its radar," Lacey added, staring at one of the photographs Embry had given out. "How many people do we have working in Sweden for us and what are our chances of getting this plane?"

"All military attachés and their staffs at both British and American embassies are working for us," Cox answered, "and I've sent Ian MacAlister to Stockholm to be England's new naval attaché. There's a reasonable chance we can obtain the aircraft. Last June a V-2 crashed in Sweden and after we gave them some radar equipment, the Swedish air force turned the wreckage over to us. Recently though we haven't been as successful as we would like. Several other night fighters have landed in Sweden in the last few months. They're being returned to the Germans."

"What are they doing about this?" inquired Lieutenant-Commander Preston, from U.S. Naval Intelligence. "For the Krauts, this must be a crisis of the first water."

"Their diplomatic activity is high. Their ambassador and Luftwaffe attaché met with the Swedish foreign and defense ministers this morning. More diplomatic personnel have arrived from Berlin, it's rumored that Von Ribbentrop himself has taken charge of this incident. If the Nazis become truly desperate, and I believe they will, given the nature of the jet, they might try a commando attack to destroy it, as they threatened last year when another of their night fighters landed by accident in Switzerland."

"If we do get this airplane from the Swedes," said Langer, of British Secret Service, "how on earth will we spirit it out of their country? Fly it?"

"In a way we can," Lacey offered. "In fact there are two ways. If the Swedes dismantle it, then we can load the jet inside one of our big transports and fly it out that way. Or there's the other, get a pilot and an electronics expert to Sweden and fly the Night Hawk out under its own power. Of course, that way would be far more dangerous than the first one. No matter how good our men are, they'd be flying an unfamiliar plane. And since the Night Hawk is still in Sweden, what are they doing with the jet? Connie told me they're as interested in it as we are."

"Shortly before you arrived, we received word that the

Royal Swedish Air Force will move the jet to their Norrköping base," said Cox, "where most interned aircraft are stored. The move should make it easier for our attachés in Stockholm to inspect the '262 and for Saab's experts to pour over it. Yes, Sweden is very interested in this jet. So interested they might even keep it for themselves. In the last few years, Sweden's aviation industry has made astounding progress. They've gone from building another country's aircraft under license, to designing and building their own airplanes. When this war is over, Sweden will have the most advanced aviation industry on the European continent.

"The latest version of their first indigenously produced bomber is the fastest example of its type in the world. Their first fighter, the J-22, is broadly comparable to Germany's Focke-Wulf 190. The Saab J-21 is their newest fighter and it's the only twin-boom, pusher-engined fighter to be produced by any nation on earth. The J-21 is the first fighter to be built by Saab, which makes its radical design even more remarkable. It's the norm for a company to be conservative with its first design. The next logical step for the Swedes is to build a jet aircraft, and possessing an Me-262 would be a tremendous boost to their aviation industry."

As Cox spoke, he held up a large photograph of each airplane he described. The first looked like a slimmed-down version of Germany's Dornier 217; the next did indeed bear a resemblance to the Fw-190. It was a little stubbier and its tail fin and elevators were more rounded, but the fighter was almost a twin for the Focke-Wulf. The last aircraft drew low, admiring whistles from several of the Americans, including Lacey. The J-21 had a sleek, futuristic appearance, as if it belonged to the next war and not the one being waged. It looked like the P-38's little brother and even sitting on the ground, it was fast.

46

"Do you think there's a chance that the Swedes will keep the jet?" asked Preston.

"In the past they've kept German aircraft that have interested them," Cox answered, "and they have every Allied aircraft that's landed in Sweden since the war began. If they do choose to keep it, I'm sure some arrangement can be made to share the data with the Royal Swedish Air Force."

"Since you're on the topic, how will we share this airplane should it come into Allied hands?" Langer requested.

"Lieutenant-Colonel Striver and I have worked out a plan for that," said Embry, jumping in ahead of Cox. "If Colonel Lacey's group is willing to help us, then the Night Hawk will be theirs and the Royal Air Force will receive all its radar, navigation and landing approach systems. The R.A.F. would like to have one of its test pilots assigned to the Enemy Aircraft Evaluation unit as well. Would those terms be acceptable to you, Colonel?"

"Since you guys need to know more about the radar than we do, sure thing," said Lacey. "And if your pilot can bring along a Gloster Meteor, I'm sure Admiral Hinton will agree. He's wanted to get ahold of a Meteor jet for more than a month now."

"The Americans already have an Me-262," said Langer, "why should they be given another? We need one for our own testing and evaluation purposes."

"The Night Hawk may be designated Me-262 but it's a completely different aircraft from the single-seater," Embry responded. "It's a unique machine in its own right and we have to give it to people who have had some experience with this type of airplane. The Royal Air Force has no experience with captured enemy jets. By giving the Night Hawk to the Americans, we can evaluate it quicker and train a cadre of pilots to handle the type, or any other German jet which falls into our hands.

47

As we all know, the Nazis are developing a wide variety of jets. Including the Arado 234 bomber and the Heinkel 162 fighter."

"I think the plan's a good one," said Cox, "and if there are no further objections, I say we adopt it."

There were a few grumblings from the other members of the team but no one said anything audible. After a few seconds it became apparent the plan wouldn't be challenged.

"Excellent, we can begin straight away. John, perhaps you should contact Boscombe Down and see if they can arrange the transfer of a Meteor and a qualified test pilot. Dennis, do you think you should call Admiral Hinton and have his official go-ahead?"

"I better," Lacey admitted, "just in case something goes wrong later on or to get help from the U.S. Navy. And it's a good idea to let your commanding officer know where you are and what you're up to anyway."

"All right, if you'll come with me, I'll make arrangements for your call. Gentlemen, this meeting is over. We probably won't meet again for some time. For the next several days the situation will be very fluid. I don't think any of us will know where we'll be but I'll try to stay in touch with you. Colonel, let's go to my office."

Cox and Lacey were the first to leave the briefing room. Constance stayed behind to collect and pack away the materials used in the meeting while most of the other team members grabbed their hats and coats from the room rack. Soon, only squadron leader Embry remained, and when Constance was finished with her chores, she took him to the secretary's office where he put through a call to the Royal Air Force test center at Boscombe Down. She then brought the photographs and charts over to Cox's office, where she found him and Lacey talking on separate phones.

"I've reached the Patuxent Naval Air Station," said

Lacey, moving the telephone handset away from his mouth. "The base switchboard is trying to reach Admiral Hinton, I hope he's not out flying . . . Yes, Admiral? Good, this is Dennis Lacey. I'm in London and Lieutenant-Commander Cox has another deal we should be interested in."

"Dennis, he's full commander now," Constance corrected. "His promotion came through yesterday."

"Okay, Colonel, let's hear it. What's your friend got for us this time?" asked the tiny voice on the phone. It almost did sound like it was thousands of miles away, but Lacey identified it immediately as Steve Hinton.

"Last night, the only existing prototype of an Me-262 night fighter tangled with an R.A.F. bomber and had to make an emergency landing in Sweden," said Lacey. "The Swedes have interned the jet and there's a chance we can get it. Charlie would like to work with us to retrieve it."

"Jesus, he really does have something. What's the deal he's offering us?"

"If the operation succeeds, our unit gets the Me-262 and the Brits will get the radar and nav systems off it. They also want one of their test pilots assigned to our unit and they're arranging to send over a Gloster Meteor with him."

"Well, thank God," said Hinton. "I've been wondering when I'd hear from the R.A.F. about that idea. I was beginning to think they weren't interested and it was a Brit, one of your Royal Navy friends, who suggested it in the first place. This is a deal I can't pass up. When do you expect to get the Messerschmitt and when will we get the Meteor?"

"We'll have only a few days before the Swedes decide what they will do with the jet. They'll either give it back to the Germans, give it to us or keep it for themselves. The Meteor will take a little longer and we might not get it if all we can do is find out the secrets of the Me-262's radar gear. At the very least we'll be able to share that information. Both British and American embassies are applying diplomatic pressure, and no doubt so are the Nazis. We'll just have to see who makes the better offer."

"OK, Colonel, you've got my permission to try. Since you're on the scene, I'll let you command the operation. Don't waste time calling me for permission to do something, go ahead and do it. Just send me a telegram from time to time, telling me about your plans. Good luck to you and the rest of your team, Dennis. Do the best you can."

"Thanks, Admiral, we will. Goodbye." Lacey returned the telephone handset to its cradle, then he looked over at Cox, who was just ending his own conversation. "I got the clearance from my C.O. I have complete freedom. I'm sorry I didn't notice your raise in rank earlier, Charlie. After all we've done, I was wondering when one of us would get a promotion."

"You'll have yours soon, Dennis," Cox replied, hanging up his phone. "I predict you'll soon be the youngest general in the U.S. Army Air Force. Well, now we really are all set to go."

"Who were you talking to, Charles?" Constance asked, "the First Sea Lord? The Foreign Office?"

"No, I talked to Sir Cunningham and the Foreign Office while you were on the continent. My call was to Scotland, I was recruiting our last volunteer. He's been on leave for the past two weeks so he was somewhat difficult to trace."

"Scotland? Who do we need from Scotland?"

"A man skilled in commando operations. If the situation comes down to it, we must destroy the jet, rather than letting it return to Germany. And if Dennis goes into Sweden, I'd still like him to have some sort of protection on the ground. So I've recruited another American I happen to know, Captain Lee Edward Roberts. He's with the U.S. Army Rangers but he's been an exchange officer with the SAS for some time. He's the best I know for what we may have to do."

Chapter Three: A Gathering of Forces
The Night Hawk Is Moved

When they entered Stockholm, Parry and Mac-Alister turned off the main road from Bromma and drove across the Västerbron Bridge to Langholmen Island, one of several islands in the center of the capital. Apart from the city's general skyline, nothing looked familiar to MacAlister, until Parry drove them through the front gate of the English-Swedish club.

The main building looked like any one of the numerous men's clubs back in London, only the windows were noticeably smaller and its light-colored exterior wasn't covered over with ivy vines. They parked in the small lot in front of the club and walked up to the double doors of its main entrance. All Parry had to do was rap on them lightly and they were swung open by a pair of footmen. Inside, he and MacAlister gave their coats and hats to the cloak room attendant, then went to the registration desk to see if their contact was in.

Carl Drache had not yet arrived, so Parry left word for him and took MacAlister into the club's bar. They chose to sit at one of the room's alcove tables instead of at the counter. They had scarcely settled in when a waiter approached them and asked what they would like.

"Do you have Finnish vodka?" MacAlister inquired.

"Yes, sir. Only the best," said the waiter.

"Good, I'll have a vodka martini."

"I'll have a pint of bitters," added Parry, "should you have any stocks left. If not, then a pint of your regular."

"This makes me feel at home," said MacAlister, after the waiter had left. "They've really improved it. This almost looks like a genuine English pub."

"I know, even when we don't have to meet someone, we in the embassy come here. Its supply of British ales has been rather spotty, but the food is excellent. Would you care to have a bite to eat?"

"No, we had a lunch, such as it was, on the air liner. It wasn't very good, though at least they served it hot and that was important. Over the North Sea, the Junkers was rather cold. In the few minutes we have before Drache arrives, is there anything you want to ask me that you don't want him to hear?"

"Still carrying on with your suspicions, Ian? Well, I suppose there are some topics we shouldn't discuss in front of him. One of them is the bomber the jet fought with last night. Lord Mallet is still maintaining that no British aircraft violated Swedish air space. We all, however, know better. Quite apart from the statements by the fighter crew, the damage to it and the run made by the bomber over Bulltofta, the Swedish air force claims to have found a Merlin engine. It's complete with a propeller and cowling, and it could only have come off a Lancaster."

"Yes, it was an Avro Lancaster," MacAlister admitted, then he went silent as the waiter came back

53

with their drinks. He didn't start up until after he had sampled his martini and the waiter was out of earshot. "The Nazis almost bagged themselves one of our top bomber pilots. Wing Commander Geoffrey Sinclair. He's only twenty-six but he's flown more than a hundred combat missions. Last night was almost his final one. In addition to losing the engine, the Lancaster suffered fire damage to its fuselage. Its wireless operator and tail gunner were wounded, and the mid-upper gunner killed. I was told he would've lived if Sinclair had landed immediately, but he wanted those photographs to reach England."

"Sometimes, hard decisions have to be made," said Parry. "Thanks for telling me, Ian. I wanted to know the bomber's fate ever since I heard of the incident."

"I can understand, you R.A.F. types are much like naval officers. Always wanting to know about ships and their crews rather than the outcome of the battle itself. Is there anything else you want to know? Or anything Drache shouldn't?"

"Yes, don't let him know how far we're willing to go in this incident. How much we want the jet or, more important, how desperate we are to prevent it being returned to the Germans. Do you know how far we're willing to go?"

"Commander Cox, the officer in charge of the recovery, will order the aircraft destroyed if the Nazis are to have it," said MacAlister. "I needn't tell you what kind of crisis that will cause."

"Greg, my old friend," roared a giant, who had suddenly appeared at the bar's entrance. "And Commander MacAlister, it's so good to see you again. Come along, my dear."

Carl Drache strode across the room and extended his hand to the two officers. Except for the girl he had with him, he was the same as MacAlister remembered him. Tall, just over six feet, and broad shouldered, Drache was an imposing figure. He had wavy red hair, wore a heavy red beard and a finely trimmed handlebar moustache. With all that facial hair, he was only modestly handsome and looked several years older than he actually was. MacAlister, however, knew the reason for it. Some years before the war, Drache had had a car accident in Germany. Both his parents were killed and his face needed plastic surgery. The results weren't entirely satisfactory, so he used the beard and moustache to hide the scars.

"Between you and Ian, I really will feel like I'm in a hole," said Parry, shaking Drache's hand. "Pleased to see you again, Ursula. How've you been?"

The woman accompanying Drache was a young blonde who started talking to Parry. She was a few inches shorter than Drache, had long, straight hair and pale blue eyes. The way her clothes draped around her, MacAlister guessed she had a fuller figure than most Swedish women he knew. Her breasts were especially large, something the heavy sweater she had on could not hide.

"Commander MacAlister, welcome back to Sweden. It's been months," said Drache, pumping the commander's hand. MacAlister wasn't quite as enthusiastic about the handshake; his was little more than a formal greeting and his hand seemed to be just along for the ride. "Commander, I'd like to introduce my confidante and personal secretary, Miss Ursula Brandt. Ursula, this is Lieutenant-Commander Ian MacAlister. The one I've been telling you about."

"I hope what Carl's told you about me has been good," MacAlister responded, taking the hand she offered and kissing it.

"It has, Commander," she said. "Carl says you are

very intelligent and resourceful."

Ursula smiled at MacAlister but it was a rather cold smile. Her English was perfect and she spoke it with a smooth, cultured accent. However, it was not a Swedish one. To MacAlister, it sounded more German.

"Boy, a double brandy for me and white wine for Miss Brandt," Drache ordered, stopping a waiter as he passed by. "Well, gentlemen, let's take our seats."

MacAlister was mildly shocked when Ursula joined them at their table. He had expected she would take her wine at the counter or make a discreet exit to the ladies room and not return for several minutes. He gave Parry a sharp, questioning look which he was immediately able to interpret.

"Don't worry, old chap. We did a complete background check on Miss Brandt," Parry answered. "She's a naturalized Swedish citizen. She emigrated from Germany in 1938 and was granted citizenship a few months later. She's worked in Stockholm as a secretary ever since and, for the last four years, in Carl's business. She left Germany as a political refugee, her father was a social democrat and the family was being persecuted. She's as clean as her employer."

"Do you object to her, Commander?" Drache asked. "If so, I could have Miss Brandt wait for me at the bar."

"No, no. It just . . . surprised me a little," said MacAlister. "We usually don't have wives or girlfriends sit in on such meetings. Have you done this before, Greg?"

"Several times, though if the conversation is about something sensitive, we advise Carl to come alone. Since the arrival of this jet is such an open secret in Stockholm, I felt she wouldn't be a security problem."

"Very well, if this is the way you've been running

the show, I guess I shouldn't complain. Let's begin."

They held off actually starting the discussion until the waiter returned with the drinks Drache had ordered. And it was he who spoke first.

"The Me-262 is in a hangar at Bulltofta, on the military side of the field. It's heavily guarded, the air force even brought in an armored car to protect the main doors. An extra show of force was made when the daily Lufthansa flight from Copenhagen arrived, just in case there might've been stormtroopers or commandoes on board it."

"When does the Swedish air force plan to move the jet?" MacAlister asked. "Greg told me they were."

"They'll move it tonight, and it will go to Norrköping, as you should already know. The jet will soon be dismantled, separated into a number of sub-sections. It'll be transported by armed convoy. The move should be completed by tomorrow morning. The air force will continue the security show at Bulltofta for several more days. It should hopefully convince the Germans and the general public that the '262 is still there."

"But will the Germans believe it's still there?" Parry inquired. "Do they know what you just told us? We know the German ambassador met with the Swedish foreign minister, we know their senior military attachés met with the defense minister and they're trying to meet with air force officials. And I understand you were at the German embassy earlier today. What's happening there? What are they doing and what are they saying?"

"There's a quiet state of panic at the embassy," said Drache. "No one less than Von Ribbentrop is watching them. They'll receive the night fighter crew in a few days and they should soon be back in Germany. But they haven't been allowed to see the aircraft and neither has the crew, not since they landed it. They're desperate for any kind of information on it. I honestly can't tell you if they know when or where it's being moved. I only went there to renew some import licenses for my company, we didn't discuss the situation much."

"I'm sure you didn't," said MacAlister. He'd been in Drache's presence for less than five minutes and already he was starting to feel uneasy. As if he were the one giving away information and not Drache. "For the moment, what the Nazis had to say isn't as important as what the Royal Swedish Air Force told you. Greg said you were meeting with them. I take it that's why you were late in arriving."

"You guess correctly, Commander. The air force was as interested as you in what was happening at the German embassy. But they're more interested in meeting you and the other attachés. One of the reasons the jet's being moved to Norrköping is to allow you and the Americans an opportunity to inspect it without being obvious. Since most of the interned aircraft at the base are American and British, it won't look so unusual for you to be there."

"When would they like us to arrive?"

"Tomorrow afternoon. Later this evening, they'll call your embassy and the American embassy to make the invitations official. They'd like to have all of your attachés visit the base. If it's possible, they want one of you to be either an expert in jet aircraft or at least night fighters."

"I'm afraid that lets me out," Parry admitted. "All I've ever flown were Blenheims and Wellingtons. The Americans won't be of much help either. Their Army attaché is an artillery man and their Naval attaché was the captain of what he calls a tin can. I believe he means a destroyer. Neither served in the air arms of their services. Do you know much about jet airplanes, Ian?"

"They're noisier than propeller-driven aircraft," said MacAlister. "That's the sum total of my knowledge on jet aircraft. But I believe I know someone who can help us. He's an expert pilot and the member of an elite group, the Enemy Aircraft Evaluation unit. He knows jet aircraft and he's even flown the single-seat version of the Me-262. He's a commander in the U.S. Navy and he just happens to be on the continent. If the Americans cooperate, and we work fast, we could have him in Stockholm tomorrow as the new U.S. Naval attaché."

"I'm sure they'll work with us. In fact I believe their current Navy man would like to return to action before the rest of the Japanese fleet is sunk. Will the Foreign Ministry object to the U.S. embassy changing its Naval attaché?"

"I don't think so," said Drache, sipping his brandy. "They didn't object to Commander MacAlister being so suddenly appointed, or to the new additions to the German diplomatic staff. If this officer is what you claim he is, then he's exactly what the Swedish air force is looking for. Are there any more questions?"

"I can't think of any," MacAlister replied. "Why? Is there some place you have to go?"

"Yes, my office. I've spent most of this day either at the German embassy or air force headquarters, and I do have a business to run. Miss Brandt is more than just a pretty decoration, she has a job to do and correspondence must be piling up on her desk. So, I thank you for the company and I'll stay in touch with you. I hope this crisis works out to our advantage. Good day, Greg, Commander MacAlister."

Drache finished his brandy and slid out of the alcove. He helped Ursula emerge from the recessed table, shook Parry's hand and left. They were scarcely out of the club before MacAlister was commenting on what Drache had given them.

"Useless," he muttered. "He didn't tell us anything we didn't already know, or could have guessed, or found out later. At least we didn't let something slip out that we didn't want him to hear."

"Ian, really. There are times when you intelligence types and your paranoia can be boring," said Parry. "You can't expect Hitler's private phone number from every contact. Carl did tell us something important. When we reach the embassy, we'll phone the Americans and start work on replacing their naval attaché. That'll give us a head start of several hours over when we would've heard the official request from the Swedes."

"Yes, I'll admit he passed us one or two useful tips. When the Swedes call us tonight, we should warn them to redouble their security efforts. Not only around Bulltofta itself but the entire region. I believe the Germans do know when and where the jet's being moved. If I were them, that's when I would attack. We have to remember how they reacted in the past, when other night fighters made landings in neutral countries.

"In April of last year, an Me-110 made an emergency landing at Dubendorf, Switzerland. We tried to obtain it but the Swiss destroyed it in exchange for a squadron of Me-109s. We later learned that the Germans threatened to send in a commando team to destroy the '110. Last October, two Ju-88 night fighters landed here in separate incidents. One's just been returned and the other destroyed, after the Germans threatened to bomb Malmö and tried to kill one of the pilots, who had defected. In each incident the Nazis threatened military action. With this crisis, with the only prototype of their most advanced fighter at stake, I'd say the Third Reich was willing to flatten Sweden in order to recover it."

"Commander Norris, what're we supposed to do with this Kraut fighter of yours?" asked the base commander, pointing at the wingless Me-410 sitting beside one of his hangars.

"Stick it inside somewhere, put a few guards on it and make sure your guys don't strip any souvenirs off it," Norris answered. "C'mon, Vince. Get your ass on the plane."

Capollini waddled towards the Lodestar sitting on the snow-swept apron, the last of a long line of men to board the recently arrived transport. As he climbed inside it, the Lockhead started its engines, making it hard for Norris to hear what the base commander and the other Army Air Force officers had to tell him.

"We just got the OK on your route back to England," said the flight operations officer for the field's bomb group. "You won't get there until nightfall, so you'll have to steer clear of the areas protected by barrage balloons and stay above minimum altitudes, or you'll have the flak guns firing at you. Good luck, Commander, and you better leave now, the sky'll be full of Invaders in ten minutes."

"Commander! Commander Norris, this just came for you," said the base communications officer, gasping for air and blowing out clouds of mist. He had run all the way from the base's radio center and had neglected to put on a winter coat or cap. "It was coded, and was sent through Ninth Air Force headquarters from London. You're not to open it until you're airborne. I'm glad I caught you before you left."

The communications officer handed a sealed envelope to Norris, which he slid inside his jacket.

"What would you have done with this if you hadn't caught me?" Norris asked.

"I was to destroy it. The message wasn't to be sent out uncoded if you were already in the air. You wouldn't have gotten it until you landed in England. Now, if you'll excuse me, I'm going to head for someplace warm before I freeze my nuts off."

"That sounds like a good idea," the base commander added. "Good luck, John. I hope whatever mission you're being put on is a big one."

After exchanging a final salute with the army officers, Norris climbed into the idling Lodestar. As soon as its cabin door was shut, the transport gunned its engines and moved off the apron. It taxied past the few A-26s which were not on the mission and turned onto one of the airfield's empty runways. It stopped briefly to check its engines, then the Wright Cyclones were opened up. The C-60 accelerated down the runway, its twin-finned tail rising off the ground as it passed the halfway marker. At 120 miles an hour the Lockheed lifted cleanly into the sky, its main gear retracting by the time it cleared the trees at the airfield's perimeter. As the sharp howl of its radial engines died out, the deeper, heavier rumble from dozens of Pratt and Whitney radials replaced it.

In a stepped formation of three-ship vees, more than twenty A-26 Invaders returned to their home field. The silver and olive drab attack bombers broke ranks by peeling off like fighters and diving at the runway threshold, their landing gear extending only seconds before actual touchdown. By then the Lodestar was a dark shadow climbing to the west.

"Jeez, we just made it out before the rush hour,"

said Capollini, glancing back at the wave of bombers descending on the air base. "What did those guys give you before we left, Commander?"

"Orders for me. I guess now is as good a time as any to open them." Norris pulled the envelope out of his jacket and ripped open the top. He unfolded the sheet he found inside and read its brief contents. "Good God, Dennis really has got us involved in this operation. I'm going to be the next naval attaché to Sweden."

"What? Why there? Are we going with you? What's our part and how about telling us what operation the colonel's got us involved in?"

"An Me-262 made an emergency landing in Sweden last night," Norris explained, handing his orders to Shannon so he could read them. "It's the only prototype of a night fighter version the Nazis are building and we're going to work with the British to get it. I don't know what your part will be, but I'm going to Stockholm. It seems like the Swedes want an expert in jet airplanes to look over the '262 and I've been tapped."

"You know, every U.S. embassy's got a contingent of Marine guards," said Shannon. "I wonder if our one in Stockholm needs a new commanding officer?"

"I wouldn't know about that. You can ask when we get to London, Chris, but I don't think they'll be able to cut you some orders fast enough to send you there in time to help me. I'm sure Dennis and Charlie Cox will have something for the rest of you guys. Remember this operation is just starting, it's less than twenty-four hours old. They probably don't know how they're going to steal the jet or what they're going to use to do it."

"How are they gonna get you to Sweden?" Capollini asked. "A military flight? I heard the Swedes intern any military plane that lands in their country."

"There's a regular air line service to Sweden," said Norris. "Swedish air lines flies the route by day and BOAC flies it at night. The Brits use Gooney Birds and Commandoes, just like the ones we use in India. They also use Mosquitoes, painted in civilian markings, for courier runs both day and night. I don't know which I'll get but when we land I'll be driven to Gatwick where I'm to board the next BOAC flight to Sweden."

"You better hope for a Gooney Bird or a C-46, Commander. Those Mosquitoes are cramped. After a few hours you'll be stiffer than hell. I wouldn't like it. I only like airplanes that are big enough to walk around in. And anyway, the Brits build those things out of balsa wood."

"I know, but save for the jet we're stealing, there isn't a night fighter in the Luftwaffe that can catch a Mosquito."

"Excuse me, could you tell me where the express from Edinburgh is arriving?" Cox inquired of the man sitting behind the information window.

"On track number five, Admiral," the railroad official answered. "And it should be arriving in the next two minutes."

"Thank you and, by the way, it's Commander. I haven't risen that far through the ranks yet."

With only two minutes left, Cox ran from the train station's entrance to its cavernous main hall. He weaved through the crowds of people, stopping at the head of each track to find out what number it was. On the fifth track he found a train inching to a halt, its locomotive enveloping itself in clouds of steam. The passengers were still on board it, and Cox started down the platform, trying to reach one of its coach cars before they began to leave.

He was at the eleventh car when the doors opened and the train conductors let the first passengers off. Cox was almost swamped by the surge of civilians and servicemen who wore uniforms of a half-dozen different armed forces. It was like two waves slapping together, and in the chaotic sea of people, Cox would never have found who he was looking for, if he hadn't known exactly who it was.

"Captain Roberts, it's good to see you again," he uttered, nearly colliding with an officer as he stepped off the train. Though his uniform was British, his shoulder patch read U.S. Rangers. "I'm glad you could make it on such short notice."

"We almost didn't," said Roberts, shaking his hand. "We arrived at the Lothian Road Station just as the express was leaving. We both had to run to catch it."

"We? Whom did you bring with you?" While Cox asked his question, he watched Roberts extend his hand to the woman standing in the coach door and help her onto the platform.

"This is my friend, Heather Maitland. If you'll recall what I told you the last time we met?"

"Oh yes. You're the young woman Lee told me he was seeing when I last saw him. I'm sorry to take him away from you but he's the best man I know for the job at hand. Is this your first trip to London, Miss Maitland?"

"No, I have an aunt and uncle who live here," the young woman answered, squeezing against Roberts's side and wrapping her arms around one of his. "I'll be staying with them. They should be here to pick me up."

"Good, I hope you told them to pick you up at the King's Cross Station," said Cox, "and not the Charing Cross Station. I made that mistake myself several times. Here, let me help you with those."

Cox took the suitcase Heather had brought with her and Robert's valise, leaving him to struggle with his overstuffed duffel bag. The platform was by now filled with train passengers and the people who had come to meet them. Leading the way, Cox weaved through the crowd with Roberts and Heather following in his wake. Several other trains had arrived at the same time as the Edinburgh Express, substantially increasing the population of King's Cross Station. Cox repeatedly looked behind him to make sure he hadn't lost his charges. Only in the station's lobby did the hectic swirl of the crowd abate somewhat, allowing Cox and Roberts to rest and Heather to look for her relatives.

"We were to meet them here," she said, scanning the room. "My uncle told me to . . . There they are! Lee, look!"

Heather pointed to an elderly couple just coming through the main entrance, then ran toward them. Moments later they recognized her and when they met, she was embraced by both. With Heather gone, Cox and Roberts had a chance to speak between themselves.

"Thank God there's someone here to take care of your girl," said Cox, "or I should say lass. That's what the Scottish call their girlfriends. At any rate, what I have to tell you is classified and I'd rather not wait until we put your girl in a hotel room before I can say anything."

"I know," Roberts admitted. "I told her what it would be like but she wanted to spend as much time with me as possible. We haven't seen each other for almost a year. I wondered if she would remain loyal to me, there are so many other servicemen in this

66

country, but she did and I think I understand how much Connie loves Dennis Lacey. Heather started crying when we entered the station just now, she really does love me."

"I know those feelings, believe me. Ann and I did many of the same things before we were married. You want the special moments to last. Here they come, see if you can do this parting quickly. It only hurts to prolong it."

Heather returned with her aunt and uncle, whom she introduced to both Cox and Roberts. There were the usual questions a civilian would have for a military officer, most of which neither Cox nor Roberts could truthfully answer.

"Oh, I understand. It's hush-hush and all that," Heather's uncle deduced. "They can't answer our questions, my dear. National security, you see."

"I'm sorry, Heather, I don't know if I'll be able to see you here," said Roberts, "but if I have a chance I'll call you. Goodbye, honey, I'll miss you deeply."

When Roberts embraced Heather and kissed her, she started crying again. He held onto her for a long time, so long Cox tapped him lightly on the shoulder.

"Time to go, Lee," Cox advised. "As you Americans would say, we've a long night ahead of us."

Roberts gave his girlfriend one final kiss, then released her and collected his duffel bag. This time he was the one who kept looking behind him, until he and Cox walked through the station's main entrance. He lost sight of Heather and her relatives as the doors swung shut.

Waiting outside of King's Cross Station was a Royal Navy staff car and driver. As soon as Roberts had his luggage stowed in its trunk, it drove off, heading due east instead of south. Leaving London instead of moving downtown. The moment they were in the car, Cox was telling Roberts of the incident and all its latest developments.

"Christ, what a coup it would be to obtain that jet," said Roberts. "It's an opportunity we can't pass up. Who have you brought in? Can I use some Army Rangers this time?"

"I'm afraid that's not possible," said Cox. "We don't have the time to go beyond the SAS for your men. As to the others, I'm bringing in some new friends of mine. A special team of Army Air Force, U.S. Navy and Marine Corps officers called the Enemy Aircraft Evaluation unit. I've worked with the Army officers before, they're quite effective. This unit is perfect for the situation, in fact one of them is being sent to Stockholm to be the American embassy's naval attaché."

"To work with Ian MacAlister, I bet. I remember him from the last time. What will my part be? Why do you need the SAS?"

"Well, there is a need for on-site security if we do send a recovery team to Sweden. I know the Swedish air force will provide their own but I'd feel more confident if I knew you were there. I have another, shall we say 'darker,' reason for wanting you. Should the Swedes refuse our offers, should they decide to give the prototype back to the Germans, I want it destroyed before it can be returned. If we can't have it, then we can't allow the Nazis to have it either. I want you to organize an assault and saboteur squad."

"OK, I'll select men who are weapons and demolition experts," Roberts replied. "Who've you told about this 'last resort' option of yours?"

"You and Ian MacAlister, as you guessed, and high-ranking officers of that American team but no one else. No one in my Threat Evaluation group or the Admiralty or the Foreign Office. I've been given a free hand and full cooperation in obtaining this Night Hawk. But if I do decide to use your men, I will go the Sea Lords for permission. I'll probably have to go all the way to Winston Churchill himself for it."

"I damn well hope so. Because if you use us, it could start a war with Sweden."

"Good evening, Mister Lindh. What's the latest word from Stockholm," asked the sergeant who opened the hangar's side door.

"We're to go ahead and move our prize," said squadron leader Lindh. "And I have been placed in charge of its safety. As if I did not already have enough problems."

Lindh entered the hangar and walked over to what had once been Germany's most advanced night fighter. As a result of the sergeant's handiwork, the sleek jet lay in several pieces. Its fuselage had been separated from its wings, and the nose section, complete with radar aerials, had been removed from the fuselage. The Me-262 looked like a giant, partially assembled model. The fuselage sections and wings were being lashed to a pair of flat bed trailers. With the exception of tarpaulins to cover the trailers, and the truck cabs to tow them, the jet was ready to move.

"You have done good work, Sergeant," Lindh observed, "especially when one considers you did not have any maintenance manuals to guide you. All right, cover it up and I will bring in the trucks. It's time to take her north."

After staying a few moments to make sure the job was started, Lindh walked out of the hangar and climbed inside an awaiting staff car. The driver gunned its engine and swung the car around sharply, heading it away from the flight line. In less than a minute, Lindh would be arriving at the air base's security headquarters, where he'd take command of the convoy being organized for him. He would return to the hangar to collect the dismantled Me-262 and then begin a winding, three-hundred-mile journey to the north, taking the jet to its new home.

"Herr Oberst, we are approximately two hundred yards from the shore line," said the captain. "We've made repeated periscope sweeps and we can spot no activity. If your men are ready, we can surface immediately."

"We've been ready to leave your boat since we boarded it," the colonel admitted. "My men are not used to such confinement. They would not make good submariners."

"I understand, it's more important that they be good saboteurs. Leutnant, periscope down, blow all ballast tanks and bring the rafts up."

The U-boat boiled to the surface of the inlet's calm, sheltered waters. It was nearly as black as the night itself and almost invisible to the naked eye. Water had yet to finish cascading off the submarine's hull when the hatches forward and aft of its conning tower opened.

First to come out were the gun crews, who manned the anti-aircraft batteries. The boat's captain and lookouts appeared on the conning tower and the life rafts were brought topside. While they were being inflated, the commando team climbed onto the hull, their commander in the lead.

"Now remember, if you become separated from the squad, you are to head for our embassy or to the

70

Norwegian frontier," the colonel told his men. "Under no circumstances are you to come back here. The submarine will be long gone. If you are captured by Swedish forces, you must tell them that you're the survivor of a U-boat which sunk off their coast. That's why you have been given navy ranks and identity tags. I hope your short stay on this sub has given you some knowledge of it, in case the Swedes question you. I'll take the first raft in. We will meet again when we are all ashore."

"Herr Oberst, all your rafts are ready," said the U-boat commander, leaning over the front lip of the conning tower. "Our lookouts have nothing to report. It's time to leave."

"Very well, Kapitän and thank you for delivering us safely. All details, to your boats."

Aided by some of the submarine's crew, the dark-suited commandoes piled into the inflated rafts. They were pushed off the U-boat's hull as a gentle swell lapped against it and almost at once their oars hit the water. The rafts paddled toward shore in a ragged line, with the colonel's raft out in front of the rest. They were less than halfway to the desolate boulder-strewn beach and the night had all but swallowed them. Only the glint of their paddles when they stroked the water could be seen by the submarine's crew. Beyond that, the rafts and the men in them were vague forms bumping across the inlet.

"Kapitän, are the commandoes being met by anyone on shore?" asked one of the lookouts in the conning tower.

"No, no one. This mission was only organized in the last twenty-four hours. That would scarcely be enough time to contact our agents in Sweden and set up a reception party. Why do you ask?"

"Because I see lights on shore. Several vehicles, I

71

think it's a convoy of some kind. A patrol convoy."

The commandoes in the rafts also saw the lights and did the best they could to hide from them; they stopped paddling and huddled inside the rafts. The lights on shore were several yards inland and appeared to be following a road. At one point they came very close to the water, where they didn't have trees blocking their view. They slowed down, and the second and fourth vehicles snapped on searchlights.

Their powerful beams swept the inlet, from their position they could cover almost all of it. The commandoes, and everyone aboard the submarine, held their breath. Then one of the searchlights illuminated the rafts. Moments later the second one was on them, and a voice boomed across the inlet, ordering them to stop and surrender in German.

"Out oars!" the colonel shouted. "Return to the boat!"

He had scarcely finished giving his order when the commandoes dug their paddles in the water and were frantically trying to turn the rafts around. The voice on the megaphone continued to warn them to stop and surrender, up until the point muzzle flashes started sparkling along the shore. Some of the commandoes unslung their Schmeissers to return fire but the contest was an unequal one. Some of the vehicles in the Swedish convoy mounted heavy machine guns and their streams of shells virtually exploded the frail rafts like they were giant balloons.

"Kapitän, they're being slaughtered," said the other lookout. "We have to do something."

"And we shall. All gun crews, fire at will! Leutnant, start the diesels! We leave as soon as we collect survivors."

The 20mm and 37mm batteries surrounding the U-boat's conning tower opened up on the convoy.

Their loud chattering covered the sound of the sub's diesel engines rumbling to life. Once out of the inlet, it was less than ten miles to Danish territorial waters, where Swedish forces wouldn't be able to follow them. One of the convoy searchlights trained its beam on the U-boat, blinding everyone topside until a burst of fire from one of the batteries shattered it.

"Pick up survivors and make for the sub!" the colonel ordered. "I hope they wait for us."

The heavy-caliber cannons raked the convoy with armor-piercing incendiaries and high-explosive shells. Whatever kind of vehicles were in it, they could not stand up to the accurate, lethal barrage. The second searchlight was knocked out and a fireball rose from the shore as a truck was hit in its fuel tank. For a time, return fire from the convoy was scattered and weak. With most of its vehicles either destroyed or damaged, none of its machine guns answered the submarine.

During the lull, the surviving commandoes reached the U-boat and were helped on board. All too quickly it ended when a series of star shells shot into the air. They illuminated the entire inlet with their harsh light. For a second or two everyone on the submarine froze; an instant later it was bracketed by a cluster of explosions.

"Mortars," said the captain. "They're using mortars on us. I want everyone out of the water now! If one of those bombs hits us, we might be too damaged to submerge. Leutnant, I want full reverse speed."

As quickly as it could, the U-boat backed out of the inlet, picking up the last commandoes and abandoning the remaining rafts as it retreated. More explosions fountained around it, several of the mortar bombs landing very close. The anti-aircraft crews lashed out at the shore line, peppering it with hundreds of rounds though without noticeable effect on the mortar crews. They continued firing at the sub and more star shells were sent up, to replace those which burned out. It was a fiercely fought battle though little in the way of real damage was done to either side. Between the rumble of the diesels, the heavy chatter of the cannons and the steady thud of mortar shells, no one heard the scream of radial engines until it was too late.

One by one a line of low-wing, fixed gear attack bombers dove out of the night sky. On their wings and fuselages were light blue roundels, with a trio of gold crowns set in them. The lead aircraft had released a pair of bombs and pulled out of its dive before the gunners on the submarine could train their weapons on it. The bombs straddled their target, showering it with spray and shrapnel.

Many of those who had just been rescued were killed or wounded by the twin blasts. More were cut down when the second Swedish air force bomber came in, firing its machine guns before dropping another pair of bombs. One fell wide of the mark, but the other exploded just in front of the U-boat's conning tower, tearing open its hull.

"This is the captain speaking. We've been too badly damaged to put to sea. I want full ahead and a hard turn to port. We have to run the boat aground or she will sink. Leutnant, send a message to base. Tell them we have been attacked by Swedish aircraft and we're running aground. Destroy all codes and coding equipment. Destroy anything else that could be of use to the enemy."

A third bomber roared in, hitting the submarine again, rending open another hole in its forward hull. It shuddered briefly as the screws were reversed, then it plowed ahead and swung hard toward the inlet's eastern shore. The lead attack bomber returned, dropping a second pair of bombs while the U-boat was in the middle of its turn. One exploded abreast of its conning tower, the other struck its after hull at the water line. By now none of the anti-aircraft batteries were firing, as if their response to the air attack had been effective in the first place. Their crews were either dead or wounded, as was almost everyone else who'd been caught topside by the planes.

The sub almost sank before reaching the shore. It developed a severe list because of all the bomb damage and practically ran onto the beach on its side. The third attack bomber broke off its return pass when its pilot realized the submarine had gone aground.

More star shells sputtered to life over the inlet. The aircraft called off their runs but circled the area menacingly, diving at the U-boat each time one of them flew by it. Those who survived the onslaught quickly abandoned the beached sub, except for a few who stayed behind to destroy sensitive equipment. The rest were met on the shore by the survivors of the convoy they had shot apart. Rather than continue the fight they surrendered to the Swedes, throwing down what few weapons they had left and raising their hands.

"I am Korvettenkapitän Ernst Wachtel," said the captain, turning his Luger over to a Swedish officer. "And I'm surrendering the rest of my crew and my boat to you. Many of my men are wounded and are in need of medical attention."

"So are many of mine," the officer tersely answered. "But you are not to worry. Our coast guard and our navy has dispatched boats from Malmö and my base has sent out another convoy. They should all arrive in the next several minutes. Your men will be looked after, and you'll begin explaining why your submarine came so far inside Swedish territorial waters. By tomorrow, everyone from Stockholm to Berlin will want to know your answers."

"Squadron leader, we have a preliminary report on the incident with the convoy," announced the air force officer, as he ran across the tarmac to a heavily guarded hangar. "They appear to have caught a German U-boat inside our waters. There's been a fierce fire fight and the Northrops we had on patrol have attacked. The last word we had is that the U-boat was damaged and is maneuvering erratically."

"Do they have any idea why the submarine was in our waters?" asked Lindh.

"No, but the convoy had first spotted a line of rubber rafts in the water before they discovered the U-boat. The army has sent reinforcements to the convoy and we should learn more about the incident once we take a few prisoners."

"Well, I cannot wait for that. My own convoy is ready to move and I feel it's safe for us to do so. This incident appears to be contained. I say the danger has passed."

"Would you not want to wait and make sure?" asked another air force officer, one of the men who had been waiting with Lindh at the hangar.

"No, we have more than three hundred miles to cover and if we don't start immediately, we will not make it to Norrköping tonight," said Lindh, checking his watch. "I'm under orders to complete this mission before dawn. If we don't leave now, we must wait until tomorrow and who knows what the Germans may try next? Tonight it was a U-boat, tomorrow they might send bombers. They might even use some of their warships based at Copenhagen. This airfield is close enough to the straits to receive a naval shelling. It's more dangerous to stay than to go. Commander, we leave at once. Alert the gate, tell the guards that we're coming through."

As the hangar's main doors were slowly cranked open, the trucks and armored cars waiting outside them were started up. Lindh climbed into one of the cars and had it move out of line. A truck which had just taken on its contingent of troops rolled up behind the armored car, then they waited. Waited for a truck towing a flat bed trailer to emerge from the hangar.

The heavy rattle of a diesel engine announced the appearance of the first rig. It joined the first two vehicles in the convoy and, together, they rolled slowly across the tarmac. The next vehicles to join the convoy were another armored car and a troop truck. With a curl of black smoke from its exhaust stacks, the second rig drove out of the hangar, hauling a trailer covered by a heavily secured, shapeless tarpaulin.

A third armored car completed the convoy, until it reached one of the side gates to Bulltofta airfield. There it was joined by a police cruiser and a pair of motorcycles from the local force. They would escort it as far as the next major town, where another local police force would take over escort duties. This is the way the convoy would make its journey north. If there were no hindrances, it would reach Norrköping in seven hours.

Chapter Four: Day Two
Making A Deal

"Commander Norris, I'd like you to meet Colonel Kenneth Whitney, British army attaché to Sweden. This is squadron leader Greg Parry, R.A.F. attaché and I've been told you already know Lieutenant-Commander MacAlister."

The officer who entered the room with Norris made his introductions as he laid aside his dark green overcoat and wheel cap, adding them to the collection of such items already filling the side table.

"Great to see you again, Ian, and thanks for recommending me," said Norris, going over to MacAlister after he dumped his own coat and hat on the table. "This is quite a welcome. I feel like I'm more in the British embassy than the American one. I haven't even seen the U.S. ambassador yet."

"Is that true, Scott?" Whitney asked of Norris's escort. "Aren't you following diplomatic protocol?"

"Protocol can wait," Scott McClory responded. "I didn't even stay at the airport to see off Captain Towns like I'm supposed to. I let one of my subordinates do that. What we've all got to say can't wait, so if you don't mind, let's get down to business."

McClory pointed to the table in the room's center and the other officers took their seats around it. As the senior American military attaché, Lieutenant-Colonel McClory took the seat at the head of the table. At his place was a map, which he unfolded as he spoke again.

"Commander, before you left London, did you hear anything about the incident near Malmö last night?"

"Yes, Commander Cox said a German sub was found inside Swedish territorial waters and attacked," Norris answered. "He thought it sounded suspicious but beyond that he couldn't say anything else. He didn't have much information to go on."

"Well, we now have quite a bit to go on. In the hours since you left, the Swedes have given us all they know about the incident." McClory pushed the map over to Norris, which he could see was a small-scale map of southern Sweden. "At approximately twenty-three hundred hours last night a German submarine, the U-705, surfaced here, in a small inlet south of Malmö. At twenty-three ten, a Swedish army patrol sighted life rafts moving toward shore. When the Swedes ordered them to surrender, they tried to flee and were fired upon. The submarine returned fire and for a while it was a pitched battle. When it seemed like the Germans would win and escape, a flight of Swedish air force B-5s arrived. They bombed and strafed the submarine, crippling it and driving it ashore, where the survivors surrendered."

"How serious was this battle?" Norris asked. "What were the casualties like?"

"The Swedes had fourteen men killed and twenty-nine wounded," said MacAlister, "and the Nazis lost thirty dead and eighteen men wounded. They also lost the U-705, one of their type Seven U-boats and its en-

79

tire crew. Which, if they were not killed, have been captured. All prisoners have been taken to the Karlskrona Naval Base where, we presume, the U-boat will be towed once some repairs have been made."

"Have the Germans tried to explain this incident? And what are the Swedes saying about it?"

"The Germans claim the sub was on a training mission," McClory explained. "It became lost because of radio failure and navigation errors. They explain away the life rafts as a landing party trying to find where they were. But they haven't explained why there were so many, heavily armed men on the submarine. Commander MacAlister totalled up the German dead and prisoners and concluded that the U-boat had twenty-one men more than its normal complement. Every prisoner taken or body found was Kriegsmarine, though again for sailors, many of them were very heavily armed.

"As for the Swedes, this whole mess has been a big shock to them. It's the worst incident of its kind since the start of the war. It's scared a lot of people in the Swedish government. After months of decline, the appeasers are out of the closet again. They're afraid of what else the Germans may do to destroy the jet. They're advising that it be handed back immediately and the Germans are making some very tempting offers for its return. I'm an artillery officer, not an airman but I'd go for the deals they're presenting."

"What kind of deals are they offering? I hope we have a few of our own to make," said Norris.

"The Nazis are being very conciliatory," said Mac-Alister. "It's rather out of character for them. Usually they're all threats and bluster after such an event. They have complained that Sweden's response was too brutal but they're now offering the Swedes a dozen Ju-88 bombers or two dozen late-model Me-

109 fighters in exchange for the jet's return. Either deal is quite good but don't worry, we have a few of our own."

"Where's the jet now? Has it been moved, and have you made arrangements for us to see it?"

"The Me-262 is here, at Norrköping," McClory answered, pointing at the map, at a town some eighty miles south of Stockholm. "It's where many interned airplanes are kept, especially ours. So it won't look out of the ordinary for us to be there. A friend of Mister Parry and Mister MacAlister made the arrangements, a Swedish businessman called Carl Drache. They told me in the past he's been very helpful. The Swedes dismantled the jet to transport it and it hasn't been reassembled. Which'll make it easier to fly out should we get our hands on it."

"Or photograph if we don't," Parry added, speaking up for the first time. "The minimum we need are photographs of the jet's radar systems and other avionics. We're hoping you can help us. Ian's told us you're something of an expert on the Me-262. If you don't mind my asking, how did you become an expert on such an aircraft? Ian gave me a few tantalizing details about your acquaintance with it."

"We have an Me-262 at our Patuxent River Air Test Center," said Norris. "We received it about a month ago. I helped reassemble it and made the first test flights on it. Since then I've been on other operations, I hope Ian's told you about them, but I have scrounged parts off of Me-262 wrecks on the continent to keep our example flying. I must point out that all my experience has been with single-seat models, nothing as advanced as the Night Hawk. And when will we get to see her? McClory told me it would be today but you people would know exactly when. You were the ones talking to the Royal Swedish Air Force while he was picking me up."

"The air force would like us to arrive at the base by noon," said MacAlister, "which means we should leave in the next hour if we're to be there on time. If there are no further questions, we should leave now. Or perhaps you should fulfill the requirements of protocol, Mister McClory, and introduce our friend to your ambassador?"

"OK, I'll go and find out if the ambassador is available," McClory replied, taking back the map and folding it up. "The rest of you can stay here. Just give me a minute and I'll be right back."

The meeting ended as McClory got out of his seat and went for the door. He picked his cap off the table, then left, closing the door behind him. Parry and Colonel Whitney got up as well and walked over to the table to retrieve their hats and coats. MacAlister and Norris remained seated, for them the meeting hadn't quite ended.

"This Carl Drache must be a real friend of yours," said Norris. "Anyone who can get us on an air base so quickly must have a lot of friends in the government."

"Drache is no friend of mine, real or otherwise." MacAlister bridled at Norris's suggestion, giving him a hard, sideways glance when he made it. "A friend is someone you trust, and Drache I don't. He is highly placed but I have my suspicions. As you Americans are fond of saying, 'I wouldn't trust him as far as I can throw him.'"

"Well, if you're that suspicious of him, why do you guys use him?"

"*We* are not suspicious of him, only I am and I don't have any solid evidence against Drache. Greg and Colonel Whitney trust him and I'm not in much of a position to argue the matter. They've been in

Stockholm for years and can point to numerous times when Drache has been marginally useful."

"If that's true, then why are you against him?" Norris asked.

"Because on really important matters he's been less than helpful, in fact he's been detrimental. Drache has supplied us with information that later proved to be dangerously false. On June thirteenth of last year, a V-2 crashed on a farm near Gräsdal. After a good deal of negotiating, we obtained some of its wreckage and discovered radio equipment in it. We paid Drache to find out if the missile was radio controlled and he gave proof that it was. Later we found he'd been wrong, after millions of pounds had been spent on useless electronic jamming gear. A week later, no less than twenty Eighth Air Force bombers made emergency landings in Sweden, after raids on oil refineries in northern Germany. Drache reported that many of the aircraft were undamaged and their crews had tried to seek asylum. It took a long time to undo the damage he did."

"Oh, come now, Ian. Don't poison your friend to Carl Drache," Parry admonished, returning to the table. "As an intelligence officer you know that from time to time the information you gather on the enemy can be faulty. It's happened to you as well."

"I know, but Carl's has proven so conveniently faulty. For the Germans and not for us."

"Ian, you're a true paranoid. You know very well that none of your suspicions can be proven, yet you persist in harboring them."

"I also know I'm not the only one to have them," said MacAlister. "The Swedish police have been conducting their own investigation of Drache. For the last few months, they've had an undercover man planted in his estate."

"Commander Norris, come along with me, please," said McClory, sticking his head back inside the meeting room. "The ambassador has a couple of minutes to spare so he can see you. Colonel, why don't you take your friends out to your car? We'll join you in the parking lot and then we can go to Norrköping."

"My friends, since I've already introduced you to each other in the hall, I say we move to the business at hand," Cox announced, taking his seat at the conference table. "I hereby call this meeting to order. We have much to discuss."

Lacey and Constance joined him at the table, as did Capollini, Shannon and Roberts. Unlike yesterday, no one from the Threat Evaluation team was there for the meeting. This time Cox had gathered all the officers who were part of the operation to steal the prototype of the Night Hawk.

"Connie told me all about the battle the Swedes had with that U-boat," said Lacey. "Sounds like it was quite a fight. More than some accidental incursion by a lost sub. What's the latest word from our embassies?"

"In spite of the success by their forces, the Swedes are in a state of shock," Cox answered. "Ian reports this was the worst clash between Swedish and German forces of the entire war. It's received heavy coverage in Swedish newspapers and on the radio, which is unusual. Most such incidents are only lightly reported, official communiqués and the like. Ian says the pacifists in the Swedish government are urging appeasement, that the press play may foretell the returning of the jet to the Germans. And they're making it very easy for them to do so.

"The Germans have apologized for the entire incident, though they still claim it was nothing more than a lost sub, and they've offered a number of deals to the Swedes. They're willing to exchange a squadron of Ju-88s for the jet or several squadrons of late-model fighters. Even without the pressure of the incident, those are most tempting offers. However, we do have a few of our own to make."

"Last night you told me the Swedes were planning to move the jet to another base," said Roberts. "Because of this incident with the U-boat, have they done it or not?"

"Yes, they went through with the move. The prototype is at Norrköping, where our attachés will soon be inspecting it. When they're finished, Ian and Commander Norris will report to me on what they saw and what type of deal they made. In light of current events, I'm afraid we won't obtain as much as we had wished."

"Or, in other words, we won't get the jet," Lacey added, making his own interpretation.

"I'm afraid you're right," said Cox. "I may have brought you here for nothing, I'm sorry. But I'd still like you to work with Connie and your team on a plan to retrieve the jet, should we be so lucky."

"What's the best we can hope for now?" Roberts asked.

"A close inspection of the '262 and some photographs. We might obtain some part of the aircraft, though it's not likely. If we are given a chance to take photographs, Ian will try to take some of the base as well. Those will be for you, Captain, to plan your operation. We've no other alternative but what I told you last night. We must neutralize the jet."

"Hey, wait a minute," said Lacey, "are you talking about that last resort option of yours? Is that what you mean by neutralize?"

"Yes, as important as it was for us to obtain the prototype, it's equally within our interest to prevent the Germans from recovering it," Cox explained, averting his eyes from the rest of the group, as if he were ashamed of what he was about to say. "If we can't have it, then neither can the Germans. Lee Roberts will organize a saboteur squad and blow up the jet while it's still in Sweden."

"Jeez, if you don't mind my saying, Commander, ain't that a little harsh?" said Capollini.

"Indeed it is, Captain. But we've been presented with a situation which may require us to be harsh. There's a good chance the jet will be returned to Germany. If that happens, we must destroy it and if we destroy it, then we could well be risking war with Sweden. That isn't something we should contemplate lightly but it could be necessary."

"With regards to our discussion last night," said Roberts, "when do I begin selecting the members of my squad and who have you told about your decision?"

"Well, my decision isn't yet final," Cox advised. "It won't be until our attachés have exhausted all their attempts to secure the prototype. However, I will be reporting to the Sea Lords once our meeting is over. They're very interested in this situation and want to be apprised of it. Gentlemen, what type of operations shall I tell them we're working on?"

"Good morning, Sergeant, I'm Colonel Kenneth Whitney, Royal Army," said Whitney, to the highest-ranking Swedish airman at the sentry post. "My friends in the back are squadron leader Greg Parry, Royal Air Force and Lieutenant-Commander Ian MacAlister, Royal Navy."

"Ah yes, you are the British military attachés," the

sergeant replied, checking a list on his clipboard. "You must be with the Americans we just checked in. I have identity tags for you, gentlemen. Please wear them at all times and don't enter restricted areas without an escort. I hope you shall enjoy your visit to our base."

The sergeant handed Whitney a set of four identity tags, one for each of the officers in the car and its driver. He saluted Whitney and motioned for the other airmen at the gate to raise the toll bar. At first the dark brown sedan moved slowly as it rolled through Norrköping's main entrance, then it accelerated to catch up with another sedan, one bearing U.S. diplomatic license plates.

Ahead of the American attachés was a Swedish air force sedan, the escort it had picked up at the front gate. The tiny convoy drove across the base, bypassing its control tower and main flight line of fighters and attack bombers for a distant group of hangars surrounded by a far more varied and unusual collection of aircraft. Ones not marked by the blue roundels and gold crowns of the Royal Swedish Air Force.

"My God, I never thought there were this many interned airplanes in Sweden," MacAlister remarked, amazed at the size of the collection. He pressed his face so close to the car's side window, he could feel his nose getting cold.

"In the last seven months there's been a considerable increase in the number of forced landings," said Parry, "for a variety of reasons. The huge increase in Allied air operations over the continent is responsible for most of ours, navigation errors and defections for most of the German aircraft you see. Please note that many of them are trainers and liaison types."

The convoy slowed down as it approached the collection, driving off the perimeter road it had been using and onto the tarmac. The foreign aircraft were arranged in two separate groups. All fighters, trainers and other light aircraft were lined up in front of the hangars; the bombers and transports faced them from the opposite side of the tarmac.

No apparent thought had been given to the order in which the aircraft were placed. An R.A.F. Spitfire sat in the middle of a row of U.S. Army Air Force P-51s and a Thunderbolt towered over the Fw-44 trainers nestled under its wings. A Russian LA-5 stood wing tip to wing tip with an Me-109 while on the bomber side a jet black Avro Lancaster sat between two silver B-17s from the Eighth Air Force.

No two aircraft in the collection wore the same exact markings. Of the five B-17s MacAlister saw, none of them carried the same combination of brightly colored wing tips, rudders and fuselage bands. A U.S. C-47 carried Russian markings and an ancient British Gladiator bore the light blue swastikas of the Finnish air force. If nothing else, the aircraft were colorful and the embassy cars slowed to a crawl as they drove through the collection.

"Jesus, they got their own little air force here," said Norris. "I see everything but seaplanes. And jets. Where's the Me-262 we're supposed to examine?"

"On those trailers ahead of us," McClory answered. "Now we'll see how much of an expert you really are."

Their cargoes still wrapped in dark green tarpaulins, the two flat bed trailers stood at the opposite end of the collection. Armed guards and an armored car watched over them, the guards snapping to attention when the convoy came to a stop beside the trailers. A Swedish officer stepped out of the lead vehicle, returning the salute of the officer in charge of the security detail. He turned to the other cars in the convoy and greeted the American and British attachés as they emerged.

"Lieutenant-Commander MacAlister, I'm told you have been to my country before," said the officer, shaking hands with the last British attaché to step onto the tarmac. "I'm Wing Commander Lennart Paulson, commanding officer of Norrköping Air Base. I have been given overall responsibility for our latest 'acquisition' by the defense ministry. Any discussions you wish to have about the aircraft, you will have them with me. And now, gentlemen, let's view the aircraft in question. Lieutenant, undo the ropes."

Paulson indicated the nearest trailer and the security officer responded by ordering some of his guards to untie the ropes holding down the tarpaulin. The attachés gathered at the trailer as the heavy canvas sheet was pulled back, uncovering the nose section and fuselage of the Me-262.

A rough wooden frame had been built around the fighter's nose cone and its fragile, wirelike array of radar antennas. The fuselage rested on the bed of the trailer and was lashed to it by more ropes. Though wingless and minus its nose, the fighter still looked sleek and lethal. It drew an appreciative murmur from the crowd which had gathered to see its unveiling. When the tarpaulin had been rolled down to the jet's tail plane, Paulson ordered the guards to stop and come off the trailer.

The fuselage had black undersides and a mottled pattern of light and dark gray blotches over its top surfaces. The fuselage crosses were simple, black lines; to the right of them were two black letters, the nearest one outlined in green. Underneath the forward canopy was a black and red shield with a white lightning flash emblazoned on it. Farther up on the fuselage, near its truncated nose, was the code number 01, in red with a white outline.

"Even in this state, she's magnificent," MacAlister commented. "May we have a closer look, Wing Commander?"

"Your experts can examine the aircraft," said Paulson, "in the presence of our own experts."

As he spoke, the wing commander made a beckoning gesture to his sedan and out of it came two more Swedish air force officers, one of whom was a woman.

"This is squadron leader Gunnar Lönnberg, of our Air Test Center and flight officer Lise Carlsson, a radar evaluation specialist from our Air Defense Command. Do your people have any objections to these officers?"

"No, if someone's going to look over my shoulder, they might as well do it with a pretty pair of eyes," said Norris. "C'mon, let's see what the merchandise is like."

Grabbing hold of the trailer's edge, Norris boosted himself onto its bed, then turned to help up the other officers. Parry came after him and, lastly, the two Swedish officers. First, they clustered around the detached nose section, where Norris bent down and opened a small access panel near its base. They quickly became involved in a heavily technical discussion over the jet's radar system. MacAlister, McClory and Whitney watched them for a few moments, then turned to have their own discussion with Paulson.

"I think we can leave our experts alone," said MacAlister. "I'm sure they can take care of themselves and we have our own topics to talk about. Isn't that right, Wing Commander?"

"Very well, I believe you already know the overall quality and uniqueness of this aircraft," Paulson replied, glancing around the area, taking note of all the guards surrounding the trailers. "I think this place is a little too crowded for our talk. Shall we go on a tour?"

Paulson waved his hand at the rest of the collection and the remaining attachés agreed that a walk among the aircraft would be fine. Whitney warned Parry and Norris they were being left alone and Paulson told the security officer to keep his guards on the trailers. Then he, Whitney, McClory and MacAlister turned and began their tour. They waited until they had walked out of earshot before any of them would speak.

"We've heard about the offers the Germans have tendered," said Whitney. "Could you tell us more about them and are they being considered seriously by you?"

"The Nazis have offered us two, sixteen-plane squadrons of their latest, K-model Me-109 fighters," said Paulson, "or a twelve-plane squadron of S-model Ju-88s, one of the fastest bombers in the Luftwaffe. Those offers are being seriously considered, especially by the pacifists in the foreign ministry and parliament. They are pressuring the air force to accept one of them and return the jet to the Nazis. They completely are against turning the aircraft over to you or even allowing you to inspect it. If they knew you were here, they would demand my dismissal and make life very unpleasant for our mutual friend, Carl Drache."

"I wouldn't mind seeing Mister Drache squirm in a spot of trouble," MacAlister sardonically remarked. "Why I might even tell the pacifists myself about our meeting."

"Commander, if you can't say anything constructive, be quiet," Whitney snapped. "I'm sorry, Mister Paulson. Lieutenant-Commander MacAlister isn't serious about informing the pacifists. I wish he would

91

join the discussion in the proper spirit."

"We have some offers of our own to make," said McClory. "Before we make them, I'd like to know what we can hope to get out of you. Has the fate of the jet already been decided, or is it still open to negotiation?"

"I'm afraid it has more or less been decided," Paulson admitted, "but the fate of the secrets the jet contains is still open. That's why we have allowed your experts to examine it. Would you care to wait until they have finished before making your proposals?"

"No, we already know from recon photos that the fighter's got some new radar gizmos. After the jet itself, that's what we really want."

"Reconnaissance photographs? How did you manage to obtain pictures of an aircraft we have had under cover since we captured it? Wait, the British bomber that overflew Bulltofta after the jet landed . . . We wondered why it risked being shot down, now I understand. Would you care to admit that a British aircraft did violate Swedish air space?"

"That's not mine to say. I'm not the British air attaché," said McClory, smiling wryly.

"Very well, I will have to ask squadron leader Parry when he's finished. Will you be satisfied with obtaining less than the complete aircraft?"

"I'm afraid we'll have to be. Well, let's get down to business. The United States government is prepared to counter the offers made by the Germans. We're willing to sign a secret agreement turning over airplanes that are superior to theirs. You can have them immediately."

"What is the U.S. Army Air Force prepared to do? Fly an entire squadron of fighters to Sweden?" Paulson mockingly asked.

92

"Why should we? The planes are already here." McClory stopped and turned to the rows of fighters, trainers and other single-engined aircraft. He pointed out the line of P-51 Mustangs and the P-47s scattered among the collection. "The P-51 is superior to every single-engined, propeller-driven fighter in Luftwaffe inventory. There's at least a dozen Mustangs in your collection here, plus Thunderbolts, plus Lightnings, plus B-17s and B-24s. All of these and more can be yours."

"The war in Europe may not last out the year," said MacAlister. "When it's finally over, where will you find the spare parts for all those aircraft the Germans have given you? On the other hand, there will still be plenty of American B-17s and P-51 Mustangs on the continent."

"More than we'd need by then," McClory added. "Washington is already making plans for demobilizing half of our military, including the army air force. That means there'll be a lot of surplus aircraft lying around and we could make them available to you at very reasonable prices. Well, what do you think?"

"I'd like to know what Great Britain wishes to offer?" said Paulson, turning to MacAlister and Whitney.

"We understand one of the reasons you'd like to retain the Me-262 is for its jet engines," MacAlister replied. "You're interested in building jet aircraft of your own."

"We know they are the shape of the future, and Sweden has no wish to be left behind."

"But you will be if you insist on using German engine technology. As Commander Norris and squadron leader Parry would tell you, German jet engines aren't quite as advanced as the air frames themselves. The Junkers turbojet on the '262 has an average life of fifteen flight hours. American and British engines are much more advanced and if you'll let us photograph the '262, then my country is prepared to share jet engine technology with you. We may even provide you with a license to produce British jet aircraft."

"Those are very desirable offers," said Paulson, slowly as if he were seriously thinking them over. "They are certainly more generous than what either the defense ministry or air force headquarters had expected. They believed you would either try to sell us more radar sets or supply more oil. On behalf of the Royal Swedish Air Force and the Swedish government, I accept both your offers, in return for detailed photographs of our most recent 'arrival.' Would you like us to do it or would you prefer to take the photographs yourself?"

"I think it's best that our experts shoot the photographs," Whitney advised, "with yours looking on, of course. When will we be able to take them, Wing Commander?"

"As soon as we have finalized our agreement. If it is your wish, we could leave for the defense ministry immediately. We could meet with the marshal of the Royal Swedish Air Force, the defense minister and your respective ambassadors in a matter of hours. You can return tonight; it would be advisable to shoot your pictures at night. There are less personnel on the base at those hours."

"OK, let's get our men and head for Stockholm," said McClory. "We'll contact our ambassadors from your ministry building, in fact they're waiting to hear from us. I think they'll be happy to hear that we've been able to reach an agreement on the jet. Do you think Commander Norris and Mister Parry are finished back there?"

"I think they're just beginning," MacAlister observed, looking at the trailers. Norris and Parry had sinced moved to the second trailer, with their Swedish escorts in tow. "If we left it up to them, they'd be happy to occupy the rest of the day examining that aircraft. I know their kind rather well, and those two in particular. I believe you could call them technophiles."

"Well, let's go pull them away from their new toy. They'll have plenty of time tonight to get better acquainted with it."

"All right, Corporal, you have the type of skills and experience we need," Roberts commented, glancing from the soldier standing at attention in front of him to the file he had in his hands. "And you show the proper determination for the mission at hand. You're on the team, Mister Barker."

"Thank you, Captain," said the corporal, beaming an enthusiastic smile. "It feels good to be working again."

Barker turned around smartly and marched out of the room. The moment the door clicked shut behind him, Cox asked Roberts why he'd been chosen.

"He's an expert in demolitions and he's been on a reconnaissance mission to Norway," Roberts explained, putting Barker's file on the smallest of several stacks before him. "He's had not only arctic warfare training but arctic combat experience as well. He's exactly what I need. I only wish you'd let me select some Army Rangers as well as SAS men."

"But he looks so young," said Cox. "I glanced at his file when you had it open. He's just nineteen."

"That's only five years younger than me, Commander. You older chaps seem to forget that war is a young man's occupation. There are nineteen-year-olds who fly Avro Lancasters, and men my age are captains of MTBs and frigates. People as old as you and Ian MacAlister are rarely seen on combat ops, you're usually working behind the scenes. And speaking of our man in Stockholm, when do you expect to hear from him?"

"Ian's latest report should arrive on the Foreign Office teletype by seven o'clock tonight. I fear it will only confirm what he stated in his earlier report. That pressure from the appeasement faction and pacifists will force the Swedish government to return the prototype to the Nazis. Though he was optimistic that the Swedes will allow Commander Norris to photograph the jet's radar equipment and other secrets. He felt certain they would accept our offers."

"It sounds to me like they want the best of both worlds," said Roberts cynically. "They'll make a deal with the Germans to hand back the bloody airplane and do another with us and the Americans to photograph it. They wish to please everyone, or should I say appease? What do the Sea Lords think of your little plan?"

"Later. I believe this is another of your volunteers."

There was a knock at the office door and it swung open, allowing in a Special Air Services sergeant. He removed his maroon beret and came to attention, announcing his name and rank. Roberts sorted through one of his stacks of personnel files, quickly locating the sergeant's records. He asked him a few questions, mostly about his training and combat experiences, then listened to the soldier's answers.

"Thank you for your time and for offering your services, Mister Davis," said Roberts, after mulling over the sergeant's qualifications for a few moments. "I'll keep you in mind for future operations but I'm afraid you wouldn't quite fit in with the current one.

Dismissed."

Like the corporal before him, the sergeant did a parade ground about-face and left the office. Roberts closed his file and tossed it on one of the other stacks on the table.

"Why did you refuse to take him?" Cox inquired. "He had much more experience than the last man, and you accepted him."

"He had the wrong kind of experience. He was involved in the amphibious assault on Walcheren Island in Holland. For this mission, I won't have need for such skills. I'll be leading a team of fifteen men and each of those men has to have the right balance of skills and frame of mind. Now how about answering my last question?"

"The Sea Lords are understandably concerned about this operation, though they do realize the need for it. Sir Andrew Cunningham and the civilian First Lord will take the plan to Winston Churchill tonight. He knows the gravity of the situation and they say he probably will authorize it. No matter how damaging or costly it may end up being."

"How well I understand that," said Roberts. "After studying the material you gave me on Sweden's defenses, I believe it's rather unlikely that my team will return. We'll probably be captured and interned by the Swedes. It's one of the factors I have to consider when I make my selections for the team. Which of these men will stand up best to the strain of imprisonment."

Roberts tapped the largest stack of files in front of him, the one from which he selected the men who would be part of his team. The other piles were for the ones he accepted, and those he rejected.

"What's Colonel Lacey and the rest of his crew doing? They were very disappointed when you told them they might not be part of the operation."

"Well, they did devise a few plans to recover the prototype," said Cox, "should Ian be luckier than we expect. The colonel and his men also volunteered to fly the aircraft for your parachute drop. Until then, they have an unexpected leave in London. And Dennis and Constance have a chance to be together for a little while."

"I'll take your coat, Dennis," Constance offered as they stepped through the doorway of the darkened apartment. "The light switch is to the right."

Lacey ran his fingers along the right hand wall, pressing in one of the buttons on the switch panel when he found it. The chandelier in the center of the ceiling clicked on, bathing the living room in a soft light, some of it multi-hued and glittering as it reflected through the chandelier's many crystals.

"This is rather fancy," said Lacey, "especially for a sub-lieutenant in the Royal Navy. How do you manage to afford this on a pay rate as low as yours?"

"I share this with a girlfriend of mine." Constance opened a closet and hung her coat and Lacey's inside it, then turned to face Lacey. "One lieutenant can't afford this but two lieutenants can. With flats at a premium in London, it's really the only way to live. And we're not too far from Whitehall. The Admiralty building is just a few blocks away."

"The Admiralty. Shouldn't we call and find out what Ian MacAlister had to report? I'd really like to know how successful he and John Norris have been."

"Reports from military attachés arrive at the foreign office first," said Constance, "and besides, they're classified. No one will read them over an open phone line. You'll just have to wait for our meeting tomorrow morning."

"That's a damn long time to wait before finding out if you're part of an operation, or on vacation. I thought I would be stealing a German jet, not going out to see movies."

"Impatience, that's something else you share with Charles. Tonight will pass quickly, too quickly for me, and soon we will know what part you're to play. We already have an inkling as to what may happen. Ian will only be able to gain photographs of the jet and Lee Roberts will have to blow it up. Your likely role will be to provide the para-drop aircraft. You were tense all through the movie, I could feel it in you." Constance wrapped her arms around Lacey and embraced him, then laid her head on his shoulder. "You're still tense, but I have a way to cure it."

"And I think I know your way. Aren't you afraid your old roommate may barge in on us?"

"No, she's off seeing her boyfriend at his flat. I don't think we'll be disturbed for the rest of the night."

Constance ran her hand down the front of Lacey's jacket, undoing its buttons as she went. She kissed him lightly under the ear as well, the twin sensations provoking a response from Lacey, who reached around her waist and started loosening her skirt.

"You're pretty good at undressing army officers," he said.

"I have to be. I'm growing tired of being poked by your eagles every time I rest my head on your shoulder."

Lacey helped Constance remove his jacket, tossing it over the back of the living room's sofa once he had it off. He then picked her up and carried her toward one of the darkened rooms in the apartment.

"This is the bathroom," she informed, just before

he stepped across the threshold.

"Sorry, remember I'm a pilot. Not a navigator."

Lacey backed up a few steps, then took Constance inside the apartment's other blacked-out room. The twin beds could be dimly seen in the weak light slanting in from the living room. He laid her on the nearest bed and started to remove her uniform, beginning with her shoes.

"There's a blanket in the closet, Dennis," said Constance, pulling off her jacket while Lacey removed her skirt and nylon stockings.

"I really don't think we'll need it," he said, "but I'll get it for us anyway."

When she only had her brassiere left on, Constance slipped between the bed sheets. Lacey stripped off the rest of his clothes as he walked over to the closet and threw them on the second bed. By the time he returned to Constance, all he carried with him was the blanket she had requested. He spread it over the bed's top cover then joined her under them, peeling away her bra after she had unhooked it and gently massaging one of her breasts.

"Make the night last as long as it can," Constance requested, her heart racing faster as Lacey stroked her.

"I will. Who knows when we'll have another like it?"

Constance slid underneath Lacey and wrapped her arms and legs around him as they began making love.

FOREIGN OFFICE SPECIAL REPORT
STOCKHOLM, SWEDEN
From: Lt.-Cmdr. Ian MacAlister — Naval Attaché
To: Cmdr. Charles Cox — Enemy Threat Evaluation

team.

The Admiralty Building, Whitehall.

THIS DOCUMENT IS RESTRICTED TO THOSE OFFICERS WITH THE RANK OF DEPUTY FOREIGN SECRETARY OR HIGHER AND MEMBERS OF: the Enemy Threat Evaluation team.

American attachés and I have concluded an agreement with the Swedish government. It was secretly signed at five p.m. local time today, between the Swedish foreign minister and the U.S. and British ambassadors. In exchange for all American aircraft interned in Sweden and British jet engine technology, the Swedes will allow us to photograph the Night Hawk prototype. We won't be allowed to take any part of the aircraft, all we can have are pictures. This is less than what we had originally hoped for, but it's the best we could obtain, considering the circumstances. It's been arranged for us to return to Norrköping at midnight tonight. I will try to take the photos you'll need of the base at that time. Wish me luck.

signed,
Lt.-Cmdr. Ian William MacAlister

"Commander MacAlister, Commander Norris, squadron leader Parry and Lieutenant-Colonel McClory," read off the sentry, moving his flashlight from his clipboard to the men sitting inside the car. "Good, you are the ones we were expecting. Lift the bar, let them pass. Please follow the truck to your destination."

This time they came in only one car, instead of two, and without a driver. They also entered the base at one of its remote side gates, instead of the main one, though they did collect an escort as they had before.

A service truck led the attachés around Norrköping's perimeter road. Little could be seen of the base, the Royal Swedish Air Force followed wartime blackout procedures nearly as well as the R.A.F., only occasionally could a darkened building be seen in the car's headlights. In spite of having been on the base only hours earlier, none of the attachés knew exactly where they were. Not until the truck ahead slowed to a stop and a pair of tarpaulin-covered trailers appeared in its headlight beams.

"Wing Commander Paulson, this is a surprise," MacAlister remarked, snapping out a salute as he emerged from the car. "I had thought you'd turn over responsibilities to one of your subordinate officers."

"When you deal with something so sensitive as photographing a top-secret German aircraft, the fewer people involved, the better," said Paulson, returning the salute and shaking MacAlister's hand. "Commander Norris, is that the camera equipment you will use? May I see it please?"

Norris came out of the sedan carrying a large, steel case. He laid it on the hood of the car and opened its lid, revealing the camera he would be using and its ancillary gear. Paulson was so interested in it all, he failed to notice the slim briefcase MacAlister had brought with him.

There were other Swedish officers who greeted the Allied attachés, the experts Paulson had introduced to them earlier in the day. Norris and Parry received the lion's share of their attention and conversation; MacAlister and McClory were almost left on their own. They walked across the tarmac to the trailers the dismembered jet sat on.

"So close we can touch it, and yet we can't have it,"

McClory commented, as they stood beside one of the trailers. "From what my ambassador told me, this plane could be back in Germany in another week."

"And the Swedes will receive their squadrons of Messerschmitts," said MacAlister. "It looks as though they're going to have their cake and eat it too. You really can't blame them. They're only working for their country's own interest."

"Sergeant, remove the cover," Paulson ordered, arriving with Norris, Parry and his own experts in tow. "Commander, you did say you wanted to start with the fuselage sections, didn't you?"

"Yes, we might as well start with the important stuff," said Norris. "Colonel, could you give us a hand?"

McClory helped Norris remove the camera equipment from its case while the Swedish guards rolled the tarpaulin off the Me-262's fuselage and nose cap. No one asked MacAlister for aid, by prearrangement he was left alone to wander around the trailers. Norris climbed onto the one being uncovered, pulling the camera body out of its velvet-lined recess in the case as McClory handed him the wide-angle lens.

"Here's the flash attachment," said McClory, unfolding a segmented disc and holding it up to Norris.

"Wait just a minute," he said. "First I have to load the camera with some film. Unpack the light meter, will you?"

By the time Norris had the camera ready, the nose section and fuselage of the Night Hawk had been uncovered. Paulson had one of the trucks standing on the tarmac turn on its headlights, bathing one side of the fuselage in their powerful beams. It wouldn't help Norris much with his photography, though at least he and Parry would be able to see their way around the trailer well enough to not stumble over something, or

103

fall off its edge.

"We'll start with the radar operator's seat," Norris advised Parry, after helping him climb onto the trailer. "That's where most of the important gear is located. I'd like to get as many pictures of it as we can."

With squadron leader Lönnberg and Lise Carlsson following them, Norris and Parry walked up to the fighter's rear cockpit and opened its canopy panel. They had to use a flashlight to see inside its black well. Norris aimed the light on the instrument panel while he decided how best to shoot it.

"Rather cramped in there, old chap," said Parry. "Are you sure you'll be able to get it all?"

"I think so," said Norris, twisting a flashbulb into the socket provided for it. "That's why I'm using a wide-angle lens. But I'll have to change to something else to make the detail shots. Miss Carlsson? Could you go over and ask Scott for the close-up lens and the plus-two diopter? Thanks, we'll be needing it soon."

Norris leaned in the cockpit as far as he could. He balanced himself by placing one elbow on the seat and hurriedly set the focus and exposure time. There was a soft crackle as the flashbulb detonated, filling the cockpit well with a brief pulse of blue-white light, and the first picture was taken. Norris popped the dead bulb out of the socket and handed it up to Parry. He replaced it and advanced the film roll before taking his next shot. He was in the middle of preparing for his third when Lise returned with the equipment he wanted.

"Now I'll take a few detail shots of the panel," said Norris, exchanging lenses. "Especially of the interception radar and the Naxos homing radar controls. Then we'll open up the panel and take more shots of

104

their interior wiring."

"Excuse me for asking, Commander, but why are you saving those bulbs?" Lönnberg asked.

"So the Krauts won't find them when they search the airplane. When you return it to them, they'll go over it with a fine-tooth comb. They'll look for any evidence that this plane has been tampered with or examined, so we have to make sure we don't leave any clues. We have to be especially careful not to scratch or mar the paint work when we open this panel up."

Once the flashbulbs had started popping, everyone's attention focussed on Norris and the other experts. Hardly any was given to MacAlister as he slowly circled the two trailers. He appeared to be on a stroll, stopping every so often to view the darkened hangars or the dimly illuminated aircraft in the rest of the collection. No one noticed how he kept pressing down the latch button under the handle of his briefcase.

"Ian, you don't seem too interested in what we're doing," said McClory as he approached MacAlister. "You asked us to leave you alone. What are you up to?"

McClory's question caught MacAlister by surprise. He had been nervous enough taking his illicit photographs, but when McClory suddenly spoke to him, MacAlister's heart nearly stopped. He also nearly dropped his briefcase; he had to grab it with both hands to prevent it from crashing to the ground.

"Damn it, Scott, don't sneak up on me like that," MacAlister snapped, more out of nervousness than anger, and it took a good deal of concentration to keep his voice low and his expression calm. "I thought you were one of our Swedish friends. Another scare and I may have a heart attack. What I'm doing has me scared enough as it is. And if you must know, I'm photographing this section of the base for that saboteur attack I told you about. A camera's been secreted in this case and I'm almost finished with it."

"A camera?" Though McClory was close enough to hear the faint click as MacAlister pressed the latch button, he still didn't quite believe it. "Where's the flash?"

"I'm using something rather new. It's called infrared film and it doesn't need flashbulbs." MacAlister felt his heart slow slightly and he picked up his stride again. He continued walking around the trailers, keeping his briefcase pointed away from them and recording the terrain. "Walk between me and the trailers, Scott. Tell me if anyone approaches us. How's the official shoot coming along?"

"They're still working on the radar man's position. Then they'll photograph the pilot's cockpit, the nose section and whatever's behind any access panel they can open on the fuselage. Norris and Parry don't know if they'll photograph the wings or not. Norris said they could spend an hour on the fuselage alone and still not cover it all. Everyone's so wrapped up in what they're doing I don't think they've noticed . . . Wait, here comes someone. It's Paulson and another Swede."

"All right, just a few more shots for good measure." MacAlister hurriedly took his last photographs and pulled a small, dime-sized patch of leather from his greatcoat pocket. It slipped neatly into the hole on the front edge of the briefcase. In the prevailing darkness, no one would be able to spot the hairline seam around the patch.

"Lieutenant-Commander MacAlister, I want you to meet squadron leader Erik Lindh," said Paulson.

"He's the officer in charge of the latest acquisition to our collection."

"However temporary it may be," MacAlister remarked, returning the salute Lindh gave him. "I heard you were up for more than twenty-four hours with moving this jet from Malmö. You did quite a job, squadron leader."

"Thank you, Mister MacAlister. I hope you understand why I did not meet you earlier today," said Lindh, "or I should say early yesterday. We have thermoses of tea and coffee in the wing commander's car. Would you and Lieutenant-Colonel McClory care to join us?"

"Well it is rather frigid out here. Especially when you don't have much to do, save for walking. I could do with a strong cup of coffee, thank you."

"Captain, what's the activity among the foreign aircraft?" asked the sergeant, standing on the wing of the airplane he was repairing. "Someone has his headlights on."

"Probably the wing commander," said the group captain. "You should not know what's happening but since you see it I guess it's all right. Mister Paulson is showing that jet fighter we have to American and British attachés from Stockholm."

"But I thought they already saw it yesterday afternoon, and have we not made an agreement with the Nazis to give them back the jet?"

"I'm told there has also been an agreement made with the Allies. I have no idea what they agreed to, but this visit is the apparent result. Have you finished working on my Northrop, Sergeant?"

"Just have to replace the access panels, sir. You had a faulty oil line and seal. They were causing your pressure loss. Another hour and your line may have failed. Could you give me a hand down?"

The sergeant turned over his tool kit to the group captain before he climbed off the wing of the Northrop 8A-1 attack bomber, one of several such aircraft on the flight line in front of Norrköping's control tower. Once on the ground, they saluted and went their separate ways. The group captain to the officer's bar and the sergeant to a nearby hangar where he would wash up and stow his kit.

All the way across the tarmac, the sergeant kept looking over his shoulder at the lights on the opposite side of the base. When he reached the hangar, he took from his locker a small pair of field binoculars and went to one of the windows in the locker room. For several minutes he watched the distant operation; the binoculars weren't much better than the naked eye, though at least he could see who was working on what. He wasn't able to identify the people but he could identify their uniforms and he was able to count them.

The sergeant then washed as quickly as he could, stowed his tool kit and working overalls and changed into his regular uniform. Parked behind the hangar was a Volvo coupe, one of the few civilian vehicles left in the lot. The sergeant climbed behind its steering wheel and drove off. He left Norrköping entirely, driving to a nearby bar where he stayed just long enough to use its phone. He let it ring only twice before he hung up.

Instead of going home he drove north, following the coast highway to Stockholm. It took him nearly two hours to reach the city; by now it was early morning. Even so Stockholm was still very much alive and the sergeant quickly found himself an open, crowded bar.

So crowded that few of its patrons took note of his uniform, except for a man at a wall table who motioned for him to come over. The man was large, almost too large for the table he was sitting at, and he had a heavy red beard and a handlebar moustache.

"Well, Sergeant Lindqvist, I hope what you have to tell me is good," said Drache, as the airman sat opposite him. "It's late and I've had a long and tiresome day."

"It is," said Lindqvist, "believe me. The air force has cheated your friends in Berlin. They've apparently made a deal with the Americans and the English. When I left Norrköping, their military attachés were examining the Night Hawk. The fuselage was uncovered and I believe they were photographing it."

"And how long ago was this? Two hours? Damn, that means by now they've unlocked all its secrets. The jet is as good as useless to the Reich. We might as well give it to the Allies. Who did you see at Norrköping?"

"The American Army and Navy attachés, and the British navy and air force attachés. I couldn't recognize the officers themselves but I did spot their uniforms. The English naval officer was talking to Wing Commander Paulson when I spotted them. I last saw him entering the wing commander's staff car."

"Ian MacAlister, I should've known it would be him." Drache slammed the table with the palm of his hand, so hard it splashed part of his drink out of its glass. "Damn him, he probably came direct from London with an offer too good for the Swedish government to reject. I have no doubt the Americans were all too willing to help the British. I believe I now know why the U.S. embassy received a new naval attaché yesterday. The British always turn to the

Americans when they're in trouble. If it wasn't for Lend-Lease, the Reich would have crushed that pitiful island."

"Mister Drache, what will you do about the attachés?" Lindqvist asked, getting the conversation back to its original topic. "It's been more than two hours since I saw them photographing the jet. They must be on the road back to Stockholm. Why not use your network to stop them?"

"No, we don't know exactly where they are and chances are as such we would not be very successful. Don't worry, Sergeant, I will deal with them. I'll notify Berlin and we will work out a plan. The pictures the attachés took are useless sitting in Stockholm. We will intercept them before they reach England. You've done well, Sergeant. You will receive a bonus in addition to your regular payment. You had better start back for home. I'll deal with Mister MacAlister and his friends."

Chapter Five: Day Three
Interception

"I thought you guys would've developed those rolls after we came back last night," Norris remarked when he entered Parry's office and found him and Mac-Alister placing film canisters inside a diplomatic pouch.

"It was nearly four o'clock in the morning by the time we returned," said MacAlister. "We were all just a trifle tired. As I recall, you fell asleep on the ride back."

"Yeah, well, I didn't have all those cups of coffee you had with the base commander. I would've liked to have seen my work before it was sent off."

"It's best to send it to London, where Commander Cox and Colonel Lacey will have access to better equipment than we have here. Well it's all ready, Greg. Give me the padlock."

MacAlister folded over the top of the heavy leather satchel and threaded its straps through the eyelets. The thick, center strap was pulled onto a peg and held taut while Parry handed MacAlister the lock he wanted. It was a rather small one but made out of chrome steel, which made it far stronger than it looked. MacAlister attached the padlock to the peg and clicked it shut. He took a pair of handcuffs and closed one of the bracelets around the satchel's handle while he slapped the other on Parry's left wrist.

"But I thought you were going to take the pics back to London," said Norris: "What changed your mind?"

"It would look rather strange for a newly installed attaché to return so soon to London," MacAlister noted. "You and I may have to stay here a few weeks before we can quietly slip out of Sweden. Don't worry about the film, we've used Greg before to transport sensitive material. Well, I think you're all set, Greg. Do you have your service revolver?"

"Yes, but I feel rather uncomfortable wearing this," said Parry, producing a thirty-eight-caliber revolver from inside his coat. "It's been so long since I last needed to. Are you absolutely certain this is necessary?"

"Of course, it's part of diplomatic tradition, old chap. In case the Germans send the Luftwaffe after you, you're to shoot them down with that. Well, I think we're all set. Shall we use one of our cars, or John's?"

Since it was already sitting in the front parking lot, MacAlister and Parry decided to use the car Norris had driven over from the U.S. embassy. Almost from the time Norris started the engine, they had to give him directions on how to reach Bromma airport. They were so busy telling him where to turn and how far to go that no one noticed the car which moved onto the sedan's tail as it rolled through the British embassy.

Norris drove uneasily through Stockholm's heavy morning traffic. He relied completely on MacAlister

112

and Parry to tell him where he was; not until he was on Drottningholm Road, which led to Bromma, did he relax a little. Just enough for him to notice what was happening behind him.

"That car, the green one, I think I've seen it before," said Norris, fixing his gaze on the rear-view mirror.

"You have," MacAlister replied. "I've seen it since we turned onto North Mälarstrand. And maybe it was in front of the British embassy, John?"

"I'm afraid not, I was too busy following the directions Scott McClory gave me. You know how difficult it is to read all these street signs that're in Swedish?"

"Yes, I know. It's a bad habit the Swedes have, using the language and all." MacAlister couldn't help being sarcastic.

"The vehicle has Swedish civilian license plates," said Parry, glancing out the rear window. "Not German diplomatic plates or Swedish police plates. Still, that doesn't mean whoever's in the car isn't an agent for somebody."

"Do you know how long it's been behind us?"

"I'm sorry, Ian. I didn't notice the car until you two started talking about it."

"Fine, I'm the only intelligence officer and I had to be busy giving directions," said MacAlister, "so it could just be some Swedes innocently heading for the airport."

"What should we do?" Norris asked. "Call it off or keep driving to the airport?"

"Greg has to make that flight. Seats on air liners are at a premium, even Swedish air liners. If he doesn't make it to this one, we'll have to wait twelve hours for the BOAC flight. So keep driving and I'll keep a watch on our friends."

For the rest of the trip to Bromma, MacAlister had his eye almost continuously on the dark green sedan which tailed them. At times, especially on the approach to the airport, it was close enough for him to identify its occupants. There were two men, neither of whom MacAlister or Parry recognized as German or Swedish agents. Still, MacAlister watched where they parked in the lot and what they did when he and Norris took Parry into the airport lobby.

"I do believe they're following us," said MacAlister as they walked through one of the lobby doors. "They're trying to be subtle about it. Entering down there with a group of tourists. John, take care of Greg for me. He has his tickets and all he has to show is his diplomatic passport at customs. I want to find out who our friends are. Goodbye, Greg, enjoy yourself in London."

MacAlister broke away from Parry and Norris, without even shaking Parry's hand. He headed for one of the lobby's rest rooms, which he only stayed in long enough to pull off his navy greatcoat, reverse it and tuck his wheel cap under his arm. When he emerged, MacAlister looked very much like a businessman wearing a black winter coat. He quickly ran up a nearby flight of stairs to the second level of the airport terminal.

For a few tense moments he was unable to spot the men who had been tailing him. All he could see were Norris and Parry at the Swedish air lines ticket counter. Then, he found them, climbing another flight of stairs to the upper level. From behind a newsstand, MacAlister watched them reach the second floor and walk to the terminal's restaurant and observation deck. Neither of them stopped at the balcony to watch Norris and Parry, nor did they scan the lobby for MacAlister. To him, their behavior was very curious.

As they walked past the newsstand, he started following them, though at a safe distance. They walked inside the restaurant and over to a table by the observation windows. MacAlister stopped at the restaurant's entrance. He felt it was too dangerous to go any farther, and he had no need to. From where he stood he could see almost everyone in the restaurant; it didn't take him long to identify who the spies were meeting with.

He never got more than a profile of the man the spies met but it was enough. The wavy red hair and full beard made him instantly recognizable. It was Carl Drache. MacAlister watched as he met the men and gestured for them to sit down. He appeared to do more listening than talking, at one point scribbling on a small note pad. Then he became visibly agitated and pointed at one of the spies, making him not only leave the table but the restaurant as well.

MacAlister turned away from the entrance and, as calmly as he could, searched desperately for the nearest exit. He bolted for an innocuous-looking door, behind which he found a set of service stairs. Practically leaping down them, MacAlister jammed his cap on his head and tore off his greatcoat. He pulled it inside out again, returning the coat to its original blue color. By the time he reached the ground floor he had his navy greatcoat back and was wearing it. MacAlister emerged from the stairwell looking like a slightly bedraggled Royal Navy officer.

"You idiot," Drache snarled. "You should have left Manfred to watch the attachés. I don't care if Parry had the diplomatic pouch on his wrist or not. It could've been changed. They have done that in the past. And I especially want to know what Ian Mac-Alister does. I believe he came here to specifically negotiate for the jet. I would like to know who boards the air liner."

"What will you do with the information we have given you, Mister Drache?" the spy asked. "It is too late to stop the British. Those photographs are now as good as in London. What chance do we have?"

"We have none, but the Reich can still interfere. I'll phone this to the German embassy, they have a line the Swedes cannot monitor. I'll let the Gestapo and the Luftwaffe deal with the air liner."

"Do you believe they will shoot it down?"

"Mistakes and unfortunate accidents can be made to happen," said Drache, at scarcely more than a whisper. "I for one know the Gestapo is very good at that."

"Well, there he goes, Ian," said Norris, waving to Parry as he walked out to the Swedish air lines Ju-52. "Where have you been? You look like you just ran the fifty-yard dash."

"In a way I have," MacAlister admitted. There were beads of sweat on his face and his overcoat flapped like a cape as he arrived. "I just saw something that confirms my suspicions. I'll tell you about it on the drive back to Stockholm. We need to go straight back to my embassy. I'd like to arrange for an escort to meet that air liner over the North Sea. I have an awful foreboding about this."

"Why? What can go wrong now?"

"I'll tell you on the drive back."

"Oh, I see. It's a secret," said Norris. "Is it too much of a secret to tell me why you've got a collar on the inside of your coat?"

116

"This is a reversible coat, standard equipment for intelligence agents and, believe me, it's as hot in here as a Swedish sauna. One of the reasons why you don't see many fat secret agents."

Just before he climbed aboard the bright orange air liner, Parry turned and waved to his friends one last time. Then he disappeared inside the plane as the first of its engines started up. The trimotor's nose engine was the first to rumble to life, followed by the port and starboard radials. The rest of the passengers filed into the Junkers while its engines were put through their run-up checks. When the boarding ramp was pulled away, and the fuselage door closed, the Ju-52 was ready to roll.

A burst of power from its Pratt and Whitney Hornet radials blew the snow on the tarmac against the departure gate's windows, creating an intense, blinding flurry. In the few seconds it took to settle, the air liner had taxied out to one of Bromma's runways. It had only to wait for an incoming light plane to land, which Norris was able to identify as a Beech Staggerwing, before departing.

The Ju-52 opened up its engines and started to roll, lifting off while it was still moving rather slowly. MacAlister and Norris waited until the Junkers had made its climb out and was heading south before they left the airport. Another party, equally interested in the air liner, waited only for it to barely cross the end of the runway before he was using the nearest available telephone.

"This is Drache, the password is vixen. Send the following message to Gestapo headquarters in Copenhagen immediately. You are not to send it to Berlin and it's to have priority status. It must be transmitted to Copenhagen within the hour. Tell them 'RAF attaché believed to be carrying Night Hawk film has departed Stockholm on Swedish air lines trimotor SE-AFT. It is imperative that you stop or otherwise intercept this air liner.' Do you have all that? Good, transmit it at once."

"Commander Cox? The aircraft you requested is ready and it's waiting on the flight line. It's the Avro Anson, serial number one-seven-five-three."

The desk officer pointed the way to the flight line for Cox, who in turn motioned for Constance and Lacey to join him. They walked through the lobby doors, turning up their collars just before they were hit by the cold, blustery weather outside. They made their way along the military flight line of Heathrow airport, staying well clear of the spinning props on many of the aircraft. When they got to the Anson, they found it more than ready. Its engines had been started and they were idling smoothly. First Cox boarded the transport, then Constance and Lacey; they had barely taken their seats when the Avro swung around and taxied off to the runways.

"How come Captain Roberts hasn't joined us?" Lacey asked, buckling his seat belt. "I'd think the leader of the commando team would be interested in which airfield we choose to launch our operation from."

"Oh, he is, but it's a matter of priorities, Dennis," said Cox. "He has his team to organize and brief. What precious little training they'll receive will be given to them today. A few days from now, Lee and his men will be parachuting into Sweden. Depending on what the photographs MacAlister has taken will show us."

"And when will we get to see them?"

"Not long after the air liner lands in Scotland. It

118

has to set down in Aberdeen to refuel. Our air attaché will disembark and turn over the film to an R.A.F. intelligence officer. He'll fly it to us in Scapa Flow, where Connie here will supervise its processing."

"After all, that was one of my jobs before I became a liaison officer," said Constance, "and I am rather familiar with the photo lab at Scapa Flow. That's where I processed the first film we had of the Frederick the Great."

"What about the film on the jet itself?" Lacey inquired. "Will you develop it as well?"

"As soon as I've done the film Ian made. Charles told me he used an infrared variety and that's difficult to develop properly. I prefer to do the difficult jobs first."

There was a sudden burst of power from the Anson's Cheetah radials, drowning out any further conversation. Constance and the others had become so involved in their discussion they failed to notice that the transport was ready for takeoff. It accelerated down the runway, its tail lifting into the air at ninety miles an hour, the main gear skipping off the ground a few moments later.

"Looks like we just got out before the rush hour," said Lacey. "There must be a half-dozen C-47s and other big planes behind us. How long will it take this plywood wonder to get to Scotland?"

"At cruising speed, we should reach the first of our prospective airfields in about two hours," Cox answered. "From your remark, I take it you're not entirely satisfied with the airplane I found for us?"

"No, not really. I'm still pissed at the Lodestar fucking up because some twenty-nine-cent part fails. At its cruise speed we could shave a half-hour off our flight time."

"I know a propeller governor sounds like a small thing, but believe me, you wouldn't want to try flying a twin-engined aircraft with a wild prop. Once your team's repaired the Lodestar, they can join us at Scapa Flow. By then we should be receiving the film from Sweden. Tell me, Dennis, have you decided which aircraft you'd like to use for the mission?"

"Yes. I know Vince is going to bitch about it, but I'd like to use a B-24 Liberator. It's got better range than a B-17 and it's built in two transport versions, the C-87 and the C-109. The Ninth Air Force transport groups have a few C-87s and Vince has a friend in one. I'm sure we can get a Lib'. How big will the SAS team be?"

"Including Roberts, there'll be fifteen men," said Cox, "not very many. Though he claims they'll be enough. He'll either join us at Scapa Flow by the end of the day or we'll fly down to him. Lee will review the photos Ian took and finalize his part of the plan. In a day or two his team should be ready and, hopefully, you'll have the right type of Liberator. Then we can all hold our breath and pray we haven't started an even worse crisis."

When it reached its assigned cruise altitude, the Anson turned due north, into a slate-gray sky and a thirty-mile-an-hour head wind. Some three hundred miles away lay the first of its destinations, Edinburgh. Which, under current weather conditions, would take the transport an extra half-hour to reach.

"Herr Heinrich, this is the latest report from our agents in Stockholm," announced Lossberg, walking up to the He-219 he'd been told was the group commander's personal aircraft. "Hurry, this is an emergency. We must act immediately."

One of two officers sitting in the night fighter's cockpit looked over the side of the fuselage. Heinrich gave the Gestapo man a disapproving stare and yet, he climbed out of the cockpit anyway. It was almost a dozen feet from the Heinkel's cockpit to the hangar floor and Heinrich had to work his way down the scaffolding erected around the plane's forward fuselage. The Heinkel 219 was a huge fighter, nearly the same size as a medium bomber. It dwarfed the men who were working on it and the three inside the hangar virtually filled it.

"For the last two days, everything you've brought me has been an emergency. Something that has to be acted on immediately," said Heinrich, taking the sheet of paper Lossberg shoved at him. He needed only a few moments to read the brief message from Carl Drache. "Then we have lost. The Allies have examined the Night Hawk and will learn its secrets before we could learn its capabilities."

"We have not lost, that's a defeatist attitude!" Lossberg stormed. "The air liner has not yet reached England! We can still do what our Stockholm agent advised us."

"What? Intercept the civilian air liner of a neutral country? Are you crazy? Do you know the kind of outrage that's created when merely a British air liner is shot down? And you're asking me to intercept a Swedish one."

"This is war and unfortunate mistakes do happen."

"No one will believe that," said Heinrich, "least of all the Swedes. Since the beginning of the war, Sweden has painted its air liners orange, with their civil registrations and the word 'Sweden' in large black letters. There's no way to mistake it for an Allied aircraft."

"It's not necessary for you to shoot down the air

liner. Merely force it to land or force it over the Danish coast where anti-aircraft guns can shoot it down. I've already had air defense headquarters place all their flak batteries in the Vendsyssel region on alert."

"You have thought of everything, haven't you? Well I will not have my aircraft kill an unarmed air liner."

"I am personally ordering you to shoot down that aircraft," said Lossberg, a cold, lethal rage in his eyes and voice. "Failure to obey will be an act of cowardice and treason."

"I'm the holder of the Knight's Cross with diamonds. Do not call me a coward or a traitor! Even if I wanted to obey you, I couldn't. As you can see, my fighter is non-operational due to repairs. So are many other aircraft in my *gruppe*. As you should also see, Herr Lossberg, my aircraft are night fighters. It would be out of place, and very suspicious, if they were to do the interception. It'd be more logical to use day fighters. Several groups of Focke-Wulfs recently transferred from the Eastern Front to Vaerlöse and Kastrup. They would be better and we could always claim they were not familiar with Swedish civil aircraft."

"Good, that I can arrange easily." Lossberg's voice softened and the murderous look went out of his eyes. "I'll order the fighters to either destroy the air liner or force it over Denmark where anti-aircraft batteries will shoot it down for violating air space in a security zone."

"I don't care how you do it," Heinrich admitted, "so long as the blood isn't on my hands. Or on the hands of my pilots. I am not like you, Lossberg. I'm a warrior and an officer. Do not make me or my men murderers. Don't involve us in an operation that will only worsen this crisis, as you did with the Kriegsmarine."

"I'll use you as I see fit, Herr Oberstleutnant. If you refuse, I may not be able to prove treason but I can ruin your career. I happen to know that several of your aircraft are not legitimate. They were not officially produced, they were assembled by a Luftwaffe maintenance unit from their stock of spare parts. As such, they have no serial numbers and their existence is unknown to the RLM. If the ministry were to be told about them, you would certainly be demoted and removed from your command. I own you, Herr Heinrich, never forget it."

"Ladies and gentlemen, may I have your attention please?" requested the air liner's pilot, his voice barely audible above the din of the trimotor's engines. "From the left side of our aircraft, you can see the coast of Denmark. Let me assure you that there's no reason to fear being fired on by German forces. We are in international air space. However, I must warn you not to use your cameras, as that would violate an international agreement."

There wasn't much of the Danish coast Parry could see. What the cloud banks didn't hide was partially blocked by the matte board placed over the window, which reduced the viewing area to just a few square inches. Parry soon gave up on the coast, it was so far away no detail could be seen with the naked eye. He settled for watching the passing formations of cumulus clouds. In the midday sun they were dazzlingly bright, it almost hurt his eyes to continue looking at them. At first he did it for pleasure, it had been months since he was in an airplane of any kind, then on purpose.

"Excuse me, Mister Parry, but you are not to do that," said the air liner's stewardess when she discovered Parry prying out the clips which held the matte board in place.

"I have to," he replied. "We're being followed. Tell your captain there are German fighters in the area."

When the last clip was removed, the board fell off the window, drastically increasing the amount of light entering the forward cabin. It also gave Parry a greatly improved viewing area and he could continue tracking the two shadows he had spotted. They flew in the opposite direction of the air liner and quickly passed out of sight, behind its tail.

"The captain says German aircraft have approached our air liners in the past," said the stewardess. "If they come too close, we will file a protest. Please do not worry, they are merely curious and you frighten the other passengers."

"I've seen Nazi airplanes enough times to know that they are not curious. I believe they're hunting us. We had better turn back to Sweden, immediately."

"The captain assures me we are still in international air space. Please, Mister Parry, you are . . ."

The stewardess's words trailed off as the cabin filled with a brief roar. Parry looked out his window to see a pair of fighters shoot past the air liner's wing tip. He saw them only for a moment, they were flying at more than twice the Ju-52's speed, but their radial engines and square-cut wing tips identified them as Fw-190s.

"If they were curious about us, they would've sat on our wing," said Parry, "not flash by it. We're being stalked, damn it. Tell the pilot to turn back to Sweden or I will."

The stewardess turned and made for the cockpit, telling the other passengers in Swedish and English to remain calm as she ran. Parry watched the Focke-

Wulfs until they made a sharp right turn and disappeared. They had simple, white crosses on their wings, black crosses on their fuselages, and yellow bands around their tails. Parry knew the bands meant the aircraft had served recently on the eastern front; perhaps they were only curious. They probably never saw a civilian air liner before. Maybe he was overreacting. However, his doubts were completely erased when the Ju-52 shuddered and tracers streaked by the wing.

Holes were punched in the wing's corrugated surface and a burst of shrapnel filled the forward fuselage. Parry ducked behind the seat in front of him. He could hear the shrapnel ricochet off the cabin walls and the passengers scream. The attack ended with another brief roar as the Focke-Wulfs shot over the air liner. Before the sound died away, Parry was out of his seat and making for the cockpit. By the time he reached it, he found he was running downhill. The Junkers had entered a dive.

"Help me! Please help me!" the stewardess cried, when she noticed Parry standing in the doorway. "We have to take him out. He's jamming the controls!"

She was tugging at the body of the pilot, who was slumped over his control yoke. Instead of helping the stewardess move the body, Parry first went for the lever at the base of the seat. He unlocked it and grabbed hold of the seat back. With one jerk he pulled it to the rear stops, where the lever locked in place again.

"Free his seat belt!" Parry shouted. "I'll grab him by the shoulders!"

There was little left to grab. A cannon shell had exploded inside the cockpit and the pilot had caught most of its blast and shrapnel. His head and chest were masses of torn flesh and bone. Blood was everywhere. It soaked the pilot's uniform and splattered the cockpit wall and instrument panels. Once his belt and harness had been unlocked, the pilot was lifted out of the seat. The stewardess helped with his legs and Parry was able to drag him to the passenger cabin where he laid the shattered body on the floor.

"See to the other passengers," said Parry, shaking the stewardess, who was crying openly. "I'll take his place in the cockpit."

Stumbling past the body of the pilot, she checked the remaining passengers to see if they'd been wounded, while Parry returned to the cockpit. He climbed into the empty left seat and tried to find a place to stow his briefcase attached to his wrist. There was blood on the seat and part of the instrument panel; and what wasn't covered in blood appeared to be damaged by machine gun fire. The co-pilot still had the Junkers in a dive. By now it was down to a thousand meters on the altimeter.

"Thank you, squadron leader!" the co-pilot shouted, so he could be heard above the gale whistling through the holes in the canopy. "I could not have flown the aircraft with him on the controls! I have the radio operator sending a distress call on the emergency channel. We must keep the aircraft in a dive until we reach sea level. Then we head across the Skagerak to Sweden!"

"No, we can't do that until we shake off those fighters," said Parry. "Turn this ship toward the Danish coast. It's the only chance we'll have to lose them!"

Parry unlocked his seat and reset it closer to the instrument panel. He put his feet on the large, cast-iron rudder pedals and grabbed hold of the outsized control wheel. Still in its dive, he and the co-pilot forced the Ju-52 to dip its left wing and swing toward the narrow finger of land jutting into the North Sea.

At a hundred meters, just under four hundred feet, the trimotor levelled off. Its controls felt heavy to Parry, much more so than those on the Wellingtons he had flown, and he hoped that wasn't the result of battle damage. The dive increased the Ju-52 airspeed to three hundred miles an hour. Almost its red line speed, though it was more than fifty miles an hour slower than the Fw-190s, which were lining up on the air liner's tail.

"They're going to make another pass," said Parry. "In a few seconds they'll be in range."

"Why are they after us?" the co-pilot asked. "We are a clearly marked Swedish air liner."

"I think it's because of me and what I'm carrying in this." Parry held up his left arm, showing off the leather case dangling from his wrist. Suddenly tracers began flying past the cockpit and the Junkers was shuddering from more hits. "Break left! Break left! If we turn right, we'll fly straight into the wing man's guns!"

The trimotor almost stood on its left wing as it banked steeply, making the turn Parry was shouting for. The lines of tracers curved away and the shuddering stopped moments after it started. When they righted their aircraft, Parry and the co-pilot saw the Focke-Wulfs climbing away gracefully, the wing man tucked in on his leader's right side. The air liner was now flying a roughly parallel course to the Vendsyssel Peninsula. With a gentle right turn, it was flying across the western shore, barely a hundred feet above the foam-capped surf.

"Axel, Mister Parry, two of our passengers have been wounded," the stewardess announced, appearing at the cockpit door. "I think one is dead. The rest are in panic. What should I do with them?"

"Make them all lie on the fuselage floor," said Parry. "Find out if there's a doctor or a nurse on board and have them treat the wounded. Break out the first-aid kits and your survival equipment. We'll need them. Watch the trees! Raise the nose, raise the nose!"

The co-pilot had allowed the air liner to drift lower while Parry talked with the stewardess. It was heading straight for the crowns of a stand of pine trees when they both hauled back the control yokes, causing the Junkers to leap some fifty feet in the air. By the time it was levelled off, the pines were a half mile behind it and another obstacle was on the horizon.

"It's a town," Parry warned. "Clear the church tower. Swing to the right, damn it!"

Only the cross-topped spire near the town's center was high enough to threaten the air liner. It roared in over the homes and low buildings and raised its left wing to avoid the spire. The Ju-52 turned slightly to the right, missing it by just a few feet, then had to immediately level itself or risk having the other wing catch the roof of another building.

On the opposite side of the town lay a collection of prefabricated barracks and huts surrounded by barbed wire. As the air liner flew past it, anti-aircraft guns opened fire, filling the sky with lines of tracers. For a second or two they bracketed the aircraft, until it passed out of sight behind a line of trees.

"Mister Parry, fuel is being lost from our left wing cell," said the co-pilot, checking the gauges on the center pedestal.

"Christ, I forgot. Civil aircraft don't have self-sealing fuel tanks," said Parry. "I'll have to switch the left engine to another source. Where are the selector cocks?"

Parry looked at the center control pedestal, where

he found the mixture controls, throttles, engine instruments of every kind, but no fuel valves.

"The selectors are in front of you, Mister Parry. The two big ones are for the wing engines."

"What? So they are. Bloody Huns, don't they know how to build an airplane right?" Parry reached past his control yoke and twisted one of two large handles on the front instrument panel. He placed it on the setting the co-pilot said was for the main fuselage tank.

"I have them!" the radio man announced, leaning out of his station and slapping the co-pilot on the shoulder. "I have contact with the Swedish air force, at Göteborg. If we can make it out of Danish air space, they will have fighters waiting for us."

"So long as we can avoid the ones after us," Parry remarked, glancing out the cockpit. "And the anti-aircraft guns. I think the fighters are trying to force us over land, so we can be brought down by ground fire and not shot down by them. Here they come, they're making a head-on attack."

The two Focke-Wulfs swung around and dropped out of the sky. They became two dark silhouettes, no features could be seen on them. Nothing until their wing cannons and cowling machine guns started sparkling.

"Break right! And watch the trees."

Its wing dipping perilously close to the forest, the Ju-52 banked and swung to the right. Most of the shells missed trimotor, though a few strikes sparkled along its tail section as it rolled out of its turn. The Junkers had barely levelled its wings when Parry manhandled it through another turn, completely reversing its direction.

"Look, the town is firing at them," said the co-pilot, pointing at the Fw-190s and the tracers bracketing them.

"Yes, I hope it means they won't be so eager to press home their attacks," said Parry. "No one likes being shot down by their own anti-aircraft guns. Is there any way we can discover our location? I'd like to know how far we are from Sweden."

"I'm sorry, but the control for the direction-finding antenna was destroyed in the first attack." The co-pilot tapped the hand crank and dial mounted on top of the instrument panel. "If it were not for this, I would be dead as well. I can give you an estimate on our location. It's less than ten miles to the end of Denmark and once there, it is thirty-six miles to Sweden."

"And all of that across open water. Well, you better pray that your air force does meet us. Or the Huns will have at least ten minutes to bring us down and they couldn't ask for an easier target."

Once set on its new, northerly course, the Ju-52 dropped to a lower altitude, virtually hugging the forest in an effort to evade the fighters and anti-aircraft guns. But its orange paint scheme was almost luminescent in the bright, midday sun; the Focke-Wulfs had no trouble following it and the guns were waiting for it.

"Another of the passengers has been killed," said the stewardess, stepping back inside the cockpit. "Whether the planes killed her or the guns I cannot say. She had a hole in the side of her head and blood covered her face. That makes three dead and two wounded. Mister Parry, what should I do?"

"Tell them to keep their damn heads down," Parry snapped. "Don't bother me now, I can't help you. The towns up ahead are heavily defended and I'll have the devil's own time trying to avoid their guns."

"Mister Parry, the fighters are returning!" the co-pilot warned, pointing at the two black specks descending on the transport's right wing.

"So, they're going to attempt a beam attack. They can chop us into scrap if they're good. Let's see if we can't put something between us and them."

Slicing through the forest of pines was a road. Paved and with a wide clear shoulder on either side to thwart guerrilla attacks, the swath it cut among the trees was just large enough for the broad-winged Junkers to fit inside. Parry and the co-pilot aligned the trimotor over the road and gingerly lowered it by a dozen feet. The forest swallowed it, denying the Focke-Wulfs a clear shot at their target.

In response they fired wildly. Their cannons and machine guns sprayed the trees with high-explosive rounds and tracers. Most of them fell behind the fleeing airliner; it scarcely received a hit. It had more to fear from the truck it encountered on the road than the Fw-190s.

"I think he overturned," said the co-pilot. "I hope he was German, and not Danish. Look, the towns."

"Yes, and they're ready for us. Let's take her up. At this altitude we'll hit a blasted school or something."

The Ju-52 quickly bounced out of the forest and climbed some fifty feet above it. Less than a mile ahead lay one of the towns the co-pilot had warned about. It was a coastal town, little more than a fishing village on the eastern shore of the ever-narrowing peninsula. Flak bursts blossomed scarcely a hundred feet over it, so low to the ground that shrapnel was imbedding itself in the roofs of buildings and the concussion blasts were blowing out windows.

"We won't make it if we try to fly through that," said Parry. "We have to go around it or above it and I'm all for climbing. Are you ready?"

131

Parry waited until they were almost on top of the carpet of flak bursts before yanking his control wheel back to the edge of his seat. The co-pilot followed his moves and the Junkers responded by climbing steeply. Its performance was hardly equal to a fighter's, but it managed to leap several hundred feet into the sky. High enough to clear the barrage being laid for it, though Parry could feel the clouds of shrapnel strike the undersides of the aircraft. After a few seconds he dove in, so the gun crews wouldn't be able to get a fix on the airliner's altitude and reset the fuses on their shells.

When the town ended so did the forest, the trees petered out to marsh lands and sand dunes. There was no longer any cover to dodge around or hide behind, though the stream of light anti-aircraft fire from the first town did dissuade the Focke-Wulfs from attacking.

The second town was already in sight. It looked like a seaside resort instead of a proper town. There were beach front hotels and cottages, all of which appeared empty, though the resort was hardly unoccupied. More flak bursts and tracer fire erupted from the sandbag emplacements surrounding the town. The Ju-52 was bracketed, the air around it filled with smoke and shrapnel.

"This is sticky. We better turn for Sweden now," Parry advised, "or we might never."

He swung his control yoke in unison with the co-pilot and the trimotor broke to the right. It roared across the calm, rolling surf of the peninsula's eastern shore, the tracers and rolling carpet of flak following it. The Junkers was battered by the fire it drew from both towns. A cannon shell punched a hole in the left engine cowling and exploded inside the radial. There was a burst of flame and dark smoke curled over the left wing; the air liner shook violently and started losing speed.

"I have feathered the port engine!" the co-pilot shouted. "You have to shut off its fuel. What else should we do?"

"Squeeze every last ounce of power from the two good ones," said Parry, reaching past his control column again and switching the left valve to its shut off position. "I pray you have a war emergency rating we haven't used. Those fighters will smell blood for sure. They'll come after us like hungry sharks."

With the dead engine's propeller fully feathered, the Junkers lost air speed, though fortunately not much. It quickly flew out of range of the anti-aircraft batteries; their shells had begun falling short before they stopped altogether. Without their explosions it became strangely quiet on the air liner. Ominously quiet, Parry knew it was only the lull before another storm.

"Where will the Swedish air force meet us?" he asked. "Do they even have any aircraft in the air?"

"They'll meet us once we reach international air space," the radio operator answered. "Which begins twelve miles out at sea. The air force claims they have launched fighters and Göteborg has a radio fix on us. They claim if we were to fly higher, they could make a radar fix."

"That would only make it easier for the Huns and they have it easy enough as it is."

"There they are," said the co-pilot. "On our right and diving!"

The Focke-Wulfs dropped out of the sky, approaching the air liner's right wing. Their cannons and machine guns stitched a path of geysers up to the Junkers, then chopped their way through it. Parry could feel the aircraft shudder and sag to the right, so much so that he had to wrestle with the controls to keep the wings level. From the passenger cabin he heard screams and, later, an unusual rushing sound. When he looked back, he could see holes blown in the fuselage skin.

"Take the survivors to the rear of the cabin!" Parry shouted at the stewardess. "And grab all the survival gear you can! We may be going down."

"Mister Parry, look. The oil lines to our center engines have been hit," said the co-pilot.

Splotches of heavy oil were hitting the windshield with soft thuds. They built up rapidly, like a sudden rain shower. In seconds they almost covered the windshield and were dribbling in through the holes that had punctured the glass earlier. Both Parry and the co-pilot could feel the oil hit their faces, still warm from the engine.

"No, don't shut it down. We need it!" said Parry, slapping the co-pilot's hand away from the center throttle.

"But if we do not, the engine will seize when all the oil is lost."

"Better a junked engine than a downed air liner. On one motor this ship won't stay in the air for long. I wish I knew how far we had to go to international air space. Are you still in touch with Sweden?"

When he got no answer from the radio operator, Parry turned to his station, and found him slumped in his chair. The radios were blown open by cannon shell blasts and the operator had wounds in his head and neck. He was bleeding to death, if he wasn't already dead. For a moment Parry froze, then looked away, glancing into the passenger cabin where he saw the stewardess doing as he had ordered. She was moving the survivors to the tail, where they'd stand a better chance of living if the plane ditched.

"Damn the oil," the co-pilot swore. "It's impossible to see out. We no longer have forward view."

"Those fighters could make a head-on pass and we'd never know it until the bullets started to hit. God I hope we're close to international air space."

Parry tried looking through the holes the first attack had left in the canopy, trying to get the best view he could. Beyond the center engine's cowling, he saw little of the sky or water in front of the plane. He saw no fighters, either Swedish or German, and was beginning to hope that he had left Danish air space when the air liner started shaking.

He noticed it first in the rudder pedals, then suddenly the entire Ju-52 was shuddering. The Focke-Wulfs had returned, and were stitching the air liner from tail to nose. The volume of fire they poured into it caused the Junkers to sway. Parry was losing control. Somewhere behind him a woman screamed; Parry looked back in time to see the stewardess grab her stomach and crumble to the floor, near the front of the cabin. She had returned to collect the survival gear and now she lay in the aisle, rolling in pain. An instant later the stream of bullets that cut her down marched into the cockpit.

Parry felt as if he were being punched in the back. The impacts threw him forward, onto his control yoke. He struggled to pull himself off it, then he found he couldn't bring the wheel with him. He turned to the co-pilot and discovered he too was draped across his yoke, a bullet wound at the base of his neck. There was nothing left to do but survive. Parry tried to climb out of his seat, only to be held down by his left arm. He finally realized that his diplomatic pouch had become wedged between the seat and cockpit wall.

It was too late. From the side window Parry saw

the ocean's surface rushing toward the air liner. Exhausted and growing short of breath, he settled back into the pilot's seat. He could taste blood in his mouth. The pain from the bullet wounds was numbing his whole body. Behind him Parry could hear someone crying, at least he wasn't the last person left alive on the plane. He found it difficult to focus his eyes on the instrument panel; he hoped he would no longer be conscious when the aircraft hit the waves.

With one pilot dead and the other dying, the Ju-52 descended on its own accord. As the Fw-190s circled above, it steadily lost altitude. The trimotor was flying very well on its own, until its huge, spatted main wheels dug through the first wave. The crippled Junkers nosed over and flipped on its back, its center engine being torn off its mounts in the first seconds. The air liner crashed with a tremendous sheet of spray, its tail slammed into the water, then rose into the air again as it slowly settled. There was no explosion when the plane ditched and whatever fires burned on board it were snuffed out by the enveloping waters.

Incredibly, the fuselage door creaked open and two passengers crawled out of the sinking wreck. By the time the forward half of the Junkers had settled beneath the waves, its tail was standing almost perpendicular. The buckled elevators and crumpled rudder creaked loudly as the tail bobbed in the swells. High above, the Focke-Wulfs circled menacingly. When they realized there were survivors they swooped in lower, as if they were preparing for a strafing run. Then they swung around sharply and flew off toward Denmark.

Seconds later they were replaced by similar low-winged, radial-engined fighters wearing dark green and light blue camouflage schemes. But instead of black and white crosses, they wore gold crowns on dark blue roundels. The Royal Swedish Air Force had at last arrived.

"Charlie, what's going on?" Lacey asked, when Cox came back from the Anson's cockpit and took his seat. "You were up there for a long time. Why are we changing course? Is it because of the weather?"

"No, we're not turning around because the weather's changed," said Cox. "We're turning because the situation has changed. That was the Admiralty on the wireless. They just received a message from the foreign office. The Swedish air liner carrying our air attaché from Stockholm was shot down near Denmark by German fighters. First reports claim there were two survivors."

"Was our man one of them?" Constance inquired. "Is that why we're returning to London?"

"I'm afraid our man didn't make it. The two survivors the Swedes picked up were civilians. We're returning because the Swedish government has apparently changed its attitude and we must change our plans."

"I thought Sweden had already made up its mind," said Lacey. "What are they going to do with the jet this time?"

"Since it was an open, unscrambled transmission, the Admiralty didn't tell me anything," Cox explained. "But if you were to ask me to read between the lines, I'd say the Swedes have decided to give us the prototype. When we land, we'll be given the complete report. And we won't be going back to London. We're heading to the base where Roberts is training his team. If our plans are to

137

change, then his mission will change and so will ours, Dennis. Perhaps you should go to the cockpit and send your team a message? Tell them to join us at the SAS base once their Lodestar is repaired. We may at last have our way."

Chapter Six: A Change In Plans
Meeting A Traitor

"Lord Mallet, Mister MacAlister, Mister Norris, may I introduce to you Defense Minister Curt Sjölund," the secretary announced, stepping away from the door he had opened, and allowing another, much older man to enter the office.

Lord Mallet, British ambassador to Sweden, MacAlister and Norris rose from their seats and shook the defense minister's hand as he came over to them. Then he walked behind the desk which dominated the room and sat down.

"Please, my friends, be seated," said Sjölund. "We have much to discuss. Let me first express my country's sorrow at the loss of your air attaché. I'm told that squadron leader Parry was a very brave man."

"And let me express His Britannic Majesty's sorrow at the loss of the air liner's crew and passengers," Mallet replied, getting the diplomatic courtesies out of the way. "Greg Parry was a good man. We were hoping you'd have some information about how he died and how the air liner was downed."

"Yes, I knew you would ask. That's why I delayed until now our meeting. I wanted to have this." Sjölund opened a leather-bound briefing book and displayed a slim folder. "This is a report from the air force. It's only a preliminary one but it will give you several important insights. When the air liner left the air force's radar coverage, it was well inside the corridor designated for civil aircraft. It was in international air space up to the time it was attacked. Only then did it enter Danish air space and overfly Danish territory in an attempt to evade the fighters. The survivors claim Mister Parry was the first to spot the Germans and, after the first attack had killed the pilot, they say he took the controls and flew the air liner. He ordered them to the tail of the aircraft and was still at the controls when it crashed."

"Flying until the moment he died. I guess that's a better way for a pilot to die than any other," said MacAlister somberly.

"It sure sounds to me like the plane was deliberately shot down," said Norris. "What happened when your planes arrived at the crash scene. What did they see?"

"The air force launched P-35 fighters and rescue aircraft when it received a distress call from the air liner," Sjölund explained. "They arrived in time to see it go down and watched the German fighters circle the crash . . . until they realized our aircraft were in the area. They departed without engaging in combat. Our P-35s stayed over the crash while a rescue seaplane landed and picked up the survivors. At no time during the operation did German forces interfere. Nor have they so far interfered with Swedish navy and coast guard vessels that have gone to the area."

"Where did the airplane go down?" Mallet asked. "Did it crash in your territorial waters or Denmark's?"

"It crashed in international waters, just outside the

Danish territorial limit. First reports from the navy say it may not be recoverable, certainly not while the war is on."

"What explanations have the Nazis given for the attack? One of the other reasons you delayed your meeting with us was the one you just finished with the German ambassador," MacAlister remarked.

"I see there isn't much my ministry can keep secret from you," said Sjölund. "I was told you were a good intelligence officer. My congratulations to you. Yes, I just finished giving an audience to the German ambassador. His excuse for the attack was that the fighters involved were only recently transferred from the Russian front. They never encountered the civil air liner of a neutral country before and they were confused. Since the air liner was in a security zone, they attacked it. And when it tried to escape, they pursued and shot it down."

"Do you believe it?"

"No, it may well be logical but it was too quickly offered. It sounded as if it were prepared ahead of time. If he had told me he didn't know why and later explained the incident, I wouldn't be as suspicious. Though I probably still wouldn't accept it. All of us here know why the air liner was shot down. It was your man, and what he was carrying in his diplomatic pouch. No amount of apologies or excuses will absolve the Germans from this heinous crime but it has obtained for them what they wanted. The prime minister and the foreign minister have bowed to mounting pressure from the appeasement faction and have ordered the return of the Night Hawk to Germany. They wish to be rid of the aircraft, and the crisis it has generated, as soon as humanly possible."

"Then we've lost," Norris observed, his heart and spirits sinking. "All our hard work and sacrifice has been for nothing. The Night Hawk will go back to Germany with all its secrets intact. And with it could go the outcome of the war."

"Not quite, my friend. Not quite," said Sjölund. "What I'm about to tell you must be held in strictest confidence. Only your top-level people must know about it. If any word were to leak out, it would precipitate an even worse crisis than what we're now facing. Do I have your word?"

One by one, MacAlister, Norris and Mallet gave hushed promises to the defense minister that they would keep secret whatever he was going to tell them.

"Good. In accordance with our usual procedures regarding Nazi aircraft, we will reassemble and repair the Night Hawk and assign it a civil registration. Of course, we must wait until the Nazis supply us with spare parts before repairing the jet. If you could give us a replacement engine and other equipment, the air force will allow you to fly the Night Hawk out of Sweden. Are you gentlemen interested in the proposition?"

"I should say we are," said Mallet, trying to keep the shock out of his voice. "With Mister Norris's permission, I feel I can speak for both the United States and the United Kingdom. We gladly accept your offer and I'm rather surprised that you would make it, considering what your government's official position is."

"As I told you before, they only wish to see an end to this crisis. Returning the jet to Germany is the most expedient way to do so. But there's a group of air force officers who don't wish to help the Third Reich win this war. They, and I, know how important the Night Hawk is and what it would mean if Germany were to regain it. Wing Commander

Paulson, Erik Lindh and many others are willing to risk their careers and their honor to see that you have the jet. Mister Norris, they tell me you actually flew a version of the jet. Do you think you can fly this one to England safely?"

"I—I suppose I'll have to," Norris stammered. "I'm the only pilot in Europe with the qualifications, outside of the Luftwaffe. If I'm to fly the Night Hawk, I'll need more than a new engine. I'll need jet fuel, ammo and one of our electronics experts to work the radar system. Give me all those things and I'll fly the jet."

"I will take what you said as yes," Sjölund replied, closing his briefing book and laying it on his desk. "Please, do not tell me anymore details. If you need someone brought into Sweden, make him part of your embassy staff and clear it with the foreign ministrsy. Take up the other matters with the air force. I want to know as little of your plans as possible. If they go wrong, I will deny any knowledge of them. That may not save my position but at least I will not be jailed. None of us should meet again until this crisis has passed. Goodbye, gentlemen, what you and the air force are about to do is very daring. You'll find Mister Paulson eager to meet with you. Good luck to all of you."

When Sjölund rose from his seat, the others in the room did the same. They shook his hand and were escorted out of his office by his secretary. Neither Mallet nor MacAlister nor Norris said anything until after they had collected their hats and coats and were leaving the defense ministry through an exit reserved for special visitors.

"This is incredible," said Mallet in a hushed voice. "I thought we had failed but instead we have a chance to make the Night Hawk ours . . . provided we can give the Swedish air force a new engine. Can we do that, Commander?"

"Hell, yes," said Norris. "That's going to be the easy part. Last month my unit scavenged the wrecks of a lot of German planes, including a few Me-262s. We have several Junkers jet engines and a small pile of spare parts. The trick will be getting them to Sweden. Should we tell Charlie Cox to fly the parts to Norrköping on a C-47 or another transport?"

"No, I don't believe so," MacAlister advised. "In thinking over what we have to do, a second transport would have to be flown in later with the jet fuel. We can chance flying one of our aircraft into Norrköping without attracting attention, not two. Besides, we have another way. Can one of those jet engines fit inside the bomb bay of a Mosquito?"

"Once you remove it from the nacelle it can. Why?"

"Because BOAC uses Mosquitoes on high-speed runs to Stockholm. They're used to carry mail, special cargoes and passengers. Even Lord Mallet and his wife have used them. They wear civilian markings but are otherwise straight military aircraft. It'd be easy to rig one of them to carry what we need. We could have the engine by tonight."

"Excellent idea, Ian," said Mallet. "Those BOAC Mosquitoes don't draw much attention anymore. I'm sure you and Commander Norris can work out the rest of the details with our Swedish friends."

"Actually, it'll be John and Colonel Whitney who'll work on the operation to rebuild and steal the Night Hawk. Something else needs my attention, a matter equally important and I'm the only one who can handle it. I have to track down the spy who killed Greg. He found out about our photography session and he could uncover our new plan. If that were to happen, we'd have more than one dead friend as a result. We'd have many friends in jail and we would be thrown out of the country. This man is still dangerous and I have a strong idea who it is."

"Oh yes, you were telling me something about that before our meeting with Sjölund. Who do you have in mind for your suspect?"

"You won't like this, it's someone you happen to know," said MacAlister, lowering his voice to almost a whisper so no one else in the hallway could hear him. "It's Carl Drache."

"Good God man, are you crazy?" Mallet asked, and the shock wasn't just in his voice, it was on Mallet's face as well. "I've known Carl Drache for years. I've met him many times. Are you positive about this?"

"In my own mind, yes. But I don't have enough solid evidence to prove my suspicions. The best I have is that when we drove Greg to the airport, we were followed — and those who followed us met Carl Drache at the airport. However, I need more proof than that. While John and the other military attachés work on the arrangements with the Swedish air force, I'll meet with the Swedish police. They have their suspicions about Drache as well, in fact they have one of their own agents in his estate. Perhaps they might let me meet him."

"We'll, don't let your meeting last too long," Norris advised. "Remember we're to have dinner with Drache and his girlfriend at six tonight."

"You mean you're actually going to meet with him?" said Mallet incredulously. "How can you do that? And why?"

"The dinner was arranged beforehand," MacAlister explained. "Drache wanted to meet with the military attachés and I agreed to it. I thought if we didn't, he might become suspicious of us. So far as I know it's still on and anyway I want to see him. I want to see how he reacts to Greg's death. There are times when even spies sit down and eat with their enemies, Lord Mallet."

"Hey, Colonel, what is this place?" asked Capollini, as he stepped out of the Lodestar, seconds after its engines had shut down. "This ain't no R.A.F. base."

"No, this is the training base for the Special Air Services regiment," said Lacey. "There aren't any squadrons stationed here. The only airplanes allowed in are those needed for specific missions. This place is top secret. If they hadn't been expecting you, they'd have shot you down."

"Gee, thanks for telling me, Colonel. Remind me to drive here the next time."

"Tell me, is Chris on board? You two are the ones I really want to see. We're holding up a meeting for you."

"He sure is, he's just finishing the post-flight check," said Capollini, then he turned and looked inside the Lodestar's fuselage. "Hey, Chris, hurry it up. The colonel's got a meeting on hold because of us."

There was a muffled, unintelligible response from someone in the transport and a moment later Shannon appeared at the exit door. After he saluted Lacey, he and Capollini were taken over to an awaiting staff car. They piled into the back seat with Lacey, who was explaining the most recent turn of events before the car had even been started.

"Jesus Christ, they shot down an air liner?" Shannon exclaimed, not quite believing what he had just been told. "I thought only the Japs did something like that. Did the R.A.F. guy survive, and what're

146

the Swedes doing about it?"

"No, I'm afraid he didn't," said Lacey. "There were two survivors and he wasn't one of them. A few Swedes are boiling mad about it and it looks like they want to punish the Germans. A preliminary report from Stockholm says they might be willing to give us the Me-262."

"Hallelujah, we're in business," said Capollini. "When are we going to go get it, Colonel?"

"Well, first we have to be sure the Swedes will give it to us. Then we have to devise a plan to get the jet, which is what we'll decide at this meeting."

The staff car drove away from the airstrip, weaving through a collection of drab, mostly temporary, base buildings to one surrounded by jeeps, other staff cars and heavy security. It wasn't the most impressive looking structure in the complex, and there were no signs to identify it, but the building was the base's headquarters.

"This, is the most recent report from Stockholm," said Cox, holding a few sheets of paper out to the other officers in the briefing room. "It was forwarded to me from the foreign office and came in a few minutes ago. We haven't had time to copy it, so I'll read it to you. 'Have met with Swedish defense minister and he confirms the death of squadron leader Parry. He reports that the downing of the air liner has frightened most of the Swedish government into returning the Night Hawk to the Germans. However, a small group of Swedish air force officers want to turn the jet over to us. If we give them the necessary parts, they will reassemble and repair it and allow us to fly it out of the country. This must be done as soon as possible, the Germans are expecting the Night Hawk to be returned to them by the end of the week.' As you can see, we have the most fantastic opportunity of the war but not much time to act on it. We have less than four days to obtain the prototype. Ian and John Norris have provided a list of parts the Swedes need and other requirements for the operation. What we must decide now is a new plan to get the Night Hawk."

"Will you still be needing my team, Commander?" Roberts asked, "or should I disband it?"

"No, despite this change, I'll still be needing your men. I'd like to use them as a security detail. I know it's a diminished role but emphasis of course has switched to Dennis and his team."

"I don't see why we just can't fly one of our big transports into Sweden and load the jet on it," said Lacey. "It's already been dismantled. That would be a lot safer than actually flying the Night Hawk."

"I know it would," Cox replied, "but our friends in Sweden are controlling the overall operation. They must appear to act normally and the normal procedure for returning Nazi aircraft is to reassemble them and give them a Swedish civil registration before they're flown out of the country. The Swedes need a Junkers Jumo Type Zero-Zero-Four B jet engine, a Riedel starting motor, an engine oil tank and related sub-system equipment. John Norris told them you have the parts. Do you, Dennis?"

"We've collected a warehouse of spare parts for German planes. We got everything they need. How'll you get them to Sweden? Will you be needing a transport?"

"No, Ian and Mister Norris have a more ingenious idea. The engine and other parts will be loaded in the bomb bay of a BOAC Mosquito. They make regular flights from London to Stockholm. They're the only British airliners which make daylight runs to Sweden. They want the parts tonight, can we do it?"

"Sure," Lacey answered, "our warehouse is located at Gatwick. All that Mosquito would have to do is taxi over and get loaded up. What else do our friends need and who's going to fly the Night Hawk?"

"They'll be needing jet fuel," said Cox, looking over the list that had come with the report. "We can supply that from our Boscombe Down test center. They'd like some wreckage of a crashed German jet, to fake an accidental fire which will consume the Night Hawk. And the pilot will be John Norris. I don't think that should've surprised you but here's something that will. Mister Norris wants a radar operator to help him fly the Night Hawk. He wants an electronics expert who's also a good pilot, and someone who has an understanding of technical German. He wants you, Dennis. Looks like you're going on a little trip to Sweden."

"Jesus Christ." It was the only thing Lacey could think of saying and as he repeated it, the hand he'd been using to prop up his jaw dropped noisily to the table. "Jesus H. Christ, how about that."

"Colonel, you're one lucky bastard," Martinez added, a touch of envy in his voice. "You're gonna go for a ride in the most advanced plane in the world. How lucky can you get?"

"Yeah, and have half the damn Luftwaffe trying to shoot his ass out of the sky," said Capollini. "I wouldn't say he's all that lucky. Commander, have you thought about giving them an escort once they leave Sweden?"

"Yes, it's quite unlikely that Dennis and Mister Norris will leave Swedish air space undetected," Cox admitted. "I had thought of providing them with a squadron of RAF Mosquito night fighters. Does anyone have another suggestion?"

"I got something that can beat your Mosquitoes,"

said Shannon. "A squadron of P-61 Black Widows."

"What, those docile cows?" said Roberts, suppressing a laugh, though not his smile. "The best description of the P-61's performance was 'pleasant.' That's not exactly the hallmark of a great warplane."

"That's the old P-61, the A-models. What I'm talking about are the new B-models. With uprated engines, paddle-bladed propellers, new radar and they've finally rectified the problems with the top turret. It's been reinstalled and it has a new fire control system, based on the one the B-29 uses. This Black Widow is a new animal, and there's a Ninth Air Force squadron here in England being re-equipped with them. I happen to have a friend in that squadron. I'm sure if I give him a call I'll get the whole bunch to volunteer."

"Excuse me for asking, but how do you happen to have a friend in a U.S. Army squadron?" Cox inquired. "You're a Marine Corps officer. I would think your contact with the Army Air Force is rather limited."

"My friend is also a Marine Corps officer," said Shannon. "Lieutenant-Colonel David Ackerman. He's an exchange officer, just like Captain Roberts. He's serving with the Four-thirty-second Night Fighter squadron. Dennis has met him, he and the rest of the squadron were sent to an air base outside of Liverpool to receive their new planes. That was about a week ago, Commander, and by now they could be ready."

"Very well, we'll see if your friend's squadron can be recruited. Though like Lee Roberts, I do have my reservations about the aircraft. Dennis and I still have to decide where we'll launch the operation and its timetable but I think we've made the most essential decisions. If there are no more suggestions or questions, I'll declare this meeting over and we can start work on our mission."

"I got one more question," said Roberts. "Why are we going to the Ninth Air Force for those night fighters? What's wrong with the Eighth Air Force? Why not them? All their bases are in England, while most of the Ninth's are on the continent. Wouldn't it be easier to get the planes we need from them? Whether or not we have friends in those units."

"We could, if they had what we want, but they don't. The Eighth Air Force is a strategic air force, all it has are heavy bomb groups and long-range escort fighters. The Eighth has never had any night fighter squadrons. Even if they did, I'd rather not work too closely with the Eighth Air Force. Colonel Lacey and I made a few enemies in it during our first operation. Those men might not be so inclined to help us, or leave us alone. Understand, Lee?"

"I think so. We have to keep what we're doing as much a secret from the Army as our enemies. What a fucking way to fight a war."

"OK, let's end this meeting and get to work, Charlie," Lacey advised. "It's growing dark outside and there's plenty for us to do before night. You said we have less than four days, let's start making every hour count."

"Oh yes, Lieutenant-Commander Ian MacAlister and Commander John Norris," said the reservations clerk, scanning the register book at his desk. "You're part of Mister Drache's party. Mister Drache hasn't arrived yet, though we have reserved a table for you. Waiter, take these two to Mister Drache's table."

Once their coats and caps had been checked by the cloakroom attendant, MacAlister and Norris were led

151

through the club's restaurant by one of its waiters. He took them to one of the tables more isolated than the others. It was empty, though it had place settings for six guests arranged on it. MacAlister and Norris ordered drinks after they were seated, which the waiter promptly brought to them.

"What is this place, Ian?" Norris asked, glancing at the rich, distinctly British furnishings of the restaurant. "If I didn't know better, I'd swear I was in London."

"That's the general idea," said MacAlister. "This is the English-Swedish Club. It's financed by British businessmen who work in Sweden, so they'll have a place to remind them of home, and by Swedes who wish to do business with England. It doesn't create much of a stir when British uniforms turn up here. It's about the only restaurant in Stockholm where we don't draw overt attention. Though you, on the other hand, might. Not many Americans come here."

"I see. You know, there are at least three other places we should be than here. We should either be with Scott and Colonel Whitney, or waiting at Bromma for the Mosquito, or waiting at your embassy for the latest report from England. Instead, we're having dinner with a man who's in all likelihood a Nazi spy."

"I know, this isn't where we should be. It's where we have to be. Through Drache, we have to convince the Germans that we're not working on any new plans to gain the Night Hawk or its secrets. Drache knows why we're in Sweden and if we were the ones who didn't show, he would guess, quite correctly, that something was up. Don't worry about Whitney and McClory, they know enough of our operation to handle the details of it with Paulson and the others. I strongly doubt any sudden news will be coming from

152

Cox's team and the Mosquito isn't due for another three hours. Until then, this is where we have to be."

"All right, but I'm still uneasy about being here," Norris advised. "What should we tell your buddy about Scott and Whitney when he arrives? I don't think you want him to know that they're meeting with a bunch of renegade Swedish air force officers."

"How strange, I asked a similar question of Greg the last time we were here." MacAlister looked down at his martini, then finished it in one swallow before he continued. "We're to tell Drache that Colonel Whitney is meeting with the Swedish military, to see if Greg's body can be recovered. McClory is tending to embassy matters which suddenly came up. We should be able to handle Drache, now that we have a good idea of what he is. And in any event we'll be finding out soon if we can. Here he comes."

MacAlister raised the finger he was tracing the rim of his glass with and pointed over Norris's shoulder. He turned to find Carl Drache and his secretary being led through the restaurant, by no one less than the maître d'.

"Smiles on. Let's be on our best behavior."

MacAlister and Norris rose from their seats when the rest of the party arrived. There were handshakes all around. MacAlister introduced Norris to Drache, who in turn introduced Ursula to Norris.

"Miss Brandt and I will have the chicken Kiev," Drache added, taking advantage of the maître d's presence at the table to put in his order. "Ian, what will you and your friend have?"

"I'll try the chicken Kiev as well," said MacAlister, "with a bottle of the house's white wine. John?"

"I'll have a steak," Norris answered, "the thickest one you have. And make it medium rare."

"Commander, you are so typically American," said

Drache, laughing jovially. "Here, let me have your drinks refilled while we wait for dinner to arrive. Tell me, why aren't Colonels Whitney and McClory with us?"

MacAlister launched into his planned explanations for Whitney and McClory's absence while he and the others took their seats around the table. As he went through them, the explanations changed everyone's mood to a more somber one.

"And Ken Whitney is meeting with the Swedish navy and coast guard at Göteborg," MacAlister concluded, "to see if they found Parry's body or any of his belongings. He'll also ask them if they're going to recover the air liner or not."

"A very sad duty to perform," said Drache, "and a very shocking incident. I first heard about the downing from a radio report. It saddened me deeply to read in the newspaper that Greg Parry was one of the people who died on the air liner. To our missing friend, may he rest in peace."

Drache raised his glass in salute and was quickly joined by Ursula and Norris. MacAlister was the last to add his glass, and he wasn't too enthusiastic about banging his against the others.

"I shall miss him," said Ursula. "He was so kind to me."

"Strange to hear you say that. Since it was your countrymen who killed him," MacAlister sarcastically noted.

"Aren't you being a little nasty?" asked Norris. "You yourself told me she was a naturalized Swedish citizen."

"We can forgive Ian's remarks," said Drache. "Greg was his friend, after all. His death must be something of a severe shock and a great loss. Ian knows Miss Brandt came to this country as a political refugee. That her father is a political prisoner and the last word we had is that her entire family is in one of Hitler's death camps."

"Yes, I know. I'm sorry Ursula," said MacAlister. "Please forgive me. It's been a very hard day."

"What was Greg doing on the air liner, Ian? Why was he going back to England?"

Before MacAlister could answer, the waiter arrived carrying a large tray. On it was everyone's dinner, which the waiter quickly laid out, along with the wine they had ordered. Beyond commenting about the meals, no one really said anything until after the waiter left.

"Since our mission's been totally ruined, I don't see why you shouldn't know," MacAlister admitted, as he prepared to slice into his chicken. "Greg was carrying all the information we had on the Night Hawk jet to London. Including photographs, the Royal Swedish Air Force allowed us to take some film of the jet. But now, it's all been lost."

"I wouldn't say that, you still have a few days before the jet is returned to the Nazis," said Drache, taking his first mouthful of chicken, its butter sauce dribbling onto his beard. "Couldn't you arrange another session?"

"I have the time but the air force and the Swedish government are now scared." MacAlister sliced his chicken breast through the center, allowing the melted butter and seasoning inside to flow out and soak the crisp exterior of the breast. "Between the air liner and the U-boat incident, your government is very scared of what the Germans may do next. I must say they stood up remarkably well to the Nazis. In a similar incident last year, they only had to mention the use of commandoes and the Swiss quickly destroyed an Me-110 which had landed in their country. Tell me, how did you know about the jet being returned and when?"

"The staff at the German embassy told me today. They're just as afraid the government will withhold the jet because of this latest incident, even though the air force is still going to turn over the jet's crew to the embassy tomorrow."

While Drache gave his answer, MacAlister concentrated on his meal, though he got no enjoyment out of it. The thought of sitting across the table from a man who, only a few hours earlier, had caused the death of his friend was almost too much to stand. The chicken Kiev tasted like lumps of wet tissue paper to MacAlister and the wine he used to wash it down had the same flavor as sweetened vinegar. He tried not to stare for too long at Drache, it made his hatred of the man boil up. Even if he could maintain a calm exterior, MacAlister knew his eyes would betray him.

"What explanation did those guys at the embassy give you for the air liner?" Shannon asked, after Drache had finished. There was an awkward silence which MacAlister was too busy with his hatred to immediately fill.

"They said the air liner was indeed in international airspace," Drache replied, "but that it was very close to Denmark, and a security zone. The fighters involved were part of a group that had been reassigned from the Russian front and they weren't very familiar with Denmark or the rules concerning aircraft of neutral countries. When the air liner tried to evade them after their first attack, they chased it and shot it down. A most regrettable action, especially with all those lives lost. Is the government going to try and recover the aircraft?"

"No, it's in about two hundred feet of water and it

sank dangerously close to a mine field the Germans have laid," said MacAlister, "so it would be a tricky recovery. The Swedish navy is also afraid that any large-scale sea operation would attract the attention of Allied airplanes. And since German fighter pilots can mistake a Ju-52 painted bright orange for an enemy aircraft, I'm sure Allied pilots can mistake salvage ships for a Nazi battle group. If the Reich's afraid that Sweden will withhold the Night Hawk, will they still use diplomacy to win its release? Or will they try more military adventures like the U-boat and the downing of the airliner?"

"They'll continue to try diplomacy, Ian, up to a point. If this crisis isn't resolved soon, they might try a more extreme type of mission."

"What kind? What could be more extreme than sending a submarine full of commandoes into Swedish territorial waters and shooting down one of its air liners? So far as I know, neither of those two incidents had ever happened to Sweden in the first five years of this war."

"The Germans will bomb Sweden," said Drache. He stopped devouring his chicken Kiev long enough to wipe the accumulated butter and food particles out of his beard. "They'll have a squadron of their bombers depart Norway and bomb the Norrköping air base. The embassy staff told me the Luftwaffe has asked them where the interned aircraft are kept at the field. It would be easy for them to level the base, their new bombers fly so fast the Swedish air force won't have time to stop them. Perhaps you might tell that to your friends at Norrköping. Now, I see everyone has finished with dinner. Would anyone care for dessert?"

MacAlister nearly gagged on the heavy, hideously sweet pastry he ordered. The rest of the dinner passed with mostly light conversation, though Drache did insist on reminiscing about Parry, which Mac-Alister was forced to join. Two hours after the meal had started, it was over. The party split up in the parking lot, with Drache and Ursula heading for his Mercedes while MacAlister and Norris climbed inside a British embassy staff car. Only then could they talk freely.

"You think Drache was telling us the truth about those bombers?" Norris asked, "and do you think he suspects we've cooked up a new deal with the Swedes?"

"No, I don't think he knows about our plan," said MacAlister, "which is why I told him about the film we shot. So he'll know that he did stop us. As for the air attack, I don't believe it. The Germans must know they've succeeded in scaring the Swedish government into giving them the Night Hawk. What Drache told us was more *dezinformatsiya*. Something to mislead us, a cleverly planted diversion. Though if I were you, I would tell our friends about it tomorrow morning."

"Me? What about you, won't you be there?"

"In time. First I have to pick up the new air attaché the R.A.F. is flying in tomorrow. He'll be carrying with him the finalized plans Cox and Colonel Lacey have devised for taking the Night Hawk. I'll drive him straight to Norrköping and then, I'm off to another meeting with the Swedish police. What I had to sit through for the last few hours only convinces me of Drache's guilt. If all goes well, tomorrow night I'll break into his estate. From what the police have already told me, I'm sure I'll find the evidence I want in there and not at his business."

"Jesus, that's a little dangerous," said Norris. "Will you tell London about your little mission?"

"I'll have to tell Ken and Scott McClory, but not London," MacAlister replied, slowing the car as he prepared to make a left turn. "This will put us on the road to Bromma. No, I won't tell London because Charles would only order me not to do it and I'd have to disobey him. Carl Drache is still a threat to us and this has become a personal thing for me. I have to find the evidence that will neutralize him and it really won't be too dangerous. The police agent in Drache's house will be warned of my visit."

"That's a relief. Did the Swedes tell you who he is?"

"No, they didn't want to take a chance on his cover being blown. Though I do know he's part of Drache's staff. It could even be Ursula Brandt, his secretary. In fact, she would be the perfect candidate for an agent."

"But she's not even Swedish," said Norris. "She's German."

"All the better," MacAlister explained. "She would be the last person Drache would suspect of being a Swedish spy. It's been my experience that naturalized citizens love their country much more than native-born ones."

"Why did you tell Ian MacAlister there might be an air raid?" Ursula asked, after she and Drache climbed inside his Mercedes. "I heard of no such plans. From what you told me, the Swedes are reassembling the Night Hawk so it can be returned to us."

"They are. What I told our friend is a plant. He will pass it on to the Swedish air force, which should give pause to any of its officers who rebel against the decision to return the jet. We seem at last to be getting what we want. I'd like to ensure that we have no more trouble at this stage."

As he spoke, Drache started the Mercedes and eased it out of the club's parking lot. He was forced to linger at the entrance for a few moments until a space appeared in the traffic flow and he was able to turn onto the street.

"Carl, do you believe what MacAlister told us? About the film being lost and his inability to arrange another deal with his contacts in the air force?"

"Yes and no," said Drache. "I believe the film was lost and that he and the Americans have been temporarily blocked. However, he is quite resourceful. He might try another deal or set up an operation for the Allies to destroy the jet. We'll have to keep a watch on Ian and his friends. We can't be certain of anything until the Night Hawk is back in the Reich."

Throughout its approach and landing, all that could be seen of the Mosquito were its landing lights and anti-collision strobe. Only when it taxied up to the flight line, on the military side of Bromma, could the DeHavilland's familiar, tapered wings and narrow fuselage be made out. Norris and MacAlister waited for the civilianized bomber to shut down its engines before joining the Swedish officers and ground crew which clustered around it.

"We had to borrow this from one of our torpedo bomber units," said squadron leader Lindh, tapping a shoe on the long dolly his crew was positioning under the bomber's fuselage. "Since you are both navy men, you should know what it is. This was the only piece of equipment long enough to handle the jet engine."

"It's a torpedo cradle," said Norris, answering before MacAlister, who was too embarrassed to admit that he didn't really know what the device was. "You better be careful when you lower the engine. You'll find it's a few inches wider than the average torpedo."

A hatch under the Mosquito's nose popped open and its BOAC pilot stuck his head out. He exchanged greetings with Norris and MacAlister, then spoke to Erik Lindh.

"Are you the officer I'm to report to for violating Swedish air space along my assigned corridor?" the captain asked in mock seriousness.

"You may, though we would rather relieve you of your cargo," said Lindh. "Could you open the bomb bay doors?"

"The bomb door selector handle is down but since the motors are off I don't have hydraulic pressure. You can wait for the doors to fall open by themselves or your crew can use this. You also use it to open the bomb grips."

The pilot gave Lindh a hand crank with a long shaft. Inserted in a slot just forward of the bomb bay and spun vigorously, the doors quickly opened, revealing a gleaming steel tube suspended inside the bay. Lindh had his crew position the dolly under the jet engine and raise its cradle portion until it fitted, very snugly, around the engine's body.

"You were right, Mister Norris," Lindh admitted. "The fit is tight. But at their maximum spread, the cradle clamps can accommodate it. As soon as we've unloaded it, we'll place it on a truck and ship it to Norrköping. The flight crew has the rest of the parts we need in the cockpit. If you could help us move them, we could be done faster. The truck is in the hangar behind us."

While the Swedes lowered the engine from the cramped bomb bay, MacAlister and Norris transferred the smaller parts from the Mosquito's cockpit to the hangar in front of it. Though nowhere as bulky as the Junkers engine, the oil tank and boxes full of hoses, piping, electrical cables and other parts barely squeezed through the cockpit hatch.

MacAlister and Norris worked swiftly. The last thing to be moved from the Mosquito to the hangar was in fact the jet engine. Some six feet long, the Jumo was covered with a network of pipes, small housings for valves and pumps and had a bullet-shaped fairing in its nose for the Riedel starting motor. Once inside the hangar, the engine was transferred to the waiting truck and secured for its trip to Norrköping. As the Mosquito fired up its engines and taxied to the civilian side of Bromma, the truck joined a small, heavily armed convoy and drove out of the base's main gate. In a few hours it would be at Norrköping. The rebuilding of the Night Hawk was underway.

Chapter Seven: Day Four
An Old Enemy

"This is D for Duncan to Speke Control, we are on final. Once we have landed, please direct us to the Aircraft Assembly unit tarmac. We're expected."

The R.A.F. Dakota already had its landing gear extended and its flaps partially lowered when it swung onto the final leg of the traffic pattern. Now the flaps came down all the way and air speed fell off to 120 miles an hour as the transport crossed the runway threshold. Though the airfield it was arriving at was in England, in fact just outside of Liverpool, hardly another British aircraft could be seen.

Speke was filled with American aircraft. Not just U.S.-built planes but U.S. Army Air Force machines. While some were C-47s, most were fighters: Mustangs, Thunderbolts and Lightnings. Aircraft which had been brought across the Atlantic on Liberty ships. They were off-loaded at Liverpool harbor and towed to Speke where they were assembled, armed and test flown before being sent to strategic Air Depots where they were assigned to operational units. Among the dozens of P-47s and P-51s filling the eastern side of the field were a handful of black, twin-boomed aircraft, which towered above the smaller fighters.

After turning off the runway, the Royal Air Force transport taxied around the congested airport to the Aircraft Assembly unit hangars, where ground handlers directed it to park beside the black giants. As its engines were shut down, a group of American officers gathered at the Dakota's side hatch.

"Colonel Lacey? I'm Colonel Martin Powers, commanding officer of the Four-thirty-second Night Fighter Squadron," said the highest-ranking officer in the group to the first man to appear at the hatch. "You got a Marine Corps major with you? One of my pilots would really like to meet him."

"I got your man, Colonel," said Lacey. "In fact most of my team and several British friends are with me. Vince, let Chris come down, his buddies are here."

The second man to step out of the Dakota was Chris Shannon. He went immediately to an officer standing behind Powers, shaking his hand and slapping him on the shoulder. Shannon's friend started introducing him to Powers and the other pilots from the night fighter squadron. For the moment those who emerged from the transport were ignored.

"This is looking like old home week among classmates," Roberts dryly noted. "If you don't mind, Dennis, couldn't we move on to more important matters?"

"Colonel Lacey, this is my friend, Lieutenant-Colonel David Ackerman," said Shannon, presenting his friend, who wore the same eagle, globe and anchor combination on his collar as Shannon did. "We first met in the South Pacific, where he flew P-70s and radar-equipped F4Us."

"Nice to meet you," said Lacey, "but I'm afraid one of my friends is right. We'll have a chance to get to know each other later. It's time to move to important matters. Colonel Powers, this is Commander Cox and Captain Roberts. Charlie, maybe you should tell him why we're here?"

"Colonel Lacey and myself are working on a highly sensitive mission," Cox informed Powers, and the rest of the officers clustered around the Dakota. "We require a squadron of night fighters, the best in England. Major Shannon claims you're the best, we're here to see if you are."

"Oh, are you here to interview my men?" Powers asked.

"No, I've come to see your aircraft. I have no doubt that your men are qualified, it's your aircraft I wonder about. Dennis Lacey and Major Shannon are quite sold on the Black Widow, I have yet to be."

"OK, Commander, if it's a selling job you want, I guess I'm the man to do it. Come along with me and I'll show you the best night fighter in England."

Introductions were still going on among the rest of the assembled officers as Powers led Cox and Lacey away from the R.A.F. transport and over to one of the P-61s sitting in front of the Aircraft Assembly unit's hangars.

Instead of the olive-drab or polished bare metal of the P-51s and P-47s, they wore glossy black paint. The Black Widows were the size of medium bombers and in fact looked like a cross between the B-25 Mitchell and the P-38 Lightning. In spite of their size, they also looked sleek and deadly. However docile they were in the air, they had the appearance of lethal war machines.

"If ever there was an airplane that deserved its name on looks alone, it's this one," said Lacey, walking up to one of the Black Widows and running his hand over its bulbous nose, almost stroking it. "I remember this plane when I was based at Muroc Field.

The Northrop plant was located at Hawthorne, California. A lot of its flight testing was done at Muroc and the Night Fighter School was based at Van Nuys. 'Sixty-ones were always picking fights with F6Fs or F4Us or Mustangs and Lightnings. Toward the end I noticed they were winning most of them.'

Cox joined Lacey at the nose of the P-61 and surveyed it with a critical eye. From their vantage point they could see the fighter's top turret, a smooth bulge shaped like a giant limpet shell with a truncated front. It mounted four fifty-caliber machine guns in its forward end, complementing the quartet 20mm cannons in the fighter's belly.

"I still don't see how anything this big can be a fighter," Cox admitted, moving away from the Black Widow's nose and walking toward its left wing. "Colonel Powers, what's the maximum speed and service ceiling of your aircraft?"

"Three hundred and seventy miles an hour," Powers answered, "and it tops out at thirty-three thousand feet. I'd also like to say that this new model can climb as fast as a P-47 and can hold its own with a Spitfire in a turn."

"The Luftwaffe's Heinkel 219 can fly more than forty miles an hour faster, and has a service ceiling some nine thousand feet higher than your aircraft. Maneuverability doesn't matter all that much, superior speed and altitude allows you to dictate when and where you accept combat."

"Not in this case, Charlie," said Lacey. "Possession of the Night Hawk will dictate combat. The Nazis will have to shoot down the Night Hawk to prevent us from keeping it. That's their handicap, and we can use it against them."

"I've found that higher speed and altitude only means your opponent can either run away or climb away from combat," said Powers. "If you're aggressive enough and use your advantages, you can take on almost anyone. With this new Black Widow and a competent crew, I can take on four single-engine fighters of any type you care to name and win."

"Your confidence is most impressive," Cox remarked. "Very well. Tell me more about your aircraft."

With Lacey hurrying over to join them, Cox and Powers began their tour of the Black Widow.

"See this wing? It has retractable ailerons and full span flaps," said Powers. Raising his arm above his head, he was just able to touch the left wing tip with his fingers. "Those allow the Widow to lift off quicker, land slower and turn tighter than any other airplane its size. With them I can almost make this plane hover in mid air, all nineteen tons of her. C'mon, let's go to the tail."

Following Powers, Cox and Lacey ducked under the P-61's left boom and walked up to the glass-covered tail of the night fighter's fuselage.

"Is this were your gunner sits?" Cox asked.

"No, this is for the radar operator. Take a look inside," said Powers, opening an underside hatch. Cox was the first to take his offer, sticking his head inside the spacious rear compartment. "The radar operator works the main radar set, the radios, the nav aids and the electronic jamming gear. In combat he doubles as the tail gunner. He rotates his seat a hundred and eighty degrees and activates his sighting station. He shares control of the top turret with the front gunner and both must relinquish control in order for the pilot to use it."

"How many radar sets does your plane have?" Lacey asked while waiting for his turn to look inside.

"We have a primary radar system in the nose and a

167

tail warning radar in the right boom. The primary set has a range of thirty miles and a scanning area of forty-five degrees. The pilot has his own scope in the cockpit and takes over the interception once the radar man has designated the target."

Lacey could only have a brief glance at the operator's station before Powers continued his tour, leading the others under the narrow section of wing between the fuselage and the right boom.

"The P-61's main armament is located here," he said, patting the airplane's underbelly. "Four twenty-millimeter cannons, in addition to the four fifties in the turret."

"What's their ammunition load? The Heinkel carries an average of three hundred rounds per gun," said Cox.

"The cannons can take two hundred rounds per gun on average. Though we can overload them with an additional fifty rounds per gun. The fifties take five hundred and sixty rounds per gun. Total load is over three thousand rounds and that's not all."

Powers reached up and tapped a short, stubby pylon protruding from the bottom of the wing.

"This version of the 'sixty-one is equipped with four ordnance pylons, two inboard of the engine booms and two outboard. Each can take a sixteen-hundred-pound bomb or a three-hundred-and-ten-gallon drop tank."

"What's the range with maximum fuel?" Lacey asked.

"We believe two thousand miles. We can only guess since we haven't had this version long enough to do any long-range fuel consumption tests. But I think two thousand miles should be enough for you. Come, we've got one more stop to make."

Powers took Cox and Lacey to the P-61's nose gear

well. He turned a small handle in the roof of the well and the main entrance hatch fell open, deploying a small ladder as it did. Powers climbed inside the cockpit first, followed by Cox, who he instructed to sit in the gunner's seat. Lacey was left to stand in the landing gear well, straining to see what little he could from his less-than-desirable vantage point.

"This is the front office of the Black Widow," said Powers, occupying the pilot's seat. "As you can see, it's very spacious. Not like the cramped cockpit of a P-70, or even a Mosquito, for that matter."

"Yes, it's rather comfortable," Cox admitted. "It certainly doesn't give you the feeling of claustrophobia which most fighters give you. The few times I've flown the Spitfire, I almost felt like I was wearing the airplane."

"If you'll pull out the locking bolt at the base of your seat, Commander, I'll show you how the turret system works."

Cox lifted the handle he found under his seat and it, along with the support column for the gun sight, rolled forward until it hit the track bumpers and locked in place. Powers then instructed him to unlock the stowage pin on the gun sight's support arm, which allowed Cox to pull the sight down in front of him. He used the height-adjusting knobs to set its reflector plate at eye level and completed the operation by unlocking the aximuth control screw.

"I feel as though I'm on some kind of amusement ride," said Cox, as the gunner's seat swivelled back and forth.

"The seat, the gun sight support stand and the sight itself will now rotate through three hundred and fifty degrees," said Powers. "The sight can be elevated from one degree below the horizon line to ninety degrees. You can literally fire the turret guns straight up if you wanted to."

"Do the gunners have to make any adjustments for the location of the turret when aiming?"

"No, Commander, that's the beauty of this system. It uses the same fire control computer as the B-29 Superfortress. All you've got to do is set the wingspan dial on the gun sight and put the cross hairs on the target. The computer automatically calculates the proper lead, you only have to remember to squeeze the triggers on the grips."

"I see. What are these flippers for?" Cox pointed to the small levers on the outboard side of each grip.

"Those are your action switches," Powers answered. "Press either one in and you'll have control of the turret. You must release both switches for the radar man to use it. There's an intercom button on one of the grips for the sight, so you'll be able to communicate with him. And here's something I'd like to show you."

Powers reached to the left side of the canopy and pulled forward a device that looked like part of a submarine's periscope. He hit a release latch at the top of the device and swung it out from the canopy. It clicked in place in front of the pilot's seat, virtually blocking off his forward view, except for what he could see through the eyepieces.

"This is a pair of infrared vision night binoculars. Even though we have radar, at close-range its resolution isn't good enough to make the kill. So we use these when there isn't enough moonlight."

"You might also use them in place of radar," said Cox. "Some German night fighters are now equipped with boxes to warn them when they're being tracked by radar. I believe I've seen enough, Colonel. Your aircraft is very well equipped, possibly the best equipped Allied night fighter in Europe. If you have

170

nothing else to show me, I say we should leave."

First Cox had to stow the gun sight, and Powers the night binoculars, before they could climb out of the Black Widow. When they emerged, they found the rest of the crowd had migrated from the Dakota to the P-61s, with many in Lacey's team inspecting them on their own.

"Well, Commander? Have you decided to use these planes?" Roberts asked, stepping up to Cox as he came out of the nose gear well.

"I think so, though I still have my reservations about them," said Cox. "At the start of the war the Royal Navy had a similar aircraft. The Fairey Fulmar was a well-equipped, well-armed fighter but it didn't have the performance to match the enemy's aircraft. Though I must admit the Fulmar did evolve into the Firefly, perhaps the one truly great shipboard airplane we'll produce in this war. Well, Mister Powers, what do you think you have? A docile cow or a lethal warplane?"

"The nastiest fucking night fighter of World War Two," he said. "Once I get full crews, I'll take on anything the Luftwaffe can dish out."

"Splendid, now how many Black Widows do you have?"

"Well, to be honest, I got a little problem there."

"God damn it, I knew there'd be trouble," Roberts swore.

"Nothing's ever perfect, Lee," Cox advised, "there are always problems. I knew your squadron was re-equipping with this new model, you were bound to have troubles. How many of them did you receive and how many can you have flying?"

"We got twelve in this first shipment," said Powers. "Eight have been assembled and are in flying condition. The other four are being put together. That means hanging the propellers and outer wing panels on 'em, arming them, installing radar and other electronics. If you give us enough time, Commander, we could have them all flying."

"How much time would you need?"

"If we work flat out, I'd say from twenty-four to forty-eight hours. Apart from these, the rest of the airplanes are in the hangar behind us. They're on priority status with the assembly unit, and I got my men working on them as well."

"That estimate works in nicely with our own timetable," said Cox. "You noted something earlier about full crews. Is that another problem you have?"

"Only a minor one. We're kinda short on gunners and radar men. I can use some of my pilots but I'm casting around the Ninth Air Force bomb groups for volunteers."

"Volunteers? Well now, since you've given me such a good 'lesson' on the gunner's equipment, would you be willing to take me on as a volunteer? Since I'll be staying here, I believe I'll have enough time to learn the gunner's duties. In between overseeing the mission and demanding you move faster."

"OK, Commander, we'll take you," Powers replied after taking a few moments to size up Cox. "Is there anyone else who'd like to join? You, Colonel?"

"No, I got other things to do," said Lacey. "I have to scout airfields in Scotland and decide which one we'll use. Most of my team will stay here though. I'm sure you'll find a few usable volunteers among them."

"I'll volunteer," said Shannon. "Since I'm the one who got you guys involved in the first place, I think you should be able to find a spot for me. Like on David's ship?"

"I'd like to volunteer to be a radar man," Martinez added, walking out from under the wing of the P-61 the others had toured. "I know as much about radar as the next guy, and I kinda like the view I'll have back there."

"You know more about radar than the next guy," said Lacey. "You see, Colonel? You'll get enough volunteers out of my men."

"If you're to inspect all those air bases, Dennis," said Cox, checking his watch, "you had better leave soon. Connie, I suppose you should accompany him. And so should you, Lee. Colonel Powers, your squadron is part of the operation. Is there someplace warm where we could discuss the details further? I think this cold is freezing all of us."

"I'm Lieutenant-Commander Ian MacAlister and this is Wing Commander Duncan Ellis," said MacAlister, pointing at a blue-uniformed officer sitting with him in the front seat. "We're expected at the foreign aircraft internment area."

"Ah yes, you are the British air and naval attachés," said the airman in charge of the gate. "You are expected. Please wear these identity tags. By now you should know the way to the internment area. Good day, sir."

The toll bar was lifted and the Bentley sedan was allowed onto the air base. MacAlister drove along a familiar network of service roads to the rows of foreign airplanes sitting in front of a remote set of hangars. He parked beside another sedan bearing English diplomatic license plates. As he climbed out of the car, the new Royal Air Force attaché let his curiosity get the better of him. He paused to admire the collection, and the canvas-covered trailers next to it.

"I thought you said our friends are reassembling the jet," Duncan Ellis whispered to MacAlister.

173

"Of course they are," he replied. "They've been at work on it since before dawn."

"Then what's that?" Ellis turned and pointed at the covered trailers. "You told me they had been storing the dismantled aircraft on those."

"It's a bit of camouflage, old boy. It's what people expect to see. Come, I'll show you the real Night Hawk."

MacAlister walked over to the nearest hangar and rapped on its side door. It opened just wide enough to allow MacAlister and Ellis in, then it slammed shut behind them. Inside they found a hangar almost filled with the wreckage of crashed foreign airplanes. In the one section of clear floor space was the Night Hawk, or at least parts of it.

The wing sections had been rejoined and were standing on a combination of the main landing gear legs and wooden support frames. Above the wings hung the Night Hawk's fuselage, minus its nose. The fuselage was held aloft by a massive crane, which was slowly lowering it onto the wings. Watching the operation, almost supervising it, were Norris and Whitney.

"Good afternoon, Ian," said Norris, turning to face the latest visitors. "You must be the replacement for Greg."

"Yes, I'm Wing Commander Ellis. Duncan Ellis. I wish we could've met under better circumstances. Squadron leader Parry was a very brave man; I hope I can measure up. I have some reports here for you and Mister MacAlister. Now is as good a time as any for you to view them."

Ellis unlocked the heavy diplomatic pouch he had dragged from the car and handed one sealed folder to MacAlister, a second one to Norris. They broke the seals and quickly scanned the contents of each.

"This is good. It's basically what we thought the recovery operation would be," MacAlister noted, reading from the folder with an Admiralty stamp and Cox's signature on it. "Charles and Colonel Lacey have devised a very easy, workable plan. I'm sure our Swedish friends can agree to this. Here's an interesting detail, they're going to use Captain Roberts and his SAS team as a security force when the transport comes to Norrköping with the fuel. What's in yours?"

"A report from Royal Air Force intelligence," said Norris, "on what unit this airplane was attached to and where it might've been based. The Night Hawk was taken on strength by the First Night Fighter Group and assigned to its tenth wing. Which is a specially organized service test unit, probably set up to evaluate the Me-262B. The tenth wing is stationed at Esbjerg, on Denmark's North Sea coast. Its regular equipment is the Heinkel 219 which, beyond the Night Hawk, is the most advanced night fighter in the Luftwaffe. Isn't that the one that has tricycle landing gear, Ian?"

"Don't ask me, John. You're the airplane expert, not me. I'm the last one to know about them."

"Yes, the '219 is a tricycle landing gear aircraft," Ellis answered, "one of the few German aircraft to be so. I flew in night fighter squadrons before being assigned to diplomatic service, so I know something about this. The '219 is fast, what you Yanks like to call a 'hot ship' and it's the only current night fighter to have a two-man crew. It would be the best aircraft to transition train for this remarkable airplane. Tell me, how is it proceeding?"

"Well it may look like the reassembly job is almost finished but it's not," said Norris, turning back to the Night Hawk to find the fuselage almost in position to be remated with the wings. "The real work starts once she's back together again. All of her electrical, hydraulic, fuel and oil lines have to be reconnected. Flight controls reconnected, systems checked and the damage which originally brought the jet down, repaired. We got the spare parts, all our friends have to do is install them. Without any technical manuals, special tools or any previous experience with jet airplanes."

Norris pointed at a long steel tube resting on a specially crafted set of wooden supports. Stacked around the Jumo were the boxes of other spares which had been flown in from England.

"I understand. It's going to be a sticky mess," said Ellis. "It sounds simple enough but it'll be a real nightmare. At least they have you to help them, Commander. I was told you've not only dismantled and assembled Nazi jets, you even flew a version of this aircraft."

"Yes, but I've never done anything like that under conditions like this. We got about forty-eight hours to reassemble this plane and prepare it not just to fly but to fight as well. I don't think the Germans will let us take the Night Hawk without a fight. Which is why I'll be glad when Lacey arrives tonight. He has the best working knowledge of electronics of anyone in my team. Which is unusual for a commanding officer. Most C.O.s don't know as much as their men do. Would you happen to know when he'll arrive?"

"Colonel Lacey will arrive tonight, on BOAC's regular flight. In London they told me he'll board the air liner at its refueling stop in Aberdeen. Your colonel is in Scotland, deciding which air base your operation will use."

"Here, you better take care of this," said MacAlister, closing the folder he held and slipping it back inside the diplomatic pouch Ellis carried. "I'm sure you and Mister Norris will be able to sell it to Wing Commander Paulson and the others. Given all the restrictions they've imposed on us, I don't think we can come up with another plan or a better one."

"What do you mean by Commander Norris and me?" Ellis requested, his face starting to drain of color. "Won't you be staying with us? You're supposed to be one of the coordinators of this operation. You were sent to Sweden for that specific reason. If you're not staying, where will you be? Back at the embassy?"

"No, I have a meeting of my own. And mine's in Stockholm, not Norrköping."

"Does yours have anything to do with our operation?"

"Only indirectly. I'm meeting with the Special Investigations division of Sweden's national police force. Greg Parry's death was no accident. His air liner was shot down on purpose and I believe I know who's responsible. The Swedes have their suspicions as well, and perhaps later tonight I'll find the evidence to prove both theirs and mine."

"Is this field also used as a passenger stop by your Stockholm flight?" Lacey asked, as he and the rest of his group collected inside the air line manager's office.

"Not usually," said the manager. "Only when there are empty seats on the air liner, which isn't often. British Overseas uses Aberdeen as a refueling stop, essentially. We also service Swedish air lines aircraft when they come in."

"I see one of your Daks has just landed," said Roberts, glancing out the window. "Excuse me, a DC-3. When it's civilian-operated, it's a DC-3. Do many flights stop here on a typical day?"

"We have six flights during the weekday and four during the weekend, which includes one flight that originates here in the morning and the nightly London-to-Stockholm flight. Past ten p.m. we have no traffic, apart from what happens on the military side. The R.A.F. has a service flight training school there, and an Air-Sea Rescue squadron."

"Students, that's the last thing we need on a top-secret operation. Still, despite that and other problems, this is the best location to launch your part of the mission. Do you have any problems with it, Colonel?"

"Not really," Lacey replied. "Even if I did, what the hell could we do about it? This is the regular stop for all Stockholm flights. If we were to change to a more secure field, like Montrose or Blackburn, we'd create more problems than we'd solve. This will do, besides we only have five hours before the air liner arrives. That's not enough time to change the location of its refueling stop."

"So what'll we do until then, Colonel?" Capollini asked. "We've been all over this country and I'm tired."

"I know, we all are but we still have one more thing to do before we can rest. We have to tell Charlie about our decisions and we can only do that from a military base. Which means we'll have to go to the flight school over there. Mister Trevor, do you have any transportation we could borrow to get to the school?"

"I can loan you our service bus," said the air line manager. "Before you go, Colonel, I have just one more question. Who else knows of your plan and who can I tell about it?"

"No one," said Lacey, Roberts saying exactly the same words at the same time. "Beyond you, no one else is to know about us. And except for you, only the captain of tonight's flight has been told anything. He's bringing me my passport and entry papers and he's been told only to give them to me or Captain Roberts here. Thank you, Mister Trevor, for all your help."

After they left the manager's office, Roberts and Lacey, together with Constance, Martinez and Capollini, were driven to the headquarters of the airfield's service flight training school. They arrived in the BOAC's service bus. Since Roberts was wearing civilian clothes, the security guards wouldn't let him enter the building until he showed them proof that he was a U.S. Army officer.

Once inside the building they met with the school's commanding officer and, after explaining what they needed, he let them use his telephone to call Cox about the latest news.

"That's all I have to tell you, Charlie," Lacey concluded. "Have Colonel Powers take his squadron to Scapa Flow. I'll meet you there in a few days with John. After I catch my flight, my group will stay here tonight and then join you in the morning. Goodbye, Charlie, see you soon."

"Does that mean your men will stay on base, Colonel?" asked the school's commanding officer, as Lacey returned the phone to its cradle. "If you wish, I could set them up in our officer's quarters and I'm sure I could find room for Lieutenant Smythe in our WAAF's barracks."

"No, thank you, I'll be taking care of them," said Roberts, answering for Lacey. "I was once stationed here during my 'apprenticeship' with the SAS, so I know this area rather well. There are some good hotels in Aberdeen and I'm sure rooms at one of them will be available. If you can afford to loan it, what we would like is one of your staff cars."

The commanding officer ended up lending them his own car and driver and, once Lacey and Roberts had picked up the flight crew of their R.A.F. Dakota, they were all driven off to Aberdeen. Roberts provided the driver with directions to the hotels he knew about, the first of which he found to be full.

"I'm sorry, this one is fully booked as well," Roberts announced, walking from the second hotel to the group surrounding the staff car. "Everyone back in, we'll try another that I know."

As they had already discovered at the airfield, jamming so many people into one car made it very cramped. They filled every available inch of seat space, and would have needed more if Constance hadn't decided to sit in Lacey's lap.

"Hey, Captain, what's going on in this town?" Capollini asked, wedged in between Roberts and the driver. "Is there a Shriner's convention or something?"

"No, it's mostly Royal Navy types and their families," said Roberts. "The desk clerks say most of the hotel rooms in Aberdeen have probably been taken."

"Hell, that's what they always say. But in the States, you know if you slip 'em an extra ten-spot they'll find the rooms you want. The next hotel we hit you let me go in with you, I'll show you how it's done."

"I don't think it will work. The clerk at the first hotel told me there's another group of American officers making their way through Aberdeen. They tried to buy rooms your way and it didn't work. The hotel simply had none left."

Roberts instructed the driver to head across the Victoria Bridge to the southern end of Aberdeen. He guided him to a small hotel near the bank of the Dee River. In spite of Capollini's offer, he went in alone again. A few moments later Roberts came out smiling;

this time he was successful.

"That's great, Lee," said Lacey as Constance climbed off his lap. "How many rooms do they have?"

"Four, and I reserved all of them," said Roberts. "One for our flight crew. One for Capollini and Martinez. One for me and, since you two want to be inseparable for the next few hours, one for you and Connie. Now I don't think you would find accommodations like that at an R.A.F. base."

"How come you got a room all to yourself, Captain? I don't think that's fair," Capollini complained.

"I might not be alone for long. When I last talked to my girl, she told me she was returning home. Her family lives a little north of Edinburgh and if I can reach her, I won't be alone tonight. Dennis, tell the driver to wait here for a minute. I might still need him."

While most of the passengers followed Roberts into the hotel, Lacey, Constance and Martinez went to the trunk of the staff car and started pulling out suitcases. The first few had to be pried out by Lacey and Martinez. Like the passenger section, the trunk was jammed to capacity as well. Martinez waddled off to the hotel as soon as he had loaded himself down with luggage, leaving Constance and Lacey alone.

"I wish we could've rested at Blackburn," Constance admitted. "That was where our first operation started. Where we first fell in love. Remember, Dennis?"

"How can I forget?" said Lacey while he sorted the rest of the luggage. "Though I don't usually think of a maintenance and storage base in romantic terms. And I'm sure we wouldn't have received the accommodations Lee got us. We would've had to sneak around like we did before and we don't have the time now. All we have are moments really, and we have to make the most of them."

181

"I hope Lee can reach his girl. I hope he can share a little time with her. I know how lonely he'll feel if he can't. About as lonely as I will when you leave tonight."

Carrying three bags apiece, Lacey and Constance pushed their way through the main doors and entered the hotel's lobby. They found the rest of their group at the front desk, signing the registration book. Lacey dropped the suitcases he was toting and squeezed past the others to stand beside Roberts.

"There, I've registered and paid for my room and the flight crew's room," said Roberts. "You can sign for and pay for the other two. Excuse me, is there a public telephone around here I could use?"

"We have one in the restaurant, Mister Roberts," the woman at the desk answered. "Just through those doors."

"Thanks, Mrs. Philips. Well, now we'll see if Heather is at home and if I'll spend tonight alone or not."

"Hey, Captain, would you mind asking your girl if she's got a couple of sisters?" Capollini asked as Roberts walked through the restaurant doors.

"Oh, is Mister Roberts in the military? I thought he was a civilian," said Mrs. Philips. "He's been here several times and he never told me or my husband that he's in the military. Is he in the Army or Navy?"

"Lee used to be in the Royal Navy," said Lacey, recalling the cover story Roberts had told him earlier. He also gave Capollini a sharp glance. "That was a few years ago, he's now with a civilian agency. The less I tell you about it, the better. He's working closely with us."

"Oh, I see, it's hush-hush. That's what the other group of Americans said to me. Their work was top secret. This is so exciting, we so rarely have Americans stay here and now there's so many of you."

"Who are these other Americans? Are they Army

like my friends and I or are they Navy?"

"They wore uniforms just like yours, Colonel. The one in charge had the same things on his shoulders." The hotel owner pointed at the eagles on Lacey's uniform, then at his wings. "And he also had a pair of those. He was much older than you, would you know him?"

"The Army Air Force is a big outfit. If I knew his name, I could tell you," said Lacey. He laid aside the pen he was using and scanned the registration book for a familiar name. It didn't take him long to find one, in fact he found several, but he didn't get a chance to use them before someone used his own.

"Colonel Lacey, this is a fortunate surprise," said an officer, standing on the stairs which led to the hotel's second floor. He wore the same uniform as Lacey and had the same rank. He was older, also shorter and had a mean, vindictive smile on his face.

"Jesus Christ. You," Capollini uttered, the suitcases he was holding slipping out of his hands. But he was too shocked to notice.

"So, we meet again, Brogger," Lacey remarked, trying to hide his own shock. "What brings you to Scotland?"

"You do. I knew you were back in Europe," said Brogger, "and a few days ago I heard you and your men were in England. Somehow, I just knew you'd eventually turn up in this area, so I rounded up a unit and drove here. Thank you for being so predictable."

Brogger came the rest of the way down the stairs as he spoke, his group following close behind him. Some of the faces were familiar to Lacey and his men, and others were not.

"It's nice to know we're wanted," said Lacey. "Why are you looking for us? You want to volunteer?"

"Parker, get the truck and bring it to the front," Brogger ordered, stepping up to Lacey. "Oh, you're wanted all right, mister. We've got a score to settle. You may be a hero to a lot of people, but to me you're still the leader of a gang of misfits and you broke enough Army regulations to land you in jail."

"Hell, Colonel, if you locked up every officer who broke a few regs, you'd have almost everyone above the rank of lieutenant in jail," said Capollini, "including Patton."

"I'll let Eisenhower deal with Patton, I've come here to deal with you and Colonel Lacey. I have warrants with me from the Eighth Air Force inspector general's office, they're for everyone in your team, Colonel. You're charged with stealing Army property, misuse of said property, endangering the lives of Army officers and causing bodily harm. I'll have you know Captain March was very badly scarred by the little game you played on us at Blackburn."

"Well, at least you'll now have something to brag to the girls about." Capollini gave Brogger's rotund aide a friendly slap on his back. "You can tell 'em it's a war wound."

"OK, Brogger, cut the crap," said Lacey, getting a little annoyed, and scared. "What are you saying?"

"You're under arrest, Colonel," replied Brogger, "and so is Captain Capollini and Lieutenant Martinez. I can't do anything about your British friends, a pity but you three are good enough for me. I'd like to introduce you to Lieutenant Neal, military police. Lieutenant, have your men arrest these three."

Since they carried no guns, no weapons of any kind, Lacey and the others made no attempt to physically resist. The MPs brushed aside Constance and the Dakota flight crew as they grabbed Lacey, Capollini and Martinez. They spun them around, pulled their hands behind their backs and slapped handcuffs on their wrists. As the military police completed the arrests, Brogger walked up to the crowded hotel desk.

"Madame, could you give me directions to the jail you have in this town?" he requested.

"Of course, sir," said the still-startled hotel owner. "Go back to the bridge, head north until you reach Justice Street and turn right. The jail is located in the municipal building. Are these men criminals?"

"To me they are and I'll soon prove that to the U.S. Army. I hear the truck outside. Are you ready, Lieutenant?"

"You can't do this. You can't," Constance repeated, her shock wearing off and her anger starting to grow. "This is England. We're on a secret operation. You'll ruin it."

"No, Connie, don't!" Lacey shouted. "Don't tell him a damn thing! Call Charlie, let him take care of it."

With their cuffing complete, Lieutenant Neal and the other MPs dragged their prisoners toward the lobby entrance. When Brogger and March opened the doors, the deep rumble of a diesel engine became more obvious. Through them, Constance could see a dark green truck pull up to the curb. As the doors closed, she saw the tailgate drop down and Lacey thrown onto it.

Chapter Eight: Day Five
Setbacks

Constance didn't remain in the hotel lobby for long. While the Dakota crew was still too stunned to act, she burst through the entrance doors in time to see Martinez being manhandled into the truck.

"Keep it up, you little spick, and we'll drop you on your face," said one of the MPs, referring to the way Martinez struggled as he was hauled inside the load bed.

"Don't do anything to make them angry, Andy," Lacey ordered. "We'll have our chance for revenge later."

"Excuse me, miss," said Brogger, making his way past Constance and climbing into the truck's cab. "Miss Smythe, isn't it? I suggest you make that call Colonel Lacey told you to make. I'm looking forward to talking with your superiors."

"You bastard, you don't know what you're doing!" she cried so she could be heard above the roar of the truck as the driver gunned its engine and drove away. Constance had grown so angry, and felt so helpless, she began to cry. Through her tears, she could see the truck turn onto the Victoria Bridge and head across the Dee River.

"What in the name of God is going on?" Roberts demanded, bursting out the doors. "Who took Lacey and his team? The Dak pilot claimed he knew who they were and that Lacey was arrested."

"He was arrested. It was Colonel Brogger, one of our enemies from our first operation. He has a long memory and a desire to avenge his humiliation. He had a whole squad of military policemen with him. There wasn't anything Dennis or the rest of us could do."

"I see, where is this Brogger taking them?"

"He wants Dennis and the others in jail, so he's taking them to the municipal building."

"I know where that is," said Roberts. "Let's see if Brogger will listen to reason. Driver."

At Roberts's command, the staff car's engine was restarted and it advanced a few feet; all Constance and Roberts had to do was open the rear door and hop in. The car hovered in front of the hotel for only a few moments longer, until Roberts had given its driver additional directions. Then it raced back to the bridge and from there to northern Aberdeen.

"I don't see the truck," said Roberts. "They must already be at the jail. Do you know this colonel very well? Do you think you can handle him?"

"Right now I'm so mad I could handle the entire U.S. Army Air Force," Constance remarked. "I'd do anything to free Dennis. But aren't you going to talk with Brogger? You were the one who said he wanted to see if Brogger would listen to reason."

"I want to see many things. A lot more than our new friends, just in case reason fails. I have a rather strong feeling that it will."

Several blocks past the Dee River, the staff car made a sharp right turn and entered Justice Street.

Roberts and Constance could see the Army truck parked in front of Aberdeen's castlelike municipal building. The staff car drove past it, then swung around and pulled in behind it. Before the car had rolled to a stop, the rear passenger doors flew open and Constance and Roberts scrambled out.

They climbed the stairs and charged through the main doors, expecting to find the local police booking Lacey and the rest. Instead, they found a sparsely populated hall. The police station was on the floor below and it took a few moments to get directions to it. When they finally arrived, Constance and Roberts discovered Brogger and Lieutenant Neal presiding over the booking of their prisoners.

"Miss Smythe, I knew you wouldn't give up so easily," said Brogger, still smiling vindictively. "Who's your friend? I hope for Colonel Lacey's sake he's a lawyer."

"I'm just part of the colonel's team," Roberts offered, using his best British accent. "I'm a research specialist."

"By whose authority are you arresting Dennis and the others?" Constance demanded.

"By the authority of the Eighth Air Force inspector general," said Brogger. "And you should know, I'm not the one who's arresting them. Technically, it's Lieutenant Neal who's the arresting officer. I'm only holding the warrants."

"He may be the glove but you're the hand inside it. You're the one responsible for this. I can't believe it's actually happening. How on earth can you put these men in a British jail?"

"There's an agreement between the British government and the U.S. Army. If a U.S. military stockade isn't available to house American personnel charged with crimes, then they'll be housed in the appropriate

British military or civilian facility. I chose this place because I had the sneaking suspicion that should I put Lacey and the others in jail on a British base either you or Lieutenant-Commander Cox would find a way to free them. I wish I had the authority to put you in jail as well but, alas, Lieutenant Neal's jurisdiction doesn't extend to Royal Navy officers."

"And I bet you would, you bastard," said Constance, this time her anger didn't produce tears but a white-hot rage. "You're only doing this for spite. Those charges of yours won't hold up in court and you know it."

"Perhaps, though it will take several weeks, maybe a month, before this case is brought before a judge. The wheels of justice grind very slowly, Miss Smythe."

"Colonel, the booking procedure is complete," Neal interrupted, turning away from the police station's main desk and the sergeant behind it. "With your permission, I'll turn the prisoners over to the Aberdeen police for detention."

"Permission granted," said Brogger. "As I told you before, Miss Smythe, you should make that phone call to your superiors. I'm looking forward to talking to them."

Neal accepted the handcuffs he had used on Lacey, Capollini and Martinez from the station's booking officer, along with copies of the booking forms. He handed the forms to Brogger, who took obvious glee in his apparent success. Until they were led away to the holding cells, the prisoners hovered behind the front desk. Under the watchful eye of the police, but close enough for Constance and Roberts to speak to them."

"I'm so sorry this happened," said Lacey, extending a hand to Constance. "I wanted to be with you so

much, I only hope you and Lee can salvage the oper
ation."

"No, I won't leave you with him," said Constance
"We'll find a way to free you. Dennis, I love you."

"Oh, how touching," Brogger commented.

"Keep your nose out of this, Colonel," said
Roberts, his own anger showing. "It's none of you
fucking business."

"And just what is your fucking business, Mister
Roberts? What do you have to do with Colone
Lacey?"

"As I told you before, I'm a research specialist."
With attention suddenly on him, Roberts was forced
to improve upon his cover story in order to make i
more believable. "I was assigned to the colonel's team
by my superiors. I don't know him too well but l
have grown fond of the colonel and Miss Smythe and
I wish you'd keep out of their private relationship."

"And who are your superiors?" Brogger inquired
"What agency or office do you work for? You're
young and healthy, a man your age should be in the
armed forces. Not unless you're part of British Secre
Service?"

"I've done my part. I was once in the Royal Navy
I was a torpedoman on the cruiser HMS *Ulysses* unti
I injured my back. Now I'm with the RMO, Roya
Meteorological Office."

"Sorry, miss, these men have to be taken to thei
cell," said a police constable, prying Lacey's hand ou
of Constance's grip. "If you wish to see him, miss
visiting hours begin tomorrow at one."

Lacey was the last to be taken down the poorly li
corridor. Constance kept her eyes on him until he
receded into the darkness. Tears started welling up ir
them when she heard a cell door slam shut a few
moments later.

"Come along, Connie," said Roberts, laying a hand on her shoulder. "I've seen enough. We've seen enough. It's time for us to leave and deal with this problem."

"Good night, Mister Roberts, Lieutenant," said Brogger, glancing up from the treasured booking forms. "The next time we meet, I trust it'll be with someone else of higher rank."

Roberts led Constance out of the police station. Instead of going up the main stairs, they went through one of the side exits. They had to walk down a corridor which took them to the opposite end of the municipal building's basement. They emerged at the back of the building and were forced to walk around it to reach the staff car.

"Why didn't you help me back there?" Constance asked. "All you did was walk around the station as if you had never seen one before. As if you were on a damned tour. And why did you insist on taking me out the rear? Look at how far we have to walk. It makes me feel like I've lost a battle and I'm crawling away in defeat."

"Sorry for that, but everything I've done and everything I'm doing is for a reason," said Roberts. As he spoke, he seemed more interested in the surroundings than in answering Constance. "In a way, I was on a tour and we still are. I've seen many police stations before, but not this one. I must know as many particulars about this station as I can. Like I told you, reason failed. Now we can either go the legal way to free Colonel Lacey, which may well take weeks and will ruin our operation, or we can do it my way. Attack the police station and break him and his friends out."

"Do you really think you can do it, Lee?"

"Of course. Remember, I've broken into prisons,

Gestapo headquarters and military bases all over occupied Europe. Compared to them, this building will be easy. Though I do find it very ironic. I never thought I'd be using my skills to break into one of His Majesty's jails."

"All right, we do a commando assault," said Constance. "At least your men will have something more to do than play security guard. What must we do now?"

"A lot, quite a lot. We'll have to contact Charles Cox. I suggest we go back for our Dakota crew and return to the air base where we can talk to him."

"Fine with me. I'd rather not stay at that hotel. I don't want to spend any more time in Colonel Brogger's presence than I absolutely have to."

"Neither do I," Roberts agreed. "So we had better get Cox here to deal with Brogger. He'll have to tell our attachés in Sweden that Dennis won't be coming tonight. I shudder to think what this disaster could do to our operation. It could scare those Swedes who are helping us into backing off. When that Sweden-bound airliner lands here tonight, we'd better get Lacey's passport from it. Christ, I should've known something like this would happen. The operation was just moving too well to be true. I wonder what else can go wrong? And I hope nothing else does."

From a distance, the estate looked like a darkened, brooding fortress. It looked unoccupied or at least no one in it was still awake, which was perfect for Mac-Alister.

After Whitney had dropped him off, he easily climbed the stone wall surrounding Drache's estate and made his way to the main house. He chose a kitchen window to make his entrance and with a little help from a glass cutter, he was able to reach in and unlock its catch. The window gave an unnerving screech as MacAlister raised it. He was sure everyone in the house heard the ungodly noise, but he climbed inside anyway and tried making less of it when he lowered the window behind him.

MacAlister stayed in the kitchen for a few moments, listening for any sounds from the rest of the house. When he was certain all was quiet, he moved out of the kitchen and onto Drache's study.

Inside it was as dark as a crypt and MacAlister moved around carefully, afraid of bumping or brushing against anything. He made his way over to the room's window, where he pulled back the drapes. The dim moonlight he allowed in was just enough to illuminate the study. At least he didn't need his flashlight to see his way around.

The first thing MacAlister searched was Drache's desk. He sifted through the papers on top of it, then opened the drawers and rummaged in them. Whenever he came across something of interest to him, he'd use a small, pen-sized flashlight on it. When not being used, MacAlister kept the flashlight clenched between his teeth.

Apart from business correspondence, a calendar with social events listed on it, financial ledgers and supplies of stationery, he found nothing. Curiously, not only wasn't there anything incriminating in the desk, there weren't any personal items either. MacAlister found no pictures of Drache's supposed girlfriend, or his parents, no love letters or mementoes of any kind. He found it rather sterile and, after making sure the desk was in its original condition, he went to the bookshelves.

Here too he failed to find evidence that would support his suspicions of Drache. There was no wall safe behind the books, no false set of volumes, not even a hidden door which led to a secret room. MacAlister drew the drapes over the window again before he left the study, going next to the front hall closet and briefly searching the coats inside it.

Again, he found nothing. When he emerged from the closet, MacAlister pulled a small notebook out of his hip pocket and studied the floor plan drawn on one of its pages. He walked to a door at the end of the hall, where he found the basement stairs.

Closing the door behind him, he sauntered down the steps. Since they were made out of stone, he didn't have to worry about any squeaks or creaking. In the basement, MacAlister produced a larger flashlight than what he had been using and played its beam around the room. He discovered what he basically expected to find: a furnace in one corner of the main basement, stacks of crates and old furniture filling the rest of it, and a small room in another corner that served as the estate's wine cellar.

As he had done before in the study, MacAlister picked his way through the terrain carefully. In a basement with virtually no windows and only one staircase for an exit, it would be fatal to send anything crashing to the floor. First he went to the wine cellar, where he did almost as much checking on Drache's taste in wines as looking for any evidence that he was a spy. MacAlister discovered no hidden niches in either the walls or the floor of the narrow, cramped room. He emerged from the wine cellar and searched the rest of the basement. He even poked through the coal bin next to the furnace, and came up fruitless again.

He was prepared to take his investigation upstairs to the second floor where everyone in the house was asleep. It would be far more dangerous to search that and the other top floors but, also, potentially more rewarding. MacAlister steeled himself to head for the second floor. Yet there was something about the basement which nagged him. He was at the bottom of the stairs when he produced his notebook and flipped through it to a diagram of the basement.

The arrangement was the same, nothing in the cellar appeared to have been altered, though it did seem to be smaller than the dimensions MacAlister had listed. He walked to its far end and did a slow, measured pace back to the stairs. He tried to walk as straight a course as he could and, after he multiplied the number of steps he took by the length of his shoe, he found the basement was more than five feet shorter than what he had listed.

MacAlister immediately checked the wall on either side of the stairs. Checked it for any seams or hidden handles and signs of wear. He even tapped the wall to see if it was real stone or false. Convinced there was nothing behind it, MacAlister returned to the far end. Here there wasn't as much wall area since the wine cellar butted up against it. The first oddity he noticed, before he had really started his search, were the wires running into the wall.

They were standard electric wires and they ran through a small hole drilled in the top of the wall. He began tapping the wall and for the first two-thirds all he got was a flat thud. Then, as he neared the corner with the basement's side wall, his tapping started to echo. Even though it still felt the same, the wall had become fake. MacAlister examined the section minutely and discovered a hairline seam. A few minutes later he found a hinged panel and behind it was a cylinder lock.

From his jacket he pulled a tiny, leather pouch and zipped it open. He took one of its thin probes and worked it inside the keyhole, tickling it until each pin had been pushed in place. The cylinder plug rotated, the bolt was freed and the false wall popped open a crack. MacAlister opened it the rest of the way and moved inside, playing his flashlight beam around the interior.

The first thing the beam fell on was a table sitting against the far wall. On top of it was a large, complex-looking, short-wave radio with the word GRUNDIG prominently displayed on its face. Lying in front of the radio was a log book and several others MacAlister identified as German code manuals. The beam swung across a bed, another table set against the opposite wall, and finally came to rest on a light switch.

Since he was so deep inside the house, and neither the basement nor the hidden room had any windows, MacAlister tapped the switch. A single, overhead bulb came on, filling the room with a harsh light. For a few seconds the glare stung his eyes. When it wore off, he went directly to the radio. MacAlister opened the logbook first, to see what time the last transmission was made and found it had been done that night. He also found who it was sent to, the length of the transmission, the code book used and the initials "HVD."

Most of the transmissions were done by HVD and many of the messages received by the station were received by him. MacAlister considered it strange. He thought Carl Drache would do it himself instead of letting some underling be the radio operator. He also wanted to have Drache's name on something to complete the indictment against him, but what he found was damning enough. MacAlister scarcely knew where to begin, which he should photograph first.

He reached into his jacket pocket again and produced a slim, rectangular camera. He smoothed out the logbook page he'd been reading, pulled open the camera body to uncover its lens, set the aperture at the widest F-stop and took his first shot. The camera gave a faint zipping sound instead of a normal click and MacAlister closed the camera body to advance the film to the next frame. He shot several more pages of the logbook before turning his attention to the code manuals.

MacAlister chose the Gestapo code book to photograph. He wished he could take it and all the other code books with him but he would have to settle for pictures. In fact there was so much for him to shoot, he started to wonder if he had enough film to get it all.

The voice split the silence like a roll of thunder, even though it was scarcely louder than a whisper. "Are you enjoying your discovery, Mister MacAlister? I should've expected it would be you."

MacAlister nearly dropped the camera as he spun around, and found Carl Drache standing in the doorway. A slight smile showed under his moustache and in his right hand he held a short-barrelled Luger, which he levelled at MacAlister when he turned to face him.

"Shit," MacAlister replied, and at first that was all he could think of saying. "Does this mean you'll be calling the police or am I your house guest?"

"I believe we're capable of dealing with you," said Drache, stepping into the radio room. He only had to take a stride or two and he was face to face with MacAlister, his Luger pointed directly at his chest. "Cover him, my dear, while I search him."

MacAlister's heart sank when the person Drache spoke to appeared in the doorway. It was Ursula

Brandt, and she trained a small, chrome-plated automatic on him as Drache pocketed his own gun and searched MacAlister.

"Don't try anything, Commander," said Ursula, her voice as icy as the look in her hard, blue eyes. "I'm a crack marksman. I never miss."

"Let's see what we have," Drache commented. "One . . . no, two flashlights. A camera, a lock-picking kit, a glass cutter, film cartridges, wire cutters. I think you should've used these, Mister MacAlister. We were alerted to your presence by an electric eye guarding this door. We also have here a smoke grenade, standard British issue, and a Beretta automatic, twenty-five caliber, with silencer. A fair choice, Mister MacAlister, with a silencer this should hardly make a noise but it's such a ladies' gun."

As he identified each item, Drache laid it in front of the radio. The table space quickly became crowded with spy equipment and weapons.

"Yes, that's what Boothroyd at the embassy told me," said MacAlister, "a woman's gun. I prefer it because it is so small and so quiet. Plus it doesn't leave a bloody mess, not like your cannon."

"I know, but then mine will definitely stop someone," said Drache, pulling out his Luger, as if MacAlister's remark made him remember he had it. He backed away from MacAlister and motioned with the gun that they should leave.

"What do you plan on doing with me? You must presume I told my friends where I'd be and if I don't turn up in the next few hours, they might come here looking for me."

"Yes, I'm sure Colonel Whitney and the Americans will come here and ask, 'Did you see a naval attaché break in here last night?' You present us with a unique challenge and a fantastic opportunity. For the time being though, I would merely like to keep you quiet."

As they filed out of the radio room, Drache fell in line behind MacAlister. Instead of turning around, Ursula walked backwards and, while Drache answered MacAlister, she began to smile. To MacAlister, it was as though she were mocking him. And to think he once considered she might be a spy the police had planted in the estate. A spark of resentment kindled inside him, and it was just as quickly extinguished by a sudden flash of pain. Something heavy slammed against the back of his head, causing him to lose his balance, coordination and finally his senses. The last thing MacAlister remembered was falling against some vases on top of a crate. He sent them crashing to the basement floor, but by then he had stopped caring about making noises.

"This is Aberdeen Control to B-Baker, after you're down, please taxi over to the R.A.F. Dak. There's a party waiting by it for your passenger."

It was a common sight for Aberdeen airfield: one of the service flight training school's Harvards gliding in for a landing. Though it was unusual to see one up so early in the morning, when most of the school's aircraft were leaving on the first mission of the day.

The brown-and-green Harvard swung off the runway and taxied past a line of similar machines that had just started their engines. As instructed it parked beside an R.A.F. Dakota, the only Dakota on the tarmac, and there was indeed someone waiting for the trainer. Before its propeller had stopped windmilling, Roberts and Constance walked over to its aft cockpit and helped its passenger climb out.

"Sorry, Charles, but this was the fastest machine

we could send for you," said Constance. "You have to remember, this is a flight school, not a fighter base."

"I understand," Cox replied, peeling his flying helmet off his head and dropping it back in the aft cockpit. "And it would've turned a few heads if I had arrived in a P-61. I think the students and instructors here would have mobbed such an aircraft."

"Well the problem here hasn't changed," said Roberts. "Lacey and the others are still being held in jail and it doesn't look like Colonel Brogger will release them. About the only good news I have to report is this."

Roberts pulled a thin envelope out of his jacket and waved it at Cox. Inside it were Lacey's passport and entry papers.

"And believe me, I had a devil of a time getting this off that BOAC captain last night. Since I didn't have a uniform on, he refused to believe who I was until I showed him my dog tags."

"All right, all right. Before you start detailing what happened with this little disaster, I have something to tell you. The situation is worse, not merely here but overall. John Norris informed me this morning that Ian MacAlister went on a job of his own last night. He broke into the house of Swedish businessman he believes is a Nazi spy. He could well be right; he hasn't been seen since. Mister Norris thinks he's a prisoner."

"Oh God, how can this happen?" Roberts turned away from Cox and Constance and held his hands up to the sky, as if asking for a divine answer. "Yesterday everything seemed to be going our way. Today, it's all falling apart. I've had operations go bad on me before but not like this. We should be thankful we're not behind enemy lines or we'd all be in the hands of the fucking Gestapo."

"Instead of just Ian in Nazi hands," Constance

added. "Charles, is there any way we can help him?"

"Well, we certainly can't leave him the prisoner of a German spy," said Cox. "If Norris is sure of Ian's location, we'll have to try rescuing him. It appears as though we may have another job for your team, Lee. That is, if you still want to go ahead with the one you told me about."

"I see no other way to free Dennis," said Roberts, "not unless you can make this 'Colonel Blimp' listen to reason."

"I doubt that's possible, I've had my dealings with Brogger before. He always seems to believe he holds the upper hand, it's damned difficult to deal with someone like that. It's impossible to reason with him, so I'll have to resort to threats of my own. Perhaps I can put him on the spot with the Eighth Air Force. I'll have to see what I can do when I meet him. Do you know where he's staying?"

"At the hotel where we had planned to stay. After Lacey's arrest, Connie and I decided it'd be better if we stayed here at the base, though it did mean Heather wasn't able to visit me. Do I have your permission to send the Dakota out to pick up my team?"

"Yes, you might as well send her now," Cox granted, looking up at the Douglas transport as he spoke. He could see its crew sitting in the cockpit; as soon as Roberts signalled them, they began their pre-start checks. "I doubt even threats will persuade Brogger to release Dennis and the rest. Is there anything else you'd care to know?"

"How are the other parts of the operation proceeding?" Constance asked. "I hope better than our part."

"Well, I've already told you about the disaster in Sweden. John Norris and a Colonel Whitney will be meeting with the Swedish officers soon. They already know about Ian's capture and Lacey's arrest. I only hope the Swedes who're helping us aren't scared off by these disasters. Apart from them, the Night Hawk is being reassembled and repaired and Colonel Powers claims he'll have his Black Widows ready ahead of schedule. They'll fly to Scapa Flow by early this evening and the Night Hawk should be ready for a ground test tomorrow. If only the people involved in this operation would work as well as the machines."

"What about this other job you want me to perform?" Roberts inquired. "Rescuing MacAlister from the spy. Has this been cleared with our Swedish friends? Do they want us to come in?"

"Why do Lee's men have to rescue Ian? Why can't the Swedish police do it?" Constance asked.

"Because Norris and the other attachés asked for them," said Cox. "Neither the Swedish police nor its armed forces have a unit with the capabilities of a Special Air Services squad. If the police tried taking this spy's house, Ian would end up dead. This spy is a well-known Swedish businessman and it'd be extremely embarrassing to accuse him and not find Ian. Not to mention what that could do to our operation."

"So you and the attachés want me to do the rescue," Roberts concluded, "as discreetly as we can, I suppose?"

"I would hardly call using an SAS unit discreet but Ian will have a better chance of being rescued alive, should an assault be necessary. There is the possibility you might not be needed. Norris told me the Swedish police have an agent in this spy's house. He may be able to free Ian but if he can't, you'll have to go in. Can you do it, Lee?"

"It'll be more difficult than freeing Lacey but yes, my men can do it. Especially if we have the floor

202

plans to the house where Ian's a prisoner. At last we have a chance of doing something more important than playing nanny to a damn jet. Now we can prove how good we are."

"Thank you for agreeing to see us so early in the morning," said Whitney as he and Norris were led into Wing Commander Paulson's office, where they found other Swedish air force officers waiting for them. "I'm afraid we have some serious problems on our hands."

"I agree," Paulson added, closing his office door. Only then did he feel he could speak freely to his guests. "I asked myself what could be worse than what has happened in the last three days? I had hoped our troubles were over but I was wrong. Mister MacAlister and your Colonel Lacey have provided the answers to my fears."

"Yes, at best we have a situation that'll only be a serious diplomatic embarrassment and a delay in our operation. At worst, an officer who knows all of our plans has been captured by the enemy and our operation might well be exposed." Whitney selected one of the empty chairs in Paulson's office and collapsed into it. He sat next to squadron leader Lindh; standing behind Lindh was another Swedish officer. One neither Whitney or Norris had ever seen until now and they were hesitant to say anything more in front of him.

"As always, Colonel, you define the situation perfectly. Before we go further, gentlemen, I would like to present Flight Lieutenant Ormand Tallberg, of air force intelligence. You need not worry, he can be trusted. He's one of the few men on this base I trust with our secret."

"Nice to meet you," said Norris, shaking Tallberg's hand. "Excuse me for asking, but why were you brought in? Yesterday. Commander Paulson thought we already had too many people involved in this operation."

"We need him because of his contacts," Paulson replied. "He works with the intelligence sections of our other services and with civilian police forces. He can learn if anyone is onto us and what has happened at Drache's estate. It's been under discreet police surveillance for several months."

"Well, can you tell us what's happened at the estate since I dropped off Ian?" Whitney asked.

"Everything is quiet and has been so," said Tallberg. "The police cannot verify that Ian is there. Not until their agent reports to them. If there's a chance, he will attempt a rescue. What have you heard on the arrest of your officer in England?"

"He was jailed by an old enemy of his," said Norris, "on some chicken shit charges that won't hold up in court. But they could fatally delay our operation. If we don't convince the shithead to release Lacey, then we'll free him our own way. We'll use that Special Air Services squad we wanted for on-site security. We can assure you they'll get Lacey out of jail."

"We were wondering if we could use the same men to rescue Ian?" Whitney proposed. "Neither your army nor the police have a commando unit like the SAS. They would be the perfect people to resolve this crisis."

"What, you want to bring in a British unit to stage an attack?" Paulson's already ashen face was drained of its remaining color and his speech became more halting as the shock of Whitney's suggestion set in. "To fight in my country? Colonel, this idea has the possibility of being an even greater disaster than what we currently face. How would we explain dead British soldiers? Or the wrecked house of a wealthy businessman? While I admit your idea could end our problem, it could also broaden it and make it much worse. Please, my friend, let the police agent in Drache's house rescue Ian."

"That would be the better way to go for the time being," Norris advised, bending over Whitney's chair to make sure he would hear. "If their man can get Ian out, great. It'd be simpler than launching a commando attack with British troops in a neutral country. And if he can't pull it off, what can happen?"

"Our agent in the estate could be compromised," said Tallberg. "His cover might even be destroyed. Then we would have two prisoners, not one and Drache would know that we are suspicious of him. Under such conditions, Wing Commander, I would advise that the British be used. They are the experts in such matters. And however disastrous the possibilities may be, they are the only ones who could end it."

"All right, I will keep their idea in mind," Paulson sighed, resigned to the fact, as if it were his fate. "And I pray this policeman can rescue Mister MacAlister. I cannot escape the feeling I have that our operation is getting out of our control. Other people, our enemies, are in charge of it. I don't know if you have the same feeling, Colonel. You don't have to come to this base and look at most of your friends as possible enemies. Mister Lindh can tell as much about it as I can."

"We know we are doing something that's right," said Lindh, speaking up for the first time. "And yet, if we are caught, we would end up in jail. We would be charged with treason, our careers and honor ruined. All that for doing something we know is right

205

and could help win this war. I realize what we risk isn't the same as combat but we hope you understand."

"I can assure you, we do," said Whitney. "It's one thing to fight an outside enemy. It's quite another to oppose your own country. We know the risks you're taking and believe me, we're most grateful. If it's your wish to try rescuing Ian with your agent, we have no objections. We won't force you to decide on our idea until after he's tried, and we do hope he's successful. We have just one request for now, we'd like to have the floor plans to Drache's estate set aside for our possible use. It would save invaluable time if they are needed. We'd like to fly them out on the first available Mosquito if we have to."

"The plans are no problem," Tallberg advised. "I can obtain them from the police unit investigating Drache. If I ask for them, there will be no questions as to why I need them. I'll hold onto the plans until it becomes necessary to use them and, like Commander Paulson, I pray they will not be needed."

"Commander MacAlister, wake up," a gentle, feminine voice urged. "Commander, please wake up. I'm here to free you."

MacAlister raised his head slightly and groaned. They were the first signs he was regaining consciousness. As he came to, his eyes half-opened and he focussed on the figure hovering over him. It was a woman, at first he thought it was Ursula but then he realized she had dark hair. She was also shorter than Ursula and slimmer. Her face had more delicate features, a smaller nose and thinner lips, and her blue eyes were much brighter, not as icy as Ursula's. The English she spoke was perfect and it was touched with a soft, lyrical Nordic accent instead of a harsh German one.

"Oh God, if it wasn't for my throbbing head, I'd swear I was in heaven," MacAlister croaked. "What's going on? Who are you, my dear?"

"My name is Karen Nilsson," said the woman. "I'm the police agent you were told about. You are in Drache's study. He and Miss Brandt have gone to Stockholm on business. They must give the appearance of normal activities."

While she spoke, Karen used a knife on the ropes which held MacAlister in one of the study's chairs. She cut away the ropes that bound his wrists to the arm rests, then went to work on the ones around his ankles.

"There, do you think you can walk?"

"I hope I can, I don't think you're strong enough to carry me," said MacAlister. He bent down and started rubbing his ankles and calves. "Damn, I must've been tied to this blasted chair for hours. What time is it?"

"A few minutes before noon. You were unconscious for a long time. Between duties, I came here and tried to awaken you several times. They must have drugged you for you to have slept for so long."

"Either that or Drache can deliver an unusually potent karate chop. What do you do here, Miss Nilsson? From the way your superiors talked, I thought you would've been the butler or some groundskeeper."

"I'm an assistant cook. Most of the estate staff are German emigrés," Karen explained as she grabbed a coat that was laying in another chair and pulled it on. "I'm supposed to be preparing lunch for the staff. So please, you must hurry if we are to escape."

Shakily at first, MacAlister stood on his feet and started walking around to get the circulation back in his legs. Karen followed him about the study, carrying a second coat which she helped him slide on. MacAlister staggered over to the curtains and opened them a crack.

The bright sunlight hurt his eyes, especially when it reflected off the cover of snow which lay over most of the landscape. From the study windows MacAlister actually saw little of the estate, just a picturesque view of Lake Mälaren and the islands of rock and pine trees which seemed to erupt out of its frozen surface.

"At least I don't see much activity," said MacAlister. "How do you plan on breaking me out of here?"

"This coat you have on belongs to Carl Drache," said Karen. "With the collar turned up you might pass for him at a distance. We will go to the servants' quarters, I have a small car there. Please, we must leave."

Karen took MacAlister by the hand and led him out of the study. They ran for the kitchen, where they found several pots on the boil, beyond which there was no other activity and no one to be seen. As they passed the stove, Karen turned the gas jets off and MacAlister paused beside the window he had used to enter the estate.

"I see they found where I broke in," he remarked, running his hand over the wooden plug inserted in the window.

"They did not find it," said Karen. "I found it. And I would never have found it if I had not seen you enter the house last night."

"Very good, they'd never suspect you of helping me after that. There's one or two people beside the servants' quarters. Should we wait until they leave?"

"No, we have to chance it."

Karen swung open the kitchen's rear door and MacAlister escorted her out. Instead of running, they walked as calmly as their pounding hearts would let them. MacAlister turned up the collar of his coat as he'd been instructed and put an arm around Karen's waist. She pointed out her car amongst the several parked beside the quarters. It would've been quicker for them to have cut across the yard but they were forced to take the pathway which had been shovelled out of the snow.

The people MacAlister had spotted earlier were still outside. They were both elderly and when they noticed MacAlister they automatically called him Mister Drache. He waved at them instead of making a verbal reply; he was thankful that the coat and, probably their poor eyesight, had allowed him to pass for Drache. MacAlister and Karen were only a few feet away from the line of cars when the sharp crunch of snow heralded the return of another.

"Damn, it's them," Karen swore as she halted in midstride. "If we hurry . . ."

"Not, it's too late," said MacAlister, cutting her off. "I think they've already spotted us and they can use that car to block the drive. Our only chance is to run for it. I know a place where we can scale the estate wall."

This time MacAlister took the lead as they broke from their leisurely stroll into a flat-out run. Drache's Mercedes had been making for the estate's garage when it abruptly stopped and veered toward the servants' quarters. Drache and Ursula climbed out and watched the fleeing pair for a few moments before Ursula drew her gun on them.

"No, they're to be taken alive!" Drache ordered. "I know where they're heading. Lars, to the house. If we're to catch them, we must have reinforcements."

MacAlister glanced over his shoulder at the

Mercedes, in time to see it pull around to the front of the estate. He knew it wouldn't take long for Drache to have his men after them, so they had to cover as much distance as they could. He and Karen followed the footprints he had made during the night when he first entered the estate.

The terrain was filled with rock outcroppings and groups of pine trees. A blanket of snow hid most of its features and dangers. Anyone attempting to run across it risked losing his balance if he didn't know where he was stepping, which made the trail of prints an invaluable guide. MacAlister remembered it had taken him almost an hour to cover the same ground during the night. Now it would take him only a few minutes to run the same distance.

"They're heading for the northeast corner of the perimeter wall," said Drache, standing in front of a small group of men who were being armed with rifles and Luger automatics. "Where a tree overhangs it. Under no circumstances are they to be killed. I want them alive. You may, however, kill anyone who's waiting to rescue them. Kurt, you're in charge of the truck. Go to the outside of the wall, you're to catch MacAlister and this girl if they make it past us."

"Please, Commander, could we stop for just a moment?" Karen asked. She was falling so far behind MacAlister it was difficult for him to keep a hold of her hand.

"All right, I'm becoming a little winded myself," he said, "but only for a moment."

MacAlister slowed his pace, then grabbed onto a tree as he stopped. He started undoing his coat buttons as he leaned against it. He'd been running for little more than a minute and already he was sweating. Drache's coat hung on him like a great tent. He would have discarded it in a second if it weren't for

210

the deep cold he felt. A cold which hurt his lungs every time he breathed and numbed his fingers.

"It's a pity you didn't think to pack along some gloves," MacAlister remarked, breathing on his cupped hands.

"I did not think to bring any," said Karen. "I just took the coat I thought would fit you. Try the pockets, I never bothered to check them."

"Well thank God for small gifts." MacAlister produced a neatly folded set of leather gloves from the coat's outside pockets. With great glee he slid them on his hands, but his smile disappeared as he looked at the ground in front of him. "There are two sets of footprints joining mine, up ahead. That means Drache knows where we're going."

"There's a car and a truck on the drive, Commander." Karen pointed to a now-familiar Mercedes and a small pickup racing away from the main house.

"Damn it, they must know. We haven't a second to waste."

MacAlister took hold of Karen's hand again and they plunged down his trail. From the drive they were visible, though only for a few moments before they ran behind a stand of pine trees. A hundred yards farther along the drive, an unpaved road branched off of it. Scarcely bigger than a footpath, it lay buried under the same mantel of snow which covered the rest of the countryside and was blocked by a wooden barrier.

Ordinarily, it wouldn't be reopened until spring but Drache needed to use it. The Mercedes veered to the left and rammed the barrier while the pickup shot by, continuing on to the estate's front gate. The wooden barricade splintered on impact, only the support posts remained intact. The sedan plowed into the heavy snow, kicking up sheets of ice crystals as it tried to push its way through. Very quickly, the Mercedes dug itself in, slowing down until its rear wheels were spinning helplessly in deep ruts.

"Everyone out!" Drache shouted, pushing open his door. "They're not far away now. Capture them!"

Drache even ordered his driver to join the chase, leaving just him and Ursula standing at the car. MacAlister caught all the activity out of the corner of his eye. He barely glanced at the approaching henchmen. His attention was focussed on escaping them and on the wall, less than a hundred yards in front of him and Karen.

"We should give our men some help in stopping them," said Drache. "Should we fire into the air?"

"I don't think that will stop Mister MacAlister," Ursula replied. "He will not hide at the sound of gunfire. We'll have to wound one of them. Which would you prefer?"

"Very well, shoot the girl. I don't want MacAlister accidentally killed, and I don't want my coat damaged."

Unlike Drache, who was armed with a Luger, Ursula had a high-powered rifle with a telescopic sight. She pulled back the bolt, then rammed it forward and locked it down, loading a cartridge into the breech. She raised the rifle to her shoulder and adjusted the focus of the sight. For a few moments Ursula tracked Karen, getting the crosshairs centered on her before she squeezed the trigger.

"Ian, my leg!" Karen screamed, her hand sliding out of MacAlister's gip as she staggered and collapsed.

MacAlister skidded to a halt and turned to find her sprawled in the snow, clutching her right thigh. The sharp crack of the rifle shot finally echoed across

212

the landscape. MacAlister glanced in its direction, then he knelt beside Karen. He carefully pulled her hand off her thigh and found an inch-long tear in her skirt surrounded by a patch of blood.

"It's a graze," he said. "They want to stop us, not kill us. Do you think you can walk?"

"No, it hurts too much," Karen gasped.

"All right, I'll have to carry you."

MacAlister slid one arm around Karen's shoulder and the other under her legs. He lifted her off the ground and turned to run in the same movement. In spite of the more than one hundred pounds in extra weight he was now carrying, MacAlister was able to regain most of his original stride, though it did hurt more to run. Not only did his lungs and legs hurt but now his arms and back did as well.

"A compassionate man," said Drache, watching the chase through binoculars. "I'd have thought he would have left her behind. Perhaps we could use this against him later."

Karen's weight also made MacAlister top-heavy, several times he nearly lost his balance. He caught himself, though each time he had to slow, which allowed Drache's men to close on him. By now the wall was only a dozen feet away, and so was the bare, gnarled tree that overhung it. The tree stood on the estate side of the wall; several of its larger branches extended over its top, which made it easy for anyone on the outside to climb in.

"As soon as we reach the tree, I want you to grab hold of the thickest branch you see," said MacAlister, in between gasps of air. "You're going to climb onto the wall yourself. I'll boost myself over, and then help you down the other side. I hope we can flag down a passing car, or something."

As he and Karen approached the wall, MacAlister

could see hands wrapped around one of the tree branches. Someone was trying to enter the estate; whoever it was, MacAlister prayed he had a car. For a moment he even thought it might be Whitney or one of the other attachés. One of them was armed with a bolt-action rifle and the other had a Luger; the chase was over.

MacAlister stumbled and sank to his knees. His lungs were bursting, every muscle in his legs and back ached and some were beginning to cramp. The adrenaline that had been surging through his body was gone. There was no longer any need for it. His arms were too tired to hold onto Karen any longer. She sagged to the ground, her arms still wrapped around MacAlister's neck, her head resting on his chest. They both felt the cold now more than ever and started shivering as they sat in the snow.

The henchmen who had been chasing them arrived a few seconds later. More guns were levelled at MacAlister and Karen, as if they were trapped animals and the hunters weren't sure if they were dangerous or not. Neither group spoke to the other; MacAlister only gave those surrounding him a cold, hateful stare. Nothing was said until Drache and Ursula arrived.

"I underestimated you, Mister MacAlister," Drache noted, stepping in front of his prisoners. "You gave us quite a surprise, and such a good chase. You too, Miss Nilsson. You shouldn't have tried leaving so soon. You are my guest and we have much to discuss. Check them both for weapons, and after you are done we'll take them back to the estate."

"Seven-B should be down there on the left," said Constance, standing with Cox at the head of the hotel's staircase. "Would you like me to come with you, Charles?"

"Yes, but all I want you to do is stand outside the door and rap on it should any of Brogger's men appear. Is there anything else I should know before I confront him?"

"We never mentioned the Night Hawk in front of Brogger, and you shouldn't either. He knows nothing of our operation and he doesn't know Lee Roberts is in the SAS. He thinks Lee's a meteorologist. Brogger doesn't know about our SAS team."

"Good, it's nice to know my final trump card is well protected. Come along, let's meet the colonel."

Cox led Constance down the hall to one of the last rooms on the left-hand side. When they reached Seven-B, he motioned for her to stand away from the door while he gave it three sharp knocks. After a brief delay, a voice inside said the door was unlocked and to come in.

"Colonel Brogger, I was told you wanted to meet me," Cox remarked, stepping through the door and closing it behind him. "You needn't have gone through all this trouble if you had wanted a little chat."

"Lieutenant-Commander Cox, I should've guessed you would be Colonel Lacey's superior," said Brogger, a look of mild shock on his face. But he was quickly able to regain his smug composure. "Misfits tend to stick together."

"I'm not a lieutenant-commander, I'm a full commander." Cox tapped the stripes of gold lace on his coat cuff. "Commander Misfit, if you wish."

"I should've guessed that as well. You do get rewards for sinking German battleships. Well, Commander Cox, I suppose you're here to beg for the release of Lacey and his men."

"I wouldn't say beg. Advise would be a better word. You've interfered with a very delicate and important operation. I advise you to release Dennis and his men or you'll find out just how important it is to a great many people."

"Are you saying you have powerful friends? Well, so do I, the Eighth Air Force inspector general for one."

"I report directly to the Board of Sea Lords and I have connections to both Eighth and Ninth Air Force headquarters. In fact, I have access to the headquarters of all Allied forces. British, American and Free French."

"Yes, I heard you were made head of some Allied brain trust," said Brogger. "Well, I don't give a damn. I don't care if you got a direct line to General Doolittle's office, it won't help you and it won't help Colonel Lacey. The inspector general's office is an independent branch of the Army. Anyone interfering with it will get in trouble, even Doolittle. You won't be able to do a damn thing until Lacey is brought before a military tribunal."

"The charges you have against Dennis and the others are rather shaky. They won't stand up in court. Chances are they'll be dismissed."

"I know my legal grounds aren't exactly firm but I'll let the wheels of justice decide that, and they do grind rather slowly. It'll take several days to transport my prisoners, get lawyers for them and arrange a hearing. By then I suspect it'll be too late for your operation."

"Yes, by then it will be ruined," said Cox. He was careful not to tell Brogger how much of a delay would destroy the operation. "Is that what you want? The destruction of a highly important Allied mission?"

216

"No, I want to take Colonel Lacey's place in your mission. If it's as important as you're suggesting it is, then you can't have a crew of misfits representing the United States Army Air Force. They have no discipline, they got no respect for authority and they don't follow procedures. Those aren't the kind of men you want on a top-secret operation. For the life of me, I can't understand why you would want them. It's like trying to make ruffians part of a marching band.

"Oh, I'll be the first to admit that Dennis Lacey and the rest lack a certain spit and polish. That they make authority earn their respect and they not only ignore established procedures and rules, they merrily trample them. They have their faults, but I wouldn't trade them for anyone else. Especially you, Colonel. They've been briefed on the situation, I know what to expect of them and they have talents I need, you don't. Now I'll only ask you this one more time. Will you come to the jail and release my friends?"

"See you in court, Commander," Brogger replied. He had become so arrogant, Cox felt an almost overpowering urge to beat him to the ground. "And if you don't mind, I'm late for dinner. I should warn you, Mister Cox, not to try any rescue attempt when the prisoners are moved. The only reason I didn't move them today is because I'm waiting for a special convoy of MPs to arrive. They're on the road now and when they arrive in Aberdeen tomorrow, we'll transport Lacey and his ruffians to an American base."

217

Chapter Nine: Interrogation
Break-in

"Osprey Twelve, this is Scapa Flow tower, you are cleared to land. If you use exit ramp C-Four, you may join your friends."

The last of the glossy black, twin-boomed fighters swung over the Scapa Flow lagoon and settled in for a landing. Since most of the base's inhabitants were Royal Navy fighters and torpedo-bombers, the appearance of an American Army Air Force P-61, much less twelve of them, was highly unusual. Off-duty air crews and flight line personnel gathered to watch the huge, ugly fighters come in. Armed guards, however, held them back from the hangar the Black Widows taxied up to.

Though a dozen arrived at Scapa Flow, only two or three were still visible by the time the last one was shutting its engines down. The rest had been towed inside the hangar and those outside were in the process of being moved. When the crew of the last Black Widow climbed out of their aircraft, they found a reception party of Army Air Force and Royal Navy officers waiting for them.

"Chris, I thought you'd like to see this," said Colonel Powers, handing over a telegram to one of the plane's three-man crew. "It was waiting for me when we got here. It's from your friend, Charles Cox."

"I can see that," said Shannon. It only took him a few seconds to read the telegram's contents. "So he's going to be a little late getting here. I knew he wouldn't convince that Army tin shit to release Dennis. A brass hat is a brass hat no matter what service he's in."

"Then what's going to happen to them, Colonel?" asked Ackerman, the pilot of the last Black Widow. "Are those guys just going to be left there? I thought we needed them."

"We do need them. And don't worry, Commander Cox will get them out of jail," said Powers. "If Chris will let you read the telegram, you'll see that Cox is going to use those British commandoes to free Colonel Lacey and his men."

"You mean a jail break? God damn it, would I love to see that."

"Excuse me, gentlemen, but you'll have to move," said a Royal Navy officer, one of Scapa Flow's original reception team. "We'll be towing your aircraft into the hangar."

The navy lieutenant had scarcely moved Shannon and the others away from the P-61 when a tow tug backed up to the night fighter and a bar was attached to its nose gear strut. In less than a minute it would be disappearing inside one of Scapa Flow's largest hangars.

"Why are you hiding our planes, Colonel?" Ackerman inquired. "Half the base must've seen us come in, not to mention those ships in the anchorage. By tomorrow morning, everyone in these islands will know we're here."

"That's not important," answered another, higher-ranking navy officer. "We have to prevent the Germans from knowing you're here. They still like to fly the odd reconnaissance mission over Scapa Flow. Lately, the Luftwaffe has been using their Arado jets, and they're damned impossible to intercept."

"In case you've forgotten, we are on a top-secret mission," said Powers. "I think Commander Cox would've shipped in our planes by submarine if that were possible."

"And I suppose that means guards are posted to keep everyone away from us," said Shannon, taking note of the security around the hangar and on the flight line. "Have we been assigned to special, segregated sleeping quarters, Colonel?"

"Yes, and we also got our own cafeteria."

"I know all this is necessary but I still don't like it. This reminds me of when I was in the Pacific and how resentful we used to get when some 'top secret' group would blow in and practically take over our field."

"I don't think we'll be here long enough for any resentment to build," Powers replied. "If we can get the rest of this mission to work right, we'll be out of here in twenty-four hours."

"Well, Commander, I hope you've been comfortable here," said Drache, on entering his study. "And you as well, Miss Nilsson. Though I think you were a little less so."

Drache circled his prisoners as he talked to them. Both were tied securely into chairs which faced his desk. As he passed MacAlister, he gave him a friendly slap on the shoulder but to Karen he wasn't quite so kind. Drache jabbed the bandage that circled her right thigh. She let out a small hiss of pain.

The wound still hurt, though not as much as he had hoped for.

"You really must forgive me. I had business in Stockholm that I had to take care of and then of course there was dinner. Oh, I'm sorry, you haven't eaten yet. Well, we'll take care of you later but first, we must have a little chat."

"You won't pry much out of me," said MacAlister. "All I'll give you is name, rank and identity number."

"That remains to be seen, Mister MacAlister. Ian, after all this time I should call you by your first name. I believe I know you well enough to. In a way I'm glad I have this chance to talk to you. There have been so many times I wanted to tell you the truth, at last I can. Come in, my dear."

Drache was responding to a knock on the study's main doors. When they opened, Ursula Brandt stepped in, carrying a leather case about the size of a portable typewriter. She joined Drache at his desk, where she set the case down and started opening it.

"What's she going to do?" MacAlister asked. "Take the minutes of our interrogation?"

"Hardly, she will be one of your interrogators," said Drache. "As it is by now obvious to you, neither of us is what we appear to be. Take Miss Brandt, for instance. Her real name is Ursula Frome. She's a German agent, not a German refugee. The real Ursula Brandt was killed in 1938. She took her place and for years pretended to be a good Swedish citizen."

"Is it really necessary to tell them this?" Ursula asked, unraveling an electric cord from her case.

"Yes, my dear, it is. You don't know how long I've wanted to tell these things to our friend here."

"She may be a spy but you're a traitor, Mister Drache," said Karen. "You are a respected business-

221

man. You have money and power and yet you betrayed your country."

"I'm no traitor, Miss Nilsson," Drache replied, his eyes ablaze with a smug arrogance as he smiled at Karen, then MacAlister. "I think Ian here understands. I'm not Swedish, Carl Drache was a Swede, I'm German. My real name, is Baron Hugo Von Drax and I coordinate all espionage activates for the Third Reich in Sweden. I was one of Carl Drache's German cousins and I've been impersonating him since September of thirty-seven, when he and his parents met with that unfortunate auto accident outside of Göttingen.

"As you should by now be guessing, that accident was nothing of the kind. The Gestapo and military intelligence arranged the crash and, of course, Carl died with his parents. In fact they were all dead before their car had even left the road. At the hospital I was substituted for my cousin and kept in isolation. Physically I was very close to him. I was the same height, had the same eyes and hair color but my facial features didn't match. I was given some plastic surgery but mostly, I grew these to hide the differences."

Drache stroked his beard and pinched the end of his moustache, which MacAllister had always been told were grown to hide disfiguring scars.

"When I returned 'home,' no one but Carl's old governess ever guessed who I really was. Of course she met with another unfortunate accident we arranged. As for me, Hugo Drax died in the crash of a Luftwaffe transport a year later. Since then no one has really suspected me. Not any of the Swedish officials I've worked with, and none of the Allied attachés or diplomats that I've known have suspected my true self. Except for you, Ian. From our first meeting you were wary of me. You were more perceptive than those other idiots your country sent over, like Greg Parry."

"Greg was a combat pilot," said MacAlister, "not an intelligence man. You couldn't have expected him to ferret out the double agents from our information sources. In his own way, he was a good man."

"But not as good as you, Ian. You were the best I ever encountered. You were the one I wanted most to tell my story to. What do you think? Is it not remarkable? Do you not see the genius behind it?"

"Of course, there always is a certain cleverness in the plans of mad men." MacAlister spoke slowly, choosing his words carefully and deliberately. However inspired the operation may have been, MacAlister wasn't about to give Drache the satisfaction of hearing him say so. "And you really must've had a good collection of sick minds to devise this one. You're the worst of the lot. You're not only a lunatic, you're a homicidal lunatic. You murdered anyone in your way, even members of your own family. I don't know if they have capital punishment in Sweden, but in England you would hang. There isn't much one can do with raving lunatics such as yourself. Often we find you commit suicide. A pathetic end to the 'master race,' dangling from some water pipe by your boot laces."

"*Schweinhunde!*" Drache exploded, reverting momentarily to his native language. He leaped away from his desk and punched MacAlister in the jaw, striking him so hard MacAlister thought his head would snap off. Drache then lifted him off the ground, along with the chair he was tied to. He held MacAlister in midair for a few seconds before dropping him to the floor and stepping back to his desk, his rage now under control. "You were foolish to have provoked me, Ian. You've only made it easier to do what we have to do. As a matter of fact, I may now enjoy this. Ursula."

MacAlister had been too intrigued by Drache's speech to notice what Ursula had been doing with her typewriter. Indeed what she had brought with her was anything but a typewriter. It sat upright on the desk, the upper half of its leather case had been peeled off it, revealing a sparse row of buttons, indicator lights, what looked like tuning knobs and a voltage meter. A power cord snaked out the back of the machine and a similar one from its top ended with a wandlike steel probe. Ursula held the probe in her hands; at its tip were two small studs. To MacAlister, they looked a lot like the fangs of a serpent.

"What's that?" he asked, "a voltmeter?"

"Not quite. It doesn't measure electricity, it dispenses it," said Drache. "The time has come for you to talk, Ian. Let's see, where shall we begin? Why don't you tell me why Miss Nilsson helped you? I've suspected she might be more than just a cook. Why is she here?"

Drache pointed a finger at MacAlister and Ursula moved toward him. She held the probe in front of MacAlister's face, making slow circles in the air with it. He was almost mesmerized by its motion, then it hit him, like a cobra striking its prey. The probe touched him on the neck, delivering a lightning bolt of pain that made MacAlister spasm uncontrollably. He wanted to scream but his throat was paralyzed and all he could manage was a harsh gargle. It would be several moments before he could speak with anywhere near a normal voice and even then, he refused to use it.

"Again," said Drache after he gave MacAlister a reasonable length of time to answer his questions.

Ursula responded by first reaching over to her machine and turning one of its dials. The needle on the meter above it jumped slightly, and when she was satisfied with the increase, she delivered a second bolt to MacAlister.

He could've sworn he heard his skin sizzle when the probe touched his neck again. It was a much more powerful jolt than the first one, it seemed to set afire every nerve ending in his body. For an instant MacAlister thought he would lose consciousness, but he opened his eyes and gave Drache a defiant, hateful stare.

"Very good, Ian," Drache remarked. "It will take much to make you talk. Perhaps we're asking the wrong person? Perhaps we should ask Miss Nilsson herself?"

Ursula turned toward Karen and waved her probe at her menacingly. She reached for the bandage on her leg and started pulling it off her wound.

"Leave her alone, you bastards," MacAlister croaked.

"No, wait," said Drache. "That's not as sensitive to pain as we would like. We should use some other part of her body. Something more . . . tender."

Drache walked over to Karen and laid a cold, maleficent hand on her. He ran it around her face, then down her neck to the collar of her blouse. He undid the first button or two, though he found it difficult to use one hand and he quickly grew frustrated. Drache tore open the rest of her blouse, eliciting a frightened scream from Karen. His fingers wrapped around her left breast and ripped the delicate, lace brassiere cup off of it. Tears started rolling down Karen's face, though she didn't cry or whimper like a terrorized schoolgirl. Instead, she breathed in short, shallow breaths, her lips trembling, her eyes fixed on the probe held in Ursula's hands.

Karen's breast shook as she breathed, so much so that Ursula had to hesitate for a moment before she stuck the probe's tip on its nipple. There was the same crackle MacAlister heard when he was hit, the sound of skin being fried. Karen did manage to get out part of a scream before the pain took her breath away. Her head crashed against the back of the chair and her fingers dug into the arm rests so violently some of her long, manicured nails cracked off.

"She's an undercover police agent," said MacAlister. He decided he might as well tell Drache some of the information he wanted to hear. It could buy them time. "She was assigned because the Swedish police think you're a little too close to your German friends. They think you might be selling Swedish defense secrets to them."

"I see, so there was someone else who was suspicious of me," Drache chuckled. "Only for the wrong reasons. I very rarely gave Berlin military secrets from this pitiful country. Beyond natural resources, Sweden has little to offer the Reich. So, you're a police agent, Miss Nilsson. Tell me, was it your idea to rescue Commander MacAlister? Or did your superiors tell you to do so? Is this a joint operation by the Swedish police and British military intelligence?"

Though the questions were all about MacAlister, they were directed at Karen. MacAlister wished he could answer for her. He knew if Drache were to find out there had been any cooperation between him and the police, he and Karen would be dead before the night ended. He couldn't give her any signals, nothing Drache could pick up on, all he could do was hold his breath and stare at her out of the corner of his eye.

"I didn't know Mister MacAlister was here until I

226

saw him in this study," said Karen, hesitating for a moment. "It was my own idea to rescue him. My superiors didn't tell me to and as far as I know, there was no contact between MacAlister and them."

"Then how did Ian know you were with the police and their suspicions of me, my dear?"

"I told him those things while I was freeing him. He was very surprised to learn we were watching you. He should know Sweden can handle its own traitors."

"And did Ian tell you why he entered my house?" Drache inquired. "Did he tell you what he was looking for?"

Drache gestured to Ursula as he asked his latest questions. She approached Karen, waving her wand at her again.

"I wasn't able to tell her much about my operation," said MacAlister. "She dominated the conversation and we were rather busy trying to escape."

"Very well, suppose you tell us now why you entered my house and more important, was this a joint operation with your friends? What are the other Allied attachés doing?"

"The break-in was my own idea. None of the other attachés helped me or believed me when I told them you were a Nazi spy. That you were responsible for Greg Parry's death. What they are more interested in doing is setting up another deal with the Swedish air force for the secrets of the Night Hawk. Thanks to your handiwork, I don't believe they'll succeed. I entered your house to find proof you were a spy, proof that you killed Greg. I wanted to find something my fellow officers would believe."

"I would say you've found your proof, Commander," said Drache. "Only you'll never have a chance to use it against me. Since you mentioned the

Night Hawk, what schemes do the Allies have for it? Are you still trying to steal it?"

"Of course we would still love to obtain it," MacAlister replied. "All we can realistically expect, however, is more pictures. Once we have those, or should the Swedish air force refuse us, we'll find a way of destroying the jet before it's returned to you. It's nearly as important to prevent you from regaining the jet as it is for us to have it."

"Very good, that's what I expected you and the Americans would be doing. Yes, what is it? I gave specific orders that we were not to be disturbed."

Drache was sharply addressing a man who had appeared at the study's main doors, one of the men who had earlier captured MacAlister and Karen.

"It's the short-wave, Herr Drache," the man informed. "There will be a transmission soon from Berlin and they want to talk with you personally. They want an update on the prisoners we captured."

"All right, we'll have to continue our talk another time, Mister MacAlister. Take care of them, Ursula."

As Drache left the study, Ursula set aside the probe to her electric shock machine and circled the two prisoners. She laid an affectionate hand on Karen's shoulder and stroked the hair at the base of her neck. Karen shivered when she was first touched and turned away from Ursula, who withdrew her hand, though only momentarily.

It came crashing back against the side of Karen's neck, a jolt of pain more powerful than the electric shock she had received. Her entire body rippled under the impact of the blow and she let out a scream before plunging into unconsciousness. When she was sure Karen had been taken care of, Ursula turned to MacAlister.

"You're a cold bitch," he said, looking up at her.

228

"You certainly are. And a bizarre one as well. Tell me, do you prefer women over men? Most of the dedicated Nazis I've met have had their odd sexual preferences. I wonder if it has to do with the fascist mind? Some latent sickness."

As MacAlister spoke, Ursula whirled around and grabbed hold of the probe lying on the desk. She also turned up the voltage output dial, the probe literally hummed when she approached MacAlister. As before, she jabbed him in the neck. To MacAlister it felt like she was burning a hole in it; the pain blotted out all his other senses. It became his entire world and it was the last sensation to stay with him before blackness enveloped him.

"Turn off your headlights and engine," Roberts told the driver. "We'll coast to the end of the street."

The truck's headlight beams died and the diesel's heavy rumble trailed off. Soon all that could be heard was the creaking of the truck's body and the soft crunch of its tires against the road's cobblestone surface. It glided to a stop a few feet from an intersection with another street. On the opposite side stood Aberdeen's municipal building, and in its basement, the Aberdeen jail.

Roberts jumped out of the truck's cab and circled around to its back where he quietly lowered its tailgate. From the load bed eleven men emerged; all were wearing military uniforms though only a few of them were armed.

"There's our target," Roberts whispered, pointing at the darkened building. "Or at least what's in the basement. Remember, all we want are those three airmen. We're not to free anyone else. Don't go wild and damage the station indiscriminately. Apart from the standard weapons locker, the station is unarmed so we'll have no problems taking it. You know what your objectives are, you know where the emergency truck is located should you become separated and our watches still appear to be synchronized. Good luck, gentlemen, and let's enjoy this one."

The group broke into three four-man teams and fanned out across the street. Two teams disappeared around the side of the municipal building; one would destroy its electrical junction box while the other would blow open the jail's rear door. The third team, commanded by Roberts, walked through the building's main entrance. Inside Roberts took the lead, the other three men trailing behind him. They tread as softly as they could, to hide how many they were; even so their footsteps echoed lightly through the darkened hall. When they reached the stairway to the basement, Roberts descended alone. The rest stayed at the top and checked their watches.

As he expected, Roberts found the police station manned by only a sergeant and two constables. It was quiet except for a BBC broadcast on the radio and some voices from the cell block. Roberts identified the voices he heard as American and one of them as Capollini.

"If it weren't for you and your fucking little stunts with those tear-gas grenades and flares, Andy, I bet we wouldn't be in this jam," Capollini swore as he paced up and down the cell he shared with Lacey and Martinez.

"And what about you stripping them parts off Brogger's personal airplane?" Martinez countered, pointing an accusing finger at Capollini. "Don't try blaming the shit pile we're in on me, Vinnie. You pulled just as many stunts as I did."

"We're all responsible," said Lacey. "Let's stop arguing amongst ourselves, that's just what Colonel Duane would like to see. We all did things that got us in trouble. You forget, Vince, that I OK'd most of those stunts. As commanding officer, I'm the one who deserves most of the blame."

"Excuse me, my name is Captain Roberts, Royal Marines," Roberts announced, loudly and with a smooth British accent. "I've been told you're holding some of my men for breaking up one of your local pubs."

"What? Would you mind repeating that, Captain?" asked the desk sergeant, a confused look on his face.

"Hey, Colonel, did you hear that?" Capollini asked, charging to the cell door and straining to look down the hallway. "It's the SAS guy, I bet he's here to spring us."

"Shut up, Vince," said Lacey. "Don't blow it for him. On second thought, don't shut up. Keep up your argument with Andy. It wouldn't sound natural for you to stop."

"What should we bitch about? You already decided the last fight, Colonel."

"Anything, Vince, and be quick about it."

"God damn zoot suiter," said Capollini, after a long, nervous moment of silence. "Why don't you boggie on back to the barrio?"

"Don't hand me any of your lip, guinea," Martinez replied, sitting up in his bunk and edging over to the door.

"Spic."

"Wop."

"Wetback!" By now Capollini was almost shouting his insults. They could be heard throughout the station.

"Sicilian greaseball, your father's a hood and your mother's a whore."

231

"Dead wetback! I'll slit your fucking throat."

"Will you damn Yanks drop it!" the sergeant demanded. "Or I'll separate the lot of you. Now, Captain, I'm afraid someone misled you. We haven't had any reports of disturbances at pubs and we haven't arrested any servicemen."

"Except for some rowdy Americans," said Roberts.

"Oh those, we didn't arrest them. Some American colonel brought them here. I wish he'd hurry back and take the buggers off our hands."

"Don't worry, they'll be off your hands soon enough." Roberts pulled his sleeve away from his wrist watch and counted down the last seconds. "Four, three, two, one."

There was a muffled crack somewhere outside the building. It was scarcely loud enough to be called an explosion, but it did its job on the junction box. The conduits running through it were torn open and the cables they protected were severed, plunging the police station into darkness.

"What the bloody hell is going on?" the sergeant shouted as he jumped up from his desk. "Captain, do you have anything to do—"

He never got to complete his question. Roberts pulled the sergeant over his desk and threw him to the ground. When he tried to get up, Roberts punched him in the jaw and he collapsed back to the floor, unconscious. The constables came running out to the desk, requesting orders from their sergeant, just as Roberts's team of commandoes came charging down the stairs.

"Flash grenade!" said Roberts, shielding his eyes.

One of his men took a grenade off his belt and tossed it onto the floor. It detonated with a dazzling, incandescent flash which blinded anyone who had his eyes open. In an instant the explosion was over and

232

the damage done; the two constables stumbled around until they were grabbed by the commandoes and handcuffed to each other.

While his men were dealing with the police, Roberts jumped the desk and ran down the corridor to the cells. Though he already knew which one held Lacey and the others, their shouts guided him unerringly to them.

"Boy, are we fucking glad to see you, Captain," said Capollini, reaching through the cell bars to shake hands with Roberts.

"Nice to know I'm fucking wanted," he replied, shaking hands with Lacey and Martinez as well. "All right, stand back. If you want to be free, I'll have to blow the door."

Lacey and the others moved to the rear of the cell as Roberts pasted a lump of plastic explosive to the door's lock. He inserted a detonator, pulled its activator pin and retreated a few feet down the corridor. After several seconds of hissing there was a deafening explosion which echoed through the entire municipal building; at almost the same moment there was another blast outside the building. Only those who'd been anticipating it knew it had gone off.

"Hurry up in there, we haven't any time to waste!" Roberts shouted, standing in front of a now-open cell door. "C'mon, we're making enough noise to wake up the whole town."

First Lacey, then Martinez and Capollini staggered out of the cell. As each one emerged a flashlight was shined in his face and Roberts assigned one of his commandoes to lead him out. Roberts was the last to leave the cell block. He reached the police station's front desk to find another team of his men waiting for him.

"We've opened the exit door, Captain," said one of

233

them. "Permanently opened it and we have the other team guarding it. If all's gone well, the truck should be waiting for us outside."

"Well done, now let's keep it moving," said Roberts. "We're not finished yet. I'd like us to be back at our base in twenty minutes."

With a commando on either shoulder, Lacey was virtually carried down the long corridor to the building's rear exit. The same was true for Martinez and Capollini, their feet barely touched the floor during their escape. Only outside were they allowed to stand on their feet and then it was just for a moment or two.

The truck that had dropped off the commandoes at the jail barrelled around the corner and pulled alongside the group. Lacey and the other prisoners were boosted into the load bed first, and they in turn helped their rescuers climb on board. Roberts was among the last to be helped in and he worked his way to the front of the load bed where he banged on the cab's rear window. The truck started rolling again, almost before the final commando had been hauled aboard and the tailgate closed. At the next intersection it swung onto North Street, then onto Saint Nicholas, which would eventually take them to the airport.

"Jesus Christ, that was fun!" Capollini exclaimed. "First time I was ever sprung by commandoes. Tell me something, do your operations always go that fast?"

"To you it may have been fast but to us it wasn't," said Roberts. "It may all be over in minutes but to me these things always seem to take an eternity. It's like I have glue in my joints, everything moves so slowly. I've heard from you pilot-types that it's much the same way when you're on a bombing or strafing run. The attack seems to last forever."

"It sure seems that way, especially when you have a dork for a bombardier. I suppose it's the same for all of us."

"What's going to happen to us next?" Lacey asked. "It won't be long before the police are looking for us."

"We're going to the airfield," said Roberts. "Charles Cox and Connie are waiting for you there. There's been a major change in our plans. I think they should explain it to you. A lot happened while you were in jail."

The truck practically flew out of Aberdeen, only when it reached the city limits did it slow a little. From there it was less than five minutes to Aberdeen's municipal airport. Instead of entering the military side of the field, the truck drove onto the civilian side, and into one of the hangars of British Overseas Airways. Inside, the hangar was empty, unoccupied except for the two figures who materialized out of the shadows and ran to the back of the truck when it stopped.

"Well, I told you I'd get him," said Roberts, jumping out of the truck after its tailgate was lowered. "And I did. Almost as easy as stealing candy bars from a drug store. Colonel, the ride's over for you."

Lacey appeared at the back of the truck and eased himself to the hangar's floor. Before he had his feet firmly planted on the ground, Constance rushed up and embraced him.

"Dennis, thank God," she cried quietly as she kissed him. "I knew they'd free you. We're so happy you're out."

"You did a splendid job, Lee," said Cox. "A simple, clean operation. I think it's time to move your men to the other side of the base. The police won't be able to look for you there."

235

"Hey, Colonel, what about Andy and me?" Capollini asked, appearing at the truck's tail.

"You're to go with Captain Roberts and his squad," Cox replied, answering for Lacey. "Everything's been arranged. Lee, the R.A.F. is waiting for you at the school's headquarters. Wait for me there, we'll be over shortly. Dennis, we have your belongings in the hangar office. We have less than ten minutes before your flight arrives and another twenty before it leaves. So we had better hurry."

Lacey said goodbye to Capollini and Martinez while Roberts joined the driver in the truck's cab. With its engine restarted, the truck swung around sharply and left the hangar; it would take the airfield's perimeter roads to the Royal Air Force's service school where Roberts and the others would hide. By the time it disappeared from Lacey's view, he was being rushed by Cox to the hangar's small office. In it he found all his luggage and, as he changed from his bedraggled uniform to a new, clean one, Cox told Lacey what had happened since his arrest.

"Christ, and I thought what happened to me was bad enough," Lacey remarked, pausing as he adjusted the knot in his tie. "What are John and the rest of our people in Sweden doing about Ian? In fact, what're the Swedes doing about him? Is anyone trying to rescue him?"

"Apparently a Swedish police agent tried to rescue Ian," said Cox, "and failed. Their agent is now a prisoner of this spy as well and they've reluctantly agreed that we should attempt a rescue. When we send in the transport with the Night Hawk's fuel, Lee Roberts and his team will also go."

"Why Lee? Why can't the Swedish military do something? Hell, we're working with their air force."

"Only with a small group within the Swedish air

236

force. They can't go to anyone else, not to any other air force unit or the Swedish army. If they did, our operation would be uncovered and they'd be arrested as traitors. Even if our friends could, the Swedish military doesn't have an elite commando unit like the SAS. When your country is officially at peace, you really don't need such forces."

"Charles, they're moving a fuel bowser out to the airliner," Constance reported, turning away from the office windows. "I think it'll be ready to go in fifteen minutes."

"So should Dennis," said Cox. "Here, this is your passport and entry papers. And this will explain to the Swedes how we'll go about rescuing Ian and their agent. Lee and I worked on it today. Give it to John and the other attachés, don't let anyone else at either the American or British embassy see it and, most especially, no one in the Swedish air force but our friends."

"How about the Swedish police?" Lacey asked. "Shouldn't they know how we're going to rescue their man?"

"Our friends in the air force will handle them. The Special Investigations division has never encountered a problem like this before and they're only too happy to pass responsibility to a higher authority. Well, Dennis, are you ready?"

"I wish I had time for a shower and a shave but yes, I'm ready to go. I just have to pack my bags."

Lacey placed the folder Cox had given him in the briefcase he would take onto the air liner; then zipped shut his garment bag and suitcase. Cox helped him carry his luggage as far as the hangar entrance, where he turned over the briefcase to Constance and the garment bag to Lacey.

"I know you two haven't had much time to be together," Cox noted, "and what little time is left you should spend alone. Goodbye, Dennis, see you at Scapa Flow."

Constance and Lacey walked out to the BOAC air liner on their own. The green-and-brown mottled Dakota looked almost identical to the Royal Air Force counterpart Lacey's team had been using. However, it didn't wear the same military-style roundels on its wings and fuselage sides. In their place was a British civil registration and a fin flash-style red, white and blue stripe. Apart from Lacey and Constance, the only other people on the hangar apron was the ground crew servicing the airliner. No other passengers were boarding it. Apart from a seat reserved for Lacey, it was full.

"I wish Charlie hadn't sent away Lee and his commandoes," Lacey admitted. "I'd like to have them around right now."

"Why, Dennis? That would spoil the last moments we can have together."

"I know, Connie. But you have to understand, I'm an escaped convict. I feel Brogger could step out of that terminal at any second and rearrest me. Now I know how James Cagney and Humphrey Bogart felt in all those gangster and prison escape pictures."

"Don't worry about Brogger," said Constance. "He was asleep in his hotel when we last checked on him. I'll worry about you from the moment this aircraft leaves until I see you again. I'm so sorry we couldn't spend more time alone."

"I know, we lost a lot. It seems like whenever we have a chance to be together, something or someone tears us apart. It should make us cherish what times we do have."

As they approached the DC-3, some of the ground crew relieved Lacey of his suitcase and garment bag.

With his hands at last free, he circled an arm around Constance's waist and drew her close to his side. A few feet short of the air liner's hatch they stopped and embraced. They held onto each other for a little longer than they knew they should but a lot shorter than what they wanted to.

"Times like these make me feel as if whatever happens between us doesn't amount to much," Constance admitted, pulling back slightly from Lacey and looking in his eyes. "We seem to do more in our jobs when we're apart than when we're together."

"Well, we won't be apart for long this time," said Lacey. "Just a few days if everything goes right. And remember, whatever we didn't have, at least we had a brief time in London. I'll be missing you, Connie."

The air liner's left engine began to whine and quickly rattled to life. The noise and the initial blast of propwash caught Lacey and Constance's attention for a moment, then they turned back to each other and kissed before separating. Lacey lifted his briefcase out of Constance's hand, which allowed him to wrap his fingers around hers as he pulled away. He finally turned and climbed the air liner's boarding steps. The instant he was on the plane, the flight attendant retracted the steps and locked the hatch shut.

Constance stepped back from the aircraft, moving out of its propwash and edging over to the hangars. She kept her eyes on the transport, watching it swing toward one of the dimly lighted taxiways. She wanted to catch one more glimpse of Lacey through the cabin windows but they were already blacked out. Constance followed the air liner so intently she failed to notice Cox approaching her until he was almost standing beside her.

Together they watched the plane taxi to one of Aberdeen's runways where it halted for a minute or two before opening up its engines. The Pratt and Whitney radials emitted a loud, flat howl as it raced across the airfield and lifted into the night sky. At last Lacey was on his way to Sweden.

"Herr Heinrich, I must speak to you in private," Lossberg demanded, storming into the *gruppe* commander's office.

"Don't you ever knock, Herr Lossberg, or wait to be introduced?" asked Heinrich, who didn't wait for an answer. "As you can see, I'm in the middle of a meeting with my *gruppe*'s maintenance chief and one of my pilots, Major Peltz. You should remember the major. The first, and so far only, pilot to fly a Night Hawk mission. We were just talking about giving the major back his '219 and how soon it can be readied. I have no secrets from these men, I trust them. What you have to say to me you can say to them."

"I don't have to tell you, Oberstleutnant, about the regulations regarding sensitive information. If these men do not leave, I'll have them arrested."

"Very well. Stohl, Ruddy, we'll continue this later."

The other two officers got out of their seats and left Heinrich's office, only saying goodnight to him and scarcely glancing at Lossberg. Neither Heinrich nor Lossberg said another word to each other, not until the office door clicked shut.

"Like almost every other Gestapo man I've dealt with, you have the manners of an ape," Heinrich remarked. "In a way I marvel at how you can order people around in their own offices. Well, what have you come to tell me? What's the news from Stockholm? What new schemes have you and Berlin come up with?"

"The news from Sweden is disturbing," said Lossberg. "The Allies are quiet and that is disturbing. Our spies strongly suggest they might be planning to destroy the Night Hawk before the Swedes return it to us. Berlin has decided that to save the prototype we must protect it."

"Why must we be the ones to protect it? The jet is at a Swedish air base. Can't they do the job?"

"We feel the Swedes will not be able to do so. The British and the Americans want to either learn the Night Hawk's secrets or destroy it and they're very determined. Our spies in Sweden think the Allies might be working with some officers in the Royal Swedish Air Force to destroy the jet. Berlin believes that the most likely time it'll be destroyed is before our people arrive at Norrköping to rebuild and prepare the jet for flight."

"And what plan do you have to protect the Night Hawk?" Heinrich asked reluctantly. "Do you know how the Allies will attack it? And what's my part in your plan?"

"The Allies could either destroy the jet by sabotage or by a commando raid or by an air attack on the base. To defend against sabotage and commandoes, I'll send in a team of SS storm troopers tomorrow night. A transport will fly them to Norrköping, some twelve hours before the Luftwaffe's rebuilding team is scheduled to arrive."

"I'm sure the Swedes will find that rather ironic. You invaded their country with commandoes and a U-boat to destroy the jet. Now, you'll invade Sweden with storm troopers to protect it. Are you aware that the Swedish air force has radar? The British gave it to them. They'll see your transport and intercept it before it reaches Norrköping."

"They may see it," said Lossberg, "but they won't intercept it. In fact, the Swedes will be expecting this

241

aircraft. Though not at Norrköping."

"You'll have to explain that better, Herr Lossberg. But for now, what part will my men play?"

"Your *gruppe* is to go on alert immediately, as will most fighter units in Denmark and Norway. If the Allies are going to destroy the Night Hawk by an air raid, they'll have to cross our territory to reach Sweden. By day, *gruppes* of Messerschmitts and Focke-Wulfs will stand on alert. By night, your *gruppe* and Nachtjagdstaffel Norway will stand ready. You'll intercept any Allied formation heading for Sweden. You're to pursue them even if they enter Swedish air space. They must be stopped at all costs. So you see, Herr Oberst, final responsibility for the Night Hawk may well rest in your hands."

"Very well, I shall put my men on standing alert," said Heinrich, reaching for his duty roster. "I'll have to contact night fighter headquarters to release my crews from flying regular operations. All available, mission-ready fighters will be armed and moved to dispersal points. Since I have more crews than aircraft, I'll set them up in rotating shifts. That way, I can assure you I'll have the maximum number of fighters available at all times. Should the Allies try an air attack, we'll stop them dead."

Chapter Ten: Day Six
Final Preparations

"D for Duncan, this is Scapa Flow tower, you are cleared for final approach. Once you are down, please follow the guide vehicle at the end of the runway. Your friends are expecting you."

The Dakota lumbered across Scapa Flow's ship-filled lagoon and settled onto the airfield's longest runway. At its opposite end a brightly colored jeep with flashing lights waited for the transport. When it finally arrived, the jeep moved out ahead of it and led it to one of the largest hangars at the air base, and the most heavily guarded.

The jeep was waved off by sentries before it entered the security zone in front of the hangar. The Dakota was guided in the rest of the way by a ground crew. They motioned for it to park beside one of its sister ships, a U.S. Army Air Force C-47. As the R.A.F. transport went through its shut down procedures, a group of American and Royal Navy officers filed out of the hangar and gathered around it.

"How come I feel like half the eyes on this base are watching me?" Cox asked as he climbed down the Dakota's set of boarding stairs.

"Because no one but your friends know who we are or what we're doing," said Powers, nodding his head at the Royal Navy officers who had come out with him. "These guys won't even tell anyone what type of planes we're flying. To most of the people on this base we're the American mystery squadron. I know we need security but this is a bit much."

"I suppose it is, though it's all for the good. We're so close to launching our operation we can't take any chances."

"Commander, how well did the operation to free Lacey go?" asked Shannon.

"As my father used to say, 'About as easy as a raid on a New Orleans whore house,'" said Roberts, appearing at the Dakota's hatch. "And almost as much fun."

"If you people don't mind, I'd rather we continue this discussion inside," said Cox, "as much for security as to escape this beastly weather."

While the gales that whipped around the tarmac made it impossible for anyone more than a few feet away to hear what was being said, it also made standing outside nearly intolerable. Even through their heavy greatcoats the officers could feel the chilling blasts of the North Sea winds. Though they had just stepped out of a well-heated aircraft, Cox, Roberts and the other new arrivals felt the cold as well and they hurried along with their reception committee to the gray, desolate-looking hangar.

They entered through a small service door; the hangar's main doors were shut and locked to keep out the gales. Inside it was still cold, though at least they were protected from the near-Arctic weather. Their frosted breath no longer swirled around the men but hung in front of them. Inside the hangar Cox found the entire P-61 squadron. All twelve fighters were packed in nose to tail and wing tip to wing tip. There was scarcely any room in the hangar for anything else; the scaffolding that had been erected around some of the planes could hardly be seen.

"Oh for Christ's sake, I knew this would happen," said Roberts. "Didn't I tell you we'd have trouble with these planes if we used them?"

"All right, Lee, all right," Cox sharply answered, then he turned to Powers. "What on earth is happening here, Colonel? These aircraft are supposed to be operational. They're due to fly a combat mission in about ten hours. What are you doing to them?"

"A few problems cropped up on the flight over," Powers admitted. "You gotta expect these things, Commander. Almost none of these planes were test flown before we came here. My number five ship had to shut down its right engine while en route because of cylinder head temperatures. My number three ship also has engine problems and others have electrical and hydraulic problems."

"If these troubles go uncorrected, how many aircraft will you lose by mission time?"

"Four will be unflyable and two more are marginal."

"Good God, that's half your squadron," said Cox. "If you lose that many, I may have to cancel the whole show."

"Charles, I think you better put a call through to One Hundred Group," Constance advised, "and have them prepare one of their squadrons of Mosquito night fighters for our use."

"Now let's not get all bent out of shape and rush a judgment," said Powers, almost pleading. "Keep your cap on, miss, we're taking care of things. We still got almost eleven hours before we're due to take off. My crews are working on the planes, the Royal Navy loaned us a few mechanics and I've sent word to my home base in Europe to send us a pair of early B-model P-61s. They'll be here in an hour or two."

"And what good will they do?" Roberts asked. "You yourself told us the earlier models can't equal these ships. They don't have top turrets and they don't have the same performance."

"I know, they might not share the same top speed but they have a lot of other things in common." The look of desperation disappeared from his face and Powers allowed a sly smile to take its place. "Such as spare parts. Many of the systems and sub-assemblies on all models are the same. I don't care if we have to strip those planes down to their wing spars, we'll get the parts we need to make this squadron operational."

"I don't see why it wouldn't be easier to send one of your Dakotas to your supply base for spare parts?" asked one of the Royal Navy officers from the original reception committee.

"Because at this stage of the mission we can't afford to waste time," said Cox, answering before Powers could. "The Dak would take two hours to reach the supply base, then we'd have to search for the parts, sign for the parts and load the parts before flying back. The colonel's way is faster, much simpler and we don't have to struggle with Army red tape. Do I have it all, Colonel?"

"You got it, Commander," Powers replied. "It'll be like pulling candies off a Christmas tree."

"Commander, this is the crew of that Army Gooney Bird," said Shannon, pointing to a new group of U.S. Army officers. "They want to know where you'd like them to put the jet wreckage they brought in."

"What did you bring up, Lieutenant?" Cox asked the pilot.

"The tail of an Me-262 and a set of outer wing panels," he answered. "We got them from the warehouse for the Enemy Aircraft Evaluation unit."

"Good, we can store them in this hangar until our own Dakota returns from Boscombe Down. Colonel, have some of your men move the pieces in here."

"OK, we'll get the wreckage inside," said Powers, who motioned for some of his squadron's personnel to go with the C-47 crew. "Could you tell us something more about your commando attack last night? Did Lacey get away to Sweden and what's going on over there?"

"I think Mister Capollini and Martinez could give you a better description of what happened than I can," Cox advised, "and I'm sure they'd enjoy it more. Suffice it to say, the largest manhunt in Scotland's history is being conducted for them and Colonel Lacey. Their 'friend,' Brogger is looking everywhere for them, everywhere but here. He'll never set foot on this base. As for Lacey, he's safely in Sweden and should be working on the Night Hawk. Connie, once the Dakota's been refueled I want you to take it to Boscombe Down and collect the jet fuel Dennis and John Norris need for tonight. Without it, they won't make it out of Sweden."

"Good morning, Mister Norris, Mister Ellis," said Paulson, turning at the sound of the hangar's side door clicking open. "And you must be Colonel Lacey. I'm so glad you could finally make it. How do you like our prize?"

Paulson swept his hand toward the Me-262 as he spoke. It was almost intact, complete except for its antenna-studded nose cap and its left engine pod. Only the upper half of the pod remained attached to the left wing. The lower half lay in several sections on the hangar floor and the Junkers engine they would eventually enclose was being worked on by several technicians. Access panels along the fuselage and wings were open as well, with still more personnel working on whatever lay below them.

"She's taking shape very nicely," Lacey remarked admiringly. "It's almost worth the delays I've had to see her. When will you complete the engine installation and how's the rest of the repairs coming along?"

"Because of the complex nature of the turbojet," said Paulson, "we stopped work on its installation when John Norris left last night. We cannot have him here around the clock. That would arouse too much suspicion, and there's already enough at this base. We had much better luck with the flight controls, hydraulic systems and the weapons.

"The flight controls are rather conventional, using push-pull rods with little power assistance. The hydraulics only operate the flaps, landing gear and brakes. Because of the low capacity of the hydraulic pumps, I'm told operation of the gear and flaps will be slow. The cannons are all operable, we will load them with shells before you depart. For such a revolutionary aircraft, it's a surprisingly conventional one."

"A plane only has to be revolutionary in the way it flies and the equipment it uses to be a threat," said Norris. "Do you have an auxiliary power unit we can use? And have the drop tanks arrived from Malmö?"

"We have a battery cart for you and we managed to locate the right kind of plugs for you to use. The external tanks arrived late last night and we checked them over, they are both in good condition."

The drop tanks sat in front of the Night Hawk, with each strapped to its own cargo pallet. They were smaller than the tanks used by U.S. Army Air Force fighters, were painted dull black instead of being left bare metal but they had the same blunt-nosed, teardrop shape as American tanks.

"We were lucky to receive those," Lindh admitted, pointing at the tanks. "When I left Bulltofta, there were no plans to save them. They would likely have been scrapped, had we not called for them. We also managed to obtain some of the original jet fuel the Night Hawk had when it landed. Once installation is complete, we can test run the engines later today."

"How'd you manage that?" Lacey asked. "A request like that should've aroused somebody's suspicion."

"Not really. We merely told Bulltofta that the Germans had demanded the fuel for when they arrive tomorrow. Twelve hours after you and Commander Norris leave, a team of German specialists is scheduled to arrive and supervise the rebuilding of the Night Hawk."

"If you had been delayed any longer, Colonel, it would have destroyed the operation," said Paulson, who then turned his attention to one of the other new arrivals. "Lieutenant, have you seen the British plans for rescuing MacAlister?"

"Yes, sir," Tallberg replied. "Mister Norris showed me the copy Colonel Lacey brought with him. It's a well-thought-out plan, they appear to have covered every contingency and have tried to make it as small-scale as possible. The same transport that will bring us the fuel and the wreckage will also bring in the commando team. It'll fly the standard air corridor used by regular London-to-Stockholm flights. The approach pattern to Bromma passes very close to Drache's estate. The transport will drop the team, then break off its approach and head here. After the commandoes finish their attack, they must be driven here as well. The British would like us to provide trucks for the trip back."

"The trucks should not be a problem. I can supply them from my base's motor pool and give you reliable drivers. You will forgive me if I'm not as enthusiastic about this plan as you are, Lieutenant. It could end most of our problems and yet could create an even greater disaster. One that would ruin us all."

"Don't underestimate what those SAS guys can do," said Lacey. "I saw them in action last night and they're true professionals. They may just be the best men in the world for the job. Lieutenant Tallberg told us nothing much has happened at the estate since MacAlister and the police agent were captured trying to escape. Have you heard anything new, Wing Commander?"

"Only the latest police report," Paulson offered, turning back to Lacey. "The Drache estate is outwardly quiet. Drache himself has been seen several times, in fact he left the estate today on business. He's trying to continue his activities as if nothing has happened. What time will those commandoes attack his house?"

"About ten o'clock," said Ellis, "if the transport leaves Scapa Flow as scheduled. Colonel Whitney and I will guide it using signal lights. We'll be there with some embassy vehicles. When Ian is freed, we'll drive him back to Stockholm and should anyone be wounded, we'll take them to the nearest hospital. I hope by the time the authorities start asking questions about where wounded British soldiers came from, this jet will be heading out of Sweden."

"Don't worry, she will," Lacey promised. "She may not look flyable now but in a few hours she will be. We'll get her out of Sweden if John and I have to carry her on our backs."

"Mister MacAlister, wake up," urged a gentle, familiar voice. "Ian? Ian, please wake up."

There was the voice but there wasn't the hand prodding, shaking him awake. The first sensation MacAlister felt as he regained consciousness was that he lay on his back. He wasn't tied in a chair, he was lying on a bed, tied to it by his wrists and ankles. He couldn't rub his eye or stretch, the only way MacAlister could wake himself up was to shake his head. Each twist his neck made brought a hot stab of pain from where Ursula had hit him with her probe. After several moments he mumbled a response to the voice urging him awake and raised his head off the pillow.

"Thank God you're all right," said Karen when he looked at her. "Can you tell me where we are? This room is unknown to me. I've never seen it before."

Only when Karen mentioned it did MacAlister become aware of the room they were in. He raised his head as high as he could and glanced around the barren, narrow room. At first MacAlister was unable to recognize where they were, but when he focussed on the radio equipment standing beyond the foot of Karen's bed, he knew where they were.

"We're in the basement," MacAlister finally answered. "We're in the hidden radio room Drache uses to contact his masters. If you've ever wondered why Drache or Ursula would go to the basement on their own, now you know why."

"To think of it, they did go to the basement often. It was not very often but it was regular, and discreet. Many times, I would not notice they were gone. How do you feel?"

"Terrible, I think they must've burned a hole in my neck. And my head's throbbing again. How about you?"

MacAlister raised his head again and looked at Karen. She was bound the same way he was, her wrists and feet were tied to the bedposts by lengths of rope. He noticed the skin on Karen's wrists was raw and bleeding. She had obviously been struggling to free herself before he had come to. Her clothes were dishevelled, her blouse still torn open and her left breast was still exposed.

"It's my neck that hurts the most," said Karen. She shivered as she spoke; the light fabric of her blouse and skirt wasn't very good at keeping out the basement's cold and damp air. "And I wish someone had thought to put a blanket on me. My wrists and ankles hurt as well, these ropes are so tight."

"Shhh, quiet, Karen. I hear something," said MacAlister, waving one of his tied hands at her. When she stopped talking, the faint hum MacAlister heard became a little more distinct. It sounded very far away, outside of the house and probably overhead. "I think that's an aircraft."

With no one talking or moving, the room became unnaturally quiet. MacAlister so tuned his ears to the soft drone he could even hear Karen breathing. He was so concentrated on these faint sounds that, when a key was inserted in the door's lock, the rasping noise and the click of the cylinder being rotated went off like a series of explosions.

The radio room's door swung in and Ursula Brandt entered. She carried with her a tray on which there were two bowls, a small pitcher and other dishes and utensils. Ursula put the tray on the table at the foot of MacAlister's bed and approached the two captives.

"Good morning, Commander, Miss Nilsson," she said, standing between the two beds. "I trust you slept well?"

252

"You should know, you're the one who put us under," MacAlister coolly replied. "You look like a zoo warden surveying his caged animals."

"How well put, Mister MacAlister. Carl told me you did have a gift for words. He regrets that he's not able to be here but he left orders to look after you. It's been so long since you last ate, I bet you're starving."

Ursula turned and went back to the tray she had brought with her. She lifted the pitcher and poured some of its contents into one of the bowls, causing the steam rising off of it to dissipate.

"Where did Carl go?" MacAlister asked. "Off to his phony business or does he have the audacity to meet with the other attachés and ask where I've gone to?"

"He went to the office," said Ursula. She stirred the bowl's contents, then picked it up and walked over to MacAlister. "From there he'll go to the German trade offices where he'll receive complete instructions about what to do with you and Miss Nilsson. Here, open your mouth."

Ursula lifted a spoonful of what looked like oatmeal from the bowl and held it out to MacAlister.

"I'd rather feed myself," he said. "I don't care to be treated as a child. If you'll just undo one of my hands."

"Carl told me to take no risks with either of you. So either open your mouth or you will inhale this."

Reluctantly, MacAlister complied with her demands and had a spoonful of hot cereal shoved into his mouth. It was hot enough to scald his tongue and he started coughing uncontrollably as he swallowed it. In a way it was more painful than the torture he had gone through the night before. It brought tears to MacAlister's eyes.

The sounds he made caused Karen to wince and

hold her breath. She shivered a little when Ursula turned toward her, then sat on the edge of her bed.

"Don't worry, my dear, I'll get to you soon enough," Ursula purred as she smiled an erotic and desiring smile at Karen. "Don't be so afraid of me, dear. You could improve your situation greatly if you warmed up to me and showed a little appreciation of what I can offer you."

"She'd be warmer if she were covered up a little more," said MacAlister, the last of his oatmeal finally down and his coughing fit ended.

"I'm sorry, I didn't realize it was so cold for you in here." Ursula grabbed hold of the torn brassiere cup and pulled it over Karen's exposed breast. As she did so, she ran her fingers around it gently and fondled its nipple. "There now, is that not much better?"

A wave of revulsion swept over Karen. She recoiled from Ursula's touch and to MacAlister she looked as though she was going to throw up. But mixed in with her revulsion and nausea was a growing hatred and when she did open her mouth it was to spit in her tormentor's face.

"I would die first then let you touch me," Karen cried, turning her face away from Ursula.

"Don't worry, my dear, when your interrogation resumes tonight, I may grant you your wish," said Ursula, wiping the spot of saliva off her forehead. "In fact you may beg me to kill you before the night is through. Such a pity, it could have been so different for you."

Ursula moved off of Karen's bed, glowering malevolently at her. Before she returned to force-feeding MacAlister, she gave Karen a quick, hard jab in her abdomen. The blow was almost invisible to MacAlister but Karen's violent reaction was easily seen. Her whole body spasmed and she started to double up, only to have the ropes that bound her feet and hands stop her. She tried turning on her side but again the ropes stopped her. Her first scream was followed by gasps for air and a low moaning. It would be some time before the pain would go away and Karen could breathe normally.

"Fox House Three to Scapa Flow tower, we're turning onto ramp C-Four and have picked up our guide vehicle. Thanks for holding traffic for us, this is Fox House Three, out."

The two P-61s swung off the runway and followed a brightly painted jeep down one of the taxiways that crisscrossed the base. They were led straight to a hangar where a small cluster of officers waited for them. The planes were almost identical to the Black Widows which had landed the day before.

They wore the same coat of black paint as the others, only theirs wasn't quite as glossy and the finish was marred by exhaust stains around the engine booms and mud splatters on the undersurfaces. Beyond that, however, the only real difference was the lack of top turrets on the arriving P-61s, which identified them as the early-model Black Widows which Powers had called for.

The guide jeep broke away from the '61s as they rolled onto the hangar apron. Some of the men waiting for them directed them the rest of the way in and signalled for the planes to shut down their engines once they were parked in front of the hangar.

Their propellers had scarcely windmilled to a halt when those waiting for them swarmed around the huge fighters. Colonel Powers went from one ship to the other, greeting the crews and introducing them to Cox while the rest of the reception group hauled out engine stands, cranes and tool boxes.

"All right, let's start stripping them," Powers ordered, once the formalities were out of the way. "Move that big engine crane out here and more scaffolds. We got work to do."

"And you have approximately seven hours to do it in," said Cox, checking his wrist watch. "That's not a lot of time, especially when you consider you have an engine change to perform. I have the notion you'll still be making repairs when the armorers start loading your guns."

"We probably will but we'll get it done, God damn it, if we have to have mechanics working on my planes up to the moment we start engines. Take the cowling panels off and let the engines cool before working on them, Sergeant. Technical problems won't defeat my squadron, Mister Cox. Damn it, these ships cost more than a B-17 or a B-24. The only warbird that costs more than a Black Widow is a Boeing Superfortress and I'm not going to let some nineteen-cent part ground one. By the way, where's Captain Roberts? I thought he'd be out here with you, complaining about my airplanes again."

"Fortunately, he has more important work to do than complain. Lee's briefing his men on tonight's assault. They're pouring over those house plans we received from Sweden, trying to figure out where Ian might be kept or where the spy might've built a secret room. By the time they leave tonight, they'll know that home as well as its owners."

"What time do you expect your Dakota to return?" Powers asked, checking his wrist watch.

"I expect it back in another hour and a half," said Cox. "It should've left Boscombe Down about forty minutes ago. The moment it lands, I'll have the Dak inspected. We've made heavy use of it in the last several days and I want to make sure it's in good condition for this, the most critical part of our operation. The last thing we need now is a vital airplane going unserviceable when we need it the most. It's one disaster we can't afford to have."

The engine cowling panels came off the P-61s as Powers had earlier ordered. Scaffolding was erected around the engine booms and a fuel truck drove up to each recently arrived fighter. Instead of filling their tanks, they started draining them, siphoning out whatever gasoline remained. Oil drip pans were set under the engines and hydraulic fluid lines were shut off as mechanics and flight crews began stripping the parts they needed to make their aircraft operational.

"Men, this is Herr Lossberg. Our regional Gestapo commander," said the SS colonel who originally called the meeting to order. "Since he knows the situation best, I have asked him to explain what the target of our mission is and where it's located. Herr Lossberg?"

The colonel relinquished the podium to Lossberg as he walked across the stage from his seat. Lossberg glanced at the small contingent of SS troops he'd be lecturing, then at the map of Sweden standing behind the podium. When he reached it, he grabbed the pointer leaning against it.

"The Reich is caught in a grave crisis," he began, staring solemnly at the men in front of him. "The prototype of our most advanced jet fighter was forced to land in Sweden some days ago, at an airfield of this city. The Swedish authorities moved it to an internment and storage base south of Stockholm called Norrköping."

Lossberg raised his pointer and tapped it on

Malmö, directly across the narrow strait from Copenhagen. Then he ran it up the Swedish peninsula, stopping at a red circle drawn at the end of a long fjord some distance below Stockholm.

"This is where the Swedes store some of the foreign aircraft which come down in their country. After hard and serious negotiations, I'm pleased to tell you they have agreed to return the jet to the Reich. But we have strong reasons to believe that the Allies may attempt to either examine the jet or even destroy it. They tried to learn its secrets earlier and failed, I don't believe they are yet finished. While Sweden has promised to protect the jet, Berlin does not believe it's safe. Which is why you are being sent in.

"You are to protect the aircraft from any attempts at espionage or sabotage. It's likely that the Allies will attempt one or the other in the final hours before a Luftwaffe repair crew is scheduled to arrive at Norrköping. It's possible that some Swedish air force personnel may help the Allies destroy the jet. Three days ago an unfortunate accident occurred, perhaps you heard about it. A Swedish air liner violated one of our security zones and was shot down by our fighters. Because of resentment over this accident, some Swedes are probably willing to aid the British and the Americans in whatever schemes they are planning.

"Latest reports say the jet is still dismantled and sitting on two long-bed trailers, next to other interned aircraft. The trailers are protected by canvas covers and are under heavy guard by base security, so they should be easy to spot when you land. How you'll arrive at Norrköping will be explained by your commander. I'm not concerned about that, I'm concerned about what happens after you arrive. Though the Swedes will not be expecting you, they will allow your aircraft to land. Once on the ground your mission is to reach the jet any way you can and supplant the Swedes guarding it.

"You are not to initiate any fighting with them, only return their fire should they oppose you. You are not to capture or destroy any other interned aircraft, no matter how tempting they might be. You must not occupy any section or portion of the air base and, should fighting break out, you are not to damage it. We do not wish war with Sweden, what we want is our aircraft protected. Remember this at all times.

"It is possible, very possible, that you may not return from this mission. It's a sacrifice any loyal soldier of the Fatherland should be willing to make and being a prisoner of the Swedes isn't as bad as being a prisoner of the Russians. Should the worst happen, should the Swedes force a fight and try to capture you, then you must escape. If you succeed, there are several safe houses in the area you can make for. We even have some in the Stockholm area should you make it as far as the city."

Lossberg tapped his pointer on a cluster of marks around Norrköping and more in the Stockholm area, the last of which was Carl Drache's estate.

"Under no circumstances are you to reveal the addresses that will be given to you later. You are not to reveal this briefing or any of the instructions you will receive. This briefing has not happened, you have not met me and you know little of the aircraft you're to protect. Herr Oberst, the meeting is yours. I suggest you call Oberstleutnant Heinrich next, to explain the jet to your men."

As Lossberg took his seat, Heinrich replaced him at the podium. He explained to the assembled squad what the Night Hawk was, what it could do and

As Lossberg took his seat, Heinrich replaced him at the podium. He explained to the assembled squad what the Night Hawk was, what it could do and what it would mean to Germany to have it back. Heinrich showed them photographs and a diagram of the jet, and told his small audience how it may have been dismantled for shipping, so they would know what to expect when the trailers were uncovered. The SS officer who had started the meeting told his men the time of their final briefing and when their plane would take off. He thanked Lossberg and Heinrich for appearing and ended the meeting. Only when they were being driven back to Kastrup airfield, outside of Copenhagen, did they talk openly to each other.

"An unfortunate accident?" Heinrich asked sarcastically, his venom coming to the surface. "By now every military man in Denmark knows the downing was deliberate. I don't care for the SS, they are more like you than me, but they are military enough for me to respect them and you should've admitted the truth back there. They deserved it, so they could properly handle the Swedes when they confront them."

"A minor point, Kommandeur," Lossberg blandly replied. "Of no consequence to the overall operation."

"To you, maybe, but not to me. Those men may die on this folly of yours. You're trusting them to protect the most advanced fighter in the Luftwaffe, the world even, and you were not honest with them. Tell me, were you as honest with the commandoes and the U-boat crew before you sent them to their deaths or imprisonment?"

"Enough, Heinrich!" Lossberg's uncaring tone suddenly became sharper and angrier. "I'm growing tired of your 'I'm a warrior and superior to me' argument.

260

I command this operation, not you. You're only a part of it and you will do as I order. I don't care about your concerns. I have more important matters to worry about. Return to your base and wait for me. After the SS team leaves, I'll be down. If the Allies try to attack the jet tonight, you might have to be the one to stop them."

"OK, let's go through this one more time," said Roberts, snatching the diagram of Drache's estate off its easel. He took it to the edge of the briefing room's stage and placed it at his feet. Using his pointer, he started tapping sections of the diagram. "From the top. Step one?"

"We parachute in and regroup," responded all the members of his squad in a clear, simultaneous shout.

"Step two?"

"We clear the ground of outside guards and move in on the house."

"Step three?"

"Take our positions and wire the house like a Christmas tree."

"Step four?"

"We set off the fireworks and waltz in."

"Step five?"

"Kill anyone who doesn't look friendly and search for those who are."

"Step six?"

"Rescue our friends and see them off."

"Step seven?"

"Wait for our taxi ride and rejoin our flight."

"And step eight?"

"Fly home and celebrate."

When they reached the end of their recital, the squad let out a cheer and Roberts tossed away the diagram.

"Would you like to say anything to them, Commander?" he asked, turning to Cox.

"Yes, I have a few words," said Cox, getting out of his chair and joining Roberts on the stage. As he did so, the small audience quickly quieted down. "I've already seen you perform, I know how good you are. You're the best, but now your objective is a far more serious one. You didn't foul it up the last time, you had better not foul it this time. If you do, you may die, the people you're out to rescue will die, our friends in Sweden will be arrested for treason and Sweden itself may declare war on the Allies. What you're doing is vital to the war, you're a small group of men with the potential to change its course. I know of no one better or more capable for the job. Good luck to all of you."

Once Cox had ended the briefing, Roberts collected his men and led them to a squadron ready hut near their heavily guarded hangar. Inside the hut all their gear and weapons were waiting for them; each man's own specific equipment was arranged in a neat pile. Cox and Constance were driven from the briefing hall to the hangar, where they found the Dakota being readed for take-off.

"Remove the covers from the engines and propeller hubs," Capollini ordered. "Roll up these hoses and get the heaters out of here. We'll be bringing in an APU in a minute."

"Captain, I've heard you volunteer to be the jump master and the relief pilot for this crew?" said Cox, stepping up to Capollini and giving him a quick salute. "I hope you understand it really wasn't necessary for you to do so."

"I know, but I ain't about to get left out of this party. There aren't anymore spots on the P-61s I can volunteer for and besides, you've been working these R.A.F. guys pretty hard, Commander. The plane got a few gallons of oil and some maintenance work, but its crew hasn't had a chance to rest. They've been flying since early this morning, so they need a relief pilot. It ain't going to do you much good to have a plane in good condition but a crew that's bone-tired."

"I quite agree. If there weren't such a demand for transports I'd use another and let this crew have a rest. However, neither the Royal Air Force nor the U.S. Ninth Air Force can spare another ship, so I'm forced to make do with what's available. Have you had any flight time on a Dak, Captain? And have you ever been a jump master before?"

"Sure, every bomber pilot has had a few hours on Gooney Birds. In the Twelfth Air Force, I even flew a few combat missions with a C-47 group when they were short of pilots. As for being a jump master, well, I never did it but I've seen it done. All you gotta do is make sure everyone goes then haul in the rip cords. Excuse me, Commander, I have to help these guys."

Capollini broke away to help the ground crew unsnap the insulated covers surrounding the Dakota's engine nacelles and propeller hubs. As they came off they had to be uncoupled from the duct hoses and folded before Capollini stored them in the transport's accessory compartment. Cox and Constance watched the crew pack up the external heating carts for a few moments, then the pilot and the rest of the flight crew arrived to take charge of their plane.

"As you can see, we have the wreckage on board and the drums of jet fuel are well secured," said the pilot, opening the Dakota's side hatch and letting Cox and Constance peer inside. "With your commandoes it'll be rather cramped in the main cabin.

You're lucky you don't have more than you do. Otherwise, I don't think I could carry everything."

"With full fuel tanks, it looks like you're going to have a maximum load," Cox observed. "If I were you, I'd use the longest runway this base has to offer."

"With this blasted wind it's not the take-off roll I'm worried about. All I have to do is fly into the teeth of it and I'm off. I wonder about this load shifting on me and throwing around my center of gravity. Will those commandoes stay where I tell them to?"

"Don't worry, they'll obey orders. You make sure you obey instructions as well. Stay inside your air corridor even after you cross the Swedish coast line. Swedish gunners are nearly as efficient as their German counterparts in firing on wayward aircraft."

"We will," said the pilot. "I promise you. This airplane has been through too much to end up shot down in a neutral country. I made sure my navigator has the right charts and the routes are clearly marked. We'll make it to Sweden, Commander. And thank you for letting Captain Capollini volunteer for my crew. We really do need him."

"I know, it's been a long day for you," said Cox, "and this is only the beginning of your mission. It's asking a lot of your men, I realize, but I have no other choice."

"Believe me, I understand. During Operation Market Garden we flew two, sometimes three, missions a day and it was all for nothing. Here at least, we know we're making a difference in the war. Goodbye, Commander, wish us luck."

Cox had barely finished saying farewell to the Dakota's flight crew when a truck drove onto the hangar apron and approached the transport. It pulled to a stop on its left side, and over the tailgate poured the Special Air Service squad. Now they came wearing their equipment packs, parachutes and weapons. Though they also wore American-style helmets, each commando had a beige beret tucked in his parachute harness. Except for their helmets, berets and parachutes, everything the squad wore was black. And except for the SAS badges on their berets, they wore no other insignia or markings. As his men filed on board the Dakota, Roberts talked with Cox one last time.

"Have any final words for me, Commander?" Roberts asked.

"Yes, I do," Cox admitted, lowering his voice. "If for some reason the Night Hawk is unable to fly tonight, I want you to perform the mission I originally had in mind for you. Don't let the Nazis have it if we can't. Destroy the jet if you have to, Lee. Again, good luck."

"Vincent? When you see Dennis, tell him that I miss him," said Constance, after Capollini was finished connecting the auxiliary power unit to the transport. "And I'll be waiting for him when he returns."

"You bet I will," Capollini replied. "That'll probably be the first thing the colonel will ask me when he sees me. I'll tell him anything you want me to, just don't ask me to kiss him."

Constance gave Capollini a quick hug, almost smothering his short, wiry frame, before the Dakota's pilot called for him to board the plane. She let him go and joined Cox as he moved off to the left side of the transport. They stood just beyond its left wing tip, in direct line of sight with the cockpit. They watched the pilot and co-pilot take their seats and run through the checklists.

"I wish I were going with them," Constance admitted. "I don't see why I can't. Sweden isn't classified as

"As I told you before, Connie, no," said Cox, giving his response a firm note of finality. "You managed to sneak aboard the first mission, I won't let you do it this time. I won't have you giving Dennis one more thing to worry about. He'll have quite enough on his mind tonight. Anyway, what I've assigned you to do here is important. You have to prepare this base to receive the Night Hawk."

"You gave me what Dennis would call a 'make work' assignment. Something to occupy my time and attention, like sending me down to pick up the jet fuel. I'm grateful for them, I know they're important, but they're not with Dennis. They can't help how lonely I feel without him."

The pilot signalled to the ground crew to clear the left engine and prepare the fire extinguishers. A brief whine heralded the start of the Pratt and Whitney radial. Its propeller ticked over once before clouds of smoke poured from its exhaust stacks and its cowling shook visibly. When they were sure the engine wouldn't catch fire, the ground crew moved the fire extinguishers to the opposite side of the transport, to cover the second radial until it started.

"We got most of our problems fixed, Commander," Powers announced, joining Cox and Constance on the flight line. "At least they look fixed. We have to test the engines to make sure. We'll begin towing out the Widows as soon as these guys leave."

With its second Twin Wasp started and running smoothly, the Dakota quivered with life. The ground crew disconnected the auxiliary power unit from it and removed the wheel chocks from the landing gear, handing them to Capollini as he closed the side hatch. For a few moments the transport sat idling, waiting for the tower to give it clearance to taxi.

Then, with a wave from its pilot, the Dakota rolled

forward, leaving the flight line and moving down to a taxiway. It joined the rest of the traffic departing Scapa Flow's other transports on supply missions, fighters and bombers going out on patrols or training flights. When a pair of Fleet Air Arm Wildcats tore off the runway, D for Duncan swung onto it. Since the Dakota had already completed its engine and magneto tests while waiting for the other planes to leave, all it did was align itself on the center line and open its throttles.

The transport waddled at the start of its take-off roll. A crosswind caused it to drift to the runway's left side, before the pilot added a little power to the right engine to correct the drift. At sixty miles an hour the plane's tail came off the ground, giving the pilots full rudder control. At eighty they could feel lift filling its wings and at just over a hundred miles an hour the Dakota skipped once on its main gear and lifted into the darkening sky.

With its weight edging near its design maximum, the Douglas climbed slowly but steadily. It chased the stubby Grumman fighters out over Deer Sound where it retracted its flaps and landing gear. The Wildcats soon turned north but the transport continued due east, gaining altitude sedately. In minutes only its navigation lights were visible against a black horizon. By that time the heavily guarded hangar it had sat in front of had opened and the mystery squadron was appearing once again. The P-61s were towed out to the flight line one at a time where they would be tested, then armed and fueled. The operation had begun.

"Good evening, Herr Drache, did business go well?" Ursula inquired, meeting Drache in the estate's foyer.

"Yes, quite well. Most revealing," he replied as he handed his overcoat and hat to his butler. "Let's go to the study, my dear. I need you to take a few letters."

Drache grabbed hold of a briefcase he had temporarily laid on a table and escorted Ursula to his study where he ordered the maid to leave and to close the doors behind her. Only when they clicked shut did he feel safe enough to tell Ursula what he had learned.

"For the time being, I want this kept secret from even our own men on the estate," he said. "Mister MacAlister is a very valuable man. Both the Gestapo and the Abhwere want him in Germany and they're making plans to move him. Our agents in Stockholm will help us do the move and are also planning to fake his death. I have all the information here. You can read it during dinner."

"He must be valuable," Ursula remarked, "for them to go through this trouble. Will we have another chance to interrogate him? And what's to be done with Karen Nilsson?"

"We'll have another chance to interrogate him tonight, after dinner. There's much in here I'd like to ask him about." Drache opened his briefcase and pulled out a folder, the only marking on which was a Nazi eagle. "When he arrives in Germany, he'll have much to answer for. By early tomorrow morning our Stockholm people will be here to remove him. As for Miss Nilsson, she's expendable. We're to kill her as part of MacAlister's cover death. She will be of use to us, in a posthumous sort of way."

Chapter Eleven: The Last Interrogation
Arrival In Sweden

"OK, that's all of it," said Lacey, fastening down the tank cap in front of the Night Hawk's cockpit. "All the jet fuel is in the forward tank. Tell the squadron leader to bring in the tug. We're ready for the test."

The sergeant Lacey was talking to left the now-open hangar and returned with a tow tug, which backed up to the finally completed jet. A tow bar was attached to its nose gear strut and, with Lacey walking beside it, the Me-262 slowly emerged from its hiding place.

Its exterior was immaculate, the wings and fuselage had been successfully remated and the lines of bullet holes in its port engine pod, wing and nose were covered with small, riveted discs. The oil stains and grime had been cleaned off the plane's surface and a thin layer of polish caused it to glisten softly in the hangar lights. It was an expert job, the Night Hawk was nearly as perfect as the day it had rolled out of the Messerschmitt factory at Oberammergau.

"Apart from the repairs, she looks exactly the way she did when I first saw her," Lindh observed, joining

Lacey as he paced the jet fighter. "We did a good job putting her together."

"Yes, on the outside she looks fine," said Lacey. "But this is the real test. Now we'll see if we got everything on the inside working right. If we haven't, it'll be panic time."

Once it cleared the hangar, the jet was turned to the right and moved toward the rows of other foreign aircraft. In addition to Lacey and Lindh, Wing Commander Ellis accompanied the Night Hawk, and Norris was already sitting in its cockpit. The Swedish crew that had worked under their direction trailed behind it, at last able to admire their handiwork.

When the jet came to a stop, it was sitting in the lane between the rows of fighters in front of the hangars and the bombers on the opposite side of the tarmac. Except for those working in the collection, no one at the base could see the night fighter. While it was being hooked up to an external battery cart, a number of other planes were also connected to battery carts.

"We will test run the engines of several fighters," said Lindh. "This should help hide the sound of our jet, and Wing Commander Paulson told me it's a normal procedure at this base. No one should notice it. I would suggest that we start the propeller aircraft first, then the jet."

"OK, and when we do I'd suggest that you keep everyone at least seven feet away from the jet engine intakes," Lacey advised, "and at least twenty-five feet from the exhausts. We don't want anyone getting sucked in by the air flow or burned by the exhausts. In addition, no one's to stand directly in front of the plane for at least fifty feet. Since we're also going to test its radar gear, I don't want anybody getting 'cooked' by it. There've been a lot of accidents with

270

radar and we have no idea how powerful the Night Hawk's intercept system is."

In addition to clearing all personnel from in front of the jet, the tarmac was also swept for any loose items. At this stage they could not afford engine damage due to foreign object ingestion either. It was still being prepared for its test when the first of the other interned fighters was started.

One by one the line of Mustangs turned over their engines. Clouds of smoke drifted back to their tails and their propellers became soft blurs. The Spitfires scattered through the collection joined in as well; by then the Night Hawk had been connected to its battery cart, its wheels were blocked, its brakes set and Norris reported all systems working properly.

"I've finished the pre-start checks," he continued, "and I've set the fuel selector valves for both engines on the main forward tank. It's time for you to get on board, Dennis."

"I'm coming," said Lacey, slipping his fingers inside the fuselage hand holds. "Squadron leader, make sure you keep everyone away from the plane's tail."

Lacey climbed up the left side of the Night Hawk and first swung one leg, then the rest of his body, into the second seat in its cockpit. He didn't bother to connect his seat belt or shoulder harness, though he did accept a flight helmet and plugged in its microphone leads. The men that had gathered around the Me-262 now pulled back from it. Almost all of them withdrew to the rows of interned airplanes, just a few remained near it and even they stayed clear of the jet engine pods and radar aerials.

"Batteries, inverter and generators are all on," Norris reported. "The throttles are closed, I'm ready to start. How's your equipment?"

"Switched on and warming up," said Lacey. "We'll

have to wait until the generators are running properly to give everything a good test. I'm ready back here."

"All right, here goes. Keep your canopy open, Dennis. If something fucks up, at least we'll have half a chance to jump out before it explodes. Opening throttle."

Norris pushed the right hand throttle forward and held it down briefly, priming the Riedel starting motor for the starboard engine. A high-pitched whine grew out of its nacelle, the first sign of life from the Night Hawk since it landed at Bulltofta six days ago. Norris pulled the throttle back to its closed position as he pressed the tachometer button on the other side of the cockpit.

The starboard engine's tachometer registered an immediate jump from zero to fifty rpm. In moments, after it had climbed to seven hundred rpm, Norris pushed in the starter button on the right hand throttle. The whine of the Riedel motor was drowned out by a deep, throbbing rumble which also grew from the nacelle. The jet engine was igniting, its compressor fan drawing in air, its burners firing up. At the same instant Lindh signalled for the Mustangs and Spitfires in the collection to gun their engines. All the idling Merlins let out an extra burst of thunder, effectively masking the scream of the Night Hawk.

"Right engine rpm is holding steady at two thousand," said Norris, scanning his instrument panel. "All pressures and temps are normal. Advancing throttle."

Norris edged the right throttle forward until the tachometer needle quivered at around three thousand rpm. Assured of a good start, he released the throttle's ignition button and began repeating the same procedures to start the port engine. Norris pushed down the left hand throttle and pulled it back, activating the Riedel motor.

This time the whine of the motor was drowned under the roar of the right engine and the thunder from the nearby Merlins. Norris had to rely on his instruments to tell him it was running and, most especially, on the second tachometer to tell him when the left engine was ready to start.

As he hit the throttle-mounted ignition button another deep rumble shook the fighter. The left engine fired up, emitting a long tongue of flame for a few moments. The flame generated a sharp bang like the firing of an artillery piece and it briefly registered above the prevailing thunder. Apart from the fireworks, the left engine started successfully and Norris quickly had it idling with the right one.

"I'm switching all my systems to internal power," Lacey advised, tapping a row of toggle switches beside his seat. "Let's see how they work on their own. How are you doing?"

"I'm increasing power to eight thousand rpm," said Norris. "Let's get this testing over and done with fast. We don't have a lot of gas to waste."

Norris pushed both throttles to their gatestops, increasing the engines to full power. The jet waddled slightly under the dramatically increased thrust. If it weren't for the wheel chocks it would have moved forward, even with its parking brakes set. Once at full power, Norris glanced over his shoulders to check the engine exhaust pipes and see if their needle valves had fully extended.

Lacey concentrated on the radar scopes and indicator panels at his station. He checked to make sure they operated properly in whatever mode he set them. It took him just a few minutes to run through the tests he had hastily devised; so far as he could tell, the systems were working.

"I got a lot of ground clutter on the scopes," said Lacey, "and the landing aids don't have any ground station to work off of, but to the best of my knowledge it's all fine."

"OK, everything up here looks fine," said Norris, "at least from what I remember of the single-seater. I'm shutting down the engines. We've burned most of our fuel already. Switch off your gear now, Dennis, let's not take any chances on weakening the batteries."

As Norris retarded the throttles, he pressed in their ignition buttons. The scream of the engines trailed off and the cone-shaped needle valves retracted back inside the exhaust nozzles, but the sound and the hot gas plumes didn't die out until Norris closed both the throttles and the fuel selector valves. With a final spurt of flame from each engine, the Night Hawk was shut down. The only activity on what had been a furiously howling aircraft was residual fuel draining from the dump valves.

"You were right to have warned me about the engine exhaust, Colonel," Lindh admitted as he climbed up the jet's side. "That flame must have been twenty feet long. I hope it didn't attract much attention. Now that the test is over, what must we do?"

"Push us back into the hangar," said Lacey. "We have to keep this plane hidden until we fly it out. When the engines have cooled they should be wiped down, cleaned of any fuel. Especially around the exhausts. Do you want to climb out, John?"

"No, let's stay here until the plane is indoors," Norris suggested. "I'd like to make sure that the exhaust nozzles cool properly. And besides, we still got warm air flowing through the vents. Why should we freeze if we don't have to?"

With the test at an end, there was no longer any

need for the other fighters to continue running. The Mustangs and Spitfires were shut down as the tug was brought back and rehooked to the Me-262's nose gear. After the battery cart was disconnected, the jet was pushed out of the collection and swung into the hangar where it had been hiding for the last three days. If all went well, it would only have to hide for a few hours more.

"There, does anyone else have a question?" Powers asked, scanning his assembled flight crews and grateful not to see another hand being raised. "Good, because we're running late and I don't have the time to answer anymore. Commander, do you have anything you'd like to say before the briefing ends?"

"Yes, I have a few words for your men," said Cox as he got out of his front row seat and stood beside Powers. "None of you should underestimate the value of this jet aircraft. It's the only existing prototype of the Nazi's latest night fighter, it could tell us all we need to know about their newest radar equipment and jet technology. This is the most valuable acquisition we've made since a Ju-88 night fighter landed in England last year. It could well be the most important one of the war. Possession of the Night Hawk will save the lives of countless bomber crews, and the Royal Air Force's contribution to the strategic bombing campaign. This escort mission will be the most important you'll fly in this war; it could easily mean the difference between winning and losing it. You're flying the finest night fighter we have and your colonel says you're the best squadron in Europe. Give us the best performance you can and good luck to you all."

Powers closed the briefing by wishing his men luck

as well and then they came to attention as he, Cox and Martinez left the room. They climbed into the first truck of a convoy that had been waiting at the briefing room's door. The rest of the squadron followed them out and they were all driven to a ready hut where they suited up. Constance was waiting in the hut for Cox. She handed him the latest reports from Sweden and a radar station in the eastern Orkneys, which had been tracking the Dakota.

"They lost it as it entered the Skagerak," she explained. "That's the strait which runs between Denmark and Norway. The station says we shouldn't worry though, the entrance to the Skagerak is the limit of their radar coverage."

"I see, and since this report is more than twenty minutes old, the Dak should already be in Sweden," said Cox, closing the folder. "If everything's gone well. Colonel, would you like to see these?"

"No, thanks, you can tell me about them once we're airborne," Powers answered. "We're still running late, Commander. Let's get going."

The same trucks drove the night fighter crews out to the flight line where their P-61s awaited them. For the first time since they had arrived at Scapa Flow, the Black Widows were out of the hangar. They stood on the same spot on the apron where the Dakota had been earlier, all arrayed in a neat row. Their underwing racks were loaded with drop tanks; their bellies were being filled with cannon shells. Royal Marine guards stood around the apron, allowing only those who had to service the fighters past them. Inside the nearly empty hangar stood the two early-model P-61s that had flown in a few hours before. Picked clean of usable spare parts, they were indeed barely standing. Most of their propellers were gone, one didn't even have engines; their nose gear struts and some of their main gear legs were missing, replaced with jack stands. The stripped fighters made a forlorn sight, though a necessary one. Because of them, the squadron was at last operational.

"All planes have full gas and ammunition loads," the chief mechanic told Powers when he jumped out of the convoy's lead truck. "The twenties have two hundred and fifty rounds per gun and the fifties have five hundred and sixty. The ammo mix is armor-piercing incendiary, high-explosive and tracer, just like you wanted. The Brits have given us battery carts for all our planes, we'll have no problems getting you off the ground."

"The problem will be keeping us in the air," said Powers, surveying his squadron. "I hope we can keep the abort rate low. C'mon, let's do the ground check, Commander."

As the rest of the fighter crews spilled out of the trucks which brought them to the flight line, Powers, Cox and Martinez did the external check of their P-61. They walked around the airplane, making sure the wheel chocks were in place, that the covers had been removed from the pitot tubes and air ducts, that the nose gear and main gear air tanks had the right pressures and the control surfaces were in good condition and free of snow and ice. When he had finished his part of the check, Martinez opened a hatch under the rear of the P-61's fuselage and climbed inside his compartment. As they finished their part, Cox and Powers made their way forward where Constance was waiting for them.

"I don't suppose you'll be needing a wireless operator?" she asked Cox, though she already knew the answer.

"Sorry, Lieutenant Martinez takes care of those duties as well," said Cox, "and you know what Dennis would do to me if I let you on this mission. This time you won't be sneaking on board our aircraft. As big as it is, there just isn't any room on this one to hide."

"I'll worry about you and Dennis. I almost wish I didn't have to go through these next few hours. The waiting will be terrible and your make-work assignment won't help alleviate it. Please take care of yourself and watch out for Dennis. I made Vince promise he'd take care of him while they're in Sweden, I want you to promise you'll watch him the rest of the way home."

"Since he's flying in the most important aircraft in the world, that will be an easy promise. I'll try to have him back soon, Connie, you can be sure of that."

Constance gave Cox a quick hug and a kiss. Neither was as long or as passionate as the ones she had shared with Lacey. This wasn't the parting of lovers but of friends. When he released her, Constance moved to the trucks. Inside one of their cabs it would at least be warm, and Cox walked over to the Black Widow's nose gear well.

"Watch your head," Powers warned, unlocking the access door in the roof of the well. It fell open in front of Cox and the ladder deployed automatically. "Be careful as you climb in, you might snag your parachute on one of the sides. This is a narrow fit."

Powers put his foot on the ladder's lowermost rung and boosted himself into the Black Widow. Cox waited under the hatch and made sure he was clear before entering it. Unlike previous times when he boarded the aircraft, Cox found the entrance more difficult to negotiate. Powers had been right. His parachute, Mae West and heated flying suit had all combined to make Cox far bulkier than he was. He could feel his suit scrape against the sides of the hatch and part of his Mae West got caught on the ladder. Once inside, Cox worked his way back to the gunner's station.

"Don't worry about the entrance hatch," said Powers. "The crew chief will take care of it. Get yourself hooked up to the oxygen and interphone system, Commander, and don't forget to plug in your flying suit."

Cox first elected to connect his seat belt and harness before tackling what Powers had advised him to do. When he finally plugged his headphones into the jack box, he could hear Powers running through his pre-start checks.

"Flight control lock, off. Ignition switches, off. Master battery switch, off. Generators, on. Parking brakes, on. Accumulator pressure, four hundred psi. Air brake pressure, four twenty-five psi. Oxygen pressure, four twenty-five. Full de-icer fluid tanks. Armament switches, off and saftied. Gun sight, off. Altimeter, set. Communications gear —"

"Your intercom system works fine, Colonel," said Cox. "Perhaps next time you won't leave the channel open."

"Commander, is that you?" Powers asked, startled. "Sorry, but since you're on the line, break out your night goggles. I'm going to test the exterior lights. Pilot to radar operator, break out your goggles for light test."

Cox slipped a pair of red-tinted goggles over his eyes, just moments before the intense glare of the P-61's landing lamps was thrown across the tarmac. A few seconds later the position lights on the wing tips and rudders sparkled briefly, followed by the recognition lights and the taxi lights. The same test was carried out by the other Black Widows in the flight line, their exterior lights coming on for several seconds as their pilots ran through their own checklists. At the end of the test, Powers ordered Cox and Martinez to switch on their fluorescent lights.

"Fluorescent tubes, on," said Cox, adjusting the controls at his station until it was illuminated by a dim, bluish glow. "I'm removing my goggles. What next?"

"As soon as Andy reports in on his equipment tests," said Powers, "we'll do the engine start sequence. If our radar is on the fritz, we won't make a very good night fighter and we'll be forced to abort the mission. My exec will take command of the squadron."

It took nearly a minute for Martinez to answer Powers's and Cox's requests. His equipment, both radar and radio systems, was operating perfectly. Powers then handed Cox one of the cards from his checklist case.

"On the old, turretless ships I used to have the crew chief run through the engine start list with me," he explained. "Since you're on board, you can help me."

"All right, let me see this," said Cox, studying the card. "Seems fairly typical. Except for this bit about water injection. When do you wish to begin?"

"Well, the more you wait, the farther behind schedule we'll be. The ground crew has already rotated the props."

"Very well, ignition switches?"

"Master ignition, off. Left and right ignition, off."

"Water injection, switch?"

"Water injection, off."

"Generator panel?"

"All circuit breakers off except for suit heaters."

"Turret circuit breakers?"

"Turret circuit breakers, off."

"Generator switches?"

"Generators, on."

"Throttles?"

"Left throttle open a crack. Right throttle, closed."

"Propeller governors?"

"Prop governors on full rpm."

"Propeller switches?"

"Prop switches, on automatic."

"Auxiliary blower?"

"Blower, neutral."

"Oil cooler doors?"

"Oil coolers, automatic."

"Intercooler doors?"

"Intercoolers, closed."

"Carburetor air heat and cleaner?"

"Carburetor heat, off. Air cleaner, off."

"Upper and lower cowl gills?"

"Gills?" Powers asked. "You must mean flaps. I wish you Brits would use the right terms. Top and bottom cowl flaps, open."

"Fuel selector switches?"

"Fuel selectors on outboard tanks."

"Fuel cross-feed valve?"

"Cross-feed valve, off."

"Master battery switch?"

"Batteries, off."

"Mixture controls?"

"Mixtures on idle cut-off."

"Master ignition switch?"

"Master ignition, on."

"Individual ignition switches?"

"Left ignition, off. Right ignition, off. OK, Commander, that's it, check complete," said Powers, reaching back for the card which Cox was just able to slip into his hand. "All I have to do is start her.

Stand by left engine!"

Powers shouted his last words out his cockpit window to the ground crew manning the fire extinguisher and the battery cart. He then flipped on the left-hand starter switch and held it down for half a minute, causing a whine to grow rapidly inside the port engine. When Powers changed the switch to its Mesh position, the propeller began to move. As it completed its first revolutions, he pushed the left ignition switch to Both and tapped the primer switch.

The engine caught partway through the propeller's second revolution. The cowling rattled as jets of flame and smoke shot out the exhaust stacks. Powers advanced the engine's mixture control lever to a much richer setting as he disengaged the primer switch. When he pushed its throttle open the engine responded with a deep, full roar and the propeller blasted away the cloud of smoke which had enveloped the engine and boom. Powers released the starting switch once he had the engine idling properly and turned his attention to the other one.

His engine firing up was almost a signal to the rest of the aircraft in his squadron to start theirs. For the next several minutes the flight line was filled with the sounds of Pratt and Whitney Double Wasps coming to life. In the dim illumination from the hangar spotlights and taxiway perimeter lights, the initial clouds of smoke the engines ejected could be seen drifting across the apron. The massive, paddle-bladed Curtiss Electric propellers became faintly shimmering discs of whirling metal.

None of the two dozen radials balked or backfired as they were started up. They purred a smooth, muted thunder while they warmed up and the pilots checked their operation.

"Fuel booster pumps, on. Master battery switch,

on, and we've been disconnected from the battery cart," said Powers, acknowledging the hand signals from the ground crew. "We're ready to roll. Scapa Flow tower, this is Osprey One. Request permission to taxi to the runway."

"Scapa Flow tower to Osprey One, you and your squadron are clear to taxi. We're holding all traffic for your departure. None of your ships need make any further transmissions, apart from informing us when they're ready to take off."

Powers waited for the ground crew to remove the wheel chocks before he released the parking brakes. Even at idling speed, the propellers made enough thrust to start the P-61 rolling. Powers switched on his position and taxi lamps, transforming his fighter from a nearly formless black mass to a collection of lights. It moved out of its position on the flight line, advancing a few yards and then swinging to the right. As it turned, Cox looked over his shoulder at the convoy of trucks which had brought the crews to their planes.

They still sat in front of the hangar where the squadron had been housed. In the cab of one of the trucks, Cox didn't know which one, sat Constance. He tried to locate her, peering intently at each vehicle in the convoy, but failed to see anyone or any movement in them. Finally, all he could do was wave forlornly at them as Powers taxied their aircraft down the flight line.

When they passed the squadron's second Black Widow it too activated the taxi lights on its nose gear strut and began moving. Each succeeding P-61 waited until the one ahead of it had rolled by before moving out of its own space. By the time Powers was on the taxiway, the rest of his squadron was strung out behind him.

When he reached the runway, he switched off the nose gear lights and turned on the more powerful landing lamps. Their beams penetrated much farther into the night than had the weaker ones, revealing an empty runway and intersecting strips. The tower had indeed held up all other traffic on the base for the night fighters.

Powers relocked the parking brakes and ran through the final ritual of tests before take-off. He tested the engine magnetoes, the auxiliary blowers, propellers, auto pilot and the water injection system. When he was sure all the temperature, pressure and tachometer readings were within their operating ranges, he called out for the other two members of his crew to read off their own checklists.

"Gunner's station locked in take-off position," Cox reported. "Gun sight stowed and locked. Turret controls, off. Turret guns are locked forward and at zero elevation."

"Radar operator's station locked forward," said Martinez. "Gun sight stowed and locked. Rear entrance hatch closed and locked. All radio and radio navigation equipment operating normally. Interception radar and tail warning radar systems are operating. I'm all set at my end, Colonel."

"Scapa Flow tower, this is Osprey One. We're ready for take-off."

All the tower did was acknowledge what Powers had said and he was free to leave. Releasing the parking brakes, he immediately stood on the rudder pedals to keep his fighter in position and pushed the throttle levers forward. The increasing power caused the Black Widow to rock back and forth on its landing gear and creep forward ever so slowly. When Powers finally jumped off the pedals, the P-61 reared back slightly, then bore down on its nose gear and rolled.

In spite of the increased power, the heavy night fighter didn't sprint away from its starting point like a runner. At nineteen tons, it took a little time for the plane to build up its speed. Half a minute later it was only passing the 100 mile an hour mark. From there on, however, the Black Widow's speed jumped dramatically. At 120 miles an hour, even Cox could feel the lift in its massive wings; it also felt like the aircraft was shaking itself apart. But Powers kept the P-61 on the ground until it was hurtling down the runway at 140 miles an hour.

When he had attained safe, single-engined air speed, Powers eased back his control wheel and the huge night fighter leaped off the ground. Almost immediately, the shaking and vibrating the plane had been subjected to ended. With its landing gear and flaps retracted, the P-61 climbed swiftly, its acceleration rivalling that of the latest single-engine fighters. At five hundred feet, Powers banked his aircraft gently and swung over the airfield.

On the ground, the second P-61 could be seen already hurtling down the runway. In a few minutes it would be sitting on Powers's left wing and the second half of the lead flight would be taking off.

"It doesn't look like the rest of your pilots are taking nearly as much time for their pre-take-off checks as we did," Cox noted, looking at the steady stream of ascending fighters.

"They probably did most of their checks while waiting for us on the taxiway," said Powers, "and you should be thankful they did that. Or we'd probably be waiting here an hour for the rest of my planes."

As they finished their climb-outs, each Black Widow turned back over Scapa Flow and joined the gaggle. The night fighters didn't assemble into a neat, tightly spaced formation like Mustangs or Spit-fires. The pilots weren't used to that type of flying and it was far too dangerous to attempt it at night. When all twelve fighters had at last rendezvoused, they made one more orbit over Scapa Flow's airfield before setting out over the North Sea on an easterly heading. As the Orkney Islands retreated behind them, the Black Widows switched off their position lights and slowly descended toward the water's surface. They became a gaggle of formless black shapes, their positions only revealed by the glow of their exhaust stacks and the occasional glint of moonlight off their polished surfaces.

"Tie him securely," Drache ordered as he held his gun on MacAlister.. "Especially his legs."

Two of Drache's men pulled MacAlister off his bed after they had freed him and dragged him to the chair Drache had brought into the radio room. He stood in front of the chair and kept his Luger trained on MacAlister until his men had started tying him into it.

"What am I going to be tortured for tonight, Mister Drache?" asked MacAlister. "More information about the Night Hawk? I'm afraid I told you all the pertinent bits."

"We're finished with our discussions about that jet," said Drache. "The question of the Night Hawk will be decided tonight. No, we will discuss a somewhat broader range of topics. Only if you become stubborn or abusive will we be forced to use this."

Drache pointed at Ursula's electro-shock machine, which she was setting up on a table beside MacAlister.

"I do hope we can be a little more cordial, this will

be our last time together, Ian, and there's so much I want to ask you. I've learned quite a bit about you."

"What do you mean this is the last time?" MacAlister inquired. "What's going on? What will happen to Miss Nilsson and myself?"

MacAlister glanced over at Karen. She still lay tied to her bed and, for the most part, had been ignored by Drache and Ursula. She, however, had not ignored anything they had said and watched intently everything they did.

"You, Ian, are going to Germany," Drache answered pleasantly. "You've become very valuable to the Reich. Miss Nilsson, I'm afraid, is not quite so valuable. I'm sorry, my dear, but you're to be eliminated."

"And how will you handle that? How will you explain away her murder to the Swedish police?"

"The answer will really be self-explanatory, at least the one we'll provide the police. Miss Nilsson and you will die in the crash of her car, along a mountainous stretch of road near here. As I told you last night, I have some experience with fatal car crashes. Yours will be a fiery crash, both your bodies will be burnt beyond recognition."

"But you just told us Ian was going to Germany?" said Karen, speaking for the first time since Drache and Ursula came into the room. "Now you will kill him?"

"No, we will kill someone who resembles Commander MacAlister in height and build," said Drache, turning to Karen. "We've already found a good double for him in Stockholm and later tonight we will abduct the man."

"You mean you will kidnap an innocent man, someone who has no involvement in the war, and kill him just to complete this plan of yours?"

"Of course, my dear. You think just because your country is neutral that your citizens can't be involved in this war? The Reich will decide when and where it'll use your country and its people. We've done it since the start of the war and will continue to our final victory after which, your country will face either surrender or annihilation."

"I can't believe it," said MacAlister. "You people still maintain you're going to win this war? With American and British armies on the Rhine, the Russians crossing your eastern frontier and our air forces coming at will over the continent, how can you still think you can win? Your cities are being burned to the ground, your industries are being smashed, your air force is paralyzed and your armies are in retreat. By all measures your country is on the verge of defeat. That lunatic paper hanger of yours has retreated to his Führerbunker under Berlin and that's where he'll probably die."

"Such conditions are only temporary," Drache replied, forcing a smile on his face and keeping his anger under control. "When the Führer leaves Berlin, he will take control of the military away from those traitorous generals and will unleash on the world a new revolution in warfare."

"I see, more wonder weapons like the Night Hawk? If you handle the rest the way you handled it, your triumphs of German technology will fall victim to German bungling."

"The Night Hawk is but a small part of our revolution. We have wonder weapons the likes of which you have only dreamed of in your nightmares. When the Führer unleashes them, it'll be the Allies who will sue for peace, not the Third Reich!"

"Carl, I don't think you should tell them anything more," said Ursula as she finished setting up her machine. "That information is top secret. It is not for them to hear."

"And why not? I doubt there's much they can do with what I'm telling them. If I cannot boast to the condemned, who can I boast to?" Drache turned back to MacAlister, a triumphant gleam burning in his eyes. "For years we have planned for this exact situation. Thousands of slave laborers have worked on the Führer's most complete redoubt and our best scientists have produced for him the latest weapons. When the Führer leaves Berlin, he will fly to a Danish island in the Baltic Sea called Bornholm.

"That is where his new headquarters has been built and he'll have at his command all German forces in Norway and Denmark. He'll have squadrons of our latest jet fighters and bombers, the entire Baltic Sea fleet, the finest divisions in the SS, V-1 and V-2 rocket batteries and something more. Our scientists have perfected a follow-on to the V-2 rocket. It's designated the A-10, its creators call it the 'New York Rocket' and the first operational base for this missile is on Bornholm."

"If it's like the V-2, then the Americans have little to fear," said MacAlister, "apart from the psychological impact of being attacked. Half the V-2s you've launched against England didn't reach their targets. I doubt one base can inflict much damage on America, even if it is run by Hitler."

"That's where you're wrong, Commander MacAlister, completely wrong. Germany has won the ultimate race. The Americans thought they would win because they had all the scientists. You thought you'd cripple us by destroying our heavy water supplies but we won the race. We proved that the 'Jewish physicists' were right after all, and to think we nearly dropped the development because of that connection.

We now have a weapon the likes of which the world has never seen before and when we use it, cities as far west as New York and as far east as Moscow will burn to the ground. We'll either win the war, Ian, or we'll exact a terrible vengeance in defeat."

"And what then? What if you are defeated? Do you have any plans for dealing with that?"

"Of course we do," Drache replied. "We have plans for any contingency but I doubt we'll need to use them. Our victory in this, the eleventh hour, is assured. If you're lucky, Ian, you may be around to see it."

"Enough, Carl," said Ursula sharply. "You should stop revelling in our future glories and start interrogating. I'm ready and we have not much time before he's to be taken away."

Ursula gestured toward her machine, the power and circuit lights of which glowed menacingly. The indicator needle on its meter quivered at around the halfway point.

"You're quite correct," said Drache. "I am forgetting what we're here for. Sorry, Ian, this is where it could become unpleasant. I received a very extensive file on you from Berlin today, and many questions they would like answered. The most important concerns what you told me earlier this week. That your American friend has test-flown an Me-262."

"I did? Well, I'm afraid I overstated Commander Norris's qualifications a bit," said MacAlister nonchalantly.

"Ian, you disappoint me. I had hoped we could remain cordial. I warned you it would be unpleasant. Ursula."

All Drache had to do was nod in MacAlister's direction and Ursula did the rest. She scooped her probe off the table and, instead of hesitating and building up fear, hit MacAlister immediately. She barely touched the back of his left hand but it was enough. His entire arm spasmed violently and the muscles in it began to contract. MacAlister could feel his arm want to rise off the chair's arm rest but the ropes held it down. The burning where the probe touched his hand was minor compared to the pain of the muscles cramping involuntarily. To MacAlister it felt as though they were being torn from his bones. He let out a long, heavy cry which seemed to echo through the narrow room. It quickly trailed off to deep breathing and in the temporary silence, MacAlister heard the faint drone of aircraft engines once more.

"Perhaps now that you realize how serious we are, Ian, you'll tell us when, where and how the Americans came to own an intact Me-262," said Drache, standing in front of the chair MacAlister was tied to. "And where they have it currently."

Outside of the estate, the drone was louder, crisper in the cold air. Still, the few people who were outside took little notice of the aircraft as it passed overhead. It was just one more air liner heading into Bromma, a little lower and slower than the others perhaps but nothing to waste attention on.

The few men Drache did have outside were concentrated around the main house, servant's quarters and the garage. In a far corner of the estate there was no one to listen to the flat drone of Pratt and Whitney radials, or to the crunch of snow as shadows dropped out of the night sky.

There was grunting and some swearing when the commandoes hit and rolled across the ground, followed by the flapping of parachute silk as their canopies collapsed around them. The first men to land released their parachute harnesses but didn't bother to collect the chutes themselves. Instead they un-stowed their weapons and armed them, then ripped off their jump helmets and replaced them with beige berets.

"Lieutenant, gather my chute," Roberts ordered as his second in command approached him. "Don't bother burying it and pass that to the others. Don't bury the parachutes, just stick them someplace where they won't blow away."

The last members of the SAS squad landed about a hundred yards away from Roberts and in a stand of pine trees, where they became entangled in branches and had to be helped down. A thousand feet above them their jump plane droned on; the Dakota was a black silhouette marked only by its wing tip, tail and nose lights.

"That's the last of 'em!" Capollini shouted after the fifteenth member of the SAS squad had disappeared out the open doorway. "Help me haul in the release lines, Sergeant!"

A thick bundle of flat cloth strips flapped through the exit hatch. Before the door could be replaced, they had to be pulled inside. With the Dakota's flight engineer grabbing hold of his belt, Capollini reached across the doorway and wrapped both hands around the bundle. He needed to use both hands because of the bundle's size and the force of the slipstream whis-tling past the hatch. It took Capollini and the engi-neer pulling together to haul the long, heavy release lines inside the transport. When they were finished, they collapsed against one of the drums of jet fuel it still carried.

"Great, now you can reinstall the door," said Ca-pollini. "I'll go forward and tell Clinton that the SAS guys have jumped. You better hurry on the door. We've already made the initial descent. We're not far away from Stockholm."

The Dakota cruised past Drache's estate, continuing its approach to Bromma for a little while longer. A few miles from its runway the transport dipped its right wing and turned to a southwesterly heading. The pilot retracted the flaps he'd been using to reduce its air speed and pushed the throttles forward. The Dakota surged ahead, returning to its original cruise speed, though not its original altitude. Its pilot kept it low, almost hedgehopping across the darkened Swedish countryside to Norrköping, which lay some eighty miles to the south.

"All right, the Americans have an example of the Me-262. An early, single-seat version," MacAlister admitted as Ursula approached him again. It seemed useless not to answer some of Drache's questions and MacAlister hoped that by answering some of the smaller ones, he might avoid the more immediate, and important, questions. "They acquired it about two months ago. They dismantled it and flew it across the Atlantic to one of their test centers."

"Oh, they didn't take it to your experimental field at Boscombe Down?" Drache inquired. "How selfish of them. Which one of their test centers did they take it to and what was Mister Norris's connection to it?"

"I'm afraid he never did tell me that. Security, you know."

"Ian, please. I'm afraid you're not telling me the truth and we must insist on that. Ursula."

Ursula turned up the main dial on her machine, causing the indicator needle to jump past the halfway point and approach the meter's red zone. MacAlister felt the increased power when the probe touched the back of his hand again. He was certain it made his heart skip a beat and for a few moments he thought he was passing out.

"My God, they're armed," said Roberts, using his binoculars on the men guarding the estate's main house. "Schmeisser MP-40s. Something big must be happening for armed guards to be posted. Have our men taken care of the guards at the servant's house and the garage?"

"Yes, Captain," the lieutenant replied. "And they're rejoining us."

There was the harsh whisper of snow being crushed as the men Roberts sent out to kill the guards at the other buildings came running back, one of them still carrying his bloodstained knife in his hands.

"All right, there are three guards at the main house that we have to take out," Roberts told his team. "Use either your knives or your silencer-equipped automatics. This time, I'll handle the first one, those of you closest to the rest can deal with them. After they're out of the way, proceed with the assault as planned. Lieutenant, you still have command of the second-story group."

Splitting into two- and three-man teams, the commando squad fanned out from their hiding spot to surround the estate's main house. Roberts and his two teammates arrived at the house ahead of most of the others and crept along its darkened side until they were almost at the front corner.

Standing at the corner was one of three guards Drache had assigned to the house. The second stood in front of its main entrance and the third was at the opposite corner. All three cradled Schmeisser submachine guns in their arms and stood casually at their posts. They weren't at attention or edgy; they seemed more like they were waiting for someone to arrive than standing guard against a possible attack. Roberts waited until the time passed for the other parts of his squad to be in position, then moved.

"Barker, he's yours," he whispered, pointing at the corner guard with his pistol. "Sergeant, cover us."

Half-standing, Roberts and one of his teammates materialized out of the shadows. Barker drew his knife from his scabbard and, clamping his free hand over the guard's mouth, rammed it into his back. Roberts jumped in front of the struggling pair and levelled his gun at the second guard. The silenced 9mm Beretta spit twice, causing two tears to appear in the guard's winter jacket, both near the center of his chest. He staggered under the impacts and started to walk backwards before he collapsed against a snowbank.

Roberts immediately turned his automatic on the third guard, who was already cocking his Schmeisser. He never got farther than that; Roberts saw a brief muzzle flash erupt from the corner of the house and the guard's hands froze on the cocking bolt and barrel. He fell forward, sprawling across one of the shrubs which decorated the front of the estate.

"I can't get my knife out of his back," said Barker, tugging so hard on its handle that it was lifting the guard's body off the ground.

"Put your foot in his back, like this," said Roberts, taking over from his teammate. He placed one of his boots on the guard's back and gave the deeply imbedded knife a sharp tug. Its blade slowly came out of the body, the layers of clothing it had to be pulled through cleaned most of the blood off it. Roberts scarcely had to wipe it before handing the knife back to Barker. "Sometimes it's harder to yank a knife out than to put it in, Corporal. C'mon, Sergeant."

Roberts and his team ran to the estate's main

doors while another two-man team came around from the opposite side and joined them, its leader telling Roberts the status of the rest of the teams.

"The lieutenant's men have anchored their grappling hook on a second-floor balcony and are starting to climb. The study team and the kitchen teams are in position and they're already planting their charges."

"So are we," Roberts answered as he instructed his own team on where to place their blocks of plastic explosive. "And in ninety seconds we'll be entering. Go and remind the other teams to search their areas as quickly as they can. We don't know where Mac-Alister and that Swede are being held in this house. Go, hurry."

His orders given, the SAS man ran to the corner of the house and disappeared around it. He stopped at each of the other teams, giving them a quick reminder of what they had been earlier told: MacAlister and Karen were somewhere in the estate's main house but no one, not British or Swedish intelligence, knew where.

He found most of the second-story team had climbed to the balcony and he had to send his message up with one of their other members. The study room and kitchen teams were already finished with their charges and were waiting for the assault to begin. He gave them Roberts's message and quickly returned to the front of the estate, where Roberts was implanting the detonation wires in the plastic explosives fixed to the main doors.

"Good work," he told the arriving commando. "We have forty seconds to go. All I have to do is hook up the wires and we'll be set. Unsling your weapons and spread along the wall."

Roberts took the weblike collection of wires and

wound them around the terminals of an electric detonator. The other SAS men flattened against the house, on either side of the main doors and held their Sten guns ready. When he was finished with his wiring, Roberts moved as far away from the doors as the lines would allow, then turned his back to them. He peeled his jacket sleeve off his wrist watch and silently counted down the remaining seconds before the attack would begin.

At this power setting, another shot could be dangerous, Commander," Ursula warned, her cold smile was the first thing MacAlister saw as he slid back to consciousness. "It could even be fatal."

"The jet was taken to Pax River," said MacAlister. When he glanced at Ursula's machine, he could see that during his short blackout she had increased the power setting on her probe. "The Patuxent River Navy Test Center. The Yanks have a special squadron there, the Enemy Aircraft Evaluation unit. It flies captured airplanes in tests against their own. John Norris is part of the unit. He was sent to Europe about a month ago to collect more German aircraft. The Night Hawk would've been the ultimate prize for him."

"Yes, and what a pity he'll never have a chance to see it again after tonight," Drache chuckled. "In fact, in less than two hours it'll be the Reich's once more."

"What do you mean? My friends in the Swedish air force told me the Luftwaffe would take possession sometime tomorrow. What's happening?"

"Berlin has decided to change the schedule. Soon, a detail of storm troopers will arrive at Norrköping to guard the Night Hawk. Some twelve hours ahead of the original schedule we agreed to. We know how highly placed your Swedish friends are, Ian. We know they could easily allow you to sabotage the jet, so Berlin has decided to use the SS to guard it. How the storm troopers will be inserted is ingenious. By the time the Swedes are aware of them, it'll be too late to stop them."

Drache let out a deep laugh as he ended his latest boast. However, it was cut short by a series of small explosions which sounded like they were occurring on the floor above them. They weren't much louder than the crash of a wine bottle and they irritated Drache more than they shocked him.

The doors didn't splinter when Roberts set off his charges. The strategically placed explosions blew out the hinges and lock and caused the heavy doors to collapse into the entrance hall. Wood splinters were still flying when Roberts's team charged inside the house; Roberts himself was the last to enter it.

"God in heaven, what's happening up there?" Drache shouted, looking at the ceiling. "Quick, Ursula, let's see what the idiots have done. Sorry, Ian, we do at times have problems with our servants. If they've broken anything . . ."

Drache hustled Ursula out the radio room's door and closed it behind them. The instant they left, a broad smile broke over MacAlister's face and he laughed slightly.

"What do you find funny?" Karen asked.

"I think some of my friends have arrived," he replied. Then he started looking around the narrow room. "I really don't want them to find me like this. If there were only some way to cut me out of this."

MacAlister's eyes fell on the probe to Ursula's electro-shock machine. She had dropped it on the table as she left the room and it rolled to the edge.

"Or perhaps I can burn my way out."

Despite being tied to the chair, MacAlister was able to lift it off the floor slightly and plant it a few inches closer to the table. He was near enough to reach over with his head and wrap his mouth around the slender probe. He had to use his tongue to work the probe between his teeth and MacAlister strained his neck so far he felt his muscles would pop.

What he definitely could feel was the electricity humming in the probe. At the power setting Ursula had left her machine on, touching the probe's end studs would cause more than a severe burn, it could cause death. Lifting the probe off the edge of the table, MacAlister brought it down on the ropes which held his left wrist to the arm rest.

"Don't go in there!" Roberts shouted when he noticed some of his men preparing to enter a set of doors on the left side of the hall. "That's the study. We already have a team in there. Go for the dining room."

Roberts had his teams move swiftly but cautiously. Following the explosions that let them in the house, it remained strangely quiet except for some shouting. Then came a muffled popping from the kitchen, followed by a heavy crash. The two-man team which Roberts had sent in through the kitchen appeared in its doorway, one of them raising his Sten gun above his head. They had drawn first blood.

The smell of burning rope filled MacAlister's nose and the smoke the probe was creating stung his eyes. He had an urge to cough but he held it in his throat. He dared not do anything which would cause him to lose his grip on the probe. He could feel the heat of the burning through his wrist and through the tears in his eyes he could see the probe's tip scorch more of the rope's strands.

MacAlister started pulling and twisting his left

arm, trying to force the rope to unravel. Almost at once it frayed and loosened. So many strands had been burned there was little left to hold his wrist down. MacAlister spit the probe out of his mouth when he was sure it had done its job and yanked his arm away from the chair. The remaining strands snapped under the pressure and the rope fell to the ground in two, unequal pieces.

MacAlister didn't waste his time savoring his victory; he pulled apart the knot on the rope that held his right arm down then attacked the ones binding his ankles. A few seconds later he stood up, free at last though still very much a prisoner.

"Basement door," Roberts warned when he caught sight of its doorknob rotating.

Everyone in the hall froze momentarily as the door pivoted open and a rifle barrel was poked out. The man holding the rifle took one step into the hall and caught a fleeing glimpse of the invading SAS teams before he was thrown back inside the basement stairway by a muffled burst of fire from the nearest commando's Sten gun.

He caught the burst in his chest and upper abdomen, the force of the impacts sending him crashing against another of Drache's henchmen. They both tumbled down the steps; by the time they reached the basement landing, the first henchman was dead.

"They're commandoes, Herr Drache," said the second man as he was helped to his feet. "Allied commandoes. They must be. I'm sure they cannot be Swedish."

"This is outrageous! Impossible!" Drache stormed. "The daring! MacAlister must be far more important than we thought. Hold the stairway, Ursula. Don't let them in the basement. I'm going back for Ian. We can use him as a hostage."

"We shouldn't try to escape from here," said MacAlister, untying the ropes around Karen's wrists. "This is the safest room to be in. We should try locking ourselves in and wait until my friends have captured the estate."

Once her arms were free, he moved to the foot of the bed and began untying Karen's ankles. MacAlister had only just started when he heard the stamp of feet approaching the door. He turned to face it and searched desperately for a weapon, anything to hold in his hands. He finally selected the hard-bound logbook, snatching it off the radio table as Drache burst into the room.

He was shocked to find MacAlister standing in front of the radio. Shocked enough to halt his stride and to forget about the Luger in his hand. He held it loosely and at about chest height. When Drache failed to level it at him, MacAlister took advantage and swung the logbook at his right hand, knocking the gun out of it.

The pain instantly brought Drache back to his senses. He caught hold of MacAlister's hand as he aimed the logbook at his head and pulled it out of MacAlister's grip. MacAlister countered by punching him in the face, but the heavy beard cushioned the blow. Drache's head scarcely moved. He gave MacAlister a hard push, literally tossing him into a corner of the room, then he went looking for his gun.

The first commando to reach the basement door was greeted with a volley of rifle fire. The bullets ricochetted off the stairwell walls, sending dust and stone chips flying. He responded by firing an ineffective answering burst and retreating back to where Roberts was standing.

"There's quite a crew down there, Captain," he advised. "Think that's where the prisoners are?"

"It could be but I want to make sure," said Roberts. "I'd like to hear what the rest of the teams have found. It'd be just our luck if Ian and the girl were hidden elsewhere and we overlooked them."

Drache found his Luger under the chair MacAlister had been tied to. He had thrown the chair onto the room's empty bed and had bent over to retrieve his gun when a shoe kicked it under Karen's bed. It was MacAlister and as he tried to wrap an arm around Drache's neck, Drache elbowed him in the stomach.

It knocked the wind out of him, and MacAlister started to double up but was quickly straightened by Drache, who turned around and punched him in the jaw. MacAlister could feel his feet leave the ground as he sailed backwards. He was airborne, though only for a moment or two before he came crashing down on the radio table. He had just enough time to look up and see Drache flying at him.

MacAlister braced himself and was prepared for Drache when he landed on him. He caught hold of Drache's hands before he could wrap them around his neck. The weight of the extra body caused the table to creak and groan, and it kept on creaking as the two continued their struggle.

While MacAlister was able to keep Drache's hands off of him, the struggle was stalemated. He took a chance and released one of Drache's hands, placing his own hand against his side while Drache finally got the opportunity to throttle him. MacAlister pushed the heavier German off him and rolled over at the same time. Now it was Drache's turn to crash as he slammed against the room's floor.

Solid stone didn't have the slight give the table had when MacAlister landed on it and the hard impact stunned Drache for a moment, which MacAlister

302

took advantage of by prying his hand off his neck and punching him in the face again, this time drawing a stream of blood from Drache's nose.

"The upper floors are empty, Captain," the leader of the second-story teams reported when he at last appeared on the staircase. "We haven't found anyone up here."

"OK, no one else has found Ian and the girl," said Roberts, "so we have to assume that they're in the cellar somewhere. Sergeant, break out the concussion grenades."

MacAlister was so busy laying blow after blow on Drache and so thoroughly enjoying himself, he failed to notice Drache reaching for one of his boots. He had to pull his pant cuff away from the top of the boot, then he got his fingers around the handle of a knife. MacAlister didn't notice it; Karen, however, did as she sat at the edge of her bed and tried to untie her ankles.

"Ian, look out! He has a knife!"

Karen's warning cry made MacAlister immediately aware of the danger he was in. He saw a flash of metal in Drache's left hand and rolled off of him. But not before he felt a spasm of pain in his side. MacAlister tried to stand as he broke away but the pain grew too sharp and he stumbled out of balance when he grabbed his side. He landed on the floor again, hitting his back against the table at the foot of his bed.

Drache wiped away some of the blood which had been collecting in his moustache; the sight of it made him even more enraged and MacAlister knew it. He looked around desperately for a weapon to kill or at least stop Drache. His Luger was far under Karen's bed and though she was hunting for it, by the time she would find the gun, it'd be too late for Mac-

Alister. The chair he'd been tied to was on top of his bed and out of his reach. There seemed nothing he could do but crawl under the table and hope he could keep Drache off with his feet. Then, out of the corner of his eye, MacAlister caught sight of something dangling off the edge of the table.

It was the probe to Ursula's machine. MacAlister grabbed hold of the long, slender rod as Drache lunged at him. He led with his left hand, the knife held in it would have the entire weight of his body behind it. If he made contact with MacAlister, the force of the blow alone would be enough to kill him, but it was MacAlister who made contact first.

The end of the probe touched Drache's left hand while he was still airborne. There was a sharp, sizzling sound as contact was made and the knife immediately popped out of his grip. The nerve-frying jolt travelled through Drache's entire body, making his muscles contract and spasm uncontrollably. He crashed onto the floor again, short of his target, his giant frame contorted by the brief shot of electricity. From the way his body trembled and jerked, MacAlister knew Drache's heart had been affected. He might even be having a heart attack. He wasn't dead, at least not yet.

Roberts stood next to the basement doorway and using one hand, swung his Sten gun into the stairwell and fired it. Without his other hand to steady the weapon, and with a heavy silencer hanging on its muzzle, it sprayed its bullets in an erratic, inaccurate pattern, though it had its desired effect. The rifle fire from the basement trailed off.

"Now, throw them now!" Roberts shouted, and the sergeant and several other SAS men stepped up to the doorway and where they hurled their concussion grenades down the stairwell.

* * *

MacAlister grabbed hold of the table's edge and pulled himself to his feet. He twisted the power output dial on Ursula's machine until the meter needle was quivering at the limit of its range. The increase in power caused the probe to literally vibrate in Mac-Alister's hand.

He turned and looked at Drache. For the moment he was a pathetic figure, fighting to regain control of his body. Soon he would have it back and Drache would be dangerous again. MacAlister sank to his knees and, hovering beside Drache, he held the probe over his chest. He didn't care how pathetic Drache looked or how helpless he was; if it was the last thing he'd do, MacAlister would kill him.

"This is for Greg," MacAlister whispered to his enemy. "Enjoy yourself in hell."

The probe hit Drache on the left side of his chest. It started burning his shirt at once and caused him to arch his back unnaturally high. Like his body, Drache's face contorted with pain; he started to scream but the rest of it was strangled in his throat as his vocal cords were paralyzed. His fingers curled in on themselves, like those of an arthritic. His entire body trembled as the surge of electricity short circuited his nervous system. When it stopped trembling, when his eyes opened fully and his pupils dilated, MacAlister was sure Carl Drache was dead.

"I'm going to the radio room," Ursula told one of the men she was commanding. "Carl should've returned with the prisoners. You are in charge until one of us comes back."

As Ursula stood up from behind a crate, a metallic rattle could be heard in the stairwell. Out of it bounced first one, then three more grenades. Their sudden arrival made everyone freeze. Ursula had just started to think about taking cover when they began to explode.

The first two blasts detonated simultaneously, their shock waves lifting Ursula off her feet. She landed on an ancient rocking chair and smashed it into kindling. Ursula was protected from the remaining blasts by crates but the damage had already been done. She struggled to her feet, scarcely able to maintain her balance. Her entire body felt numb and her ears were ringing so loudly she could scarcely think. Somehow, Ursula had managed to keep her hand on her automatic. The pistol felt like it weighed a ton but she gripped it tightly and staggered off to the radio room; the only thought in her mind was to find out what had happened to Carl Drache.

"Ian, I have Carl's gun," said Karen, rolling away from the edge of her bed and displaying the Luger in her hands.

"Good, but let's stay in here until the fight's over," MacAlister warned, reaching for the controls on the electric shock machine and switching it off. "If one of us goes out there armed, we might be shot by the very people who came to rescue us. And I don't feel quite like running about."

"I forgot about your wound. How bad is—"

Karen didn't complete her sentence; her words trailed off as the radio room door opened. Ursula stumbled in, her hair and clothes in disarray and a worn, exhausted look on her face. When she saw Drache's body on the floor, her expression changed to one of anger and she trained her gun on MacAlister. Ursula needed both hands to steady her chrome-plated automatic, but Karen only required one to aim and fire the Luger.

The first bullet hit Ursula in the left side of her

306

stomach, rupturing her spleen. The impact threw her against the radio room's end wall. As she placed her left hand over the spreading patch of blood, her right dropped to her side, the automatic slipping out of it. Karen took careful aim and fired again. The second bullet struck Ursula in the center of her left breast, about where Karen thought her nipple would be. The second wound didn't bleed as profusely as the first one. Just a small stain of blood expanded around the hole torn in Ursula's shirt. She looked down at her breast and cupped her blood-smeared left arm around it.

Then she died. The bullet had gone through her breast and struck a rib as it entered her chest. It had fragmented and several pieces punctured her heart. Ursula sagged into the corner formed by the end wall and the false side one. Her body spasmed a few more times and stopped, even the blood flowing out of her stomach wound ceased. When MacAlister looked over at Karen she had a slight smile on her face.

"I was right. That cannon does leave a bloody mess," MacAlister remarked, "though I must admit I didn't mind witnessing it."

MacAlister pushed himself off the table the electro-shock machine stood on and, stepping past Drache's body, managed to reach Karen's bed. She dropped the Luger and took hold of him, easing him onto the bed. She placed a hand on the wound in his side and held his head up with the other.

Outside the radio room the muffled, staccato bursts of machine gun fire and an occasional rifle shot filled the air. The rifle fire stopped after less than half a dozen shots, the machine gun bursts ended a few seconds later. Then a figure appeared in the radio room's doorway, dressed in black, armed with a Sten machine gun and wearing a beige beret.

"Rescuing people is becoming quite a habit with me," said Roberts, stepping over Ursula's body. "Looks like you two had quite a fight in here. How do you feel, Ian?"

"Better, now that I know it's you," MacAlister answered. "Karen, I'd like you to meet Captain Lee Roberts, Special Air Services. If he sounds like he's an American, that's because he is. Lee, I'd like you to meet—"

"I know, Karen Nilsson. We were told you'd be here. Ian, you look like you're wounded."

"Drache stabbed him," said Karen. "He needs a doctor. Please help him."

"That's what we're here for, lady," said Roberts, stepping past the bodies on the floor and sitting next to MacAlister. "Some of my men have medical training and the British embassy is supposed to have an ambulance for us. This doesn't look too bad. You'll bleed a lot, Ian, but you'll be OK. I should get my sergeant in here."

"No, no, wait," said MacAlister, grabbing Roberts as he started to rise off the bed. "The operation, are you still going according to plan?"

"Yes, if I push things I may get to Norrköping in time to see that damn jet we've worked so hard for take off."

"You have to hurry. This bastard told me something. The Nazis have changed their plans." MacAlister found it difficult to continue speaking. He knew if he stopped he would pass out from shock and blood loss. "They're going in early. They're sending in the SS to seize the jet. In two hours they'll arrive in Norrköp—"

"Jesus, how will they arrive, Ian? How?" Roberts asked, shaking MacAlister, but it was too late. He had already slipped into unconsciousness. "Ian, please. God damn it, sleep some other time. Miss Nilsson, did you hear how the Nazis planned to arrive?"

"The only thing Drache said about that was their arrival would be ingenious," Karen reported. "I'm sorry."

"Don't be, at least I have something to work on. I'll get you help right away. Sergeant, get in here!"

Roberts jumped off the bed and shouted his command again at the radio room's door. He waited just long enough for the sergeant to appear at the door before he ran to the basement stairs. On the ground floor Roberts met his lieutenant and ordered him to round up the squad. He then charged out the front doors and stopped at the end of the walk, beside the body of the guard he had killed. Roberts pulled a Very pistol from his equipment pack and quickly loaded it. He fired the pistol into the air, sending a bright green ball arcing high above the estate before exploding.

As the sputtering fireball drifted back down, a line of headlights appeared in the distance. It took a little over a minute for them to enter the estate grounds and weave up the drive to the main house. The first vehicle in the convoy, a car with British diplomatic plates, stopped beside Roberts. Behind it was another sedan, a dark blue one with "Flygvapen" stenciled on its doors, and behind it were three trucks with similar markings. Bringing up the rear of the convoy was an ambulance, its crew already opening its doors.

"Captain Roberts?" asked the first officer to climb out of the embassy car. "I'm Wing Commander Ellis. Have you found Commander MacAlister and Karen Nilsson?"

"Yes, they're inside and they've both been

wounded," said Roberts. "You'll find them in the basement. I suggest you get them to a hospital at once. Who's in charge of these Swedish trucks?"

"I am," said Tallberg, emerging from the dark blue sedan. "I'm Lieutenant Ormand Tallberg. What do you want, Captain?"

"You got a radio? It's vital that we contact your base."

"No, I'm afraid I do not. Why is it vital?"

"Because the Nazis are jumping the gun on us. I just found out they're sending a team of SS storm troopers to Norrköping. They want to hold the jet until their repair crew arrives tomorrow."

"Good God, could we try contacting the base by phone?" Ellis suggested.

"No, this information is too sensitive to use an open phone line," said Roberts. "How long will it take us to get to Norrköping?"

"We needed two hours for the drive up," said Tallberg. "Perhaps we could take less for the return trip."

"It had better take a lot less. Those storm troopers are supposed to hit your base in two hours, so we haven't any time to waste. I want my men on your trucks immediately. We should've left here five minutes ago."

Chapter Twelve: Airfield Attack

"Jeez, will you look at that," Capollini marvelled as he stood behind the Dakota's pilot and co-pilot seats. "It looks like we landed at an army air depot. The last time I saw this many B-17s was at an Eighth Air Force base."

"It is impressive," said the pilot. "Most impressive. I hope we have a chance to look over these aircraft while the jet is being fueled. Can you see the jet?"

"Yeah, there it is. They're pulling it out of that hangar." Capollini pointed across the pilot's field of view, almost putting his finger in his nose. "God, what a sight."

"Restrain yourself, Captain. I see it well enough now. Go back and help the flight engineer with our cargo. We'll be shutting down in another minute."

The Dakota rolled another hundred yards before turning onto a taxiway which led directly to Norrköping's internment area. Part of the ground crew that was working on the Night Hawk guided the transport in. They instructed it to park alongside the canvas-covered trailers at the end of the collection. As the Dakota killed its engines they finished towing out the Night Hawk and swung the jet around behind it.

"Fancy meeting you here, Colonel," said Capollini when the cargo loading hatch on the transport was opened.

"What the hell are you doing, Vince?" Lacey asked. "I thought you would've volunteered for the Black Widows."

"Well, they wouldn't let me fly one but this bird needed a relief pilot and a jump master. Commander, it's nice to see you after all this time. How's Sweden?"

"Great country," said Norris, shaking Capollini's hand after he jumped onto the tarmac. "I can't wait till I get back to someplace where they're shooting at me. This is a hell of a way to fight a war. Our friend's in enemy hands and not only couldn't we help him, we had to be fucking nice to the enemy. I hope you got what we need to fly out of here."

"Sure do, we got high test and more high test. Straight from Boscombe Down. Have you heard anything about the commandoes we dropped. Did they free your friend?"

"We don't know yet," McClory admitted, joining the group. "And we won't know until they get here. Captain, I'm Lieutenant-Colonel McClory, Army attaché to Sweden. We've got a lot to do to make this jet airworthy, gentlemen. If you'd like to continue your discussion, I suggest you do it while working on the plane. Have you seen the Night Hawk, Captain?"

"Only from out there on the runway," said Capollini. "I'd like to have one look at it close-up."

The Night Hawk had been positioned behind the Dakota's tail to provide the shortest route to move the drums of fuel. The group of U.S. Army and Navy officers was joined by the R.A.F. flight crew as they walked back to the jet. Apart from a few whistles and appreciative swearing, they admired it silently. While they walked around it, part of the Swedish ground crew continued to work on the jet, opening the gun bay access panels and removing the ammunition boxes for the Night Hawk's battery of cannons. The rest of the Swedes were busy placing a ramp up to the transport's main hatch so the fuel could be off-loaded.

"As you can see, the cannons are still empty and we haven't hooked up the drop tanks yet," Lacey told Capollini. "How many drums did you bring with you?"

"An even dozen, Colonel," said Capollini, "and we had one hell of a time trying to figure out where to put them, those commandoes and that jet wreckage."

"Let's see, at fifty-five gallons each that'll give us six hundred and sixty gallons," said Norris, running the calculations through his mind. "That's more than enough for us but we'll have to squeeze every drop we can into her. It's a long way to England by the route we're flying."

"Commander Norris, we have the ramp in place and we're ready to unload the fuel," Lindh advised, stepping up to the American and British officers. "We can begin whenever you wish."

"What? Ain't you guys going to use a forklift to move those drums?" Capollini asked.

"We wanted to, but it broke down and I dare not go for a second one. It might look suspicious."

"So you're gonna move them by hand? Jeez, this'll be just like North Africa, when we had to unload our gas by hand. It hurts my back just to think about it."

"Be lucky you don't have to do it," said Lacy, "and let's hope nothing else breaks down until we reach England."

* * *

Tallberg ordered two of the three trucks he had brought to Drache's estate to keep their engines running. As he gave his final instructions to the men he had brought with him, Roberts loaded his own into the idling trucks. Roberts himself climbed inside the first truck's cab, together with Colonel Whitney. When Tallberg returned to his staff car, it swung out of the convoy line and raced down the drive, the trucks close on its tail.

At the end of the drive the vehicles turned east and for a time appeared to be heading for Stockholm, then they drove across the bridge that spanned Lake Mälaren. At last they headed south, following a series of back roads and only slowing when they had to go through a town or village.

"Wing Commander Ellis knows what to look for at Drache's estate," said Whitney, responding to Robert's questions. "He'll take all the evidence we need to prove Drache was a spy and destroy the rest."

"Destroy? How will he do that? And will the Swedes let him do it?"

"The Swedes will help him. Tallberg said the police and military intelligence decided a long time ago that if Drache was a spy, it'd be too much of a scandal to release. His estate will be destroyed by fire and since you already killed everyone in it who was a German agent, you've made their job that much easier."

"I see, and I was thinking our rescue mission would've created more problems for the Swedes than it would solve," said Roberts as he glanced at the truck's speedometer. "C'mon, Corporal, you're not doing more than forty miles an hour. We can do at least seventy."

"Please, Captain, these roads are dangerous," the driver replied. "They have many curves and there's the ice. What if we encounter any slower traffic?"

"Right now we're the slow traffic. We're losing sight of Tallberg's car and I think the truck behind us is going to try passing us, so move it. We still have almost seventy miles to cover and I don't know what the Nazis' exact timetable is. I don't want to arrive after they do, I want to be there to welcome them."

Reluctantly, the driver shifted to a higher gear and pushed the gas pedal a little closer to the floor. The lead truck accelerated slowly, closing the distance between it and the staff car. Tallberg was by now almost a mile ahead of the trucks. At times they could not see him, especially when he disappeared around a curve. Even when they did, his car was little more than a set of red tail lights.

Occasionally, another vehicle would appear on the road. Those on the same side as the convoy would be passed first by Tallberg's car, and a few seconds later by the trucks. Beyond them, there was no sign of life on the roads the convoy traveled, which suited Roberts perfectly. The fewer obstructions and delays they encountered, the sooner they would arrive at Norrköping.

"RO to pilot, looks like there's something wrong with one of our planes," Martinez warned. "I think it's that guy DeVega. He's breaking formation and approaching us. I think he has engine trouble."

The Black Widows flew in a loose gaggle of two-ship elements. Not used to flying or fighting in formation, the night fighters flew across the North Sea in a seemingly unorganized cloud. The pairs, however, did fly at the same altitude, Powers and his wing man in the lead. The rest of the squadron trailed them, until one of the P-61s broke from its own wing man and pulled abreast of Powers.

"He's flashing his position lights," said Powers. "I think he's going to send us a message in Morse code. Take it down, Commander. You'll find paper and pencils in the data case."

"All right, I'll try, but I warn you," Cox advised, "I'm not very good at translating code transmissions."

"But I thought with you Navy guys Morse code was second nature. Didn't you learn it?"

"Of course I did, but the last time I used it I was a sub-lieutenant assigned to a Swordfish squadron."

Cox found a note pad and a bundle of pencils in the data case located between the gunner's seat and the pilot's seat. The P-61 which had joined the lead pair sat on Powers's left wing. The initial flashing of the position light in its wing tip had been to warn that it wanted to send a message, then it waited for Powers to flash his lights before actually transmitting it. Cox had to bring up the fluorescent lights at his station so he could see what he was writing and he took down the message silently, not bothering to pronounce the words as he spelled them.

"Well, what's wrong with him?" Powers asked, growing anxious and frustrated with Cox's silence.

"Right engine, rough. Low oil pressure and high temp," said Cox, reading the message after it had been transmitted. "Cannot keep up, must abort. May I have escort? It sounds like he does have engine trouble. Will you be giving him an escort back to Scapa Flow?"

"I wish we could but we need every plane we can get. I know he has a long flight ahead of him across what, for all purposes, is enemy air space but I can't afford to lose a second plane. He knows our procedures, he'll identify himself as a ship in trouble and he'll pick up an escort of British Mosquitoes or Beaufighters. Well, I guess I have to tell him the bad

316

news."

Powers reached down for the electrical control panel next to his throttles, and started flicking one of its toggle switches. The wing tip lights of his P-61 flashed the message for the stricken fighter to abort the mission but there would be no escort for him. He acknowledged his orders and banked away from the lead element. He climbed slightly, the entire squadron was so close to the sea he would've crashed had he dove, and swung around until he was flying in the opposite direction, due west to Scapa Flow. As it left the rest of the P-61s behind, the strickened fighter jettisoned its set of external tanks and reduced power. Eventually, it would feather its starboard propeller and climb for a higher, safer altitude.

"Pilot to RO, how did you know DeVega had engine trouble?" Powers inquired after the P-61 had departed.

"When he broke with his wing man, I could see the exhaust stacks of his right engine weren't glowing too brightly," said Martinez. "That's always a sure sign it's engine trouble. And I also heard DeVega telling his crew he still had engine problems back at the briefing."

"Did you hear anyone else complain about their aircraft?" Cox asked. "I'd like to know how many other ships we have a chance of losing."

The orphan wing man joined the nearest pair of P-61s, turning the element into a three-ship vee. The reduced squadron continued on its easterly heading, skimming over the North Sea's foam-capped surface at barely a hundred feet. With no exterior lights on and just an occasional ray of moonlight breaking through the heavy cloud cover, the Black Widows were all but invisible. Only their thunder and their glowing engine exhausts betrayed their presence.

Soon, the squadron would be changing its course to avoid the Danish coast line and would thread its way into the Skagerak, the seventy-mile-wide strait between Norway and Denmark. On entering the Skagerak, the squadron would be less than an hour's flying time from Sweden.

"We're losing him again," said Roberts as the staff car vanished around another bend. "Step on it."

The driver pumped the gas pedal, causing the truck's speed to jump, until it reached the bend where the driver was forced to briefly slow it. Even with his foot on the brakes the truck still hit the curve doing better than fifty miles an hour. It slid across the road's center line, Roberts was grateful they encountered no traffic driving in the opposite direction, and came around the bend almost travelling sideways. The driver was still trying to straighten the truck out when he and Roberts realized that the tail lights ahead of them weren't of Tallberg's staff car but of some other, slower moving vehicle.

"Good Lord, we're too close!" Whitney shouted. "We're too close to stop!"

"Go around him, go around him!" Roberts ordered. "Steer, damn it! Get your foot off the fucking brakes."

The driver started spinning his control wheel frantically. However, the truck had yet to respond fully to the change in direction before a jarring crash sent it skidding forward. The second truck had come around the curve as well but hadn't seen the danger until it was too late. The resulting collision threw everyone in the lead truck's cab against the seat back. Its force kicked the vehicle in the direction its tires were now turned, to the left.

While bolting out from behind the slower moving, civilian car, the truck clipped it in its rear bumper. The sedan started to fishtail wildly, its driver fighting to maintain control. He lost it completely when the second truck brushed against him, crumpling one of his rear fenders. The car spun around and shot off the road, coming to rest on its side.

"Captain, please. We should go back and help them," said the driver, pleading with Roberts and Whitney. "What if we hurt someone?"

"I'm sorry, it couldn't be helped," said Roberts, "and we can't help them. If we stop now, a lot of your friends and a lot of mine will be dead. It's a hard decision, but it's the way things have to be."

"Then could we at least slow down and prevent another accident?"

"No, we're behind as it is and we have to catch up to Tallberg's car. We're not slowing down until we reach the gates of your air base."

When he noticed the driver easing his foot off the gas pedal, Roberts stamped his own on it, sending the truck racing down the road at an ever-increasing velocity. Only after he got the driver to promise that he would keep the truck's speed high did Roberts take his foot off the pedal. A few minutes later they caught up to the staff car on a straight stretch of road.

"Flash your lights at him," Roberts ordered. "It's useless for us to keep up with him."

All the driver had to do was flick his headlights from low beam to high beam a couple of times and Tallberg's sedan shot into the night. The sole acknowledgment Roberts got was a hand reaching out one of the car's side windows and briefly waving at him.

"What's that?" the driver asked. "What is he doing?"

"A prearranged signal," said Roberts. "Before we left the estate, Lieutenant Tallberg and I decided if we couldn't stay with him he would race ahead and warn your base. We were going to do this when we got near the field, so the gate would be open for us. But this way at least our friends will get a little advanced warning."

"Does this mean we can slow down?"

"No way. Just because we can't match his speed doesn't mean we give up. You keep your foot on that pedal or I'll break it. Understand, Corporal?"

The staff car rapidly pulled away from the trucks; soon its tail lights were just a small, red glow in the distance. Eventually Roberts lost sight of the car, and he hoped he wouldn't see it again until after he drove through the gate at Norrköping.

"Herr Oberst, we have made our initial contact with Norrköping air base," said the pilot when the SS colonel entered the cockpit. "I gave them our cover story and they accepted it. We have clearance to land and they will illuminate a runway for us. Everything is perfect."

"You're right, the plan is going perfectly," the colonel replied, a satisfied smile creeping onto his face. "I had wondered if it would, I have no doubts now. I'll tell my men, we have to prepare for landing and so should you."

"Yes, if the Swedes are to believe engine failure then we must have a dead, cold engine. Leutnant, prepare to shut down starboard engine and feather propeller."

The colonel turned and walked back to the transport's main cabin. In it he found his squad resting in their seats, talking, reading or just looking out the windows at a starry night sky partially obscured by clouds.

"Men, I want your attention," he said, and everyone in the cabin stopped what they where doing and looked up at him. "Phase two of our operation is complete. Norrköping air base has given us permission to land. They believe we are who we claim to be. We have about fifteen minutes before we land, time to prepare our gear and arm weapons. In five minutes the pilots will change us to red lights, so our eyes will acclimate to the night. Should you feel our aircraft dip to one side and lose air speed, don't worry, one of our engines is being intentionally shut down. Let's begin."

Their orders given, the storm troopers started to pull on their equipment backpacks and checked their Schmeisser machine pistols and Lugers before loading clips into them. They stowed extra clips in their jacket pockets and accepted the hand grenades being passed out by the squad's master sergeant.

Somewhere during their preparations, the transport did indeed tip to one side, as the colonel had warned. The DC-3's starboard engine sputtered noisily as its throttle and mixture control were closed and its ignition switch turned off. It gave out its last cough while the propeller ground to a halt, fully feathered, knife edge to the wind. The loss of the engine also caused the aircraft to lose some of its air speed. It wasn't much but it would be several precious minutes behind schedule by the time it reached Norrköping.

"OK, that's enough!" Capollini shouted, pulling the hose out of the fueling vent atop the Night Hawk's fuselage. He quickly put his thumb over its end, to prevent any excess fuel from dribbling onto the jet. "I'm clear, you can start rocking her, Commander."

After Capollini had climbed off its fuselage, teams of men on either side of the Night Hawk started pushing it, rocking the plane gently from side to side. They kept it up for half a minute, then let Capollini back onto the jet to check the level of gas in its main tank. While the Swedish ground crew and American officers were still shaking the plane, a dark blue sedan drove into the internment area and Paulson climbed out.

"What are they doing, Mister Lindh?" he asked as he walked up to the squadron leader.

"A special fueling procedure," said Lindh. "Perhaps the Americans should explain it to you. Commander Norris and Colonel Lacey were the ones who requested it, sir."

"All right, let's hear what their reasons are," Paulson replied, turning to Norris and approaching him. "Excuse me, Commander, but is this the way jet aircraft are supposed to be fueled?"

"You mean the jiggling?" Norris deduced. "No, that's an old trick the long-distance flyers in the twenties and thirties used to increase range. The shaking makes air bubbles in the gas tank rise to the surface. That way, we can add a few extra gallons of fuel and, believe me, we need every drop we can get."

"Are you almost finished?"

"They're just topping off the front main tank. We got the front auxiliary and the rear auxiliary filled but we still have those to do."

Norris pointed at the two drop tanks hugging the Night Hawk's fuselage aft of the nose gear well. As streamlined as they were, they detracted from the Me-262's sleek lines and gave it a rather "pregnant" look.

"We have loaded its cannons, a hundred shells for each upper gun and eight rounds apiece for the lower guns, and even the gun camera has film in it. Once Lacey gets back here we can begin our pre-flight checks. Right now he's suiting up and McClory is giving him a list of radio frequencies and code words we'll have to know."

"I see you also brought us the pieces of jet wreckage you promised," said Paulson, glancing at the tail section and outer wing panels stacked against the nearest interned fighter. "What will you do with the surplus jet fuel? Will the British take it back to England?"

"I'm sure that after all the sweat and hard work it took to get those drums out," said Norris, "your men and that flight crew would like to load one back inside the plane. You can use it to help create your fake fire. Jet fuel burns a lot differently than aviation gas. In fact this stuff may burn differently from German fuel. They use a brown coal oil similar to kerosene while ours is a more refined fuel that has some new additives to ease engine wear and increase thrust."

"Commander, the main tank's full," Capollini advised as he tightened the vent cap in front of the cockpit. "We're doing the drop tanks next and that shouldn't take long. We won't be shaking the airplane to get them full."

The fueling detail uncapped one of the black pods shackled to the Night Hawk's fuselage and ran their hose into it. One of the men started working the hand pump on top of the open drum. It would take another minute or two for the drum to be emptied and even then the drop tank wouldn't be full. At least two of the three remaining drums would be needed to fill the tanks.

"Well, I know the suit's a bit baggy but how do I look?" Lacey asked, approaching Norris and Paulson. Like Norris, he had traded in most of his uniform for a flight suit, flying jacket, insulated boots and gloves. He also carried with him a helmet, parachute and Mae West.

"Like I should've gotten you a flight suit a size smaller," Norris admitted, "but that was the best one I could find amongst the gear these guys took from our interned crews. Let me help you put on your 'chute and Mae West and then we can check out the jet."

Lacey placed his helmet and flotation vest on the wing of the Me-262 while Norris and Paulson helped him slide his parachute on his back and connect its straps. When they would get done with him he'd look as bulky as Norris but he would be ready to fly the Night Hawk.

"What's happening here?" questioned the sergeant in command of the gate. "He must be crazy."

Even inside the guard house he and the other airmen could hear the distant roar of a car engine and the screeching of its tires as it came out of a turn. The sergeant stepped out the door and immediately caught sight of the car racing along the service road beyond the base fence. It didn't slow until it was almost on top of the gate. The sedan nearly spun out of control trying to slow and clipped a snowbank making a turn onto the gate's entrance road, sending up a spray of ice crystals. Its arrival was dramatic enough to have every guard train his rifle at the sedan, despite the fact that it had Flygvapen stenciled on its doors.

"Sergeant, I'm Lieutenant Tallberg," said the car's passenger, leaning out the rear window and showing the guards his identification. "Ormand Tallberg. Has anything unusual happened here? Any aircraft land?"

"Apart from our own aircraft on training flights, no, sir," said the sergeant. "And nothing in the last hour."

"Thank God, they haven't arrived yet. Look, there will be two trucks driving through this gate in a few minutes. They are air force trucks, they're on a vital mission and they will not stop. If you don't raise the barrier they will crash it. They must not be hindered. Understand?"

"Completely, Lieutenant, completely. I'll let them through. Why is their mission so vital?"

"That's top secret, though by the morning you'll probably know all about it. Driver, the collection."

The toll bar was raised just in time for the sedan to pass. It swung to the right and sped off, racing toward the internment area at the highest speed the narrow, ice-covered road would allow.

"There's the field," said the pilot, pointing to a pattern of lights laid out on the darkened landscape. Beyond them, the only way Norrköping could be spotted was its control tower beacon. "We will begin initial let-down procedures, Herr Oberst. Go back and wait with your men. We have a little while still."

"What do you mean, a little while?" the colonel repeated. "How far away is that base? I can almost reach out and touch it."

"Illuminated objects look closer at night than they really are. At times that makes it difficult to land. Go back to your men, I'll tell you when we are on final approach."

When the colonel reappeared in the main cabin, he informed his men about the field having been sighted and reassured them that the mission was on schedule. He went to the rear of the cabin where he sat beside the main hatch. After the transport had landed, he would be the first to stand and the first to leave the plane.

"What the hell's happening?" Lacey asked as the approach and marker lights to one of the runways suddenly came on. "It's a little early for us. You think this has anything to do with Paulson getting a call on the hangar phone?"

"We'll find out in a second, here he comes," said Norris. "Commander, what's with the lights?"

"Gentlemen, we have trouble," Paulson announced, out of breath from running back to the Night Hawk. "A Lufthansa airliner has declared an in-flight emergency and will be landing soon."

"You mean a German air liner?" Norris asked, more than a little incredulous. "How the hell can that happen? This is a military field."

"There's a treaty. Any German civilian air liner or military courier aircraft may land at a Swedish air base if it's in trouble. This base has been designated as an emergency field for all Stockholm-bound aircraft and the air liner in trouble is Lufthansa's regular, nighttime flight from Copenhagen. The only other field available is Malmslätt and since it is near our largest aircraft factory, it's our test center. A very sensitive installation."

"I know," said Lacey. "That would be like using Wright Field or Muroc for emergencies. Or Pax River, right outside of Washington."

"OK, I see it his way," Norris relented. "When do

you expect this plane in and how long will we be delayed?"

"Ten minutes, perhaps less," said Paulson. "The tower crew told me the pilots can see our runway lights. You cannot take off until the passengers and crew have been taken to a building. Once inside they will not hear your engines. You'll be delayed a half hour, perhaps an hour at the most."

"Wait a minute, what's this?" Lacey warned. "He's driving like a bat out of hell."

Lacey pointed at a staff car barrelling onto the tarmac. It drove through the collection of interned airplanes and screeched to a halt a few feet away from the Night Hawk and the men assembled near it.

"Wing Commander, I just came from Drache's estate!" Tallberg shouted, the moment he jumped out of the car. "The Germans will be arriving here at any minute."

"Yes, we cleared them to land," said Paulson automatically. "Wait. How did you know their air liner was making an emergency landing."

"An air liner?" Paulson's quick response caught Tallberg off guard and he slowed his stride for a moment before he made the connection between what he knew and what Paulson had told him. "So that's how they plan to do it. It is ingenious. Sir, before Drache died he told Ian MacAlister that the Germans are sending SS soldiers to take the jet from us. They were to guard it until their repair team arrives tomorrow. They must be on the air liner."

"You mean it's carrying soldiers?" Paulson gave Tallberg a puzzled, uncomprehending stare, as if he couldn't believe what he was being told. "But how can that be? It's a civilian air liner."

"In a totalitarian state there's little difference between civilian and military," said Lacey. "You're right,

Lieutenant. It is ingenious. A Luftwaffe transport trying to sneak into this country would've been spotted. But who watches an air liner on a regularly scheduled flight?"

"Where are those SS commandoes?" Norris asked. "Are they still at the estate? And how's Ian? Is he alive?"

"MacAlister is injured but alive. The British are driving here in the trucks. They're a few minutes behind me and I hope they arrive very soon."

"They're not going to arrive soon enough for us," Lacey advised. "We better move the jet. Hide it on some other part of the field. As soon as the Germans see this British C-47, they'll know something's up. Squadron leader, hook up the tow tug. Vince, are you finished?"

"Sure thing, Colonel," said Capollini. "We just finished capping both drop tanks. We still got about forty gallons in that last drum. What should we do with it?"

"Get it out of the way. We're moving the Night Hawk. John, you better climb aboard now."

"Colonel, we better trade places," Roberts told Whitney. "When we reach the base I'll be wanting to make a quick exit to join my men."

Roberts had been sitting next to the driver ever since they left Drache's estate. Now, as he leaned forward, so far forward he was pressing his face against the windshield, Whitney slid under Roberts and he took Whitney's spot beside the passenger's door. With a little more room to move around in, he was able to change the empty clip in his Sten gun for a new, full one.

"There, there's the base," said the driver, pointing at a slowly rotating beacon in the distance. "We have almost arrived. Can I slow down now, Captain?"

"No, not until we're approaching the gate," said Roberts. "What the hell's going on? They got a runway lit up. Don't tell me they're welcoming the bastards?"

"They could be," Whitney advised. "It could also be a training flight. Don't jump to a rash conclusion. We should wait until we talk to base authorities. Wing Commander Paulson in particular. Whatever's happening, there's the aircraft. I'd say it is four to five miles out."

"Reducing speed to one hundred and twenty miles an hour," reported the pilot, retarding the left throttle. "Give me thirty-five degrees on the flaps and lower the landing gear."

"Flaps coming down, thirty-five degrees," said the co-pilot. "Look, I can see the interned aircraft. There, on the left side of the base. That group has so many large bombers it has to be them."

As the DC-3 slowed, first its flaps then its main landing gear were lowered. Because of its dead engine the gear took longer to extend than usual and it caused the air liner to sway until the pilots jumped on the rudder pedals to correct the problem. At five miles out, the airplane was seen as a formation of wing tip and fuselage lights and the faint muttering of its one good engine could be heard in the internment area.

"The drum's out of the way," said Capollini returning to the Night Hawk. "What about the battery cart, Colonel?"

Capollini pointed at a small, two-wheeled cart sitting about a hundred feet away under the nose of a

B-17.

"Shit, it's too far away and we don't have the time to get it," said Lacey. "If we have to, we can use the plane's internal batteries to start the engines. Grab that fire extinguisher and climb aboard, Vince. I'd like to have someone along who really understands English."

With Norris inside the jet's cockpit and the tow bar reconnected to its nose gear, it was ready to be moved. And in fact Lacey started the jet rolling before Capollini managed to return, dragging the fire extinguisher with him.

The Me-262 lurched forward on the initial pull from the tug. Lacey and Capollini rode on the tug, behind its driver and carefully balancing the extinguisher between them. Lacey motioned toward a perimeter road running off from the tarmac; he wanted to take it instead of a taxiway that was closer to them. After some haggling with the driver, the Night Hawk swung onto the narrower strip of asphalt. Its wing tips barely cleared the snowbanks on either side. The taxiway would've given it much more room, but it was heading for one of the few patches of forest on the otherwise clear airfield. In a little over a minute the jet would be out of sight.

"At least that's safe," said the Dakota pilot, watching the Night Hawk disappear. "What about us, Colonel? Should we move the Dak?"

"No, it's too late for that," McClory answered, "and where could you hide her? I think you better arm yourselves and hide somewhere. I'm glad I decided to bring this along."

McClory slid a Colt .45 from under his coat and pulled back its slide bar to cock it.

"I only wish I brought more than one extra clip of ammunition for it."

"In addition to our side arms, we have two Sten guns aboard the aircraft," advised the pilot. "I'm going back for them. Fraser, you just volunteered to come with me."

As the pilot selected one of his crew to help him retrieve the machine guns from their Dakota, the rest followed McClory to find a hiding place among the hangars and other parked airplanes.

"Cowl flaps, closed," read off the air liner's co-pilot. "Landing gear down and locked. Tail wheel, locked. Brake pressure is normal. Switching on landing lights."

What had been a dark silhouette barely outlined by anti-collision lights became a glowing nova when its powerful landing lamps were snapped on.

"Jesus Christ, I think I see a swastika on its wing!" Roberts exclaimed, training his binoculars on the rapidly approaching air liner. "And there's something on its nose. Luft . . . Lufthansa, that's the German air line, isn't it?"

"Yes, but do you really think the Nazis would use a civilian air liner to fly in storm troopers?" Whitney asked.

"Of course, it's brilliant. That's what the spy Ian killed told him. OK, you can start slowing, Corporal. But don't stop under any circumstances. Whether it's closed or open, you go through that gate."

The trucks finally began to slow as they approached the first gate in the airfield's perimeter fence. As they had been ordered, the guards lifted the toll bar and waved the trucks in. They each sideslipped going through the turn coming dangerously close to the guardhouse. They drove past the entrance and turned sharply again, taking the same route Tallberg did to reach the internment area while the air liner dropped toward the runway threshold.

"Holding air speed at one-twenty," said the pilot. "Five hundred feet to go. Give me full flaps."

"Flaps down, full," replied the co-pilot, glancing at his commander, then beyond him. "Something's wrong over there. Where the jet is stored. There's a British transport sitting next to the trailers. We should tell our passengers about this."

"I will. I will. Once we're down."

Hidden behind a stand of pine trees, the Me-262 was at last out of sight of the arriving air liner. But the piercing beams of its landing lights could be seen and the rumble of its struggling engine filled the air.

"I don't see any trucks coming to the rescue, Colonel," said Capollini. "All those Nazis have to do is look under the covers on them trailers to know what's happening. It won't take them long to find us. You carrying a gun?"

"Just a standard .45," Lacey admitted, shifting his glance from the DC-3 to Capollini. "And Norris has one as well."

"So do I, but I don't think three automatics are going to stop a plane full of storm troopers. If things really got hot, maybe we should launch the jet ourselves?"

"We might have to. But I'll decide when and if we do it. Those SAS guys were good when they rescued us the first time, I'm sure they'll do it again."

Its right wing dipping slightly, the air liner settled

onto Norrköping's illuminated runway. Its tail was just touching down as the SS colonel ran from the back of its main cabin to the cockpit.

"I see what you mean," he said, looking out the cockpit's left window. "The Swedes are doing something. I think we caught them trying to double-cross us. Berlin was right to send us in. The British are trying to steal the Night Hawk. Take the next taxiway, get us as close to that area as you can."

"Turn off your headlights," Roberts ordered, watching the DC-3 land. "Turn off your lights, Corporal."

"But, Captain, we still have a long way to go," said the driver. "This road is narrow and it would be dangerous without lights."

"It'll be a hell of a lot more dangerous if they see us." Roberts nodded at the plane swinging off the runway. "Turn them off, damn it. Don't worry about the truck behind us. My lieutenant will know what we're doing."

The lead truck switched off its head and tail lights an instant later; a few seconds afterwards the lights on the second truck also flickered out. Now a pair of dark hulks, they continued toward the internment area. From a distance, they were almost invisible.

"The Swedes have apparently done a deal with the Allies," the colonel informed his men as he made his way downhill to the hatch. "There's a British transport sitting beside the trailers holding the Night Hawk. I have no idea what we'll encounter, but our mission is even more critical. Leutnant, you and your men are to remain with this aircraft. The rest of you are to follow me. The fate of our most advanced fighter, and the Reich, is in our hands."

At the back of the cabin, the colonel waited for the DC-3 to start slowing before he opened its main hatch. Propwash from the left engine caught the door and blew it the rest of the way open. The cabin filled with a blast of frigid air and the roar of the Pratt and Whitney. It was so loud the colonel had to shout his orders for his men to disembark.

The air liner was still creeping along when he jumped onto the taxiway. He swept the terrain with his Schmeisser as the balance of his squad poured out the hatch. They grouped into four-man teams before the colonel signalled them to charge the collection. Moments after the last man jumped from the air liner, all its exterior lights blinked out. It too became a dark, nearly invisible hulk.

"What does that mean?" Paulson asked when the DC-3 extinguished its lights. "Mister McClory, what does it mean?"

"I'd say the Germans are getting ready to attack," said McClory, glancing out from his hiding place in the hangar. "And I'm afraid we're going to be the only ones who can stop them. The SAS won't arrive on time."

The snow field bordering the taxiway was almost two feet high, forcing the storm troopers to charge across it as if they were wading through heavy surf. A dozen yards in front of them was the collection's line of bombers and transports. The individual aircraft were easily discerned, as was any movement around them. Of which, ominously, there was none.

"Something's wrong here," the colonel warned. "I don't see any guards. Everyone, stay alert."

"They're almost on top of us," said one of the Dakota's crew men. "Should we open fire, Lieutenant?"

"I don't think so," answered its pilot. "Colonel, what do you advise?"

"Don't fire until they're on the tarmac," said Mc-Clory. "The only thing we got going for us is surprise. We have to hit as many of them in our opening shots as possible."

"So long, gentlemen. I have to be going," said Roberts, opening the passenger door slightly. "Corporal, slow down when we reach the airplanes. Drive all the way through them and when you get to the other side, stop the truck and abandon it. You too, Colonel. See you after the battle."

Roberts swung the door open the rest of the way and climbed out, using whatever toe holds and hand holds he could find to hang onto the cab. He waved to his lieutenant in the second truck and, like Roberts, climbed out of the cab. Several faces peered around the lead truck's tail; Roberts shouted for them to prepare to jump and they acknowledged him with quick salutes.

As they reached the internment area, the trucks slowed drastically. In moments they were going barely faster than a crawl; for Roberts it was easy to leap off and hit the ground running. His men started pouring over the truck's tailgate the instant they saw him. The commandoes in the second truck repeated the maneuver with the lieutenant jumping off its cab and the rest dropping out the back.

The harsh rumble of diesels rolled across the tarmac, preceding the trucks and taking everyone by surprise. By the time it reached the opposite end of the collection, the lead truck was empty and it drove by the Dakota without drawing a shot from the Germans. Only when the second one appeared did they respond.

"Open fire! Open fire!" the colonel shouted, training his Schmeisser on the dark hulk moving through the airplanes.

A dozen flashes of fire answered his order, though none could get a clear shot at the truck because of the aircraft. Stray slugs tore holes in its canvas sides, only when it emerged from the rows did a full burst lace its cab. The driver was hit in the chest and died almost immediately; he slumped against the wheel of the truck, locking it in a right turn.

Picking up speed rapidly, it grazed one of the trailers which had once held the Night Hawk, causing some wreckage hidden under its tarpaulin to shift and roll off. The truck scraped past the trailer and plowed into the tail of the Dakota. It came to a stop, crushing the right stabilizer against the fuselage.

"I don't think they've located us yet," said Roberts, using the landing gear leg of a B-17 for cover. "Sergeant, let's announce ourselves. Let's tell them it's the SAS."

Roberts pointed to a team of four men running past the tail of another Fortress. They wore dark gray uniforms instead of black, and carried MP-40 machine pistols. Roberts and the SAS men around him opened up with their Sten guns. The muffled spitting contrasted with the sharp rattle of the MP-40s being fired at the truck. One by one the Germans Roberts had spotted staggered and slumped to the ground. None of them heard the gunfire that killed them.

"Corporal, *panzerfaust*," the colonel ordered, pointing at the crippled Dakota. "Complete its destruction."

The corporal armed the launcher he'd been carrying with one of his anti-tank grenades. He sighted in the transport and fired the rocket-propelled charge. It went hissing out of the launcher and hit the Dakota in its nose, just behind the cockpit. The grenade had almost punched its way out the other side of the fuselage by the time it exploded. The blast tore apart the nose section, disintegrating the cockpit and shearing off the rest of the section. Debris came raining down on the tarmac as the storm troopers continued to occupy the internment area. The sound and the initial flash of the detonation were heard and seen all over the airfield.

"Jesus, this is getting serious, Colonel," said Capollini, flinching at the explosion. "Things don't sound too good for our guys."

"No, they don't. It's getting out of hand," Lacey observed, "and I can't see where that air liner is anymore. We better move the jet, and I better climb on board."

"Bastards, they shouldn't have done that," said the Dakota's pilot. "Not to my airplane."

He jumped out of his hiding place in the hangar and ran to its front. Using one of its side posts for cover, he fired his Sten gun at the figures advancing across the tarmac. Its loud, unsilenced bursts, along with gunfire from others inside the hangar, drew the attention of most of the Germans."

"Return their fire!" shouted the colonel. "And take the trailers. Seize them!"

"Captain, watch it!" the sergeant warned, nearly tackling Roberts to bring him down.

An instant later, the glazed nose of the Heinkel 111 Roberts had been moving by was shattering with a burst of machine gun fire. Before he could train his weapon on the man trying to kill him, the other SAS commandoes answered with theirs. The storm trooper was hit with full bursts in his stomach and chest and the force of the impacts threw him onto the wing of a Spitfire.

"Thanks, Sergeant. That really saved me," Roberts admitted, being helped to his feet by his team. "You too, Barker, that was good shooting. How the hell did he get over there, on the opposite side of the collection?"

"They must be infiltrating that side farther on down," said the sergeant. "Where most of the heavy fighting is."

"Probably, and since none of our men are over there, we better clear it. Barker, cover the sergeant and myself, then we'll cover you."

Crouching low, the two black figures scuttled across the center lane like a pair of crabs. A moment later they were joined by the other member of their team and together, they moved through the rows of fighters and trainers, searching for more storm troopers.

The first two Germans who managed to climb on top of the prized trailers were shot off them by a barrage of gunfire from the open hangar. Their bodies tumbled to the ground, where the rest of their detail was pinned by the barrage.

"Panzerfaust," the colonel told his man with the grenade launcher. "I don't care if you destroy the whole hangar, just stop them."

The corporal quickly armed his launcher with another grenade and fired it into the hangar. However, it failed to hit a building support beam or other solid object. The anti-tank weapon punched a hole in the back of the hangar and exploded several hundred feet behind it, creating a loud blast but causing no damage.

"Colonel, we better try regular hand grenades," advised a sergeant as his commanding officer joined him beside the trailers. "We should save the tank weapons for other uses."

The colonel barked more orders and several wooden-handled grenades were thrown at the hangar. Each of the heavy-ended sticks spun through the air and hit the asphalt in front of the hangar entrance. They did little damage when they went off, except for one which clattered into the hangar. Its explosion lifted two men into the air. When they came back down, they were dead.

With the tug's engine whirring softly, the Night Hawk moved farther along the perimeter road, leaving the trees behind it. In the open, the sounds of the growing battle were louder, they seemed to be following the jet. At an intersection with a taxiway, the tug brought it to a halt and Capollini ran back to its cockpit.

"Colonel, Commander, where do you want us to take you?" he asked.

"The farthest runway from the internment area," said Norris after consulting with Lacey. "If the Nazis win, we'll need as much time as we can get to start this thing."

The sharp rattle of Schmeissers caught Roberts's attention as he moved through the back row of fighters. It came from the front row and sounded very close. Creeping around a forest of landing gear struts, Roberts led his team to the source of the lethal rattling and found storm troopers hiding behind the massive tires of a P-38 Lightning.

"Captain, they have some of our men pinned down," the sergeant advised. "They'll kill them if we don't help."

"Climb onto the wings of this airplane," said Roberts, "and break out grenades. You better make them concussion types. The Swedes have been promised these planes and I don't know if any of them are filled with gasoline."

Roberts and his team climbed onto the wings of the P-51 they'd been hiding behind. The aircraft in front of it was the Lightning and by peering over the top of its wings, they could see the Germans, intent on slaughtering the commandoes they had trapped under a bomber. First Roberts, then his team members hurled their grenades at the storm troopers. They had only just become aware of the grenades when they detonated. Though protected by the Mustang's wings, Roberts and his team still felt the shock waves from the multiple blasts. They looked back over the wings to find the Germans either rolling on the ground or attempting to stand.

"Take care of them," Roberts ordered, jumping off the leading edge of the wing. "If they so much as lift a finger in resistance, kill them!"

Roberts turned to find one of the storm troopers leaning against one of the Lightning's propellers, and pulling a Luger out of its holster. A muffled burst of gunfire sent him crashing to the ground. Roberts moved under the P-38 and quickly surveyed the other stunned Germans while his men tied them up. He came across one whose leg was twisted grotesquely, the blasts had thrown him against a landing gear strut and had broken his leg.

"You poor bastard," Roberts uttered, then he realized the German was reaching for his machine pistol and he brought one of his combat boots down on his hand, breaking it with a sharp crunch. "I suddenly don't feel too fucking sorry for you."

Roberts lowered his Sten gun and flicked its trigger. A half dozen slugs hit the German in the chest. He spasmed once, twice and died.

"Why did you kill him?" Barker questioned. "Cap-

340

tain, he was helpless. He was injured."

"Not so helpless that he didn't try to kill me," said Roberts sternly. "You either capture the enemy or kill him, and if you give him half a chance he'll kill you. Now get those two tied up and follow me."

"What on earth is this?" the colonel asked, crouching behind the engineless, tailless fuselage of an Me-109. "Where did it come from?"

"It rolled from the trailer when the truck hit it," said one of the storm troopers hiding with him. "It must be part of the jet we came to protect. Isn't it, Colonel?"

"No, I'm not in the Luftwaffe but I know aircraft. And this isn't part of the jet we came to protect. The Swedes and the British have done something with it. Go tell the men at the air liner about this, Private. Tell them the Night Hawk has been hidden on this base somewhere. I want the rest of you to provide cover fire for me. I'm going to find out what's on this trailer."

On the taxiway, there was much more room for the Night Hawk. The tug driver didn't have to worry about it scraping against the snowbank and was able to increase his speed. So much so he had trouble slowing down as he approached the distant runway. Norris had to use his main brakes to help reduce their speed just before they swung off the taxiway.

"I think that was a little close," said Capollini after they had come to a stop. "You unhook the bar from the nose gear, I'll see what the pilot wants."

Capollini set the fire extinguisher on the ground as he left the tug and ran to the jet. This time he climbed the side of the Me-262, and found Norris and Lacey already doing their pre-start checks.

"Keep all electrical systems off," Norris advised. "That includes your flight suit heater, helmet mike,

341

everything. We have to save all our battery power for starting the engines."

"I got it," said Lacey. "It's going to stay mighty cold and dark in here. Vince, you got your flashlight with you?"

"Sure thing, Colonel." Capollini handed his flashlight over to Lacey, who in turn handed it to Norris. "How do you think I did the checks on the drop tank caps? What do you guys want us to do?"

"Move that towing mule away from us," said Norris. "Tell the driver to take it back to the taxiway. You stand by as fire guard. Want to add anything, Dennis?"

"Yes, watch the internment area for us. If you see something happen, tell us."

Capollini climbed down from the cockpit and relayed Norris's orders to the tug driver. As he was moving the fire extinguisher to the right side of the jet, he could hear Norris running through his checklists.

"Oxygen regulator, normal. Oxygen pressure, four-twenty psi. Batteries, off. Generators, off. Pitot heat, off. Fuel selectors, off. Throttles, closed."

Roberts didn't wait for the sergeant or Barker to join him. He made his way around the rows of aircraft, hunting for more Germans. He didn't have to look very far. He found one crouching behind the tail of a fighter in the back row. By the time he sprang up, Roberts had his Sten gun trained on him and it popped. Once.

Roberts squeezed the trigger again but nothing happened. There had only been one bullet in his gun and now it was empty. The German staggered from the impact but managed to regain his balance. He forced his hands off the wound in his abdomen and wrapped them around his Schmeisser. Roberts made

342

a grab for his Beretta, only to have Barker step out of the shadows and fire a long burst from his Sten. The storm trooper was thrown against the hangar behind the aircraft and slid to the ground, dead from more wounds in his stomach and chest.

"Barker, you stay with me," said Roberts, changing the empty clip in his submachine gun for a full one. "This is the second time you saved my life. My thanks, again."

"Captain, where do we go now?" asked the sergeant, joining Roberts and Barker.

"To the end hangar. That's where most of our people are and if we join them, we can rout the Germans completely. We can push them back to their airplane."

"Leutnant!" shouted the private, fighting his way through the snow to the air liner. "Leutnant, the colonel says the jet isn't here. He sent me to warn you, it's hidden somewhere else on this base!"

The storm trooper was met by other soldiers at the edge of the taxiway and brought to the air liner where he repeated his message to the officer left in charge.

"Corporal, go ask the pilots if they can see anything from the cockpit," the lieutenant ordered. "Did the colonel tell you what he plans to do next?"

"No, but he wants you to move and seize the jet if you spot it," said the private. "If you have to, destroy it so the British cannot have it."

"I've seen enough. This is a trick," said the colonel, sliding off the trailer he had climbed on. "It's filled with the parts of other machines, not the Night Hawk. We had better make plans to withdraw."

"Colonel, you should see this," warned one of his

other men, scurrying from one trailer to the other. "We killed two soldiers near one of the bombers. They wore no uniforms, no insignia except for these caps."

The soldier handed his commanding officer a beige beret with a badge showing a winged sword. For a few moments, the colonel examined the beret with first surprise, then shock.

"My God, this is from the Special Air Services," he remarked. "England's best commando force. We had better withdraw, we can't match them. Spread the order, everyone leaves. Destroy that transport, that should occupy the English."

Those with the colonel pulled hand grenades off their service belts and hurled them at the crippled Dakota beside the trailers. The truck that had damaged it was still resting beside the plane, its engine still running. The grenades bounced and rolled under both of them, a few seconds later they exploded.

Initially the blasts ripped open the underside of the Dakota's fuselage and flipped the truck on its side. The unused drum of jet fuel erupted a split-second afterwards, creating a fireball that engulfed the transport and split the night sky. A powerful shock wave rippled through the collection, shaking the hangars and knocking down anyone within a hundred yards of the explosion. It was seen, heard, even felt across the air base.

"Jesus H. Christ, it sounds like the Germans are winning the war," said Norris, looking over at the internment area. For a brief time the fireball was brilliant enough for him to read his instruments. "I'm ready to leave with or without this damned plane. Are you ready?"

"Ready, John," Lacey replied. "Hurry up and light this thing. And remember, don't waste battery power.

This isn't equipped with a starting crank."

"OK, here goes." Norris was afraid to begin the ignition sequence, afraid to ruin it and drain the batteries. Yet he was more fearful of being captured by the Germans, and the Night Hawk was the only way to escape. "Batteries, on. Generators, on. Inverter, on. Opening throttle."

Norris pushed the right throttle forward, to its gate stop and snapped it back, priming the Riedel motor. Its whine could scarcely be heard above the continuing roar of the explosion. He pressed the tachometer button and watched the needle on one of his gauges climb slowly. The plane's batteries were now powering the Riedel motor and bringing the right engine to life.

The tachometer needle didn't rise as fast as it had during the earlier test run. It wasn't quite touching the seven hundred rpm mark when Norris hit the starter button on the right hand throttle. He felt if he waited any longer the batteries would lose their charge. He was rewarded with a deep, vibrating rumble and a long tongue of flame from the starboard engine pod. The sharp bang it emitted was all but drowned out by a second, more powerful blast in the internment area.

The consuming fireball had found the Dakota's fuel tanks. What remained of the transport was disintegrated, melted by the intense flash. Those just getting to their feet were blown back off them, the tarpaulins on the trailers were set afire and some of the planes near the blast site were damaged. All that would remain of D for Duncan after the fires had died would be its engines and wing tips.

"Oh Christ, there goes our ride home," Roberts sighed, rising to his feet. "Looks like we're going to be guests of the Swedes."

"Well the Germans don't look like they want to be," said Barker. "The survivors are heading for the air liner. Captain, what's that screeching sound?"

"I've only heard it once before. That's the sound of a jet plane. Colonel Lacey and his pilot must've decided it's time to leave, and they sure picked one hell of a time to do so. The Germans can probably hear this, that's why they're retreating to the air liner."

"What can they do there? Except provide us with an easy target."

"They can use the aircraft to block the runway the Night Hawk's on. Sergeant, gather up some men and tell the rest to chase down the Nazis. Barker, you're with me. We're commandeering that truck."

Roberts pointed at the Swedish air force truck which had brought them to Norrköping. It sat beside the open hangar, in the same condition as when it had been abandoned.

"Engine speed, three thousand rpm," said Norris, checking his instruments. "Generators are running. We can switch on the rest of our systems. Stand by for number two engine."

Lacey flipped on one of the switches at his station, and the fluorescent light tubes on either side of his seat buzzed softly and cast a bluish glow over the instruments. He also plugged in his helmet's microphone leads and heard Norris repeating the start procedure for the left engine.

"Riedel motor, engaged. Throttle, closed. Left fuel valve, off. Left tachometer gauge, on."

A few moments after his private recital, the port engine began to throb and a tongue of flame exploded out its jet pipe; the sharp crack it made echoed across the base. Even those who didn't pay attention to the roar of the first engine noticed the ignition of the second.

"Leutnant, the pilots have spotted the jet!" announced a storm trooper, appearing at the DC-3's hatch. "It's on another runway, on the opposite side of the field. They say it's intact. It looks ready to fly."

"Tell them to start the other engine," said the lieutenant. "They must take us to that runway. We must stop the Allies from stealing the Night Hawk."

"Leutnant, what about the colonel and the rest of our squad?" asked the private who brought them the news.

"We can't wait for them. They must fight a holding action. Keep the British off us until we can move."

The DC-3's right engine fired up easily, its rumbling warned the storm troopers around the plane that they should board it. The stairs were left down after the last man climbed inside and the engines emitted a louder, flat howl. Rolling forward a few yards, the air liner picked up enough momentum to swing around sharply and head back down the taxiway. During the turn its landing lights came on, their beams swept over the internment area, briefly illuminating the Germans struggling through the snow to reach the air liner and the SAS commandoes pursuing them.

"Is this all you managed to round up?" Roberts asked as the sergeant returned with only three other commandoes.

"Afraid so, sir," the sergeant replied. "The lieutenant's leading the rest on a mopping up sweep."

"All right, get them in the load bed. Cut some slits in the canvas sides to use as gun ports. Prepare for a wild ride. We're the only ones who can catch that

Nazi air liner."

Roberts climbed into the truck's cab and, with the keys the driver had given him, turned its diesel over. A heavy plume of black smoke shot out its stack as the truck backed away from the hangar it was hiding beside. Roberts grinded a few gears before he shifted it to first and it lurched forward when he jumped on the gas pedal. He selected a taxiway instead of the perimeter roads because it would get him to the aircraft faster. Even so, Roberts had a lot of ground to cover and the Germans had a head start.

"Good luck, Colonel! See you guys in England!" Capollini shouted, backing away from the Me-262, and dragging the fire extinguisher with him.

Lacey and Norris each gave him a quick wave, then pulled down their sections of the Night Hawk's long, framed canopy, thankful that the freezing winds no longer swirled around them and the engine noise didn't pierce their ears so painfully. They quickly made the rest of their checks.

"Rudder trim, neutral. Stabilizers, plus three degrees," said Norris, pushing a small lever on the left side of the cockpit. A gauge in front of it showed the position the tail plane was taking as he moved the lever. "This is a lot different than the old trim wheels. Easier to use too. Setting flaps at twenty degrees. You'll have to help me check them, Dennis. There's position marks on their upper surfaces."

While Norris glanced out the left side, Lacey glanced out the right. Since his seat was almost in direct line with the wing's trailing edge, Lacey had a much easier time watching the flaps drop and the white marks on their top surfaces appear. When he looked up, he could also see a set of powerful beacons moving across the field. He immediately recognized them as landing lights.

"John, there's another plane on the runway," Lacey warned, "at two o'clock. I think it's that German air liner the SS arrived in."

"I see him, what the hell's he doing?" Norris asked.

"They must've heard our engines ignite. Don't you see, they're out to stop us. I think they've turned onto the runway that intersects with this one. If they reach the intersection, we won't have enough room to take off."

"And there isn't enough time to beat them out," Norris added. "They'll make it to the intersection before we will. They have to be stopped, and there's only one way to do it. Arming cannons."

On the control stick below the grip was a large button that Norris pushed in, activating the Night Hawk's battery of 30mm cannons and loading shells into their breeches. He also tapped a switch under his gun sight, causing a bright yellow circle and cross hairs to appear on its reflector plate. After he adjusted their size and weakened their intensity, Norris unlocked the brakes and the Me-262 began to roll forward.

Using his throttles, and brakes, he slewed the jet to the right. He was almost immediately rewarded with the dim outline of the air liner appearing in his sight's reflector plate. Norris pressed the control stick's trigger and the whole jet vibrated as the cannons fired. The muzzle flashes lit up the nose and its radar aerials, and four converging lines of tracers sparkled into the night, missing the DC-3's tail by several feet.

"Aim ahead of it," Lacey advised. "Let the bastard walk right into your fire."

The Night Hawk moved again, straightening out

and rolling forward before turning to the right. Before he stopped it completely, Norris added a little extra power to his right engine, pointing the jet's nose ahead of the taxying air liner. He didn't need to sight in his target, in fact he realized it was better for him not to. All he did was jump on his foot pedals and squeeze the trigger.

This time the lines of cannon shells shot past the air liner's nose, then under it and an instant later were puncturing its left nacelle. High-explosive shells blew coweling panels off the engine and exploded behind its firewall, severing fuel and oil lines. Armor-piercing incendiaries penetrated the engine itself, killing it, and even tore through the plane's fuselage.

A blossom of flame rent open what remained of the engine nacelle. One cannon shell managed to hit a landing gear strut and smashed it, causing the rest of the gear to collapse. With its left wing scraping across the runway, the airliner spun to the left and plowed into a snowbank. It came to rest with its tail still on the runway, a crippled, burning wreck.

"That takes care of them," said Norris. "Let's get the hell out of here before someone else tries to stop us."

Norris realigned the jet on the runway's center line and, giving his controls and gauges one last check, released the brakes and opened the throttles. The roar of its engines grew dramatically, though its speed did not. If anything, it was off to a sedate roll.

"God, they shot the aircraft off the runway," said Barker, leaning forward to get a better look. "Did you see that?"

"Of course I did. But it doesn't mean we're not needed," Roberts answered. "They may have stopped the plane. They haven't stopped the men inside it."

* * *

"Everyone out!" shouted the lieutenant, grabbing men and pushing them past him toward the still-open hatch. "Everyone out, move! We still have our mission!"

Dazed by the crash, those storm troopers who weren't injured stumbled and fell out of the DC-3. Because its left engine was still burning, they scrambled to the runway where the lieutenant joined them. The air was filled with the scream of jet engines. In the distance the advancing Night Hawk could be seen.

"We are several hundred feet from the intersection," said the lieutenant. "If we run, we might beat the jet. Let the crew take care of the air liner. Follow me."

Jogging at first, the storm troopers quickly advanced to a flat-out run. They slung their Schmeissers over their shoulders instead of carrying them in their hands; it proved easier to run that way.

"John, can't you push this thing a little faster?" Lacey asked. "If this was a Mustang or some other propeller job, we'd be airborne by now."

"I know, but I can't race the engines," Norris replied. "I can't be too fast opening the throttles. If I do, I'll start cavitations in the compressor fans. The engines won't get a smooth air flow and we won't get full power. The engines could even catch fire if I race them."

"There they are," said Roberts, turning onto the runway the air liner had been using. "I knew it. I knew they wouldn't stop. I'm turning off our headlights. They won't see us until we're on top of them."

Roberts also shifted to high gear and put the gas pedal to the floor. As the truck's headlights were extinguished, it accelerated, becoming a dark hulk racing to catch a group of figures ahead of it.

"Air speed, one hundred miles an hour," said Norris calmly. "Another thirty miles an hour and I'll have take-off speed."

"Well, you better get it soon," said Lacey. "There's someone on the runway. And I think they're German."

As the truck approached the crippled air liner, gun barrels popped out its cab windows and through slits in the canvas cover over its load bed. Roberts brought out his Sten gun as well, balancing it on the window sill. Like his men, he fired a short burst at the plane's flight crew, scattering them. He was saving his ammunition for the storm troopers and he didn't have long to wait.

They had gone less than a hundred yards and the barrelling truck easily overtook them. With its lights out and the thunder of turbojets drowning out all other sounds, none of the Germans realized it was approaching them. The silencers on the Sten guns meant they didn't even hear the bursts of fire which killed them.

One by one, most of them staggered and fell, lines of holes in their backs. Barker emptied his gun at the lone German who actually turned and saw the truck, and Roberts managed to kill the last one. His submachine gun empty, he aimed the truck at the lieutenant and ran him down. The collision sent his body sprawling over the asphalt; he had scarcely stopped tumbling when Roberts swung the truck off the runway. It sent up a cloud of ice crystals and came to a halt after travelling a few yards. It was the safest, surest way Roberts could use to stop his vehicle short of the intersection.

Moments later the Night Hawk screamed by. At 120 miles an hour Norris pulled the control stick back slightly, raising the nose wheel into the air. The jet bounced gently on its main gear. It was almost ready to fly. At 130, it screamed off the runway.

Finally airborne, the Me-262 climbed away from Norrköping at a shallow angle. Its camouflage scheme quickly blended in with the night sky. Soon it would only be tracked by its brightly glowing exhausts. In minutes the Night Hawk would have to turn south; all Lacey and Norris had to do now was get it to England.

Chapter Thirteen: Rendezvous Battle Over The North Sea

"Braking wheels, retracting landing gear," said Norris as they crossed the runway threshold. "How are things with you?"

"I'm putting all radar systems on full power," Lacey replied. "Now I'll see what this gear can really do."

The main landing gear wheels were still spinning furiously after the jet's take-off. Norris applied the brakes to stop them before pressing the gear retract buttons. A soft grinding indicated the hydraulic pump was working, slowly retracting the nose gear and main gear struts. Because of the pump's operation, it would take almost a minute to bring them in.

The Night Hawk had barely cleared Norrköping's perimeter fence when a convoy of more Swedish air force vehicles came barrelling across the field. In addition to trucks there were ambulances, fire trucks and even the armored car which had originally been stationed in the internment area. Most drove to that section of the base, but a few surrounded the Lufthansa air liner and one picked up Roberts and his men. They were taken back to the collection where they found the Swedes busy fighting the fires started during

354

the battle, treating the wounded and taking charge of the captured storm troopers.

"We lost three men killed and two wounded," the lieutenant informed Roberts as he stepped down from the truck. "And one of the wounded is in serious condition. The Dakota crew has lost one killed and the pilot has been wounded. The Swedes have three dead, I don't know how many were injured."

"What about the krauts?" Roberts asked, watching the Swedes spray foam on the furiously burning remains of the Dakota. "How many did they lose?"

"We counted fifteen bodies. There were four survivors, all of them wounded. The Swedes have them. One of the wounded is the German CO, I thought you'd like to know that."

"Really? I'll have to meet him. Show me where he is."

Roberts was led to one of the ambulances parked on the tarmac. Three of the four men in it were laying on stretchers, the last one, an SS colonel, was sitting up, having his leg wound treated and arguing with Wing Commander Paulson.

"You're not in a position to make demands or threaten me," Paulson angrily replied. "You attacked my airfield, you invaded Swedish territory under the guise of a civilian air liner in trouble. All this in violation of our neutrality."

"You allowed the Allies to steal Germany's most valuable aircraft," said the colonel, wincing as a tourniquet was wrapped about his leg. "The Reich will not look kindly on that."

"For the sake of avoiding an even greater crisis with Sweden, I don't think the Third Reich will say much about this incident. Your actions give us the perfect pretext to declare war on Germany and move into the Allied camp. Sweden can mobilize an army of a quarter of a million men and our air force has almost a thousand combat aircraft. We are one more enemy you can't afford to have."

"Wing Commander? Excuse me, but I'd like to introduce my superior," said the lieutenant, interrupting the argument. "This is Captain Lee Roberts, Special Air Services."

Both Paulson and the SS colonel introduced themselves to Roberts, and both even congratulated him on a successful mission.

"We in the SS have great respect for you, Captain," the colonel added, a hint of admiration in his voice. "You are the best the Allies have. But you must admit we did come close to stopping you. It could have so easily been different. You and your men could've been lying here, dead, instead of mine and the Night Hawk would be in our hands."

"Well the situation isn't different," said Roberts. "You could've had the Night Hawk had you played the game right but you didn't. You can always count on a dictatorship to do the worst thing in its own self-interest. We didn't get that jet because we worked a better deal than you, we got it because you fucked up. You have only yourselves to blame."

"The prototype isn't in England yet, Captain. You and your American friends might still lose your prize to the Luftwaffe. They have a long and dangerous flight ahead of them. I hope you understand why I will not wish them luck."

"I understand," Roberts answered pleasantly, giving his counterpart a salute and a quick smile. "Fuck you too. And if you'll excuse me, I have my own wounded to look after."

Once its landing gear and flaps were retracted, the Night Hawk gained altitude swiftly. As it climbed to cruise level, Norris swung the jet onto a southwesterly heading. At cruise speed it would take him and Lacey just over half an hour to reach Sweden's eastern coast line.

"Levelling off at fifteen thousand feet," said Norris. "Setting cruise speed at three hundred miles an hour. How are things with you, Dennis? You on oxygen?"

"I'm on oxygen," Lacey advised, "but I'm having a little trouble with my gloves. I don't think the electric heaters in them are operating."

"Try fiddling with the plug. If that doesn't work, open up your warm air vent. I'm going to switch us over to our drop tanks. We better start using them before we reach German air space."

Next to the engine throttles was another pair of levers; each controlled a fuel selector valve for the Messerschmitt's two engines. Norris first moved the right lever forward, switching the starboard engine's fuel supply from the plane's internal tanks to one of its external ones. There was scarcely a sputter from the Junkers turbojet, its fuel flow was hardly interrupted.

The left hand lever proved harder to move. To Norris it felt a little too tight, as if it needed some lubricating oil, but he was able to make it creep forward. The problem took most of his concentration off his flying and, more dangerously, when the lever clicked out of the "front tank" position it did not automatically click into the the next one up.

"Stubborn little bastard!" Norris shouted at the control. "C'mon, move another half-inch."

"John, something's wrong," Lacey warned. "We're losing speed and there's a trail of white smoke from the port engine."

Norris immediately scanned the engine instruments on his panel and found the tachometer, fuel pressure gauge, injection pressure gauge and tail pipe temperature for the left engine were all falling. With its fuel supply interrupted, it had flamed out.

"Hold on, I've killed the port engine," said Norris, grabbing the left throttle and closing it. "I'm going to have to redo the whole starting procedure to fire it up again."

Like the engine readings, air speed fell rapidly. It dropped from three hundred to under two hundred miles an hour in seconds. With Norris preoccupied with closing the left throttle and running through the engine shut-down steps, the Night Hawk's nose started to rise, decreasing air speed further. By the time Norris was finished the jet was at stall speed.

Its port wing dipping slightly, it lost all forward momentum and slid off to the left. Norris felt the jet enter a spin, the night sky and darkened landscape gave him no visual references; he could only tell by the beginnings of centrifugal force and the reactions of his flight instruments.

"You better hurry and stop this thing," said Lacey, trying to find something around his seat to grab hold of. "Or we're going to find out real soon how well we put it back together."

The first rotation of the spin had barely been completed and already the Night Hawk's air frame was groaning. Norris jammed the rudder in the opposite direction of the spin and threw his control stick about the cockpit. The spin slowed, then stopped altogether before its second rotation had been completed. However, the Night Hawk was still in a dive and Norris had no intention of ending it.

"At Pax River we were ordered not to relight a jet engine above ten thousand feet," Norris told Lacey. "It would start a fire if we did."

"Well that was Maryland, where the tallest mountain is a hundred-foot-high molehill. This is Sweden, where there's a lot more mountains and they're a lot taller."

"It looks like we don't have a hell of a choice. Either we risk catching fire or we make a one-point landing on a mountain peak. I'm opening the fuel dump valve to drain out the excess fuel in the port engine or that too could start a fire."

Its gyrations stabilized, the Me-262 continued its dive at a shallow angle. It descended rapidly from fifteen thousand to ten thousand feet, dropping closer to the darkened landscape of pine-forested mountains and narrow lakes. An occasional glint of moonlight off an ice-covered surface and the sparkle of town lights were the only hints of any terrain features on the black and gray mantle below. Until they hit engine restart altitude, Norris remained silent. The moment the altimeter needle dipped to three thousand meters, he jumped into action.

"Air speed, one-eighty. Throttle, closed. Fuel pump, on," he quickly read off. "Ignition, on."

Norris pressed the button on the left throttle, causing an immediate jump in the dead engine's tachometer to several hundred rpm. At a thousand rpm he released the starter button and slammed the fuel selector lever from closed to its external tank setting. He was rewarded with a soft but satisfying click as the lever reached the setting, and a sharp bang from the left engine. A brief jet of flame shot from its end pipe and the Night Hawk swung slightly to the right as engine thrust built up.

"We're at about eight thousand feet," said Norris. "Your radar showing anything like a peak in front of us?"

"I'm not picking up anything but ground clutter," Lacey advised, his face pressed against the view finder over his primary radar screen. "You have to remember, this is interception radar. Not navigation or bombing radar and German equipment has a different style of scope from ours."

"OK, I'm going to pull her out. If we hit anything along the way, I'm holding you responsible for it."

Easing his control stick back, Norris began to gently end the Night Hawk's dive. Using his artificial horizon and altimeter, he levelled the aircraft off and pointed its nose skyward. Once he equalized throttle settings, he pushed both forward, increasing speed to 280 miles an hour. The dark horizon line quickly dropped under the jet's nose, replaced by a star-sparkled sky partially covered by cloud banks.

"OK, emergency's over," Norris sighed, "for now at least. Whatever this jet fuel has, it's got a real kick to it. It's a lot better than that coal oil crap the Germans made. I wonder if we'll have anymore problems like this on the way back to England?"

"Who knows what we'll have?" said Lacey. "This plane was just put back together by an inexperienced crew who didn't have a single manual to work with. If it weren't for the fact it's the most advanced fighter in the world, I wouldn't be sitting in it. I'll be very happy when we land."

At just under three hundred miles an hour, the Me-262 soon returned to its cruise altitude and was back on its southwesterly heading. For the time being the danger had passed.

"Well, there goes our second abort," said Powers as he watched another shadow climb away from his wing and turn onto a westerly heading. "I wish I could've given him an escort. Are you sure you translated his message properly?"

"Yes, he reported that his radar had failed and

360

much of his electrical system was going," Cox replied, glancing at his note pad again. "It's a wonder your pilot could even tap out this message with his position lights. I wish you could have sent along an escort as well, I have my doubts he'll make it to Scapa Flow, but we need every single aircraft. It was a hard decision for you to make and I'm sorry you had to do it."

"I feel like I'm abandoning him, though I think we'll be seeing Morelli again when we return home. He's a good pilot and he's gotten out of tough scrapes before. What I'm more worried about is my squadron. If I lose many more planes I won't be of much use to you. Should it get that bad, will you abort the whole mission?"

"I don't care if we're down to just this ship by the time we meet the Night Hawk, we're going ahead. By now, it's in the air and if it has to land at another Swedish air base, it'll be daylight before we can try again. And by then Germany will have half the Luftwaffe waiting for that aircraft. I don't think Dennis and John would like those odds."

Now reduced to ten airplanes, the squadron reformed into five pairs of fighters and continued on toward Sweden. In an hour they would reach its southwestern coast and would start climbing for the altitude they expected to find the jet cruising at. The P-61s would wait until it arrived or they received word that it had been delayed and the mission postponed. In the latter case, the chance of getting the Night Hawk to England without Germany learning of it would be lost.

"The latest report from Sweden, Herr Kommandeur," Lossberg announced grimly. He tossed out a single sheet of paper from his attaché case and

Heinrich managed to grab it before it fluttered to the ground. From the defeated look on the Gestapo chief's face, and the casual way he treated the report, Heinrich knew the news wouldn't be good.

"How did you manage to collect information like this?" he asked while still reading the report.

"We received a radio message from the air liner before it landed at Norrköping. The crew saw a British transport sitting beside the trailers that contained the Night Hawk. They thought the Allies might be trying to smuggle the jet out of the country. Our radar stations in Norway went on alert and, approximately ten minutes later, watched an aircraft lift off from the airfield. Based on its speed and climb rate, they claim it's not a transport but a high-performance machine. They say it's a fighter. I think it's the Night Hawk itself. You might as well show that to your pilots, let them make their own conclusions."

Once Heinrich was finished with the report, he handed it to the pilot standing beside him and turned to the others in the crowded ready hut.

"I think Herr Lossberg could be right," he told them. "We must operate on a worst-case basis and the worst here is that, somehow, the Allies helped the Swedes reassemble the prototype and now it's being flown to England. Since it was a British Dakota the air liner spotted, it's likely that the British are responsible for this. We don't know how they managed to repair it, or how well it's been repaired, but we can't allow the jet to reach England. We must destroy it."

"How will you do that?" Lossberg asked dejectedly. "This machine is completely superior to your fighters. You, everyone has told me that.

"We will exploit its weaknesses. Even an aircraft as revolutionary as the Night Hawk has its problems. The most critical is its range. From Sweden to England the distance is between six hundred and seven hundred miles. That is at the outer limit of its range. If we can engage it in a sustained dogfight, it may not be necessary to actually destroy the jet. Fuel starvation will bring it down. This will not be an easy kill for us, and not merely because of the nature of the target. Gentlemen, it's virtually certain the British will give it an escort. My bet is Mosquitoes."

Heinrich's last remark drew an appreciative murmur from his assembled pilots and radar operators.

"Perhaps we can finally take on the best the Royal Air Force has. To your fighters, we have not much time to stop the British. Take off individually and formate at ten thousand feet. I'll explain my plan to you once we are airborne. Good hunting and remember, either the Night Hawk itself or its secrets are in enemy hands. We are the only ones who can stop this disaster."

With their briefing at an end, the crews collected their flying gear and streamed out of the hut. Once he found the discarded report, Lossberg ran out and joined Heinrich in his own staff car. A variety of trucks and cars were used to drive the crews across the base to the dispersal points. All combat-ready fighters were kept at widely scattered hardstands, far away from the hangars and other base buildings, far away from the usual targets of night intruders. They were set in the forest surrounding the base, some distance away from any open ground.

Heinrich's car followed a taxi strip after crossing the runways and it seemed to Lossberg that they drove deep inside the forest before the group commander's night fighter appeared in its headlight beams. The driver pulled off the hardstand and parked near the ground crew's tent. With the headlights no longer illuminating it, the Heinkel 219 became a dark, brooding creature sitting in the middle of a clearing. It was like a dragon from some medieval legend, and it was hardly a silent, inactive one.

From the moment the staff car appeared, the Heinkel's ground crew was piling out of the tent and climbing over their charge, pulling the insulating covers off its engines and canopy and hooking auxiliary power lines to it.

"We last ran her engines about an hour ago," said the crew chief as he walked alongside Heinrich. "All systems checked out. She's as good as the day she left the factory."

"Excellent, she will have to be at her best," said Heinrich. "We may be hunting Mosquitoes. An elusive prey, the most worthy opponent in the world."

"You sound conceited, Kommandeur," Lossberg remarked. "You sound as if you are joining a game. May I remind you that it's you who will be held responsible if the Night Hawk is lost to the Allies. Do not treat such a responsibility so lightly."

"And don't you tell me how to approach this battle. This is what I do best. All your little schemes and murderous plans have only worsened this crisis. You didn't succeed with what you are best at, so now it rests on me and what I am best at. As I told you before, Herr Lossberg, I'm not like you. I'm a warrior, just like the men I will hunt and kill. They are likely to be the best the Allies have, but my men and I are better. Soon you will see how good we are. Sergeant, give me a boost."

Though its rail-thin boarding ladder was deployed, Heinrich still needed the help of his crew chief to climb up the side of his He-219. Finding hand holds in the dark was hard, even for someone experienced with the plane, and dangerous; by the time Heinrich reached the cockpit he was more than a dozen feet off the ground. He unlocked the hinged section of the canopy and pushed it up and to the right. With one leg in the cockpit, he straddled its edge while placing his parachute in his seat and arranging its harness. When Heinrich finally climbed in, all he had to do was slide the harness straps around his body and buckle them up.

Heinrich's radar operator had to use the same ladder and many of the same hand holds to reach his station. He sat directly behind the pilot, with little more than their armored head rests separating them. He faced the rear of the aircraft instead of forward, his radar scope and most of his other gear set against the back of the cockpit. Once he buckled his parachute, seat belt and shoulder straps, Heinrich started his checklist.

"Erich, make sure your suit-heating cord is plugged in properly," he warned. "I don't want you freezing like you did on the last sortie. Ejection system?"

"Seat ejector, armed," said the radar man. "Catapult handle locked and safetied.

"Same here. Oxygen system?"

"Oxygen line connected. Pressure meter reads full."

"Herr Heinrich, I though you were making an emergency take-off?" said Lossberg, standing below the cockpit. "The British could be in England by the time you finish."

"This is a night fighter, Herr Lossberg, not a car," Heinrich snapped. "You don't just turn a key in the starter and drive off. This is a complex aircraft, in many ways more complex than a jet. If this procedure is not followed to the letter, we could crash on take-off. Now, where were we? Oh yes, flight control lever, unlocked. Rudder control lever, unlocked."

Heinrich pushed down two handles on the left side of the cockpit, freeing the pedals under his feet and his U-shaped control yoke.

"Sergeant, turn the propellers."

While Heinrich continued his checks, the ground crew split into two teams and grabbed hold of the fighter's enormous, paddle-bladed, VDM propellers. They rotated them by hand, four rotations each, in order to clear accumulated oil from the engine cylinders.

"Batteries, off. Electrical system on external power," said Heinrich, flipping a pair of switches on the right side of the cockpit. "How are your systems performing, Erich?"

"All systems, coming on line," said the radar man, hunched over, his face pressed against the view finder of the main radarscope. "All readings look normal so far."

"Good, I'm almost finished here. Fluorescent cockpit lights, on. Auto-pilot system, off. Fuel pumps, off. Landing gear handle, locked. Flap handle, locked. Propeller switches, on automatic. Ignition switches, off. Fuel tank switches, on outboard tanks. Fuel mixture levers, on cut-off. Coolant flaps, closed. Sergeant, prepare for port engine start. Stand by to disengage external power."

"Herr Heinrich, remember, if you fail to stop the Night Hawk, do not bother returning!" said Lossberg, shouting his final threat as he backed away from the Heinkel.

"Herr Lossberg, if I fail, you better hope I return. If I don't, Berlin will have no one to blame but you. You may yet have to explain failure to Adolf Hitler."

After he issued his own warning, Heinrich raised his hand and pointed at the left engine. A few moments later a whine grew from its nacelle and the VDM propeller began to tick over. The shrouds covering the engine's exhaust stacks prevented the ignition flames from being seen. But they couldn't hide the smoke which enveloped the nacelle and left wing, or muffle the sound of the engine exploding to life.

When he was sure it had made a good start and would stay running, the sergeant motioned for the external power line to be disconnected. In the cockpit, Heinrich had already changed his fighter to internal power; the switch registered as a short blinking out of the fluorescent lights. He pulled the canopy down over himself and his radar man and locked it. The roar of the Diamler-Benz sitting behind his left ear was now muted and the cold winds no longer swirled into the cockpit.

As the right engine on Heinrich's '219 started, the sounds of more Diamler-Benz inlines coming to life were heard. The coughing and bursts of thunder drifted through the trees from the other hardstands. They were like the sounds of night creatures awakening and filling the forest with their calls. Then the landing lamps on the Heinkels were activated, creating islands of light scattered around the forest.

One by one, the creatures began moving toward open ground. Heinrich's '219 was the first to emerge from the forest; it moved down the taxiway he had driven across earlier and swung onto a dimly lighted strip of concrete. While it sat and ran its engines up for the final battery of tests, the rest of the squadron fell in line behind it.

In all, a dozen He-219s gathered on the taxi strip, the full, operational strength of Heinrich's group. After nearly a minute his checks were completed and he opened up his throttles and released his brakes. The bomber-sized fighter lurched onto its nose gear and rolled forward. The power of its Diamler-Benz inlines quickly had it speeding along the runway. At the halfway marker the nose wheel lifted off the ground and for a few moments the Heinkel rode on its main gear. The second time it bounced the fighter lifted into its natural element.

At full take-off power it climbed swiftly to ten thousand feet; when it reached that altitude there were two more He-219s chasing after it and a fourth hurtling down the runway. In minutes the entire squadron was airborne and wheeling above their darkened base in a great, loose cloud. They made one orbit, to allow the wing men to join their leaders, then headed due north, across the Denmark peninsula to the Skagerak, where they would make Germany's last attempt to stop the Night Hawk.

"You sound like a kid in a toy store," Norris remarked, becoming curious about the noises and appreciative swearing Lacey was making. "What's going on back there?"

"The Germans have come up with some fantastic equipment," said Lacey. "The Nazis don't use centrimetric radar like we do. They use radar in the meter range and the displays are all different. I have one scope that shows me distance and numbers, another shows me altitude. The resolution on this gear is much better than on the older systems and its range is forty kilometers, about twenty-five miles, three times the range of any other interception radar on a German night fighter.

"We have a tail warning radar and a special box on the IFF system. This box does more than identify friend or foe, it tells you who it is and where they are. This could be the heart of the jet's effectiveness. Combined with its improved radar and its speed, this could free the Night Hawk from the Himmelbett Line. It could roam at will across Europe, not tied to any

368

ground control."

"How does this IFF box work?" Norris asked. "Is it another radar set?"

"No, it's more ingenious than that. It homes in on the radars used by other planes. Every fighter and bomber on a night mission uses radar for navigation, bombing or interception. This gear detects it and can even tell you what type of plane you're tracking by the wavelength it picks up. It identifies both German and Allied planes, so you don't shoot down one of your friends."

"God, what an idea. We'd have to blind all our planes to protect them. Can you make that thing work, Dennis?"

"Easily. It's already got a target. An R.A.F. bomber, type unknown. Distance, thirty-six miles and twenty degrees to our left."

The Night Hawk banked gently, breaking away from the course it had been flying for the last fifteen minutes. Norris steered according to Lacey's directions. He could see nothing in front of the jet except for scattered clouds and a bright star field. Two minutes after they began hunting the bomber, it registered on the radar system. A blip at the thirty kilometer range and cruising at eighteen thousand feet.

Norris put the jet in a shallow climb and increased power to keep its speed at three hundred miles an hour. He levelled off at the bomber's altitude where, several minutes later, Norris finally caught sight of a black silhouette scraping across a layer of clouds.

"I got him, Dennis," he said, elated. "I got him at eleven o'clock. God damn, this was easy. Even for an amateur night fighter pilot like me."

"Think of what a plane like this could do in the hands of experts," Lacey advised. "Think of what a hundred could do. They'd destroy hundreds of bombers in a single night."

"I understand. Can you tell me what kind of bomber we have here? It's got radial engines and twin tail fins but it's not a Liberator."

"It's a Halifax. After the Lancaster, it's the most important bomber in the Royal Air Force."

As they closed on their four-engined target, Norris and Lacey could make out more details. Its glowing exhaust stacks, the glint of moonlight on its upper surfaces, the bright red squadron codes and fin flashes.

"You think this guy's inbound or outbound?" Norris queried.

"Whether he's going to his target or coming from it, he's lost if he's over Sweden," Lacey said calmly, before the plane lurched violently, throwing his head against the canopy. "Jesus, what's going on?"

"The asshole's firing at us! Now I'm getting fire from the tail turret!"

Norris reacted the instant he saw muzzle flashes on the Halifax's top turret. He threw the Night Hawk into a steep dive and rammed the throttles forward, almost to their gate stops. The combination immediately accelerated the jet to over four hundred miles an hour, shoving Lacey against his seat back. Despite the violent maneuvers, tracers still curved out from the bomber and flashed menacingly close.

As it dove past the black giant's twin tail fins, another stream of fire erupted from the turret sitting between them. It passed only inches above the Night Hawk's canopy. Lacey was certain it would hit the tail. However, when the jet failed to shudder from any impacts, he breathed a little easier.

"We're doing almost five hundred miles an hour," said Norris, clearly elated with the Me-262's performance. "Is this one fucking machine?"

The jet quickly shot out of range of the Halifax's

guns, though not until it was miles away and thousands of feet below it did Norris level off. He pulled the throttles back to their original settings, causing the Night Hawk's velocity to ebb back to cruise speed. He also returned it to its original course heading; they were once again on their way out of Sweden.

"Oh God, that was a close one," Norris admitted, his delight with their success giving way to nervousness. "To be almost shot down by one of our own planes. We won't be able to trust anybody until we rendezvous with our escort."

"We're going to have to watch ourselves as much as the next guy," said Lacey, "and not get carried away with our new toys. I think the fun's over for this flight."

"Gray Fox Leader to *gruppe*, divide into two-ship flights," Heinrich ordered, after making sure all his fighters were with him. "Climb and reform into a stepped formation between twenty and thirty thousand feet. I will be lead flight. Gray Fox Eleven, you will be last. When you are in position, we will all accelerate to maximum cruise speed. We should make it to the Skagerak before the Night Hawk. If it holds to its last reported altitude, we will make diving attacks. That's the only way we can overcome its speed advantage. If we are all ready, execute change."

At Heinrich's command, the Heinkels broke ranks and, in pairs, began climbing. Heinrich quickly lost track of most of his fighters, the only one he could be sure of was his wing man, tucked in on his left side. He nudged the throttles forward and pulled back his control stick, putting his giant fighter in a gentle climb.

From ten thousand feet it would take just under

seven minutes for the He-219s to reach the first level of their new formation. At around fifteen thousand their superchargers automatically switched to high-blower, giving a fresh surge of power at a time when many of the Heinkels were mushing down, their climb rates dropping. The first to reach twenty thousand feet was Heinrich, who levelled out and checked to make sure his wing man was still with him.

Another pair of bomber-sized fighters climbed past his left wing tip and his radar man informed him there were more appearing off their other wing and behind them. Heinrich glanced through the roof of his canopy and could see some of the He-219s arranging themselves as he had ordered. The last of the two-ship sets he could not see and had to wait for them to report to him before he knew they were in position. When Gray Fox Eleven reported he was at thirty thousand feet, Heinrich and the rest of his squadron increased their speed by almost 100 miles an hour, to 390. From the center of Denmark, it would take less than twenty minutes for them to reach the Skagerak.

"We're getting close to the rendezvous point," Powers advised his crew. "We better start arming our weapons. Commander, activate your station. Lieutenant, I'd rather have you at your radar scopes for now, but be prepared to activate yours at any moment."

"Understood, Colonel," said Cox, lifting the handle under his seat. "Here we go, activating stations."

With the seat unlocked, the gunner's station rolled forward until it hit the track's end bumpers and clicked in place. Cox unfastened the stowage pin on the gun sight's support arm, which allowed him to pull the sight down in front of him. He set its reflector plate at eye level by adjusting the control wheels on the mounting column. He unlocked the azimuth control, then reached for a small control box on the right side of the cabin. Cox flipped on the turret power switch and camera switch, and placed the fire selector on Gunner, which gave him and Martinez control of the overhead turret. His station was now armed.

"Osprey One to Osprey Squadron, arm all weapons," said Powers, hitting the armament toggle on his electrical panel. "Stand by to salvo external tanks."

"Top turret, on," Cox reported. "Camera, on. Turret guns, armed. Gun sight, on. I'm all set here."

"RO to pilot, I've switched on my station's systems," said Martinez, "but I haven't activated the station itself. I'm still on my scopes and they're still clear."

"Good, you sing out the minute you pick up so much as a sea gull," Powers replied. "In about ten minutes I'll start contacting Commander Norris and Dennis Lacey. We could be going into action any time now. This is where the real fun begins."

To test his station, Cox swung his seat from left to right. He could hear the whirring of the turret drive motors behind him and, out of either corner of the canopy, he was just able to see the muzzles of the turret guns. Outside the canopy Cox could also see the top turrets moving on some of the other P-61s. They rotated and trained their guns menacingly on themselves. The sleek, black giants were now alert; ready to attack or be attacked by whatever they encountered.

"Well, there it goes," Lacey observed, glancing out either side of the canopy and watching a light-sparkled coastline slide under the Night Hawk's tail. "We're leaving Sweden. We'll be in international air space in another two minutes."

"So far so good. Shouldn't we be trying to raise

those Black Widows?" Norris asked.

"No, we actually left Norrköping a few minutes early. In spite of all the shooting back there. Charlie Cox and our escorts weren't supposed to reach the rendezvous point for another few minutes. We'll be on our own for a little while."

"Maybe I should slow us down? What kind of activity is your gear picking up?"

"Lots of Royal Air Force bombers and night intruders," said Lacey. "So many they're overloading this IFF system. Quite a few Nazi night fighters as well. Just Me-110s and Ju-88s. Nothing that can touch this bird if we open her up a little and nothing in our immediate area."

"OK, I'm slowing her down."

Norris retarded the throttles a fraction of an inch, reducing the Me-262's speed by fifty miles an hour. The slowdown was barely felt by Norris and Lacey, it showed up as more of a drop on the air speed indicator and a softening of the turbojet's whine than anything else. A few more miles and the Night Hawk would be entering international air space, where the Luftwaffe would get its one chance to stop it.

"This is Jäger Division Two Control to Gray Fox Leader, we have your target. It's been handed over to us by Jäger Control Norwegen. It's still at fifteen thousand feet but it has reduced air speed to two hundred and fifty miles an hour. There are no other aircraft around it and we're keeping the rest of our fighters away from it. We can vector you in at any time."

"Thank you, Division Two," Heinrich replied. "We're ready for the vector. Bring us in right on top of him. Gray Fox Leader to *gruppe*, let's make this run quick and deadly if we can. The prototype has no escort yet.

374

Let's rendezvous with it before they do. We can enjoy a Mosquito hunt later. Accelerate to maximum speed."

Their throttles pushed to their gate stops, the He-219s boosted their air speed to between 410 and 415 miles an hour. The minor differences were due to altitude. The lowermost flights were faster because the slightly thicker air increased the efficiency of their paddle-bladed propellers. The higher ones were slower and would fall a little behind the rest. They would be arriving late at the rendezvous point being set for the Night Hawk.

Just past Denmark's north coast the Heinkels all swung around gently, onto a more northeasterly heading. At maximum speed they were only minutes away from Sweden. From their altitudes Sweden's southern coast spread out before them. Already the higher pairs were dropping behind Heinrich and the others. Almost at once their radar emissions were being picked up by the Night Hawk's detection gear.

"John, I got something new," said Lacey as he watched more warning lights on his IFF homing system light up and activity on his radar scopes increase. "And it's something big. A large formation of planes just appeared on my scopes. I'd say there's at least a dozen and the warning light for the Heinkel 219 just went on."

"I've heard of that ship," said Norris. "It's a hot one. As I remember, it was only two days ago Duncan Ellis was telling me about it. Apart from what we're flying, the '219 is the hottest thing in the Luftwaffe and the trials unit this jet was assigned to was equipped with them. You think these could be the same guys?"

"They have to be tracking us, so I wouldn't put it past the Luftwaffe to use their best unit to stop us."

"What type of formation are they flying and how far away are they?"

"They're flying in a loose, stacked group between twenty and thirty thousand feet," Lacey advised, hunching over his scopes. "They're in two-plane flights and the closest is about twenty miles away. Their speed must be at least four hundred and, combined with ours, means our closure rate is six hundred and fifty miles an hour. They'll be on top of us—"

"In one minute and fifty seconds," Norris completed, putting the figures together in a faster time than Lacey. "Shit, that doesn't give us much time. Can we avoid them?"

"They're being directed by the finest and most experienced night-defense network in the world. They're flying flighters that are second only to ours and, let's face it, we're damn good but those men are the best night fighter crews in Germany. Any way you look at it, we're in for a fight. You better jettison those tanks."

"What, you mean the drop tanks? If I get rid of them, we might not make it to England."

"If you don't, they'll blow up and fry us. All it would take is one cannon shell."

"I know," said Norris. "I know. Just give me a minute to think. There's gotta be a way around this."

"Jäger Division Two Control to Gray Fox Leader, you are on target. You are eleven miles and closing. We have no Allied aircraft in your area. You should have the target on your interception sets."

"Gray Fox Leader to Jäger Division Two, we have him," said Heinrich, glancing down at the radar screen on his front panel. "Let us know if any Allied fighters enter our area. Gray Fox Leader to *gruppe*, arm cannons, including your jazz music mounts. Activate your gun sights."

Heinrich pressed two buttons on the lower half of

his control stick, charging the batteries of 30mm cannons in the Heinkel's belly and just aft of its wings. He switched on the Revi gun sight atop his instrument panel, then reached for a second, simpler gun sight on the roof of the canopy and turned it on as well.

"The prototype is maintaining speed and altitude, Gunnar," Heinrich's radar man reported. "You should see it in the next minute."

"Strange, we should be on his radar scope by now. One of the few advantages we have over the Night Hawk is we know exactly what its capabilities are. Either its Allied crew couldn't make the radar work or they're planning something. Let me know immediately if anything changes. Erich."

"Wait, I got it. I'll open the fuel transfer lines," said Norris, finally latching onto an idea. "I'll switch the engines back to the main tank and transfer fuel to it from the external ones."

"OK, at least you'll be able to fill it," Lacey advised, "and save some of the gas we'd lose when the tanks are released. Go ahead, we don't have much time."

Norris reached for the selector valve levers and froze before wrapping his hand around them. He remembered the trouble he had with shifting the levers earlier. If either jammed now, the disaster would be immediate and fatal. Norris hesitated another moment, a moment longer than he should have, then grabbed both levers and yanked them back. He nearly pulled them out of their slots but at least they didn't stick. They clicked back to the forward main tank setting; there was scarcely a sputter from either engine as the change was made. Norris didn't waste time congratulating himself, his hand flew over to the switch for the transfer valve and activated it, opening the lines from the external tanks to the main one. He was rewarded with the needle on its gauge moving up instead of down.

"How much fuel do you have to make up?" Lacey asked, nervously eyeing the blips on his glowing screens.

"About forty gallons," Norris answered. "We have to replace the fuel used to start the engines, take off and climb out. Planes use more then than at any other time in their flight. And remember, we're using fuel from the same tank. The more we use, the longer it'll take to fill."

"Well, it better not take too long. The lead pair is four miles out. I want you to jettison those tanks once the attack begins."

"We'll see. I'm switching on my gun sight."

The Revi sight's reflector plate was illuminated once again with the dim image of a circle and cross hairs. Since its intensity had already been set, all Norris had to do was adjust the diameter of the circle to match the wing span of the He-219.

"I have him, Erich! God in heaven, it is the Night Hawk!" exclaimed Heinrich as a tiny, gray arrowhead of a plane materialized out of the darkness. "A miracle it's flying. What a pity we have to destroy such a triumph. Gray Fox Leader to *gruppe*, I'm going in! Attack in sequence. Gray Fox Two, stay with me."

Heinrich pushed his control stick forward and he dropped away from his wing man, who was a fraction of a second late in nosing down. Already flying at top speed, Heinrich's He-219 accelerated to better than five hundred miles an hour in the first moments of its dive. Soon it would be flying almost as fast as the

"Here goes, get ready for some fireworks," said Norris, jamming his throttles forward and pulling his control stick back. "They're Heinkel 219s all right."

"Have you jettisoned those tanks?" Lacey asked.

"Not yet, the main one isn't full."

The Me-262 reared on its tail and shot into the sky, climbing steeply. Despite their size, the Heinkels looked incredibly thin and spindly. When Norris put his cross hairs on the lead ship he realized that its fuselage was narrower than its engine nacelles, so narrow it almost disappeared behind the central aiming dot on the reflector plate. The Heinkel almost looked too frail to be a lethal machine. Only after it started firing did Norris's doubts vanish.

The battery of cannons under its nose flared brightly. Norris reflexively squeezed his trigger and unleashed his own barrage of tracers. The streams seemed to merge with each other. However, the Heinkel's fire drifted wide of the Night Hawk, itself a small target, while Norris's fire was more accurate. It flashed perilously close to Heinrich's canopy, forcing him to break attack. He rolled to one side and plummeted vertically. His wing man challenged the jet for only a moment longer. He quickly followed Heinrich when Norris shifted his fire to him.

"Gray Fox Leader to *gruppe*, the target is carrying external tanks! Aim for them. Burn him from the sky!"

As he righted his ship, Heinrich yanked his control stick to the edge of his seat. The He-219 was virtually standing on its nose as it began to pull out. It groaned and shuddered under the stresses but it levelled off and in seconds was zoom climbing, regaining the altitude it had lost.

"Gray Fox Three to Leader, we understand. We'll burn it."

Tracers from the second pair of Heinkels flashed underneath the jet, seeking out its thin-walled external tanks. It took Norris a few moments to realize what they were aiming for and he put the Night Hawk in a vertical climb, shoving the throttles up to the gate stops. For a time it did rise vertically, then it was climbing on its back, entering the top of a loop.

For the seconds the Messerschmitt was on its back Norris glanced down, through his canopy roof, and caught sight of the '219s below him, and another pair about a thousand yards behind them. He eased the throttles away from their gate stops, reducing the scream of the Junkers turbojets to an idling purr.

"What's the reason for cutting power?" Lacey asked. "There's another half dozen fighters we gotta tangle with."

"That's exactly why I'm chopping our speed," said Norris. "If we complete this loop too quickly, the next pair will nail us. If we slow it up, maybe we'll get them. This may damage the flaps but I'm going to risk it."

The reduction in power had slowed the Night Hawk's velocity but it started to build again as the plane slid out of the top of the loop and entered a dive. To stop the increase, Norris pressed two buttons ahead of his throttles and lowered the flaps by about ten degrees. The disturbances they caused to the air flow around the jet buffeted it, however; the action had its desired effect. The Night Hawk's air speed hung at around 450 miles an hour while the oncoming He-219s were doing better than 500.

The jet was still diving as the third pair of German fighters passed under it. Norris managed to get a brief shot at one of them as it appeared in his gun sight. He only fired a handful of shells, though one of them did strike the Heinkel in its fuselage, tearing open a hatch and blowing away the emergency life raft the ship carried. Norris immediately retracted his flaps and opened the throttles a little; the Night Hawk came out of its loop doing over five hundred miles an hour.

"If you don't jettison those tanks I'm going to reach around your seat and do it myself," Lacey warned.

"I will," said Norris. "The main tank's almost full."

"Well, it better hurry up. I have three more flights on my main scopes and the tail warning radar just came on."

"Great. We have 'em coming from both directions. The ones in our six o'clock worry me the most. We can avoid the others, not them. Let me know what they're doing and how far away they are."

Norris banked the jet steeply and swung it to the right, paralleling Sweden's western coast line. The fourth pair of Heinkels, already committed to their attack, dove harmlessly past its left wing. Before the remaining pairs could start their runs, Heinrich advised them not to.

"Gray Fox Leader to Gray Fox Nine and Eleven, hold and orbit. I'll let you know when to attack."

At the end of his zoom climb, Heinrich used the rest of the momentum it had generated to pivot his fighter on its right wing. The '219 only needed to have its nose pointed to the earth to begin another dive and, with his wing man beside him, Heinrich tore after the fleeing jet.

"They're closing on us, fast," said Lacey, glancing over his shoulder at the rapidly approaching gray shadows. "I'd give anything to see our P-61s right now. If you'd hit your throttles we could outdistance them."

381

"I want them to close on us," Norris replied. "I'm going to try a trick some P-38 pilots once told me about."

The Heinkels levelled out behind the Me-262 and almost seemed to pounce on it. Both Heinrich and his wing man held their fire. They both wanted to close to optimum range before doing so.

"I can make out their radar aerials," said Lacey, growing nervous. "Soon I'll be able to make out the cannon shells with our names on 'em. Whatever you're gonna do, do it now."

"How far away are they?" Norris asked.

"About a hundred and fifty yards."

"OK, watch this."

Norris pulled the jet into a climbing right turn and, as its nose started to rise above the horizon line, he switched off the fuel transfer valve and pressed the bomb release button on his control stick grip. There were two heavy clunks under the cockpit floor and the Night Hawk wobbled slightly as the drop tanks fell away.

They tumbled backwards, gyrating wildly because they lacked control fins and had fuel surging around inside them. The He-219s obediently matched Norris's maneuver, initiating their own climbing turns. For an instant, Heinrich thought he saw something black flip past him. In the last moments of his life, the pilot of Gray Fox Two could clearly see the black, teardrop-shaped tank careen toward him.

It struck the night fighter squarely in the nose, crushing the forest of radar aerials it carried and splitting open, shredding, on impact. Somewhere there was a spark, that was all it took to ignite the remaining fuel in the tank. A sheet of flame enveloped the forward fuselage as it was breaking apart under the collision. The Heinkel staggered in midair and began to roll to one side. Then it exploded, tearing open what was left of its fuselage in a dazzling fireball. Its wings folded in on themselves and what remained fell to earth like a comet, neither of its crew escaping.

"Jesus Christ, did you see that, Commander?" Powers asked, taking quick glances at the distant fireball.

"Most certainly," said Cox in a hushed voice. "I don't care to wait anymore, Colonel. Break radio silence and contact Dennis and Norris. And pray that wasn't them."

"God in heaven, I can't believe what happened," said Heinrich's radar man. "I was looking right at them. Did something go wrong with their aircraft, Gunnar?"

"No, those pilots in the Night Hawk are responsible," Heinrich angrily replied. "Somehow, some way, they are. Gray Fox Nine, Gray Fox Eleven, bring your flights around and join me. We'll finish them off now!"

"Only one? What a pity, I was hoping for two for two," said Norris, after being told the results of his trick. "In the Pacific, those P-38 pilots told me they got quite a few Jap planes this way. Only they couldn't claim them because they didn't have gun camera film of—"

"Holy shit, they're here!" Lacey shouted, interrupting Norris. "Switch your intercom to the transmitter channel. The cavalry's arrived."

Norris turned a small knob on the side of his cockpit and Lacey's announcement was replaced with a calm voice repeating the same message.

"This is Osprey One to Hawk Masters, come in

please. This is Osprey One to Hawk Masters, come in."

"Osprey One, this is Hawk Master," Norris replied, pressing a button on his radio control panel before Lacey could reach his. "You're the best thing we've heard since we took off. We got trouble up here, we're wondering if we could bring it your way?"

"Whatever you have we're ready for it," said Powers. "We are just outside of Swedish air space. Near a big group of lights called Göteborg. We're at five hundred feet and we're climbing to meet you. Osprey One to squadron, jettison tanks."

Ever since Scapa Flow the P-61s had been running on their external tanks. Their outboard pairs had been exhausted over the North Sea and were dropped. Now, the tanks nestled between the engine booms and the fuselage of each Black Widow slipped away from their pylons. Free at last, the Northrop giants went from cruise settings to full power and began to climb, with Powers and his wing man taking the lead.

"RO to pilot, I got lots of activity on my screen," said Martinez, his face pressed against the view finder on his main radar scope. "I count at least nine planes, one of 'em looks like he's diving at us. You should have this on your screen."

"Pilot to RO, affirmative," said Powers. "It's all on my scope. You can go ahead and activate your station, Andy."

Martinez unlocked his seat and turned it 180 degrees to face the tail of the fighter. Because of its nose-high attitude, when he hit a second release lever his seat rolled downhill and slammed against the track bumpers. His view out the plexiglas-covered tail of the fuselage pod was magnificent, obstructed only by the plane's slablike stabilizer. He could see the dimly shimmering waters of the Skagerak and Sweden's light-sparkled coast line fall away from him, as well as the other pairs of Black Widows trying to catch their leader. By the time Martinez had unstowed his gun sight and set it up, they were passing through a layer of gray-black clouds at five thousand feet.

"We still have one guy behind us and he's gaining," Lacey reported. "With our drop tanks gone we could open up and really walk away from him."

"I do that and we might end up swimming the last few miles to Scapa Flow," said Norris. "Besides, we'll be picking up enough speed real soon."

Still climbing to the right, the Night Hawk suddenly rolled on its back and dove, catching Heinrich by surprise. Even without increasing engine power, its air speed quickly passed the five hundred mile an hour mark.

"Why would he dive when his ceiling is higher than ours?" Heinrich asked himself while the jet fell from his view. "Not unless he's—"

"Gray Fox Leader, this is Jäger Division Two. A formation of unknown aircraft has just appeared in your area. They are passing five thousand feet and are believed to be hostile."

"Understood, Division Control, thank you. Gray Fox Lead to *gruppe*, the Night Hawk's escorts have arrived. The Mosquito hunt begins now."

Heinrich flipped his '219 on its back and yanked his control stick into his stomach. The bomber-sized fighter rolled cleanly and dropped after the Me-262. Moments later Heinrich was joined by two pairs of He-219s, his own reinforcements had arrived.

"Night Hawk to Osprey One, we're going to meet you halfway," Norris advised. "Be prepared for a fight. We got someone behind us who's mighty pissed."

"We got someone behind us who's still gaining," Lacey corrected. "If we don't do something we'll be in firing range. And four more Heinkel 219s have appeared."

"Good, I still have one trick up our tail. That is if the Swedes did what they promised they would. Watch this."

Norris lifted a safety bar off a set of buttons on the left side of the cockpit and pressed them all before hitting a toggle switch above the panel. Only Lacey could hear the slight clicking which resulted in a flare being ejected out the Me-262's tail and only he could see it sputter into the night where, seconds later, it ignited.

It became an incandescent, glowing star sailing toward the lead Heinkel. Startled, and wary of what the jet might've done to destroy his wing man, Heinrich jerked the control stick back to avoid the flare. The fighter snapped out of its dive, even started to climb, before Heinrich realized what the jet fired at him was harmless. By then the four He-219s he had called in were diving past him.

"Those pilots are good, Erich, very good," Heinrich told his radar man. "Someone worthy of us. To destroy them will be quite an achievement."

"Osprey One to Hawk Masters, I have you," said Powers. "I see you brought some of your friends along. Get ready to pull up on my command. We'll take care of the rest."

Powers watched the blips on his radar screen for a moment before he pulled forward his pair of infrared binoculars. When they reached the end of their track they unlocked and swung in front of Powers. He adjusted the focus on the eyepieces as he peered through the binoculars. Though they restricted his view, he could clearly see the approaching Me-262 and the

Heinkels behind it. The turbojet pods and the exhaust stacks on the propeller-driven fighters glowed especially bright. Using the gun sight through the binoculars was difficult but Powers was able to put his aiming circle of orange diamonds on one of the planes behind the jet.

"Out of the way, Hawk Master," he ordered. "Your friends are in range."

The Night Hawk pulled out of its dive a thousand feet above the lead Black Widow. It had barely cleared his view when Powers touched the button on the left arm of the control wheel. The 20mm cannons in the Widow's belly rattled the entire ship as they fired, spitting tracers at one of the four Heinkels pursuing the jet. Cox had locked his gun sight on one of the other '219s, the bright aiming circle almost washing out its dim image.

Armor-piercing and high-explosive cannon shells battered the German fighter; Powers concentrated his fire on one of its glowing engine nacelles. The Diamler-Benz inside it was hit by half a dozen shells and exploded. A shower of hot engine fragments and flames erupted out of the nacelle. When the wing spars were hit by more shells, the right wing's outboard panel twisted and folded back. Eventually, it ripped away.

Cox raked his fire along the slim fuselage of his Heinkel before it broke away and pulled out of its dive. The remaining two fighters received withering fire from more P-61s but managed to escape as well. Only the '219 Powers hammered at fell toward the North Sea; the crew ejecting from the doomed plane before it entered a lopsided spin.

"Let's see, that's two down and ten to go," said Norris. "We're doing pretty good."

"No, we're not. That only means we've evened up

the sides," Lacey countered, glancing over his shoulders as he noticed the tail warning radar lights were still on. "John, five o'clock high. The rest of our friends are joining the party."

"I got it, Dennis, thanks. Hawk Masters to Osprey One, more '219s in your twelve o'clock."

"Roger, Hawk Master we'll take care of 'em. Osprey One to squadron, fan out. The rest of those Germans are coming after us. Whatever you do, keep them away from the jet."

The remaining pairs of Heinkel 219s descended on the Black Widows as they broke formation. They managed to get a few, brief shots at the American fighters though mostly they encountered empty air space. The P-61s hit their water injection switches, boosting their power and increasing their climb rates as they spread through the night sky.

"Our tail warning radar has come on, Gunnar," Heinrich's radar man advised. "I have a target at twenty-five hundred feet. He's climbing after us and closing fast."

"Good, he has us right where he wants us," said Heinrich, "and he's right where I want him."

Heinrich aimed his fighter at a looming cloud bank and inched the throttles back from their gate stops. The speeding Heinkel slowed a little, to just under four hundred miles an hour, allowing the Black Widow to reduce the gap to where it could open fire. Tracers flashed around the He-219 as it plunged inside the cloud bank.

Heinrich immediately cut the throttles almost back to their shut-off positions. He also dumped the Heinkel's flaps, the resulting deceleration was like hitting a wall. The fighter was on the verge of stalling when Heinrich pushed its nose down. He dove a few hundred feet and levelled out, slamming his throttles forward again. When he emerged from the cloud bank he glanced up to find the pursuing night fighter above him and moving ahead of him. It was just as he expected, and yet it was not what he expected.

"It looks like an American P-38," Heinrich remarked, taking a second to closely study his adversary. "A Lightning. But it's much larger and has radial engines. Wait, I have it. It's a Black Widow. One of the new, American night fighters. These aren't Mosquitoes, they are the latest the Allies can offer. Their best. A magnificent challenge."

The He-219 accelerated rapidly with its power restored and climbed up to the P-61. Heinrich didn't position himself directly under it but offset himself slightly. He concentrated on his overhead gun sight and aligned his massive fighter so the sight's cross hairs rested on the Black Widow's right engine boom.

"Steady, don't shake so much, my pet. Let's give them a sample of our jazz music," Heinrich told his airplane. He placed both hands on his U-shaped control stick and pressed one of two triggers on its handle tops.

Immediately aft of the Heinkel's wings were two holes, muzzles, almost flush with the fuselage skin. Spurts of flame suddenly erupted out of them and a twin steam of 30mm cannon shells arced over the fighter's canopy. They shot upwards at an oblique angle, striking the Widow's right engine cowling and walking back to the landing gear well. The first shells were enough to blow the engine off its mounts. The rest tore open the landing gear doors and severed oil and fuel lines. Almost the entire front half of the starboard boom exploded, its Double Wasp radial, its cowling and propeller falling away. The outer wing panel detached and the rest of the P-61 rolled on its back. By the time it began its final plunge, Heinrich had broken off and was diving as well.

"I'm levelling her out," said Powers, pushing his control wheel forward and steadying it. "Was that explosion one of theirs or ours?"

"I think it might've been one of ours," Cox answered, looking in the direction of the flash. "These Germans are very aggressive to take on an airplane like the Night Hawk."

"RO to pilot, my tail warning gear is on!" Martinez cried, "I think I see him. Commander, gimme control of the turret!"

Cox released the levers on either side of his gun sight grips and the top turret swung around to face the tail. Martinez trained his sight on the gray shadow diving on the P-61. He waited until its wing tips touched the rim of the aiming circle before firing. The turret's four fifty-caliber machine guns sprayed the oncoming Heinkel with a heavy barrage of shells. Hits sparkled all over its forward fuselage and wing root area. The '219 was damaged, though not enough to bring it down; its pilot wouldn't allow that. He snapped it away from the Black Widow, allowing Martinez an extra shot at its undersides before diving below the turret's field of fire.

"Our enemy is as good as we thought he would be," said Cox. "If you can't lock onto another Nazi, I suggest you raise the Night Hawk. We're here to provide it with an escort. We had better do so."

"John, how slow are we going?" Lacey asked as he felt the Night Hawk decelerate after it levelled off its climb.

"I got us down to three hundred and fifty miles an hour," Norris advised.

"Isn't that rather slow for us in a combat zone? Those Heinkels must still be doing four hundred."

"Maybe it is, but if we continue to go racing around we might not have the gas to make it to England. We'll have to let the P-61s do our fighting."

"Well, they're not doing enough of it. Our tail warning set is still on and I think I have him. Bandit, five o'clock low and climbing. He'll be under our tail in another second."

"Not if I can help it," said Norris, pushing the control stick to the left side of the cockpit and working the foot pedals.

The Night Hawk dipped its left wing and started a diving turn. Banking it steeply, Norris brought the jet around; in moments he had a slim-bodied, gray shadow centered in his reflector plate. He caught the Heinkel while it was still climbing. For a few seconds it would be helpless and Norris took advantage of it.

The Night Hawk's battery of cannons flared brightly, unleashing a stream of tracers which caught the '219 in its right engine nacelle and aft fuselage. Its cowling panels ripped open by explosions, the starboard engine sputtered and died, its propeller windmilling to a halt. Norris wished he could give the night fighter a sustained burst, but he only had the few seconds he originally guessed he had before overshooting it.

"We crippled him all right," Norris answered, pulling the jet through another turn, reversing its direction again. "I say we go back and finish him."

However, by the time Norris and Lacey caught sight of the Heinkel once more, it was diving toward the North Sea, trailing a streamer of fire from its right engine.

"At least, we beat him off," sighed Lacey. "Tail warning radar is clear, John. How about high-tailing it out of here and continuing to England on our own?"

"No, we wait for our escorts. We could run into a hell of a lot of trouble without them. Remember what that British bomber almost did to us? We're in as much danger from our own side as the Nazis. We stay until the battle is decided."

"Dave, he's getting away from us," said Shannon, observing the He-219 through his station's gun sight.

"I know. Shit, even with water injection he's escaping," Ackerman swore, watching the fighter he'd been pursuing climb away from him. He retarded his throttles, unlocking the water injection switches he had tripped when he first shoved the throttle levers beyond their gate stops. "Damn it, this airplane is still underpowered."

"He won't be going far. We're already inside Sweden and he's flying deeper into it. Why don't we wait for him?"

"No, our first duty is to protect the jet. Maybe we can get lucky later."

"RO to pilot, if you'd like to bag a kraut there's one behind us. Six o'clock low and closing."

"Gunner to RO, you want the turret?" Shannon asked.

"No, this guy's below the horizon line. In fact he's nearly underneath us."

An instant later the radar operator was screaming that they were being attacked as a twin stream of tracers flashed between the engine booms of the P-61.

"Flip us over, Dave!" Shannon ordered. "Let's see if this turret can fire straight up!"

With a flick of his wrists, Ackerman rolled the bomber-sized fighter onto its back. As it rotated, the P-61 received a single, jarring hit in one of its engine booms, the only damage it would receive. Shannon pushed his gun sight until it was directly overhead. In its cross hairs he could see the Heinkel 219 cruising several hundred feet below him, its narrow fuselage and long, tapered engine nacelles clearly seen against the illuminated Swedish landscape. Fighting the dust and debris that rained on him from the cockpit floor, Shannon aimed for the Heinkel's nose and opened fire at the same moment a second burst erupted from its jazz music cannons.

The slower-firing cannons managed to get off only a few rounds before the top turret's battery of machine guns had sprayed the entire forward fuselage of the He-219. Unprotected by either its armor plating or bulletproof glass, the crew was killed by the hundreds of shells which rained down on their ship. The encounter was over in seconds. The Black Widow righted itself and swung toward international air space; the Heinkel flew deeper into Sweden with a dead crew at its controls. Somewhere near its Baltic Sea coast the aircraft would eventually lose its stability and crash.

"Gunnar, I think I have the Night Hawk," said Erich. "It's three thousand feet above us and on our right side. Its air speed is far below four hundred miles an hour."

"Its crew must be waiting for their escorts to finish us off," Heinrich remarked. "That will give us our chance to finish them off."

"Wait, wait. Our tail warning radar has been activated again. Single target, one thousand feet out. He must be diving on our tail." The radar operator looked up from the view finder to his main scope and saw the unknown descending, a sleek, black giant with huge radial engines. "Gunnar, it's an American!"

That was all Heinrich needed to hear. He grabbed his U-shaped control stick with both hands and threw it to the left side of the cockpit. The '219 responded by racking into a tight left turn, moments later streams of tracers shot by the cockpit. They drifted away as the Heinkel banked and flew through its turn. Heinrich glanced over his left shoulder and saw the P-61 cutting inside him. More tracers began spitting from its underbelly, forcing him to reverse course.

Heinrich pushed the control stick to the right and advanced the throttles to their gate stops, after just having eased them away. In the middle of its left turn the German fighter abruptly swung to the right, catching the Black Widow by surprise. For several moments it stopped firing, by the time it resumed the He-219 was climbing steeply, though not yet out of range.

Tracers flashed around the cockpit again and Heinrich felt his aircraft jar repeatedly as it was hit by cannon shells. There was an explosion behind him and the cockpit filled with the smell of cordite. If the plane was burning, he and his radar man would have to abandon it, and the Night Hawk would probably escape.

"Gray Fox Leader, this is Gray Fox Nine. Hold your course and we'll deal with the American."

The Heinkel took hits for a few seconds more, then suddenly the heavy thuds stopped. Heinrich glanced out each side of the cockpit, and on the left he caught sight of the P-61 for the last time. Its port engine boom was being raked by fire from one Heinkel 219 while another hammered at its fuselage. The top turret was trying to return fire but it was too little, too late. The doomed aircraft dropped away, trailing a sheet of fire from its battered engine.

"Gray Fox Nine to Leader, we did it. That makes three," the radio announced as a He-219 slid onto Heinrich's left wing, followed by another on his right. "There's yours, and Gray Fox Four scored the second. We have more on our scopes, should we hunt them?"

"No, we have a bigger prize to kill. We've spotted the Night Hawk on radar. Erich, are you still tracking it? Erich? Erich?

Straining to look around his armored headrest, Heinrich caught sight of his radar man slumped to one side of the cockpit. He knew at once Erich was dead. Heinrich could see the holes in the rear canopy glass, the damaged instrument panels and the blood splattered over it all. It took a little while for the shock to wear off and for him to realize someone was calling his name.

"Gunnar, this is Gray Fox Nine. What's wrong?"

"We will have to use your radar man," Heinrich finally answered, turning away from the torn body slumped behind him. "Mine is gone. The Night Hawk is three thousand feet above us and was originally on my right. Do you have it?"

"Oh no. Shit, not now," Lacey swore, banging his fist on top of his instrument console. "Not now of all times."

"What's wrong back there?" Norris asked.

"Our main radar set just stopped working. The scope, everything, just fizzled out."

"What do you mean, everything? Have all our systems gone out?"

"No, it's only our interception system," said Lacey,

pulling Capollini's flashlight from his jacket, and a small tool kit as well. "The tail warning set, the IFF box and our nav aids are all OK."

"Then don't worry about it. Switch your intercom back to the radio and you'll hear our escorts joining us."

"Osprey One to Hawk Masters, stay on your present course and we'll catch you," Powers advised before releasing the button on the left arm of his control wheel. "I got 'em, Commander. They're four thousand feet above us and heading west. We'll be joining them in about three minutes."

"I'm afraid you'll have to delay our rendezvous," said Cox. "Heinkel, ten o'clock low. I think he's going after one of our fighters. Dive and I'll try to hit him."

Powers had just started pulling his control wheel back when he was forced to push it forward. The Black Widow tipped its nose up slightly before dipping it below the horizon line. The heavy fighter picked up speed immediately, and Powers could see the He-219, about a hundred yards ahead of him and off to his left. It was diving as well and far below could be seen the black silhouette of another P-61.

Cox had his gun sight's cross hairs on the tail of the Heinkel from the moment it appeared in the reflector plate. He squeezed the levers on his grips, returning the turret to his control and automatically training it on the target. Then he waited a few seconds more to make sure he had the range before pressing the triggers.

Above and behind him the turret emitted a deafening rattle as it unleased a stream of tracers. Hits sparkled all over the Heinkel's tail section and rear fuselage. Cox kept his guns trained on the aircraft, even as Powers swung in behind it and opened up with his own weapons.

The heavier cannon shells did more damage than the fifty-caliber bullets, tearing holes in the rear fuselage and blasting apart one of the twin tail fins on the He-219 before it pulled out of its dive and snapped to the left.

"He's lucky his whole damn tail didn't come off," said Powers, releasing his cannon button. "That was pretty good shooting, Commander. You're really getting the hang of that turret. You want to hunt him down and finish the job?"

"No, you promised Dennis and Commander Norris we would give them an escort," Cox replied. "We better make good on it. Especially since we'll be a little late."

"RO to pilot, there's another plane climbing on our right," Ackerman's radar man advised. "I think it's another P-61."

"Osprey Seven to unknown 'sixty-one, please identify. Chris, you better get your turret ready. Osprey Seven to unknown 'sixty-one, identify. Over."

Ackerman lifted his thumb off the radio transmitter button to listen for a reply. He had to make another request for identification, almost a demand, before his headset crackled with an answer.

"Osprey Seven, this Osprey Ten. Oh boy, are we glad to see you. Colonel Powers put out a call for all ships not engaged to escort that jet. It's about a thousand feet above us and eight miles to the west."

"I didn't hear it," Ackerman admitted, "but thanks for telling me. You can count me in. I think if I said no my gunner would shoot me."

When the second Black Widow formated on Ackerman's right wing, the pair increased speed and began to climb. They changed direction slightly, to a heading which would allow them to rendezvous with the Night Hawk.

* * *

"I'm slowing us to three hundred miles an hour," said Norris, retarding the throttles a bit more. "That should allow the 'sixty-ones to catch up to us, wherever they are. How's things with you, Dennis?"

"I got the panels off but I don't see what could've caused the failure," said Lacey, hunched over the console. "Why can't it just be a simple short? A hundred things could've caused it. I hope our escorts arrive soon. I don't like flying a blinded fighter."

"Gray Fox Nine to Gray Fox Leader, the prototype has reduced speed. My RO says we enjoy a speed advantage of over a hundred miles an hour."

"Good, we will intercept it that much sooner. When we close, you two will hold back. I want to make the first pass, alone."

In the distance, Heinrich could see the orange-red glow of turbojet engines. They were just above him and heading for a cloud bank. If the Night Hawk made it to the bank before he could intercept it, Heinrich would have to let the other '219s, with radar men, close in and destroy it.

"Ackerman and Hanks will help us escort the Night Hawk," Powers told Cox, their aircraft finally climbing to meet the jet. "In fact they'll get there before we do. I don't know how many planes I still have, or how many Germans are left, but I'll try to find out when we rendezvous."

"Osprey Seven to Osprey Ten, bogies have just appeared on my screen," said Ackerman as two, then three, blips materialized on the scope below his gun sight.

"Osprey Seven, I got 'em too. How the hell did they just appear like that?"

"They must've climbed into our radar search cones." Ackerman pulled his infra-red binoculars forward while he spoke and swung them in front of his face. The moment he focussed the eyepieces he could see the Heinkels ascending in front of him. "Yes, there's three all right and they're Germans. We're still above them, so we're not yet on their tailwarning sets. Tell the jet they're about to get hit."

First Ackerman's Black Widow dipped its nose and dove and a moment later Osprey Ten followed. They selected the two Heinkels trailing the leader; Gray Fox Nine and his wing man wouldn't know they were being hunted until the instant before the cannon shells started to fly.

"Hold on, Dennis, we got company!" Norris shouted. "What the hell's wrong with our tail radar!"

Norris slammed the throttles to their gate stops, causing the Night Hawk to kick forward as the engines exploded to full thrust. The surge pulled Lacey back to his seat, scattering his tools, the access panels and his flashlight. Once in it, he could see the status lights on the tail warning set blazing away, as they had been for some time.

"Gray Fox Nine to Leader, we're being jumped!"

The cry brought Heinrich out of his concentration on the glowing pipe exhausts ahead of him. Looking past his shoulder, he caught sight of the Black Widows diving on the other Heinkels. He could only afford them a moment's regret that he couldn't help them as they had helped him before he turned his attention back to the Night Hawk.

Ackerman placed his aiming circle of orange diamonds on the center section of Gray Fox Nine and opened fire. The P-61 shook as the 20mm cannons in its belly poured a stream of tracers onto the He-219. Hits sparkled all over the fuselage aft of its canopy and its wing roots. High explosive and incendiary shells detonated inside the ammunition trays held in the wing roots and the fuselage fuel tanks. The Heinkel disintegrated into a storm of burning scrap metal; Ackerman had to roll his fighter to the left in order to avoid it.

"Dennis, how many planes are behind us?" Norris demanded.

"Jesus, there goes one now," said Lacey, watching a blossom of fire erupt out of the night. "And another just blew up! Hold it, I don't think that's all of them."

Silhouetted against the brilliant fireballs of his squadron mates was Heinrich's '219. Its Diamler-Benz engines howling at war emergency power, they were literally tearing themselves apart; however they were pulling the bomber-sized machine closer to the Night Hawk. For the time being the Heinkel was out-accelerating it, and Heinrich would only need a few minutes to complete his mission and destroy it.

"Hawk Master to Osprey One, we're under attack. We've got a kraut on our tail and he's gaining."

"Roger, Hawk Masters, we see the fireworks," Powers replied. "Turn to your left and dive. We'll set a trap for him."

Norris racked the jet through a steep left turn and

pushed its nose below the horizon as he had been told. Heinrich tried to follow, but his giant fighter wasn't able to match the same hard maneuver. It side-slipped and lost air speed, falling several hundred feet behind the Night Hawk.

"What kind of trap are you making?" Cox asked, when he noticed Powers retarding the throttles.

"I'm going to use one of the oldest tricks a night fighter pilot knows," said Powers, "and you're gonna help. You're pretty good with our top turret. Think you can shoot down the plane chasing Lacey and Norris."

"Give me a good chance and I'll cut it in half."

"That's what I wanted to hear. I'm lowering the landing gear and, with them, the landing lights. Once the jet is in range, I'll order it to pull up and I'll flip on the lights, blinding the Heinkel's pilot and giving you your chance. It'll be all up to you, Commander. When I lower my wheels, I won't be able to use my cannons. You still want to do it?"

"I've taken a chance like this once before and it worked," Cox recalled. "I don't see why this can't."

"All right, here goes the shooting match," said Powers, checking the air speed gauge before he pulled the gear control lever. "Pilot to RO, I want you back on your scopes. You'll have to help me set this up."

Even though its air speed had fallen to just over two hundred miles an hour, the Black Widow's nose dropped suddenly as first the nose gear, then the main wheels were extended. Along with them, the powerful spotlights in the outer wing panels were lowered as well. After Powers checked the radar screen one last time, he swung the infrared binoculars back in front of his face. With the binoculars in place, he would not be able to use the radar and would have to rely on Martinez to identify the jet and direct him onto a collision course with it.

"He's still behind us," Lacey advised, "and I don't believe it but he's holding his own."

"That's one of the little problems with jets," said Norris. "They're faster than prop planes but they can't outaccelerate them. But I have heard General Electric is experimenting with something called an afterburner. Well, if he's still back there perhaps I can shake him loose. A good trick is always worth using twice."

Norris reached for a toggle switch on the right side of the cockpit and flipped it, ejecting another flare from the Me-262's tail. The glowing ball shot toward the Heinkel, only this time Heinrich ignored it as it flashed harmlessly over his wing.

"It didn't work, John," said Lacey, looking out the rear of the canopy. "This is one determined son-of-a-bitch."

"I'll say. Whatever your Colonel Powers has cooked up had better work," Norris remarked, "but I still have one more trick up my sleeve."

"RO to pilot, I got the jet," said Martinez, sitting back at his radar table. "It's about ten degrees to our right and eight miles out."

"Got it, Andy," said Powers, dipping his control wheel to the right. "Are you set, Commander?"

"Ready and waiting," Cox answered. "In fact I think I see the jet in my sights."

The Night Hawk and the Black Widow flew toward each other at a combined speed of nearly seven hundred miles an hour. Heinrich kept pace with the jet though he was a few hundred feet behind it. At that range he couldn't see what was waiting in front of it and the jet created a blind spot on his radar screen. More important, Heinrich didn't care to see anything except the Night Hawk. His concentration on it and determination to destroy it were total.

Cox nervously fingered the triggers on his gun sight grips as he watched two gray shadows loom larger in its reflector plate. Martinez called out the range at one mile intervals, which seemed to come every few seconds. It made Cox more nervous, though at least the swift closure rate didn't allow him the time to become scared.

"Two miles and closing," Martinez recorrected.

"All right, that's enough," said Powers. "Osprey One to Hawk Masters, pull up! Pull up sharp!"

Norris reacted instantly to the command; he jerked back both the control stick and the stabilizer trim lever. The lever caused the entire horizontal tailplane to angle up by several degrees. Enough to snap the Night Hawk onto its tail and send it climbing steeply; in the twinkling of an eye it reared up and vanished from Heinrich's view.

Powers watched it clear the line of fire. The moment the Heinkel was in full view he hit a pair of toggle switches on his electrical panel. The landing lights under the Black Widow's wings flared to life like twin flashes of lightning. They emitted a pair of dazzlingly bright beams, surprising and blinding Heinrich.

Cox found his target illuminated perfectly. All he had to do was nudge the gun sight a little to put the cross hairs on its nose. He pressed the triggers in and felt a reassuring vibration shake his station. The streams of half-inch shells the top turret spit into the night converged on the '219, which had just begun to raise its right wing tip.

Heinrich could hardly see his instrument panel, let alone the aircraft that was blinding him. He put his right hand to shield his eyes and between his fingers he saw the tracers pouring at him. Almost on its own his left hand pulled the control stick to its side of the cockpit but it was too late. His fighter shuddered as hits sparkled all over its forward fuselage.

The windshield was shattered immediately and even the heavy plate of armored glass began splintering under the heavy fire. The instrument panel in front of Heinrich exploded and the cockpit was filled with glass shards, pieces of torn metal and shrapnel. Heinrich could feel his body being ripped by the storm. All he could do was use his right arm to shield his head. The instruments and controls on the cockpit's right side exploded next. Heinrich even heard the hiss of shells passing him as they blasted through the company. Suddenly, the storm was over. The cockpit grew quiet but the Heinkel continued to shake as the stream of fifty-caliber bullets hammered the right engine nacelle.

Cox followed the He-219 as it swung lazily into a left turn. It wasn't a sharp or fast maneuver; it allowed him to walk his fire through the right nacelle. The straining Diamler-Benz inside it took just a brief shower of hits before catching fire and dying. The nacelle's landing gear doors were blasted open and the landing gear strut, its hydraulic lines severed, dropped partway down. Cox even managed to chop off part of the Heinkel's right tail fin before it passed out of his range.

"Hawk Masters to Osprey One, did you nail him?"

"You better believe it," Powers answered, pushing the binoculars out of his way. "I'm going to bring us around and see if we shouldn't finish him off."

With the infrared binoculars safely stowed, Powers lifted the landing gear lever and the P-61 wobbled as the wheels were retracted. Cleaned up, he eased his fighter through a right turn and overtook the mortally wounded '219. As the P-61 drew alongside it, Powers and Cox could see what was left of the canopy fly off

404

the fighter; its pilot was preparing to bail out.

"If we're taking a vote, I say we kill him, Commander," said Martinez. "He tried like hell to kill Colonel Lacey and Mister Norris."

"I know, but he was only doing what he was ordered to do," Cox advised, seeing his enemy for the first time without a gun sight in front of him. "He's a professional, just like us. He was good, almost too damn good, and he has my respect."

"And mine," Powers added. "Quick, before he bails out. Bring up your cockpit lights, Commander."

Cox and Powers brought their fluorescent lights to full intensity and switched on every panel light they had. In addition, Powers activated the position and anti-collision lights; the black mass sitting on Heinrich's left wing became a constellation of multicolored lights.

The strobing beacons were the first things to catch Heinrich's eye. He froze in the middle of his bail-out procedure and looked at the Black Widow. He was helpless, and knew it; it would take just another burst from the Widow's top turret to kill him. In its cockpit, Heinrich could see its pilot and another crewman. They were illuminated by cockpit lights and, for one eternal moment, he stared at them.

Then Cox and Powers raised their right hands and saluted him. Heinrich could only return their salutes with a brief wave; his right arm was too badly injured for him to do much else with it. As it was he could barely get his right hand to close around the ejector seat lever and pull it back. With a shot of compressed air Heinrich and his seat were lifted out of the Heinkel. Above and behind it they separated; Heinrich managed to jerk open his parachute before his pain and blood loss rendered him unconscious.

He drifted eastwards, with the prevailing winds at

his altitude. He would eventually come down inside Sweden, near one of the coastal towns above which part of the air battle had been fought.

"This is Hawk Masters to Osprey One, we're throttled back to two hundred and fifty and we've picked up Osprey Seven and Ten as escorts. We're heading west again and if you want to join us we're at fifteen thousand feet."

"John, don't you think two hundred and fifty is a little slow?" Lacey asked after Norris finished his message.

"You bet it is," he admitted. "But after all the fuel we used up in this dogfight we have to fly that slow. And when we've passed the entrance to the Skagerak, I'm going to reduce her to two hundred miles an hour. I know it's dangerous, though no more dangerous than flying without radar. You get working on that gear and give us back our eyes."

"Osprey One to Hawk Masters, we're climbing to join you," Powers announced, opening his throttles and raising his nose above the horizon line. "I've made contact with the rest of my squadron and three more fighters will be joining us. Three don't answer my calls and a fourth says he's too badly damaged to make it home. I've given him permission to crash land in Sweden. My radar man has made contact with some R.A.F. fighters and they'll help us escort you to England. We may just recruit the whole damn Royal Air Force to get you home."

While Lacey scrambled to gather his tools and flashlight, more Black Widows gathered around the jet. Eventually, there would be a vee of P-61s riding on each wing tip. What was left of Heinrich's squadron fled to Denmark. Most of the survivors were damaged and they all flew to Luftwaffe airfields around Copenhagen where they made emergency landings. Out of twelve aircrafts, only five came back.

Several minutes after the P-61s had formated with the Night Hawk, the Royal Air Force started arriving. In pairs the DeHavilland Mosquitoes joined the growing umbrella around the Me-262. By the time they reached the entrance to the Skagerak, nearly two dozen American and British night fighters were protecting it. Some four hundred miles to the west lay Scapa Flow, where Allied experts were waiting nervously for their first real look at the Night Hawk. The operation was almost over.

"Oberstleutnant Heinrich? I am Doctor Andersen," said a shadowy figure standing beside Heinrich's bed. "You are in a Swedish civilian hospital. You are going into surgery soon. We have contacted your embassy. Is there anything you wish to tell them? Or our military?"

"The war is over for me," Heinrich managed to answer, his words slurring together. "I wish to remain in your country. I wish to defect."

"I will tell the Army of your decision. It's a wise move." Andersen spoke in short sentences and pronounced them slowly, so his patient could understand through the haze the painkillers had created. "You lost your battle. And your country will soon lose the war."

"Yes, I lost. I lost the Night Hawk. But in a way, I didn't lose." Even though it hurt, Heinrich began to smile and laugh weakly. With great effort, he turned his head toward the doctor's obscured figure. "I have a small victory. I wonder how Lossberg will explain failure to Hitler?"

Epilogue: The Parting

"Commander, your luggage and Mister Capollini's is being loaded on the air liner," Wing Commander Ellis advised, walking from the BOAC desk to the waiting lounge at Bromma's customs station. "You two should be boarding in the next ten minutes. I'm sorry, Ian, but she hasn't shown up yet."

"Don't worry, she will," said MacAlister. "Her superiors promised she would be here. If she wanted to be . . . well, I'm sure she'll come. Thank you, Duncan, you're a good friend."

Ellis shook MacAlister's hand, then Capollini's before he turned to leave. He headed for the terminal's observation deck, where he would watch the take-off of the BOAC Mosquito being readied on the flight line.

"Jeez, and to think a few days ago I was talking about this plane," said Capollini, glancing at the civilian-marked DeHavilland bomber. "Now I'm gonna have to fly in one."

"Are you looking forward to the flight?" MacAlister asked.

"Hell no. That thing may be fast but it's a God

409

damned balsa wood toy. It's cramped and I don't like airplanes I can't stand up in. I'd rather take the Gooney Bird we had, if it still existed. What's going to happen to its crew, and those commandoes?"

"The crew will be treated like those of any other interned airplane. They've flown their last combat mission. As for our SAS friends, their adventure in Sweden has just started. Lee Roberts and the survivors of his team are in the British embassy. I met with him before Ellis drove me here. In a few days they'll be taken to the Karlskrona Naval Base. From there, they'll head for Bornholm Island. Allied high command is extremely interested in what's going on there. I personally haven't been told much about the Night Hawk. What's happened to it since it landed in Scapa Flow?"

"Last thing I heard they were still celebrating," said Capollini. "They haven't dismantled the Night Hawk yet. When that's done, it'll be loaded into the biggest transport we have and flown to Pax River. Commander Norris will probably go with it. Half the reason why I want to leave Sweden is to join the colonel and all the others in that party. Hey, Commander, ain't this the girl you've been waiting for?"

Capollini had turned away from the flight line and was looking at the lobby. He tapped MacAlister on the shoulder and pointed to a woman being escorted to the customs station; though once alerted, MacAlister hardly needed any help to pick her out of the crowd.

"Karen, thank God," MacAlister replied, a wave of relief spreading over him. "Wait here, Captain, this won't take long."

Karen's escort stopped short of the station and allowed her to continue on alone. MacAlister left his cap, briefcase and overcoat with Capollini and rushed, practically ran, to meet her. She physically looked much better than when he had last seen her, but different. Despite the soft makeup she wore, the new hairstyle and clothes, she appeared to be sad.

"Ian, I'm so sorry I couldn't see you until now," she said when they met at the lounge entrance and embraced. "And I'm sorry you have to leave Sweden."

"My superiors want a full report on what Drache told us," MacAlister answered. "As you can guess, they're most interested. I rather liked the way your superiors and the Swedish military handled Drache's death. It's a pity they had to actually burn down the estate's main house to prove there had been a fire. Why wouldn't they let me see you?"

"Security. They didn't want the press to link us together. They're already linking you with Ursula. That you may have had a fight with Drache over her on the night of the fire. I'm so sorry, in a way I wanted to see you as well."

"Well, don't be, we can see each other again. This war won't go on forever and then, I won't need special orders to come to Sweden. I could come on my own and spend as much time with you as you'd like me to."

"Ian, please, you make it so difficult," Karen pleaded as tears started to roll down her cheeks, carrying with them some of her makeup. "I think I love you, but I can't see you."

"Why? If it's your job, my dear, I can wait until you're due for a vacation."

"No, it's not my work. It's the rest of my life. Do you see the man I came with?"

For the first time MacAlister took a good look at Karen's escort. He looked several years younger than MacAlister, about the same age as Karen. He was blond-haired, ruggedly handsome and better than six feet tall. If it weren't for his Swedish police uniform, MacAlister would swear he had just stepped off a Viking longboat.

"I will marry him, in another three months."

"I see. I see," said MacAlister, his heart sinking, the fantasies he had concocted about him and Karen dissolving into empty illusions. He couldn't hide the hurt look in his eyes from her, but sighed and managed to force a smile on his face. "I'm jealous of him. I hope he appreciates how special you are, my dear. I'm sorry if I caused you any problems. My flight is almost ready to leave. I'm afraid I have to be going. I'll always remember you, Karen, and what might've been."

MacAlister didn't want to say goodbye, instead he held out his hand and he and Karen touched each other for the last time. When he released her, he turned and walked back to Capollini, who handed him his overcoat.

"I'm sorry, Commander." Capollini handed MacAlister his cap and briefcase once he had his coat on. "Just like me. I can win a girl's heart but I can't keep her."

"In a way, you're right. Commander Cox has said much the same thing to me. Well, as much as I don't want to, it's time to leave Sweden. And as much as you don't want to, it's time to board the aircraft."

When Capollini was as warmly dressed as MacAlister, they left the customs station and walked out to the BOAC Mosquito in front of the terminal. They climbed inside its specially equipped bomb bay and, after its doors had been closed, the brown and green DeHavilland started its engines. It taxied away from the terminal, following a Swedish air lines Ju-52 out to the runways.

The civilian bomber had to wait for the bright orange trimotor to depart before it lifted into a cold, clear morning sky. Along with Ellis, Karen watched the Mosquito's take-off from the observation deck and quietly shed a few, brief tears as if flew out of sight. The Night Hawk operation was over.

Author's Note

Only three prototypes of the Me-262B-1a/U1, alias the Night Hawk, were built by the Third Reich. Of these, there is just one survivor still in existence. Half forgotten, the Night Hawk is on display at the Willow Grove naval air station, Pennsylvania. How and where it was acquired by Allied forces is a mystery. There are some who say this is intentionally so.

ASHES
by William W. Johnstone

OUT OF THE ASHES   (1137, $3.50)

Ben Raines hadn't looked forward to the War, but he knew
it was coming. After the balloons went up, Ben was one of
the survivors, fighting his way across the country, searching for his family, and leading a band of new pioneers attempting to bring America OUT OF THE ASHES.

FIRE IN THE ASHES   (1310, $3.50)

It's 1999 and the world as we know it no longer exists. Ben
Raines, leader of the Resistance, must regroup his rebels
and prep them for bloody guerilla war. But are they ready
to face an even fiercer foe—the human mutants threaten-
ing to overpower the world!

ANARCHY IN THE ASHES   (1387, $3.50)

Out of the smoldering nuclear wreckage of World War III,
Ben Raines has emerged as the strong leader the Resistance
needs. When Sam Hartline, the mercenary, joins forces
with an invading army of Russians, Ben and his people
raise a bloody banner of defiance to defend earth's last
bastion of freedom.

BLOOD IN THE ASHES   (1537, $3.50)

As Raines and his ragged band of followers search for land
that has escaped radiation, the insidious group known as
The Ninth Order rises up to destroy them. In a savage battle to the death, it is the fate of America itself that hangs in
the balance!